P9-CAD-954

3 9223 037106179

JAN 2013

Kokomo-Howard County PUBLIC LIBRARY

220 North Union St.
Kokomo, Indiana 46901-4614
(765) 457-3242
www.KHCPL.org

The Dog Stars

Center Point
Large Print

**This Large Print Book carries the
Seal of Approval of N.A.V.H.**

The Dog Stars

PETER HELLER

KOKOMO HOWARD COUNTY PUBLIC LIBRARY
KOKOMO, INDIANA

CENTER POINT LARGE PRINT
THORNDIKE, MAINE

This Center Point Large Print edition is published in
the year 2013 by arrangement with Alfred A. Knopf,
an imprint of The Knopf Doubleday Publishing Group,
a division of Random House, Inc.

Copyright © 2012 by Peter Heller.
All rights reserved.

This is a work of fiction. Names, characters, places, and
incidents either are the product of the author's imagination or
are used fictitiously. Any resemblance to actual persons,
living or dead, events, or locales is entirely coincidental.
The text of this Large Print edition is unabridged.
In other aspects, this book may vary from the original
edition. Printed in the United States of America on
permanent paper. Set in 16-point Times New Roman type.

additional copyright information on page 379

ISBN: 978-1-61173-613-7

Library of Congress Cataloging-in-Publication Data

Heller, Peter, 1959–
The dog stars / Peter Heller.
pages ; cm.
ISBN 978-1-61173-613-7 (library binding : alk. paper)
1. End of the world—Fiction. 2. Survival—Fiction.
  3. Large type books. I. Title.
PS3608.E454D64 2013
813′.6—dc23

                                                  2012035181

The Dog Stars

To Kim

BOOK ONE

I

I keep the Beast running, I keep the 100 low lead on tap, I foresee attacks. I am young enough, I am old enough. I used to love to fish for trout more than almost anything.

My name is Hig, one name. Big Hig if you need another.

If I ever woke up crying in the middle of a dream, and I'm not saying I did, it's because the trout are gone every one. Brookies, rainbows, browns, cutthroats, cutbows, every one.

The tiger left, the elephant, the apes, the baboon, the cheetah. The titmouse, the frigate bird, the pelican (gray), the whale (gray), the collared dove. Sad but. Didn't cry until the last trout swam upriver looking for maybe cooler water.

Melissa, my wife, was an old hippy. Not that old. She looked good. In this story she might have been Eve, but I'm not Adam. I am more like Cain. They didn't have a brother like me.

Did you ever read the Bible? I mean sit down and read it like it was a book? Check out Lamentations. That's where we're at, pretty much. Pretty much lamenting. Pretty much pouring our hearts out like water.

They said at the end it would get colder after it gets warmer. Way colder. Still waiting. She's a surprise this old earth, one big surprise after another since before she separated from the moon who circles and circles like the mate of a shot goose.

No more geese. A few. Last October I heard the old bleating after dusk and saw them, five against the cold bloodwashed blue over the ridge. Five all fall, I think, next April none.

I hand pump the 100 low lead aviation gas out of the old airport tank when the sun is not shining, and I have the truck too that was making the fuel delivery. More fuel than the Beast can burn in my lifetime if I keep my sorties local, which I plan to, I have to. She's a small plane, a 1956 Cessna 182, really a beaut. Cream and blue. I'm figuring I'm dead before the Beast gives up the final ghost. I will buy the farm. Eighty acres of bottomland hay and corn in a country where there is still a cold stream coming out of the purple mountains full of brookies and cuts.

Before that I will make my roundtrips. Out and back.

★

I have a neighbor. One. Just us at a small country airport a few miles from the mountains. A training field where they built a bunch of houses for people who couldn't sleep without their little planes, the way golfers live on a golf course. Bangley is the name on the registration of his old truck, which doesn't run anymore. Bruce Bangley. I fished it out of the glove box looking for a tire pressure gauge I could take with me in the Beast. A Wheat Ridge address. I don't call him that, though, what's the point, there's only two of us. Only us for at least a radius of eight miles, which is the distance of open prairie to the first juniper woods on the skirt of the mountain. I just say, Hey. Above the juniper is oak brush then black timber. Well, brown. Beetle killed and droughted. A lot of it standing dead now, just swaying like a thousand skeletons, sighing like a thousand ghosts, but not all. There are patches of green woods, and I am their biggest fan. I root for them out here on the plain. Go Go Go Grow Grow Grow! That's our fight song. I yell it out the window as I fly low over. The green patches are spreading year by year. Life is tenacious if you give it one little bit of encouragement. I could swear they hear me. They wave back, wave their feathery arms back and forth down low by their sides, they remind me of women in kimonos. Tiny steps or no steps, wave wave hands at your sides.

I go up there on foot when I can. To the greener woods. Funny to say that: not like I have to clear my calendar. I go up to breathe. The different air. It's dangerous, it's an adrenalin rush I could do without. I have seen elk sign. Not so old. If there are still elk. Bangley says no way. Way, but. Never seen one. Seen plenty deer. I bring the .308 and I shoot a doe and I drag her back in the hull of a kayak which I sawed the deck off so it's a sled. My green sled. The deer just stayed on with the rabbits and the rats. The cheat grass stayed on, I guess that's enough.

Before I go up there I fly it twice. One day, one night with the goggles. The goggles are pretty good at seeing down through trees if the trees aren't too heavy. People make pulsing green shadows, even asleep. Better than not checking. Then I make a loop south and east, come back in from the north. Thirty miles out, at least a day for a traveler. That's all open, all plains, sage and grass and rabbit brush and the old farms. The brown circles of fields like the footprint of a crutch fading into the prairie. Hedgerows and windbreaks, half the trees broken, blown over, a few still green by a seep or along a creek. Then I tell Bangley.

I cover the eight miles dragging the empty sled in two hours, then I am in cover. I can still move. It's a long way back with a deer, though. Over open country. Bangley covers me from halfway out. We still have the handsets and they still recharge with the panels. Japanese built, good thing. Bangley has a .408 CheyTac sniper rifle set up on a platform he built. A rangefinder. My luck. A gun nut. A really mean gun nut. He says he can pot a man from a mile off. He has done. I've seen it more than once. Last summer he shot a girl who

14

was chasing me across the open plain. A young girl, a scarecrow. I heard the shot, stopped, left the sled, went back. She was thrown back over a rock, a hole where her waist should have been, just about torn in half. Her chest was heaving, panting, her head twisted to the side, one black eye shiny and looking up at me, not fear, just like a question, burning, like of all things witnessed this one couldn't be believed. Like that. Like fucking *why?*

That's what I asked Bangley, fucking why.

She would have caught you.

So what? I had a gun, she had a little knife. To like protect her from *me*. She maybe wanted food.

Maybe. Maybe she'd slit your throat in the middle of the night.

I stared at him, his mind going that far, to the middle of the night, me and her. Jesus. My only neighbor. What can I say to Bangley? He has saved my bacon more times. Saving my bacon is his job. I have the plane, I am the eyes, he has the guns, he is the muscle. He knows I know he knows: he can't fly, I don't have the stomach for killing. Any other way probably just be one of us. Or none.

I also have Jasper, son of Daisy, which is the best last line of alarm.

So when we get sick of rabbits and sunfish from the pond, I get a deer. Mostly I just want to go up there. It feels like church, hallow and cool. The dead forest swaying and whispering, the green forest full of sighs. The musk smell of deer beds.

The creeks where I always pray to see a trout. One fingerling. One big old survivor, his green shadow idling against the green shadows of the stones.

Eight miles of open ground to the mountain front, the first trees. That is our perimeter. Our safety zone. That is my job.

He can concentrate his firepower to the west that way. That's how Bangley talks. Because it's thirty miles out, high plains all other directions, more than a day's walk, but just a couple of hours west to the first trees. The families are south ten miles but they don't bother us. That's what I call them. They are something like thirty Mennonites with a blood disease that hit after the flu. Like a plague but slow burning. Something like AIDS I think, maybe more contagious. The kids were born with it and it makes them all sick and weak and every year some die.

We have the perimeter. But if someone hid. In the old farmsteads. In the sage. The willows along a creek. Arroyos, too, with undercut banks. He asked me that once: how do I *know*. How do I know someone is not inside our perimeter, in all that empty country, hiding, waiting to attack us? But thing is I can see a lot. Not like the back of the hand, too simple, but like a book I have read and reread too many times to count, maybe like the Bible for some folks of old. I would know. A sentence out of place. A gap. Two periods where there should be one. I know.

I know, I think: if I am going to die—no If—it will be on one of these trips to the mountains. Crossing open ground with the full sled. Shot in the back with an arrow.

Bangley a long time ago gave me bulletproof, one of the vests in his arsenal. He has all kinds of shit. He said it'll stop any handgun, an arrow, but with a rifle it depends, I better be lucky. I thought about that. We're supposed to be the only two living souls but the families in at least hundreds of square miles, the only survivors, I better be lucky. So I wear the vest because it's warm, but if it's summer I mostly don't. When I wear it, I feel like I'm waiting for something. Would I stand on a train platform and wait for a train that hasn't come for months? Maybe. Sometimes this whole thing feels just like that.

★

In the beginning there was Fear. Not so much the flu by then, by then I walked, I talked. Not so much talked, but of sound body—and of mind, you be the judge. Two straight weeks of fever, three days 104 to 105, I know it cooked my brains. Encephalitis or something else. Hot. Thoughts that once belonged, that felt at home with each other, were now discomfited, unsure, depressed, like those shaggy Norwegian ponies that Russian professor moved to the Siberian Arctic I read about before. He was trying to recreate the Ice Age, a lot of grass and fauna and few people. Had he known what was coming he would have pursued another hobby. Half the ponies died, I think of heartbreak for their Scandinavian forests, half hung out at the research station and were fed grain and still died. That's how my thoughts are sometimes. When I'm stressed. When something's bothering me and won't let go. They're pretty good, I mean they function, but a lot of times they feel out of place, kinda sad, sometimes wondering if maybe they are supposed to be ten thousand miles from here in a place with a million square miles of cold Norwegian spruce. Sometimes I don't trust my thoughts not to bolt for the brush. Probably not my brain, probably normal for where we're at.

I don't want to be confused: we are nine years out. The flu killed almost everybody, then the blood disease killed more. The ones who are left are mostly Not Nice, why we live here on the plain, why I patrol every day.

I started sleeping on the ground because of the attacks. Survivors, it seemed like they picked it out on the map. On a big creek, check. So water, check. Must have fuel, check. Since it was an airport, check. Anyone who read anything knew, too, that it was a model for sustainable power, check. Every house with panels and the FBO run mostly on wind. Check. FBO means Fixed Base

Operator. Could've just said the Folks Who Run the Airport. If they knew what was coming they wouldn't have complicated everything so much.

Mostly the intruders came at night. They came singly or in groups, they came with weapons, with hunting rifles, with knives, they came to the porch light I left on like moths to a flame.

I have four sixty watt panels on the house I don't sleep in, so one LED light all night is no problem.

I was not in the house. I was asleep under blankets on the open ground behind the berm a hundred yards away. It is an old airport, it is all open ground. Jasper's low growl. He's a blue heeler mix with a great nose. I wake up. I beep Bangley on the handset. For him I think it was like sport. Kind of cleaned out his carbon, the way for me going up to the mountains.

It was a high berm, just a big mound of dirt, we made it higher. Tall enough to walk behind. Bangley, he saunters up and snuggles down beside me at the top where I am already watching with the goggles, and I smell his rasping breath. He has them too, the goggles, in fact he has like four, he gave me one. He said at the rate we use them the diodes will last ten years maybe twenty. What happens then? I celebrated my fortieth birthday last year. Jasper got a liver (doe), I ate a can of peaches. I invited Melissa and she came the way she does, a whisper and a shiver.

In ten years the additive will no longer keep the

fuel fresh enough. In ten years I'll be done with all this. Maybe.

Half the time, if the moon is up or if there is starlight and snow, Bangley doesn't need the goggles, he has the red dot, he just centers the red dot on the moving figures, on the ones standing still, crouching, whispering, centers it on the shadow by the old dumpster, puts the red dot on a torso. *Bang.* He takes his time, plans out the sequence, *bang bang bang.* Breath gets heavier, raspier just before. Like he's about to fuck someone which I guess he is.

The biggest group we had was seven. I heard Bangley lying beside me counting under his breath. Shit on a shingle, he murmured and chuckled like he does when he is not happy. I mean a lot more not happy than usual.

Hig, he whispered, you are going to have to participate.

I have the AR-15 semi-auto, I am good with it, he fitted me with the night scope. I just.

I did.

It was three of them that survived the first volley and after that we had our first bona fide firefight. But they didn't have night goggles and they didn't know the terrain and so it didn't take long.

That's how it started, the sleeping outside. I was never going to get trapped in the house. Like the dragon sleeps on the pile of treasure, but not me. I stay back a ways.

After the second summer they tapered off, like turning off a faucet, drip drip. One visitor a season maybe, then none. Not for almost a year, then a band of four desperados that almost cleaned our clock. That's when I started flying regular like a job.

Now I don't have to sleep on the ground. We have our system, we are confident. The Fear is like a memory of nausea. You can't remember how bad it was or that you just about asked to die instead. But I do. Sleep on the ground. Under a pile of blankets in winter that must weigh twenty pounds. I like it. Not boxed in. I still sleep behind the berm, I still leave the porch light on, Jasper still curls against my legs, still dreams in whimpers, still trembles under his own blanket, but I think he is mostly deaf now and useless as an alarm which we will never let on to Bangley. Bangley, you just don't know with him. He harbors. Might resent the meat I share who knows. The way he sees it everything has a use.

I once had a book on the stars but now I don't. My memory serves but not stellar ha. So I made up constellations. I made a Bear and a Goat but maybe not where they are supposed to be, I made some for the animals that once were, the ones I know about. I made one for Melissa, her whole self standing there kind of smiling and tall looking down on me in the winter nights. Looking down while frost crinkles in my eyelashes and feathers in my beard. I made one for the little Angel.

Melissa and I lived on a lake in Denver. Only seven minutes from downtown, the big bookstore, the restaurants, movies, we liked that. We could see grass, water, mountains out the big window of the little house. The geese. We had a resident flock and a flock of Canadas that came in fall and spring in great chevrons, mixed with the locals, maybe mated, then moved on. Took off again in raucous waves. I could tell the transients from the wild ones. I thought I could.

In October, November walking around the lake on our evening pre-prandial we'd point them out to each other. I thought she was always wrong. She'd get half mad. She was so smart, but she didn't know the geese like I did. I never thought of myself as really really smart but I always knew things in my bones.

When we got the puppy Jasper I was confirmed: he would chase the wild ones who were skittish but not the mean residents. My theory anyway.

We had no children. She couldn't have. We saw a doctor. Tried to sell us treatments we declined. We were okay with just each other. Then she did, like a miracle. Get pregnant. We'd gotten used to the other and I wasn't sure I could ever love someone more. I watched her sleeping and I thought: I love you more than anything.

Sometimes back then, fishing with Jasper up the

Sulphur, I hit my limit. I mean it felt my heart might just burst. Bursting is different than breaking. Like there is no way to contain how beautiful. Not it either, not just beauty. Something about how I fit. This little bend of smooth stones, the leaning cliffs. The smell of spruce. The small cutthroat making quiet rings in the black water of a pool. And no need to thank even. Just be. Just fish. Just walk up the creek, get dark, get cold, it is all a piece. Of me somehow.

Melissa part of the same circle. But different because we are entrusted with certain souls. Like I could hold her carefully in my cupped hands, like to bear her carefully carefully, the country I cannot, but her I can, and maybe all along it was she holding me.

The hospital St. Vincent's was right across the lake. The orange helicopters landed there. At the end we talked about flying west but it was too late and there was the hospital, we went to the hospital. To one of the buildings they took over. Filling with the dead.

★

Bangley just shows up. I'm changing oil. He could rap on the steel siding of the bay but he doesn't he likes to give me a heart attack. Shows up beside me like a ghost.

What are we monkeying with now?

Jesus, if I have a coronary who will fly your patrols?

We'd find someone wouldn't we? Put an ad in the paper.

His grin straight across his eyes never smiling.

Anyway I bet I could fly this sucker.

He says it every now and then. It's like a warning. For what? If he wanted this windy place to himself he would have. A long time ago.

Now Jasper is awake on his dusty blanket and growling. Jasper can't stomach Bangley unless it's like an emergency visitor situation in which case he keeps his trap shut, he's a team player. Once just after Bangley showed up Jasper snapped at his arm and Bangley unholstered a sidearm big as like a skillet and aimed and I yelled. The only time. I said You shoot the dog we all die.

Bangley blinked he had that grin. What do you mean we all die?

I mean I fly patrols from the air, the only way we know we can secure the perimeter.

That word. It was the only one that hit its target. I almost saw it go in his ear and through the tubes into his brain. Perimeter. Only way to secure. He blinked. He worked his jaw side to side. He stank. Like old blood like when you butcher a deer.

Only reason I am still alive. How do you think I live here by myself?

So that's how the bargain was struck. Without

even a negotiation. No words but that. I flew. He killed. Jasper growled. We let each other be.

I was saying: I'm changing the oil in the Beast and he shows up beside me like a ghost.

Why do you visit the Druids? he says.

They're not Druids they're Mennonites.

He grunts.

I put down the filter wrench. Lay it on a rolling box. Pick up the safety wire pliers.

Bangley is standing there. I smell before I see him. I feed the wire through the hole in the flange at the filter's base, twist it with the pliers. It's safety wire. Holds the filter on in case. All to spec. FAA regs. Wouldn't want the oil filter to vibrate loose, fall off, spill all the oil midair and the engine tears apart. Has happened. They used to say all FAA rules resulted from a real accident. So the .032 mil wire is maybe a kind of memorial to some pilot. Maybe his family too.

Bangley is picking his teeth with a splinter of wood, watching me. On top of the tool box is a shop rag a square of old t-shirt. The graphic is faded but I can see rows of smudged pink cartoon women: big breasted little breasted all shapes and underneath "melons" "peaches" "jugs" "plums" "raisins" a big "Cabo" bannered across the top. I read all the fruit before I reach in and wipe everything down one more time. Stab of pain. Just that. Fold it. A cartoon. That we are so hard wired that way. That two little arcs or circles of a cartoon boob could stir up memory, a temperature, change, a tightening of guts, a crawling in the groin. I think it's curious. I half gulp, stand still for a second, breathe.

Melissa was cantaloupes.

Cabo is out at the end of a nine hundred mile peninsula. Plenty of fish probably. Is there some survivor like me out at the old municipal airport changing the oil in an antique Maule, flying recon every day, using a Ski Colorado t-shirt as a shop rag? Fishing of an evening off some dilapidated pier that still stinks of creosote? Wondering what it's like to ski.

Why didn't Colorado shirts ever have tits on them? I ask Bangley.

Not much of a sense of humor in old B.

Walk to the north wall of the hangar slide a case of 50 straight weight Arrowshell off the stack. Set it down on a wooden stool. The sunlight is retreating back across the concrete slab to the open doorway. Bangley is wearing his honking sidearm. Night and day. Once he went to the pond in the creek bottom to hook a catfish and a bearded stranger built like a bear rose out of the Russian olive and attacked him. He says. Bangley shot him through his shaggy head. Brought an entire leg back still wearing three sets of ripped pants and a bandaged boot. The left. Threw it down in front of the hangar.

For the dog he said. Angry. Because I didn't do

my job. To him. I didn't guarantee the perimeter.

Why do you visit the Mormons? he says again. He is fucking with me. He is ramrod straight and inclines forward real subtle when he is pissed.

I pull at one flap of the cardboard box of motor oil. The glue is heavy, I tear it open tear the other side, four rows of three black quarts. The pale waxy line down the side of each tall rectangular bottle is translucent for reading the level, they remind me of tuxedo pants. One stripe of piping. Twelve little groomsmen.

How do you know that I do?

Bangley gets mad in gradations of increasing internal pressure like a volcano. The veins in his nose turn purple. Madder I mean. He is like one of those volcanoes in Ecuador that is always threatening to blow even when the top looks wisped with clouds like any other mountain.

We agreed, he says. Seismologists at the USGS or wherever seeing portentous tremors on the graph. A certain vein in his forehead just under the bill of his Ducks Unlimited camo cap beginning to throb.

No, you agreed. With yourself.

Off limits. It's off limits.

What are you? The Base Commander?

I should never talk to Bangley this way. I know it as I say it. I just get sick of the attitude sick to death of it. He's working his jaw back and forth.

I put the funnel, just an old oil bottle cut off

halfway, back down on top of the other quarts. I face him.

Look Bangley relax. Want a Coke?

Once every two months I land on a cleared boulevard in Commerce City and restock ten cases of the oil. On the way over one day I found the Coke truck. I always bring back four cases, two for him two for me. A case of Sprite for the families which I don't tell him about. Most of the cans have frozen too many times and burst but the plastic bottles survive. Bangley always goes through his Coke a lot faster.

You'll kill us both. We agreed.

I get him a Coke. Here relax. It's not good for your heart.

He had arteriosclerosis. Has. Once he said: I'm a time bomb. Which he didn't have to tell me.

I open it so he has no choice. At the crack of the top and the sound of the fizz he winces like one more Coke down, one less in the world.

Here.

Hig you will kill us. He drinks, he can't help himself. I can see it work in his throat and down into his barrel chest.

He makes himself stop before he drains the whole bottle. You know just one cough, he says. That's what they said at the end. Not just through blood.

Sharing bodily fluids. I'm not fucking a Mennonite.

A cough is a bodily fluid. Land in your eye. Open your mouth to speak.

I don't think that was ever proven.

What the fuck does it matter if it's proven. You want to get this far and die of the blood?

This far. I'm thinking not saying it. This far. Bangley and Jasper and a low fat diet. Well.

You can't choose for me Hig.

I breathe.

Everything we do is risky. Once in a while they need my help.

For what? For fucking what? They have what? Two, three, five years tops? The luckiest? Every few months one dies. I can tell by how you mope around. For what? Boils and rash and bloody coughs and burning?

They are people. They are trying to stay alive day by day. Maybe some can survive it. There were rumors of survivors.

He is still inclined forward, still throbbing the vein with a dribble of fresh Coke on the stubble of his chin.

They are no threat to us Bruce.

The sound of his given name widens his eyes. He never told it to me, it was always just I'm Bangley, which like I said I rarely use.

The families know to stay fifteen feet back. I've trained them. Not once not ever have they showed any aggression, nothing but gratitude, kind of embarrassing gratitude when I fix a pump or show them how to make a fish trap for the creek. Truth is I do it as much for me as them: it kinda loosens something inside me. That nearly froze up.

Bangley works the jaw stares at me. That last thing—it's like I just spoke perfect Japanese, a whole paragraph ending with a slight bow. Like A, he can't believe I fucking said it, and B, he doesn't understand a single syllable. Psycho spiritual language it leaves him, well, less than cold.

Once I asked him if he thought there was something more. We were sharing two rare Cokes on the front porch of my house I never go in, under the bulb I leave on at night that used to work like a bug zapper for attackers. It was evening and the October sun was making for the mountains. Like some old couple taking their ease. Two wicker chairs losing their paint and cricking when we shifted our weight. His chair had a rhythm like he remembered what it was to sit in a rocker. Only time I can think of he told me anything about his life before. He grew up in Oklahoma. That's what he told me.

It's not like you think, he added. Long story.

That was it. A little cryptic. I hadn't really thought anything. He never elaborated. Still, seemed like we were making leaps and bounds intimacy-wise.

I told him I used to build houses.

What kind of houses?

Timber frame. Adobe. Odd custom stuff. Wrote a book too.

A book on building houses.

No. A little book. Poetry. Nobody read it.

Shit? He took a measured sip of Coke watching me as he tipped back the bottle, watching me as he set it back down on his thigh, kind of appraising me with a new appreciation, not readable good or bad. Adjusting the context.

Wrote for magazines now and then. Mostly about fishing, outdoor stuff.

The relief it swept his face like pushing off a cloud shadow. I almost laughed. You could see the gears: Phew, outdoor stuff, Hig is not a homo.

Growing up I wanted to be a writer. A great writer. Summers I worked construction, framing. Like that. Tough to make a living as a writer. Anyway I probably wasn't so good. Got married bought a house. Led to another thing then the other thing.

Long story, I said.

Bangley held his Coke in both hands in his lap. He kind of hunched over himself maybe remembering. Suddenly remote like his spirit retreated to a safer distance. To watch. From a distance. Still rocking the chair that didn't rock.

We didn't speak for a long time. The sun touched one of the higher peaks, broke slowly like a bloody yolk. Wind stirred, rattled the dried rabbit brush at the exact moment. Cold.

I asked him if he ever thought there was anything more than this, than just surviving day to day. Recon, fixing the plane, growing the five vegetables, trapping a rabbit. Like what are we waiting for?

His chair, *crick crick,* stopped. He got very still like a hunter that smelled an animal on the wind. Close. Like he woke up.

Say again.

More than this. Day to day.

He worked his jaw, his mineral eyes graying in the fading light. Like maybe I'd tipped over the edge.

Gotta go he said. Stood up. Hooked a finger in the breast pocket of his flannel shirt, fished out the bottle cap, screwed it on. Carried his Coke off the porch, boot cracking the broken step.

That was maybe the second year. So now in the hangar I know the stuff about thawing out inside will not exactly exact sympathy. Half the time with Bangley I'm thinking about all the stuff I should never say.

I crack a quart of oil and tip it into the funnel made from a cut off bottle and snug it down into its twin. Leave it to drain. Face him.

Who knows maybe one day *we* will need *them.* We can't know.

Ha. A cough of contempt dismissive. Never happen Hig. For funeral detail maybe.

He had consigned them, wished it. All of them dead.

You want to be the only one left? You'd be just as happy. The only goddamn human being left on earth.

If it shakes out like that. Better than the alternative. Anyway I got you. He tipped back the Coke watched me past the bottle.

He meant the alternative if everyone's going to die. I think. I didn't say it: One day I'm gonna climb in the Beast and fly west and keep going.

No you won't he said.

What?

What you were thinking. There is no other safe place. Maybe on the planet. We got the perimeter, water, power, food, firepower. We got mountains close enough if the game gets scarce. We got no internal strife no politics cause it's just you and me. We got no internal to tear apart. Like the Mormons like everybody else out there who ain't alive anymore. We keep it simple we survive.

He grins.

Country boys will survive.

His favorite phrase.

I stare at my only friend on earth. I guess he's my friend.

Don't go killing us, he says and leaves.

★

Still I go when they ask. The patrol goes west to the mountain front then south. I follow the line of

33

trees that mark the river. At the stacks of the power plant and the reservoir I swing back northwest. The Mennonites are on the creek. In an old turkey farm. Eight metal sheds in two rows of four set at angles like diagonally parked cars. Tall century old trees strung along a windbreak and clustered into a grove in the middle of which cants the asphalt roof of a big brick farmhouse. Two ponds fed by the creek. In one I can see floats, an empty canoe. An array of solar panels to the south of the sheds and two windmills, one mechanical for drawing water. Why they came here in the first place.

In the yard, in the clearing, a thirty foot flagpole, flag long since gone, maybe stripped for a baby blanket. When they need help they hoist a ripped red union suit. Signal and wind sock. In a strong wind it splays legs and arms out stiff like a headless man.

I land on the straight dirt drive that Ts from the old county road to the west. I can see the sign swiveling in the wind. At the head of the drive they wired a metal sign to two posts it has a red skull and crossbones says DANGER WE HAVE THE BLOOD. The drive floods, gets sliced with ruts. They come out with shovels and fill the holes. They aren't good at maintenance, they're most of the time too weak, but the landing strip is one thing they keep clean. Almost always a strong crosswind from say 330. I slip the Beast so she comes down cocked, almost sideways to the drive, left wing low, nose ruddered over hard to the south, then kick her straight at the last second, the kids in the yard jump up and down, I can see they are laughing from two hundred feet, it's the only time I ever see them laugh.

★

Jasper used to be able to jump up into the cockpit now he can't. In the fourth year we had an argument. I took out the front passenger seat for weight and cargo and put down a flannel sleeping bag with a pattern of a man shooting a pheasant over and over, his dog on three legs, pointing, out in front. Not sure why I didn't do that before. The dog doesn't look like Jasper, still. I carried him. Lay him on the pattern of the man and the dog.

You and me in another life I tell him.

He likes to fly. Anyway I wouldn't leave him alone with Bangley.

When I took out the seat he got depressed. He couldn't sit up and look out. He knows to stay back of the rudder pedals. Once in a shear he skidded into them and nearly killed us. After that I fashioned like a four inch wood fence but scrapped it after he inspected it and jumped out of the plane and like refused to fly, no shit. It insulted him. The whole thing. I used to worry about the engine roar and prop blast, I wear the headset even though there is no one to talk to on the radio because it dampens the noise, but I worried about Jasper, even tried to make him his own hearing protector, this helmet kind of thing, it wouldn't stay on. Probably why he's mostly deaf now.

When I picked up oil etc I moved the quilt to the top of the stack so he could look out.

See? I said. At least it's good half the time. Better than most of us can expect.

He still thought it was lame I could tell. Not half as excited. So now when I'm not picking up, just flying, which is most of the time, I bolt the seat back in, it just takes a few minutes. Not like we don't have time. First time he sat up straight again and glanced at me like What took you so long? then looked forward real serious, brow furrowed like a copilot. His mood it lifted palpable as weather.

He's getting old. I don't count the years. I don't multiply by seven.

They bred dogs for everything else, even diving for fish, why didn't they breed them to live longer, to live as long as a man?

★

One weird thing: the GPS still works. The satellites, the military or whoever put them up there to spin around us and tell us where we are, they still send their signals, triangulate my position, the little Garmin mounted on the yoke still flashes a terrain warning if it thinks I am getting too close to high ground.

I am always too close to high ground. That's the other thing about the end of everything: I stopped worrying about my engine failing.

There's a Nearest button on the Garmin. Somebody was thinking. It tells you fast which way is the nearest airport and how far. It pops up a list of the closest airports, their identifiers, distance, bearing, tower frequency. When I used to worry about stuff the Nearest button was my pilot's best friend. Any kind of weather or trouble or just getting low on fuel and I tapped it and there was the list and if I scrolled down and highlighted I could just press Go To and *pop* it gave my vector. Steer the arrow back to the center of the arc. Slickest thing.

Still useful but after nine years so many of the runways are unusable or you have to know where the two foot pothole is exactly and rudder around it. Surprising how fast. How fast it turns back to grass and ground. Back before, there was a TV show: *Life After People.* I watched every one. I recorded it. I was gripped. By this idea: New York City in a thousand years would look like: an estuary. A marsh. A river. Woods. Hills. I liked it. I can't say why. It thrilled me.

That fast. Because it is amazing how fast girder steel corrodes when exposed to water and air, how fast roots break shit apart. It all falls down. Oh, so the runways: nine years doesn't sound like a long time but it is for the tarmac unmaintained and it is for a brain-cooked human trying to live it. I could make a list. Nine years is pretty fucking long:

To live with Bangley's bullshit.

To remember the ad hoc flu ward and.

To miss my wife after.

To think about fishing and not go.

Other stuff.

But. I lost a cylinder one evening south of Bennet. I was flying the city which I do now and then not too low just to see and. *Tap tap tap* vibration like a mother. Best to get down and troubleshoot, might be just a fouled plug. I didn't need the Garmin to tell me Buckley the air force base was just to the west maybe twelve miles. I banked around and came down with the gold sun straight in my eyes, banging louder, now kind of alarming like it would suck to throw a bearing and practically blind with the sun, using the left pavement edge as a guide, and a hundred feet after I touched down still tearing ass, maybe seventy indicated, *WHOMP,* and had it been the nose gear and not the left main the Beast, and me too, we would be toast. Jasper too. I walked back and checked. The hole was waist deep practically, neatly rectanguloid, it looked like it had been dug out by prairie dogs with little backhoes. Fuck. My back. The jolt. I sat down with my legs dangling in the hole, Jasper sat too and leaned against me like he does, and glanced up at me real quick and polite, and real concerned. Sitting that way reminded me of a Japanese restaurant Melissa took me to once that had instead of chairs, instead of mats and pillows, like a well for your feet, like cheat floor seating for stiff Westerners. The sun threw our shadows about half a mile long down the runway. As it was, the impact cracked the strut, which is when I learned to weld and also it's possible to weld with solar power.

I sat with my feet in the hole and shook myself by the shoulders and said, What's wrong with you? Is this a game to you?

That took a while to answer.

Do you want to live today?

Yes.

Do you grant that you may want to live tomorrow? And maybe the next day?

Yes.

Then get methodical. You got nothing but time.

So I made a survey. I took the chart we call a sectional and flew every airstrip within a hundred miles. I flew Centennial, I flew Colorado Springs, the Air Force Academy, I flew Kirby, formerly Nebraska, I flew Cheyenne. I flew them all at probably thirty feet in good light and made notes. Surprising how many would have killed me. At Cranton we almost did when I came in for the fly-by real low and parallel to the runway and some xenophobe put a high powered hole through the fuselage. I knew because it exited right through my side window up and out. That's how I knew we had neighbors in Cranton.

So the Nearest button still works but about half I can't use anymore at all. Better to land in an old field. Used to mean Nearest Haven now means Nearest Maybe Death Trap. All good information.

★

I still monitor the radio. Old habits die hard. Every airport has a frequency so traffic can talk to each other if there's no tower. Important to know where everybody is when you're taking off or entering the pattern. Used to be. Collisions used to happen every year. Between airports there's no designated way to communicate but there's an emergency frequency 121.5. What I do when I'm approaching an airport is flip to the old channel. When I'm within five miles I make a call. Call a few times.
Loveland traffic Cessna Six Three Three Three Alpha five to the south at six thousand en route Greeley. Repeat. Anybody? I'm the only goddamn plane up here and likely to be til the end of time. Maybe on another planet in another universe they will again invent the Cessna. Ha!

I laugh. I hoot. It's kinda morbid. Jasper glances sideways with mild canine embarrassment.

I have a book of poems by William Stafford.

It's the only thing I went back for: my poetry collections. Landing at night on no power, no lights, in the old King Sooper's parking lot, one row a thousand easy feet between low cars, the wings went over and no light poles. Just over a mile from there to the house. Fires burning west and south, some punctuating gunshots. Waiting in the plane with the AR-15 between my legs waiting to see if anyone was left to bother the Beast for the half hour I'd be gone.

I took the rifle and jogged around the lake like so many times before, morning and evening. Used to jog. I ignored the pictures on the mantel, along the stairs, didn't look, packed an old backpack and a duffel full of books, just poems. Fingered *We Die Alone* which is the first book Melissa gave me which was creepily prognosticant in the title only: the protagonist is a true real Norwegian commando back in the last good war. He out-skis two entire divisions of German troops and survives to pose handsomely in distinguished middle age in a rollneck fisherman's sweater for the back of his memoir. I had always envied that guy, a war hero in hearty Norway who must have had a cabin up in the fjordland and a thousand friends and too much mulled cider or aquavit or whatever they drink at parties, and enjoyed skiing now just for fun. If that man could have imagined hell on earth probably. He'd seen its shadow. I fingered the book, didn't read the inscription and slid it back on the shelf. Done. I'd decided I was done with crying about anything.

When I got back to the parking lot I circled in from the outside rows and there were two figures leaning into the open doors of the plane, one about to climb in. I cursed myself and checked the safety, heart hammering, and stood and yelled to get the fuck away, and when they grabbed hunting rifle and shotgun I shot them at twenty yards the first ones. For poems. I gave their guns to Bangley, refused to answer when he asked.

The Stafford book is called *Stories That Could Be True*. One poem is called "The Farm on the Great Plains" and it begins:

A telephone line goes cold;
birds tread it wherever it goes.
A farm back of a great plain
tugs an end of the line.
I call that farm every year,
ringing it, listening, still

He calls his father. He calls his mother. They are gone for years only a hum now on the line but he still calls.

When no one responds from the airport I'm about to fly over I flip back to the emergency frequency and make a pro forma call

Mayday mayday Cessna Six Triple Three Alpha feeling awful lonely.

In year seven someone answered. I took my hands off the yoke and pressed the headset into my ears. The hair stood up along my arms like it does in an electric storm.

It came out of the static with a doppler fade.

Triple Three Alpha . . . tailing off into aural snow.

Triple Three Alpha . . . Gust of static . . . **Grand junk.** Whomp like hit with magnetic wind.

Grand Junction . . .

I waited. I shook my head. Actually knocked my temple in the headset. Keyed the mike with the thumb button on the yoke.

Grand Junction? Grand Junction? Triple Three Alpha over Longmont. I'm over Longmont holy shit! Didn't copy. Repeat: didn't copy!

I circled. I circled higher. Climbed to fifteen thousand feet and circled til I was dizzy with hypoxia. Descended to thirteen and circled for two hours til the fuel flow gauge told me I had fifteen minutes left, then I banked east.

Whoever it was was a pilot or a controller.

The one and only time.

★

I cook my meals in the hangar. About a month after Bangley showed up I got him to help me dolly over a Vigilant woodstove from the kitchen of a fancy Mcmansion on the east side of the runway. Maybe the provisional nature of eating in what's essentially a mechanic's garage makes me feel like none of this is permanent. Part of why I don't live in a house. Like living in a hangar, sleeping outside, I can pretend there's a house somewhere else, with someone in it, someone to go back to. But who's kidding whom? Melissa is not coming back, the trout aren't, and neither is the elephant nor the pelican. Nature might invent a speckled proud coldwater fighting fish again but she will never again give the improbable elephant another go.

Still last summer I saw a nighthawk. First one in years. Flitting for bugs in a warm dusk, wing-bars blinking in the twilight. That soft electric peep.

So the hangar is where I cook and eat. I tried eating in my house at the kitchen table like Bangley does, tried it for a few days but it didn't sit.

All the firewood we could use in our lifetimes is stacked up in the walls of the houses around the airfield. A sledgehammer and a crowbar gives me all I can use for a week in a few hours. Not to mention fine furniture.

Took a few winces to get used to battering apart finish carpentry, cherry and walnut, and maple flooring for firewood. But. Value relative to need. Still I'm taking apart the crummy houses first. Not sure if I'll ever get to the four or five really beautifully built mini-mansions the ones with exotic hardwoods, if I do by then they will hold no cachet probably. Probably just look to me like some refreshingly different scents in the burning. By another unspoken agreement we began harvesting wood in the cheaper houses on the west side of the runway, him working north and me south. That leaves me a not-so-long wheelbarrow roll back to the hangar.

Often Bangley wanders over and joins me. He can't cook I can. Can't train the man to knock ever, or at least not whisper in like some ghost, which creeps me out a little cause I never know how long he's been watching.

Dinner early tonight.

Fuck Bangley, I nearly scalded myself.

You cook like you enjoy it.

Huh?

The way you move around with the skillet, the knife, like it's a kitchen. Like it's one of those cooking shows.

Bangley's nostrils flare with a gill-like rhythm when he's particularly enjoying himself.

I stare at him for just a moment.

You hungry?

Like one of those cooking shows where they tie on an apron. Like cooking a frigging dinner is some kind of dance. Tra la la.

I put a pan full of fresh new potatoes down on the stove. In the beginning I tried using venison fat for lard but it went rancid so fast.

Well I'm not wearing an apron, as you can see, and I'm not dancing.

Almost no oil in the pantries of houses at the end the last few months they must have been drinking it for the calories. Then in the basement of the big Bauhaus across on Piper Lane I found two five gallon barrels of olive oil. Hidden behind a stack of new bricks.

You were singing though. He flashes that straight across grin. Just makes him look meaner.

The stove is hot with Canadian fir two by fours, the best frying wood for flash heat. The oil is spitting and I prod at the cut potatoes until most of them are in contact with the bottom of the pan. With the steel spatula I reach down and joggle the chrome lever that closes the side vent to the stove to slow it down. I think: If I were made of different stuff, if I thought I could defend this place myself I would shoot Bangley where he stands and get it over with. Would I? Maybe. And then I would miss this sparring every day. Probably feel it like a big void. We really have become like a married couple.

I don't think I was singing, I say finally.

You were Hig, you were. Wasn't Johnny Cash either. He grins.

Like that was the only approved sing to yourself music in the Book of Bangley.

Well what the fuck was it?

He shrugs. Hell if I know. Some pop girl stuff. From the radio I distantly recall.

Distantly recall. Standing there with a smile of triumph and his scruffy week old beard. I swear. I start to laugh. That's what he does to me: aggravate me all the way to the point of laughter. To the point of ridiculous and then a fuse pops, flicks a switch, and I laugh. Lucky for both of us I guess.

Sit down Bangley. Pull up a stool. We're having catfish, dandelion salad with basil, new potatoes *au* something not *gratin.*

See? he says. Just like one of those shows. If you aren't just a little light in the loafers I'm a jew.

I look at him. I laugh harder.

★

I play music sometimes. I have mp3s, cds, vinyl, everything. I wired my hangar to the main battery bank at the FBO the one that pulls from the wind turbine so power isn't a problem. The mood has to be just right. I have to be careful or it sends me back to that place I don't want to ever be again. Can't be anything we used to listen to: we were a sucker for the decades old singer-songwriter, climb out of the bottle, country road stuff, Whiskeytown to Topley to Sinead. We loved the Dixie Chicks, who wouldn't. Amazing Rhythm

Aces. Open Road, Sweet Sunny South, Reel Time Travelers, the scrappy fine bluegrass and old timey groups just before before. We thought it was heartbreaking then. Try playing it on a fine early spring morning with the hangar door open and a single redtail gyring over the warming tarmac:

And I remember your honeysuckle scent I
*   still adore*
I can't believe that you don't want me
*   anymore . . .*

Or the sweet wrecked mountain tenor of Brad Lee Folk singing

Hard Times.
Head hung down and homeless, lost out in
*   the rain . . .*

I never thought I'd be an old man at forty.

What I can play is blues. She was never that into blues. I can salve with Lightning and Cotton, BB and Clapton and Stevie Ray. I can blast Son Seals singing Dear Son until the coyotes in the creek raise up a sympathetic sky ripping interpretation of the harmonica solo. Piercing howls and yelps. Sounds like it's killing them and also like they love it. Which when you get right down to it is the blues.

At night I lie with Jasper against the back of the berm. It's early spring, some late or very early hour with Orion toppling backward onto the serrated edge of the mountains and not crying out but silent, silent as he tries to shoot the bull before it tramples him. Sometimes he is very peaceful not tonight. Tonight he is fighting for his life.

Jasper is unleashed, sleeping on my left thigh but my thoughts are leashed tight. I allow them to circle tight. To brush the green house, the hangar, the possibility of a spring hunting trip for spring bear when the bear are careless with hunger.

He is snoring softly like he does, a little snort on the inhale and maybe a whimper on the way out. Then against all plan I begin to remember the call from Grand Junction. Coming in like a train out of a snowstorm, whomping the bandwidth then receding back into the static blizzard with a long mournful tail of dopplered distance. Lost. **Triple Three Alpha . . . Grand Junk . . . Grand Junction . . .** The voice older, kind, concerned, like a grandparent calling up a steep flight of stairs.

How many years ago? Two or three. It was summer I remember. I remember the smoke from the summer fires, circling the Beast up into the smoke, and the sunset that night like a massacre. How I circled and climbed and made the circles broader and keyed and keyed the mike. Frantically worked the squelch. Some skip in the atmosphere maybe, how could it travel that far with none of the repeaters working anymore years since. The competence in the voice. An older man. I remember that. It came through the noise. Another pilot, I was sure it was another pilot.

I can fly to Gunnison and back on my tanks maybe Delta the other way. Maybe—if the wind is right in both directions. Which rarely happens. I have thought about it. Again and again. Junction less than half an hour beyond. And then. What? Another pilot at another airport probably much less secure. But.

They had power somehow. They—he—had survived seven years. Maybe still so.

Jasper shifts, straightens his legs in a dreaming stretch and pushes back against me, wakes himself up. Sniffs. Lowers his head again.

I lift my head from the pillow
I see the frost the moon.
Lowering my head I think of home.

Li Po's most famous poem.

Even then: long before before the end, the bottomless yearning. Almost never home, any of us.

I lie back against the duffel bag stuffed with foam I use as a pillow. Doesn't get dirty as fast, doesn't remind me of my old bed. Rub the band of the wool hat back down on my forehead. The sky is bell clear, the forest fires don't start til mid-June, and the Milky Way is a flowing river of stars profoundly depthless. I mean deeper than can be reckoned. Jasper sighs. Almost no wind. What there is is cooling my right ear, a lazy breeze from the north.

Would I be more at home if I met a pilot from Grand Junction? If Denver to the south was a bustling living city? If Melissa were sleeping on the other side of Jasper as she used to do? Who would I be more at home with? Myself?

Still I think of the pilot's voice. The competence and the yearning. To connect. I think I should have gone there. Pushed the fuel, backed off the throttle, flown slow, maybe eighteen square, picked my morning and gone. To see. What, I don't know. Still I didn't come close. To going. Admit it: I was scared. Of finding the interrupted dead as I had and had and had again. Nothing but. And running out of fuel before I was even back to Seven Victor Two which is Paonia, the airstrip up high on the narrow flat butte like an aircraft carrier. Running out of fuel in the 'dobe flats east of Delta. Going down in the shadow of Grand Mesa.

Before, I read that they found Amelia Earhart. Conclusive I guess. On the island that had been checked off in 1940 as Searched. Opened clam shells, a jackknife shattered apart for its blade, for maybe a fishing spear. A fire pit. Ancient crumbling makeup. A plexiglas airplane window. A woman's shoe. Bones. Chips of bones. The DNA verified against a living female Earhart cousin. Of course it was her island, she and the navigator castaways for how long until they succumbed to what? The coral atoll from the air: elliptical oasis with a central lagoon. Flat outer reef at low tide like a parking lot. The Lockheed Electra with a landing configuration stall speed of fifty five mph, she'd need seven hundred feet, no more. Wading the meager provisions to shore maybe injured. Maybe not low tide, maybe the gear torn off by water. Maybe blood in the water. Running out of fuel over the Pacific taking gratefully what comes. That they made that tiny island at all. Living off of shells and rain.

Shells and rain.

And the company of another, just one.

Starvation. Slowly burning through time like a fire in wet wood. Attenuating to bone, to walking bones, then one dies, then the other. Or attacked by passing islanders maybe better.

Missing what most the whole time? The babbling faceless agora, the fame, the parties, the pop of flash bulbs? The lovers, the gaiety, the champagne? The solitude carved out of celebrity, poring over charts by a single lamp on a wide desk in a venerable hotel? Room service, coffee before dawn? The company of one friend, two? The choice: All of it or not? Some or none? Now, not now, maybe later?

I have none of that now. Those choices. And yet. I do not want to run out of fuel and go down in the high desert grass of the western Gunnison valley and die trying to walk with Jasper three hundred miles home. Home. Meager as it is. Nothing to lose as I have. Nothing is something somehow.

★

Jasper growled. I had slept in my reverie.

Low, mean, serious.

I held my breath, listened. Sat up slow. He is mostly deaf, yes, but his nose is good.

Could be coyotes. Or wolves. The mountain wolves in the last two years: drifting down from the mountains in ragged packs. Growing pressure of the growing repopulation. Because they used to be there in numbers enough and are again.

Jasper growled now in the night and I sat up in the blankets heart thumping. I whispered *Stay* and crawled to the top of the berm.

Jasper knows. He knows when the shit's serious.

He sat back on his hindquarters and cut the noise mid-growl and looked at me with real concern and also with the taut poise of a hunter who is enjoying himself. He was amped. So was I. This hadn't happened in a long time, maybe half a year, and I felt a little sluggish, a little out of practice. A couple of years ago and I would have been at the top of the berm by now and scanning with the goggles with my left hand on the receiver of the AR. As it was I had to dig the rifle out from between the cold damp tarp and the back of the duffle. Next to it the goggles inside an old wool sock. At least I still thought to bring them out with me when we slept. I set the goggles against my brow and stretched the strap over the back of my head and slowly, quietly, tugged against and pulled the charging handle that racked the gun. Climbed the berm slowly, more cautiously.

Jasper stayed still. Straining against the urge to chase down the smell in the dark. Or maybe some sound, some sound in some frequency that penetrated his near deafness. I climbed the steep back of the berm slowly. Prayed it was coyotes, even wolves. Not in the mood for killing, not one bit. Not myself, not to spot for Bangley.

At the top I slid the rifle flat over the smooth top and lowered myself to cold dirt and wriggled upwards until my eyes cleared the lip.

In the light of the porch bulb I saw them. One two threefourfive . . . *break onetwothreefourfive pigeonsjustlikethat* . . . Five men all fullgrown except maybe one smaller maybe younger.

Shit.

With great effort that first summer we had levered and toppled the dumpster back south maybe a hundred feet further from the house. It was on its side, the open top gaping black. The creek bank was sheer and deep. The stream ran around it so that the airport sat in an oxbowed bite. Perfect moat. The only good ford was a trail that led out of the bottom to this house, the only one we lit. So they naturally clustered against the dumpster, south of it in the shadow of the bulb, shielded from the house where they—anyone not a professional soldier—would imagine the threat and the prize.

Fish in a barrel. Whatever other hapless metaphor for the hapless soon to be dead.

I kill deer. I have no problem killing deer. Dressing, butchering, eating.

Heart now thumping like a blind thing trying to bang its way out of the ribcage. I felt down to my belt and squeezed the sides of the radio, keying the mike button with my thumb three times. Then three then three. Then I counted. Before I got to two hundred Bangley would be sauntering up behind me carrying two guns: M4 assault rifle and a light sniper, probably an AR-10 .308. Counted to myself and shifted the rifle up and over one of the sandbags at the top and snugged the stock into my right shoulder and sighted. Ninety feet. We had measured it to the inch.

Onethirtyone onethirtytwo

They were crouched and talking among them-selves, whispering, I couldn't hear them. The wind was light, cool against the back of my neck, westerly from me to them. Carrying sound. Very slowly I thumbed the safety to fire, heard the click, wince, seemed loud, eased the small lever forward to full auto.

Oneseventynine oneeighty

They were not even not pros. They were crouched together as one target at this distance one alone filled the scope, way more than filled it. They were farmers insurance men mechanics. Probably. Haplessly clustered. But. I shifted the scope, just the slightest pressure from the inside of my shoulder, and swept them and they had guns, each one. As I swept, the sight picture tremored with the hammering of my heart. At this stage they were killers. I mean this stage in our mutually culpable history. Who to say how many or how cruelly. At this stage they were gathered in the posture of armed assault. On who knew what remnant of family had managed to survive in that house. And.

The cruelty of it struck me: they in relation to the house, the fictional family, me to them, that any of us should be in this position. *Don't fucking think, Hig. You will get us all killed* Bangley liked to bark.

TwoOfive twoOsix. No Bangley. What the fuck. Never happened not once he wasn't here by two hundred, usually earlier.

I eased my eye off the eyepiece and twisted my head around to the left. No shadow. No figure, no

Bangley approaching. *Fuck.* Eye back on the scope. Hand on the trigger guard trembling. Starting to tremble.

They were talking among themselves. I flipped the lever that unlocked the scope with my trembling left hand and released it from its rail. Lay it to the side out of line of the iron peep sight. It opened up my field of view.

Even as a boy, the killing part was my least favorite. I loved to hunt with my Uncle Pete. He was an unreconstructed man of letters and of action in the mode of Ernest Hemingway and Jack London, except that he taught ballroom dancing. On cruise ships. He and Aunt Louise did that for like twenty years and she died, and my normally exuberant and talkative uncle got quiet, more serious. Still fun. He wasn't very good at either one, either the action or the letters, but I idolized him for a long time, longer than was necessary and went on my first elk hunt with him when I was twelve.

I was good. I mean I quickly understood terrain and habitat almost as if I had grown up with People of the Deer, and I was quiet and careful about the direction of the wind and the sound of twigs whizzing along the cordura of my pack, and the covering sounds of water, and I was an adept stalker and helpful in camp and nearly leapt out of my bag into the icy five a.m. chill of what was still a mountain mid-November night. I adored it all, and it seemed I didn't have any problem putting the cow elk in my sights, but the way she stumbled over the rockfall when I shot, tripping forward and somersaulting over her own neck, and the way her eye shone up at me and she scrabbled her useless legs sideways over the rocks before I shot again right into the head in a panic, and the life went out of her eye and her legs, and then the way when I dressed her the blood spilled onto the frozen ground and mixed pink with warm milk from her still feeding teats—

Didn't like it. Did it every year for years afterward and loved it all including having elk in the freezer, but not that. Don't even like to kill a bug.

Twotwentythree twotwentyfour

No Bangley. I had tried negotiating once. Closest I ever came to dying.

Old rules are done Hig. Went the way of the woodpecker. Gone with the glaciers and the government. New world now. New world new rules. Never ever negotiate.

He loved to say that before he set up to plug someone.

Five was a big bunch, biggest we'd had in a couple of years. They were crouched, the biggest closest to the dumpster had a rifle with scope, was twisted back doing the talking, signing with his right hand, touching the watch cap cocked on his head, the one just beside him had some sort of

58

assault rifle probably an AK, the three others: two shotguns and a ranch rifle all clear at ninety feet with the goggled eye. The third from the left with a shotgun wore a cowboy hat a short man in a big hat. They were bunched and nodding and they were about to move. My hand shook. They would never be this tight a target.

I planned to sweep right to left. Full auto. Set the peep in the middle of the last one's bulk and planned to cut across through the midline of the bunch.

Moved right index finger onto the cold trigger, took a deep breath, a deep living breath to let out slow the way taught and

Cracked open. The night. Not me. Erupted pulse of flame peripheral from down to my right, the hulk carcass of a truck, the concatenate blast of rapid fire, the group in my sight coming apart entropic, the red dot flying across like a lethal bug throwing their shadows upwards and out to land, to be swallowed by the green ground.

Not me.

I hadn't pulled the trigger.

A shriek and scream, one moaning another writhing, and whimpers, I saw Bangley step out from behind the truck, unholster his .45 walk calmly across the open ground and three shots, the ones crying suddenly silent.

Light wind, cold. Blood rushing in my ears, rinsing the cries. Quiet.

He picked up the scattered guns, slung all five. Walked around the berm, unslung the guns, heard them chink together on the ground, talked low to Jasper, climbed up to me where I was still prone, I would say still frozen on the trigger but more like just stilled with disbelief.

What the fuck.

Good he said. Good job. Not sure you still had it in you.

He meant that I would. That my finger was moving on the trigger. Before he took over.

What the fuck Bangley. Not sure I still had what in me?

Silent. Knew I knew what.

I've never had it fucking in me. But I do it. What the fuck were you thinking? What if I'd seen you and thought you were one of them?

Never happen: You see me. Unh unh. Not that way.

I opened my mouth, closed it. I said, Unfuckingbelievable. What if they had broke apart. I mean just launched. Sooner.

Silence. Knew I knew now that he had them covered from the get go.

Well how the hell did you know I was about to pull the trigger and why didn't you? Let me?

Silence. Knew that I knew now that he was scoping me more closely than he was scoping them. Scoping my frigging finger while he kept half an eye on the men that could have frigging killed us. Had them sighted all along. Let loose only when he saw me take the big breath maybe. I see him in my mind's eye pulling the trigger on the first man not even looking, watching me first in the good night scope on its own legs, watching me jerk back in alarm in surprise, then casual but efficient tuck down to his weapon and sweep the rest of the group. Not sweep. Bangley doesn't believe in full auto. Two shots probably to each panicked leaping shadow. *T-TAP.* Each one that fast. Maybe he was laughing at my confusion all the while he harvested this bunch of souls.

C'mere Hig. Show you something.

Goes over the top and down the berm. Jasper still down there, this side, trembling. Not with fear. I can see him in the starlight. Sitting on his haunches following my movements with concern, restraining himself from action, somebody doing their job just their job the way they are supposed to.

C'mon. I whistle soft. He jumps, not like the old days but still fast enough up to the top of the berm and over. Bangley is down there among the black figures sprawled. Jasper already moving one to the other, not stopping, nosing, the low growl.

Look at this Hig. They never should have done it.

He doesn't sound unhappy.

Bangley has reached up and switched on the LED headlamp banded to his cap. His cap is on backward. He shines it on the short man, the one in the cowboy hat, the hat now tumbled into a drainage furrow a few feet off. It's a boy. Maybe nine. About the age. Melissa seven months pregnant when. Nine years ago. This boy is thin, hair matted and tangled. A hawk feather tied into it.

Face hollow, a shadow smirched with dirt and exposure. Would have been born into this. Nine years of this. Piecing the jigsaw puzzle of this world into some dire picture in his head to end cast as an extra in Bangley's practical joke.

He grunts. Arms in the hands of babes. Should have left him behind.

Where?

Bangley shrugs, swings his head up, the light up into my eyes, blinding.

I wince down against the harsh white blare but don't turn.

Then when he wandered out of the creek starving tomorrow you would have shot him just like the others, but in full daylight and at three hundred yards not thirty.

I can't see anything but the light, but I know Bangley's grin is straight across and grim.

Hig you haven't learned a goddamn thing in all this time. You're living in the past. Makes me wonder if you appreciate any of this. Goddamn.

He walks off. He means do I deserve it. To live.

I walk away leave Jasper to his business. We will bury them tomorrow.

This is what I do, have done: I strip off haunches arms breast buttocks calves. Slice it thin soak in salt brine and dry to jerky for Jasper for the days between. You remember the story of the rugby team in the Andes. The corpses were corpses already dead. They did it to survive. I am no different. I do it for him. I eat venison, bottom fish, rabbit, shiners. I keep his jerky in airtight buckets. He likes it best of all his food I'm sure because of the salt. Tomorrow I will do it again but not the boy, I'll bury him not with any tenderness or regret just in one piece with his hawk feather.

That we have come to this: remaking our own taboos forgetting the original reasons but still awash in the warnings. I walk back around the berm. I am supposed to lie back down in our blankets and sleep with the berm at my head like a wide headstone. So I am fresh for tomorrow to fly. I will not sleep all night. I lay the gun down, just the gun, snug it back under the duffel and keep walking.

II

Back then I took up flying with the sense of coming to something I had been meant to do all my life. Many people who fly feel this way and I think it has more to do with some kind of tree-top or clifftop gene than with any sense of unbounded freedom or metaphors of the soaring spirit. The way the earth below resolves. The way the landscape falls into place around the drainages, the capillaries and arteries of falling water: mountain slopes bunched and wrinkled, wringing themselves into the furrows of couloir and creek, draw and chasm, the low places defining the spurs and ridges and foothills the way creases define the planes of a face, lower down the canyon cuts, and then the swales and valleys of the lowest slopes, the sinuous rivers and the dry beds where water used to run seeming to hold the hills and the waves of the high plains all together and not the other way around. The way the settlements sprawl and then congregate at these rivers and mass at every confluence. I thought: It's a view that should surprise us but it doesn't. We have seen it before and interpret the terrain below with the same ease we walk the banks of a creek and know where to place our feet.

But what I loved most from the first training

flight was the neatness, the sense of everything in its place. The farms in their squared sections, the quartering county roads oriented to the cardinal compass points, windbreaks casting long shadows westward in the morning, the round bales and scattered cattle and horses as perfect in their patterns as sprays of stars and holding the same ruddy sun on their flanks, the pickups in the yards, the trailer parks in diagonal rows, the tract homes repeating the side-lit angles of roofs, baseball diamond and kart track ovals, even the junkyards just so, ragged lines of rusted cars and heaps of scrap metal as inevitable and lovely as the cottonwoods limning the rivers, casting their own long shadows. The white plume from the stack of a power plant tended eastward on the morning wind as pure as washed cotton. This was then. From up here there was no misery, no suffering, no strife, just pattern and perfection. The immortal stillness of a landscape painting. *Nor ever can those trees be bare* . . . Even the flashing lights of an emergency vehicle progressing along the track of a highway pulsed with the reassuring rhythm of a cricket.

And for a time while flying, seeing all this as a hawk would see it, I am myself somehow freed from the sticky details: I am not grief sick nor stiffer in the joints nor ever lonely, nor someone who lives with the nausea of having killed and seems destined to kill again. I am the one who is flying over all of it looking down. Nothing can touch me.

There is no one to tell this to and yet it seems very important to get this right. The reality and what it is like to escape it. That even now it is sometimes too beautiful to bear.

Also I wonder how Bangley is built inside and everyone like him. He is as at home with his solitude as the note reverberating inside a bell. Prefers it. Will protect it to the death. Lives for protecting it the way a peregrine lives for killing other birds midflight. Does not want to communicate what the death and the beauty do to each other inside him.

I took him flying in the first week of his arrival. He wanted to recon our perimeter, our weakest approaches. Squeezed him into the passenger seat and gave him a headset so he could talk to me. I made widening circles outward and climbed like a climbing hawk. It was a clear morning with the gullies still shadowed and a flock of seagulls shocked white between us and the ground. At ten miles and a thousand feet he said

Druids. Go lower circle.

I'd never heard the word.

Met them on the way in, he said. They have the blood sickness. Yelled across the yard. Shot two that came too close. Wish I had incendiary now.

I glanced at him. The shock of it. Never heard

that story but of course how could they know he ended up with me, my partner.

A few of the ragged kids ran out of a turkey shed and waved, jumped up and down. Bangley turned his hunched shoulders in the cramped seat to look at me.

They know you?

Yup. I help them. They're not Druids, they're Mennonites.

I felt his eyes on the side of my face then not. He said nothing the rest of the trip, not even when we flew up close along the mountains and saw the fresh snow blowing off the rock ridges.

III

So I wonder what it is this need to tell.

To animate somehow the deathly stillness of the profoundest beauty. Breathe life in the telling.

Counter I guess to Bangley's modus which is to kill just about everything that moves.

★

On the night of the one sided firefight in which I didn't pull the trigger I walked straight past the west hangars and kept going. Jasper has a good nose and I knew that if he looked up and got worried he would just follow. Didn't want to whistle him away from his party, and I knew Bangley well enough that he'd had enough killing in one night not to fuck with my dog. I had no goggles no gun. Bangley always wears a belted sidearm, I'm sure he wears it to sleep. I have never seen him asleep but I wonder how many nights he has watched us at the base of the berm snoozing. There is much about the man that creeps me out but this is the worst, the unrelenting sense of being surveilled. I've learned to live with it the way the Cree in Canada must live with swarms of mosquitoes. Did live. But there is the nagging fear: if he decided the attacks had tapered off enough to defend this place himself or if my visiting the families was too much of a risk he might kill us both, me and Jasper, unimpeded with an easy two shots fifty steps from his front porch. So in this sense I am crazy to sleep in the open, but then if Bangley wanted to kill me he would have limitless opportunities in any one day, so I decided from the beginning to make my daily choices without including Mr. Death in the calculus.

And so, in this way, I thought as I walked past the last hangars west and away from our one burning bulb on the one porch into the not total darkness of the starlit plains, I thought that in this way the visitation by the five men paid a kind of surety against my survival at least for a while. For a while Jasper and I were indispensable, though Bangley had dispatched the group, the killing part, with literally one eye on the ball.

I walked around the old gas tank which was green in daylight, now black, bulked in the tall sage brush, and my feet found without thinking the worn trail to the mountains. My trail. The one Jasper and I had worn over nine years, and Bangley out to his tower. Erie airport had no control tower, it was an uncontrolled field, meaning that the pilots just talked to each other and worked things out according to long used protocol, but Bangley and I had built our own tower four miles out onto the plain, halfway to the mountain front, and this tower was for killing. It had taken us two months to build, salvaging the lumber out of a painstaking teardown of an ugly, blocky, modern, wooden thing on Piper Lane that reminded me of a grade school from the Seventies. We hauled the lumber out to the site in his pickup when it still ran, and in his dry van trailer, the one he had showed up with that was full of guns, weapons of every murderous phylum, and mines and canned food and ammo. We hauled out a generator too from one of the electricity free hangars on the north side, and we ran it on avgas to power the saws and drills. Bangley was not a born carpenter and it was the first and only time I saw him do a manual job with any kind of éclat, the work fired I know now by a vision of the clean, long shots he'd get with his .408. He couldn't wait to get to the top platform and install the bench rest and locking swivel he had spent hours at his desk designing. A separate permanent mount for his spotting scope and another for his laser range finder. None of which—the gun nor the scope nor the range finder—he ever left on the tower. But he left a windspeed/direction indicator out there on its own pole where it wouldn't be queered by wind deflecting and eddying off the roof, and he left his ballistics tables in a neat dove jointed drawer which I crafted for him.

His preferred range was fourteen hundred yards. Close enough with his skills to pretty much guarantee a kill but far enough to flatter his pride.

Which meant that there was one spot on the trail that was a place where many people over the years had seen their last living look of the sad world. It was a place literally soaked in blood. The ground here, the dirt between a tall sage on the south side of the trail and tall bushy rabbit brush on the north, was black with the coppery minerals of spilled blood, stained the way the place in a yard or dirt drive where a man changes the oil in his car is stained. That night I covered the four miles plus four hundred yards in much less than an hour. I didn't notice the distance and I didn't notice the time. By my calendar it was the night of April 21st which to my knowledge is not some solstice or equinox, but seems significant anyway to me like all 21sts of the month. It was also Melissa's birthday. She didn't like parties so we never had one. We had quiet dinners, usually sushi, which she regarded as a ridiculously decadent form of nutrition but adored never-theless like twice a year. Her favorites were gone by the end, the tuna and yellowtail and wild salmon, and the prices were so high for most of the rest we just stopped going.

I always gave her a book. An old hardback from the same section in the used bookstore where you'd find Hardy Boys and Nancy Drew, and musty scrawled-in *Hobbit*s, the painted paper covers often ripped or gone. But some motif from the cover illustration was stamped on the cloth of the hard cover itself, a rearing horse or an ancient elm, so that you could close your eyes and run your hands over the grainy surface and feel the fleet curves of the bucking bronco, the brachial patterns of the spreading tree.

My favorite was a sort of illustrated guidebook of pond creatures on which a very young child had written in pencil on each page under the picture of an otter

I love otter

Under a muskrat:

I love muskrat

Beaver:

I love beaver

★

I walked past the tower in the dark. The path through the brush absorbed and gave back the light from the Milky Way and was clear in its windings. I walked over the target spot, over a black staining that was not the shadow of the sage. I did not shudder or feel much of anything. I felt the wind. It was west down from the mountains and it should have been cold-snow cold, but it was warm and smelled of earth, and of the cedar on the lower slopes and the spruce higher up. Like rock emerging from ice. Lichen and moss. I thought it did. It smelled like spring.

Too early in mid-April for a real thaw, but

anymore the old seasonal benchmarks were mostly nostalgia. We had snow in the mountains this winter but there were two years running where the peaks were dry holding almost nothing. This scared me more than attacks or disease.

Losing the trout was bad. Losing the creek is another thing altogether.

I still fished in the mountains. The trout were gone because the streams got too warm, but I fished suckers and carp, nymphing the bottom like before, and overcoming the revulsion when I got a sucker, the sluggish resistance that couldn't be called a fight, and the distended lips and the scales. I made myself get used to the taste and the bones. Now that the trout were gone the carp had learned to occupy the niche and feed more and more on the surface, so I even sometimes fished dry flies. Never brought them back for Bangley because he wouldn't have understood. The hours spent. The danger in being so absorbed along a stream which was the thoroughfare for both animals and wanderers.

But I did. He would have called it Recreating, which he called with scorn anything that didn't directly involve our direct survival, or killing, or planning to kill which amounted to the same thing. *Christ Hig we're not Recreating here are we? Good goddamn.* Deer hunting was one thing. The amount of quality protein in one successful trip divided by the risk. The fact that I wanted to go, that I needed it—to get up there, to get away, to breathe that air—he overlooked. Had I hated it, he would have liked that better. Same with flying. He knew that flying for me was life somehow and yet he couldn't count on two hands the times we were arguably saved by the intelligence from some patrol.

He wasn't my boss and I did what I did, but he made sure his disapproval grated hard, and after a while it was easier to not put this stuff in his face. A matter of keeping the needle in the green day to day.

I fished. I'd set down my pack against a still green tree. The kayak sled. My rifle. I passed up the beetle kill, the standing dead trees that broke and fell in a hard wind, and walked further into the green. I always fished a stretch of woods that had not died, or that was coming back. I set down the pack and breathed the smell of running water, of cold stone, of fir and spruce, like the sachets my mother used to keep in a sock drawer. I breathed and thanked something that was not exactly God, something that was still here. I could almost imagine that it was still before when we were young and many things still lived.

I listened to the creek, and to the wind and watched it move the heavy dark boughs. In a pool below me the dark surface was dusted with green pollen. The roots of a tree exposed in the bank snaked over the water and in their spaces old spiderweb swayed in the wind and glimmered along the threads with its rhythm.

I took out the four pieces of the rod wrapped in flannel and snugged them together, sighting along the guides and twisting the shining metal loops so they lined up true. It was a Sage pack rod, a little number four I'd had since high school. My father gave it to me for my sixteenth birthday just after I came to live with him. He died of pancreatic cancer the next year before he could ever show me how to use it, but I ended up teaching myself and learning from Uncle Pete.

I pulled out the Orvis reel he had given me with the rod, which I'd kept cleaned and oiled when no other part of my life was working smoothly if at all. I slid the tang of the reel foot into the aluminum slot in the top of the cork handle and tightened down the nut. The nut went around the whole rod and rod seat and was stamped with a deep diamond pattern that made it easy for the thumb and forefinger to grab. It turned easily and locked down tight.

All of this, these motions, the sequence, the quiet, the rill and gulp, the riffle of the stream and the wind soughing the needles of the tall trees. As I strung the rod. I had known it all hundreds, probably now thousands of times. It was ritual that required no thought. Like putting on socks. Except this ritual put me in touch with something that felt very pure. Meaning that in fishing I had always all my life brought the best of myself. My attention and carefulness, my willingness to risk, and my love. Patience. Whatever else was going on. I began fishing just after Pop died and I tried to fish the way I thought he would. Which is a little weird thinking about it now: trying to emulate a man I had never seen wield a rod, and with the fierceness of a son this man had never had much of a chance to father.

When I lost my high school girlfriend, I fished. When in a fit of frustration and despair I quit writing anything, I fished. I fished when I met Melissa and barely dared to hope that I had found someone I could love in a way that surpassed anything I had known. I fished and fished and fished. When the trout got hit with disease, I fished. And when the flu finally took her in an Elks Hall converted to a hospital and crammed with the cots of the dying not five hundred yards from our house, I fished.

I was not allowed to bury her. She was incinerated with the rest. I fished. In the increasing chaos of dwindling supplies and longer gas lines and riots, I fished. By then I was nymph fishing for carp just to get away and follow a stretch of creek, the curves and moods of which I knew as well as I had known the body of my dead wife.

In all the years at the airport I kept bringing my rod into the mountains. I'd set down the pack and put together the rod and breathe and Jasper would take his cue and lie down on the bank where he could get a good view of the action. I put on the light wading shoes which were like hi-tops with sticky rubber on the soles, and stepped down to the smooth stones that were dusty and gray in air and stepped into the water. As soon as these riverbed rocks were wet and covered they came alive with color, greens and russets and blues. I did too. Felt like that. Soon as the cold shocked my feet and pressed my shins.

Never used waders anymore. I just liked the feel of cold running water against my legs.

I was thinking, remembering this as I followed the path toward the mountains and I thought how I hadn't fished in over a year, not at all last summer, and wondered why, and wished now that I had the rod and Jasper, just a pack for a day and no gun and fuck Bangley I wasn't even going to pretend I was going hunting. But I didn't. Have any of it. I'd been walking for as much time as it took Orion to decline over the mountains, probably an hour and a half, and I stopped. I breathed and looked around me for the first time and realized I was very close to the first trees of the mountain front. And I was alone. I came out of reverie and almost called out for Jasper and realized that for the first time I could remember he wasn't with me. An icy fear contracted my guts and I turned and trotted all the way back to the airport.

IV

It warmed fast. Spring gave way without resistance. Two weeks earlier than last by the calendar I had scrawled onto a board in the hangar. I judged the threat of night frost over and furrowed and strung the rows of the garden, and drilled and planted under a benign sun which warmed the back of my neck and turned the fur of Jasper's back pleasantly hot under my hands.

I planted the same crop I planted every year: string beans, potatoes, corn. Also had spinach which I grew in a cold frame along with the little tomato plants I'd started.

In the final days when I decided I would have to bail out of the city fast, those are what I took out of my own cold shed in the backyard. A dirt crusted basket of seed packets and a bucket of seed potatoes. The same five, this now our tenth planting. I'd need to trade seeds with the families soon to keep the plants strong, why I hadn't done it already I'm not sure. A couple of years I used the warm conservatory room of one of the mansions to start seedlings but they died in a hard frost each time when the cold overcame the stored heat in the brick floor. I couldn't be bothered to put in a woodstove and keep them warm. Then I made the cold frame for the spinach so we could have it all year and for tomato starts in the spring.

It worked usually. I planted the potatoes later than normal so that we would get a late harvest and have them all winter. With what we had, and with just me and Bangley, I canned more than we could use and stored the jars and a heap of potatoes in a cold room in the basement of my house, the one with the bulb. I never told Bangley but I dropped off fresh vegetables in the summer, and jars too later in the year, to the families who also had a garden but were hapless in their efforts due to the disease.

On this afternoon in late April I worked slowly, enjoying the warmth of the day and letting the sun soak into my winter bones. I talked to Jasper the whole time.

We need a hill, I called, picking up the spade. We need two rows built up nice for the potatoes.

Jasper furrowed his brow and agreed, happy just to lie on a pile of sunwarmed dirt and supervise.

Hey where are the old stakes for the beans? Where did we put em?

Jasper's ears came up and his mouth opened in his version of a smile. He didn't know. He didn't give a fuck.

Were life that simple, I thought, as I had many times before. Simple as a dog's life.

I spaded up the hills for the potatoes and buried the pieces, each with its eye. I found the split lumber we'd used as bean poles and dug them in and guyed them out with string and strung three lines laddered for the climbing vines over six feet high. There was almost nothing on earth as satisfying as a wall of beans, leaves fluttering taller than you are.

I was in no hurry. What we didn't plant today we'd plant tomorrow. Probably warm enough even to plant the corn. Our shadows puddled to the north at midday and lengthened over the furrows as the spring sun made its transit into the northwest. I hummed almost tunelessly. Melissa always ribbed me for the unconscious near melody I repeated day after day when I worked. Always the same non-song. The comfort. I made a little trough for the beans, sprinkled them along it, covered them firmly. Dirt from shoveling furred the hairs on my arm and smudged my face when I rubbed my nose with the back of a fist. From the dammed-up pond in the creek, I siphoned into the shallow ditch at the head of the garden and broke it in four places with the tip of the spade to run water into the furrows. The silver runnels in the turned earth went ruddy and molten with the low sun. Staining the dirt to either side. By the middle of the night the whole planting would be wet.

I was tired. Tomorrow I'd plant the rest, the tomatoes and corn. The next day if the weather was good Jasper and I would take the sled, and this time the fly rod, and go up to the mountains for a spring buck.

The deer wandered the plains but they knew

somehow to stay away from the airport and I hadn't had much luck stalking them on the open prairie. I was a mountain hunter and anyway I wanted to go up there before the creeks got too high.

Bangley sometimes set up on the second floor of his house with a sandbag in an open window and made sport long-shooting what he could. He killed two gray wolves at great distance but then they too steered clear. He sewed the fur of a ruff onto the hood of his winter fatigue coat and wore it like a trophy.

I stood back of the new garden watching the sun touch the mountains and ruddle the turned dirt and the threads of water and I can say there was something moving inside that resembled a kind of happiness.

I would never have named it. Not then. For fear. But I name it now.

C'mon, Jasp.

I speared the spade into the loose earth for tomorrow and turned for the hangar and heard the muffled clapping as Jasper shook himself and came trotting behind me.

★

Couple days, I said. Maybe three.

I pushed two gallon Ziplocs of Jasper's jerky into the bottom of my pack. Long since over the nausea. My Uncle Pete told me, You can get used to stepping over a dead goat on the doorstep. How about a dead person?

Why three? Bangley said.

I stuffed in my down sweater, the bulky stained brown one I had ordered from Cabela's in my late twenties and taken with me to the woods every trip since. On top of it I lay the bags of my own jerky, the venison, and the folded nylon tarp I used for shelter, and a roll of parachute cord.

Why a couple, three? Plenty snow Hig. The deer should be down low.

I couldn't think of a reason so I said: That last trip in November I saw elk sign. I swear. I know you think it's crazy talk but I saw it. Tracks of a big cow. I want to look some more. Christ, if we could get an elk.

I didn't look at him. Silence.

We were like a married couple unable anymore to speak the truth about the most important things. I had never lied to Melissa about anything except the conviction that she would pull through the flu. She knew it was a lie and did not hold it against me. She was too sick anyway to worry about whether she might survive. She had dysentery-like nausea and diarrhea and her lungs were filling up like pneumonia which was terrifying. In the end she just wanted it to be over. Pillow, she whispered to me. Her eyes were glassy and unfocused, her hair wet with sweat, her hand terribly light, almost desiccated on mine. And cold. Pillow. I'd been crying. I tried with every ounce not to, not to weep as I saw my world, everything in it of any importance, vanishing from my grip. In almost a panic, I can say now, I adjusted her one pillow behind her head on the cot, not sure what she wanted adjusted, so that it bunched a little and raised her head.

No, she breathed. Barely breathed. Her hand scratched the back of mine like a claw, like she was trying to grasp it and couldn't.

Use it.

I stared at her.

Hig. Two, three breaths short, unable to get enough oxygen. Please.

Her eyes glassy, still blue gray, I always thought like a clear sea on a cloudy day, now deepening in color, struggling to focus on mine.

Please.

Please.

I looked around the hall filled with cots for a doctor or orderly, in some desperate hope to forestall, but they were almost all sick anyway, or starting to throw up and cough, this was like some ring of hell, there was no one. A stench, the clamor of coughing and sickness.

Her hand scratched at mine her eyes would not leave my face.

I gently lifted the back of her head off the pillow and laid it back down on the stained sheet and brought the pillow around and said I love you. More than anything in God's universe. And her eyes were on mine and she didn't say a word and I covered her face and used it. On my own wife.

She heaved twice, struggled, clawed lightly, went still. The clamor in the hall did not stop the moans and coughing. Did not stop.

I loved her.

This is what I live with.

I lift my head off the pillow
I see the frosted moon.
I lower it down I think of home.

Bangley said, What's wrong with you Hig? You look kind of fucked up.

I shook myself. The way Jasper does.

Nothing.

Maybe you need a vacation Hig. You been working too hard in the garden. Men weren't meant to be farmers the way I see it. Beginning of everything fucked up.

He meant take a vacation lying in the hammock I strung in the shade of the house. Between two ornamental trees, a Norway spruce and an aspen that always looked to me a little lost down here, and like they were shaking their limbs longingly at the mountains where they belonged.

I breathed. Yeah, maybe you're right. But listen

I want to go up there. If there are elk. Jesus. We'd be like kings.

We are like kings Hig. It took the end of the world.

He began to laugh. Gravelly, a little like a cough. Unpleasant.

Took the end of the world to make us kings for a day. Huh Hig? Captains of our fate. Ha!

Then he really did cough. A short fit. When he came out of it he said, Well you go up there. Do a little fishing. *Recreating.* Unwind. Get us a goddamn ghost elk. But get a deer, too, why don't you Hig. Something we can eat.

He smiled straight across, stared at me with his eyes that sparked like gravel in a streambed.

Not more than three days. I mean it. Every day you're gone fucking around we are vulnerable.

I cocked my head and looked at him. It was the very first time he had admitted to my usefulness.

I don't sleep that good he said. To tell the truth.

He coughed once more and spat out the hangar door. Well, good luck, he said, and walked off.

He didn't sleep well when I was gone. Like a wife. Fucking Bangley. Just when I thought I wished him really gone.

★

We would leave the next morning in the dark. I could cover the eight miles under cold stars and

85

make the trees with the air getting gray and grainy. I packed the pack for three days though I thought if we got on an elk it could be longer. Bangley would have to deal. I could tie the pack into the sled and drag it, but I kept it light and I preferred it on my body with the sled almost weightless behind on the way out. I knew the creeks and I moved from drainage to drainage so I packed two quarts of water only.

I decided to make one more flight. Both to scout the hunt and to give Bangley one more day of security in three directions. The afternoon was fine with just a light breeze stirring off the mountains, warm in the sun but almost winter cold in the shadow of the hangar. I had the woodstove going and the kettle on, steaming. I made tea from the jar of summer flowers, leaves that I dried: wild strawberry, black raspberry, mint, and sat in *Valdez*, the recliner I had pulled out of the home entertainment room of one of the mansions. It was named after the Exxon tanker that had wrecked and spilled in Alaska.

It was a split double recliner for husband and wife presumably, but now for me and Jasper, with a lever on each side and covered in the finest calfskin. It was very soft. I put an heirloom quilt on his side, patched with prints in blues and yellows, and with a repeating pattern of a log cabin made from squares and triangles in printed cloth, every piece different but with the same twist of smoke coming out of each chimney, paisley or polka dot or ribbed with color, so it gave an impression of a fanciful village evenly spread over a country of geometric fields and flowering crops, and at a retiring hour when everyone was indoors enjoying the warmth of a fire. As we were. It was comforting to look at and comfortable sitting in the deep chair in the waves of heat from the stove, levered halfway back and drinking tea.

I could almost imagine that it was before, that Jasper and I were off somewhere on an extended sojourn and would come back one day soon, that all would come back to me, that we were not living in the wake of disaster. Had not lost everything but our lives. Same as yesterday standing in the garden. It caught me sometimes: that this was okay. Just this. That simple beauty was still bearable barely, and that if I lived moment to moment, garden to stove to the simple act of flying, I could have peace.

It was like I was living in a doubleness, and the doubleness was the virulent insistence of life in its blues and greens laid over the scaling grays of death, and I could toggle one to the other, step into and out of as easily as I might step into and out of the cold shadow of the hangar just outside. Or that I didn't step, but the shadow passed over like the shadow of a cloud that covered my arms with goosebumps, and passed.

Life and death lived inside each other. That's what occurred to me. Death was inside all of us, waiting for warmer nights, a compromised system, a beetle, as in the now dying black timber on the mountains. And life was inside death, virulent and insistent as a strain of flu. How it should be.

It was memory that threw me. I tried hard not to remember and I remembered all the time.

Spencer was his name. Going to be. Sophie if a girl. Very English. In the second trimester we decided we wanted to know. Melissa's family was Scottish. Came over from Melrose when she was seven, enrolled in a West Denver primary school and was made to stand in front of the class and repeat words like *arithmetic* while all the kids giggled and the teachers died of cuteness assault. She said she lost the accent completely in two months. Adaptable as only a seven year old can be.

Her father's name.

Not sick, not once, the whole time. Never nauseous. Never craved avocados and ice cream.

She didn't like to hunt at all but she loved to fish. She fished with me when she could. In some ways she was better than me. She didn't have the distance and accuracy in her cast but she could think more like a trout than probably anyone alive. She would stand on the bank of a creek and just breathe and watch the bugs flying in and out of the sunlight.

The guides, the freaks, did stuff like pump out

the stomach of their first fish with a rubber bulb to see what they were eating right now. As if being caught, netted, held in the scalding air wasn't traumatic enough. They put the fish back, but did they live after that operation? They claimed they did, I doubted it. She didn't do anything like that. She snugged the halves of her rod together, strung it, pulled the line straight down from the top guide with a whizz of the reel and let her slender fingers slide down the length of the leader, the tippet, and pushed back the brim of her Yankees cap, and then she asked me.

Hig what should I put on?

I studied the hatch flitting in the sunlight or swarming the surface, turned over a few rocks to look at the larvae.

Eighteen Copper John on the bottom, a Rio Grand King, pretty big, on top.

She'd move her lips around looking at me like I was putting her on. Then she'd tie on a bead head prince and an elk hair caddis. Big and small just the reverse. Or she'd go with a purple wooly bugger, the one with the brass conehead, which is like a swimming minnow mimic and an entirely different strategy.

Why do you ask me? I said. I think you ask and then do just the opposite.

Her smile, bright and sudden, was one of my favorite things on the planet.

I'm not disrespecting you Hig. I'm doing a

survey. Kind of calibrating what I'm thinking against the finest fisherman I know.

Flattery now. Jeez. Fish on.

She usually outcaught me. Except on the big rivers, the Gunnison, the Green, the Snake, where a long cast was helpful. The last time we went fishing we had a terrible fight.

I drank the tea. It occurred to me that Jasper owned more special quilts than any dog in history. He had his *Valdez* recliner log cabin quilt, his flying hunting dog quilt, his outside sleeping quilt covered in Whos from Whoville. He was lying flat on his side with his butt against me and his legs sticking off the cushion and he was snoring.

Is it possible to love so desperately that life is unbearable? I don't mean unrequited, I mean being *in* the love. In the midst of it and desperate. Because knowing it will end, because everything does. End.

I drank in the beginning. Every kind of food, even the horses, were all consumed in the first year, but the booze was still tucked in cabinets and closets, in basements. Bangley and I used it for treating cuts. Bangley never drank because it was part of his Code. I'm not sure if he thought of himself as a soldier or even a warrior, but he was a Survivor with a capital S. All the other, what he had been in the rigors of his youth, I think he thought of as training for something more elemental and more pure. He had been waiting for the End all his life. If he drank before he didn't drink now. He didn't do anything that wasn't aimed at surviving. I think if he somehow died of something that he didn't deem a legitimate Natural Cause, and if he had a moment of reflection before the dark, he would be less disappointed with his life being over than with losing the game. With not taking care of the details. With being outsmarted by death, or worse, some other holocaust hardened mendicant.

Sometimes I think the only reason he kept me around was so he had someone to witness his prowess in the winning of each day. I wonder if the stunt the other night was just to let me know that it was him. That he vouchsafed our survival every day. Remember that, Hig.

I heard a joke once about a shipwreck. I heard it way back when a model named Trippa Sands was the woman in the posters on the walls of teenage boys. The cover girl of cover girls, the paragon of sexiness. She is on vacation on a big cruise ship that hits a reef in the Caribbean and sinks. She washes up on a desert island with my buddy Jed. The only survivors. They wash up onto the beach, the waves christen them with foam, they are in tatters, mostly naked, and they look into each other's eyes with the dawning apprehension of their unique solitude, and love hits them like a falling coconut. They fall hopelessly. Luckily, the island is replete with low hanging fruit and sweet fresh water, and oysters and fish that jump into their woven baskets, so that sustaining themselves is a breeze and they have a lot of leisure time just to gaze into each other's eyes and make the kind of fierce love I imagine an apocalypse affords. About a week into it Jed says, Tripp?

Ahh. Hmmm. Yes, my fragrant studliness.

I have a favor to ask you.

Of course, my sandbrushed power drill. Anything. For you.

Can you wear my cowboy hat for a few days?

Oh sure, why not!

Next day he says, Trippa?

Yes, Pooty?

I have a favor to ask you.

Anything my little mango.

Can you use a bit of this charcoal and draw on a moustache?

Hmm. Well for you, you big Cumquat, anything.

Next day they've just made love nonstop for an entire tide cycle. They are sitting on a tortoiseshell bench watching a thunderstorm sweep over the azure water, Trippa in her hat and moustache, and Jed says, Hun?

Yes Poots.

Um, can I call you Joe?

Well, ah sure, you plunging hammerhead shark you.

Jed grabs her and shakes her shoulders.

Joe! he cries. Joe! Joe! I'm fucking Trippa Sands!

Still makes me laugh. Can't help but think of me and Bangley which isn't so funny. That he wants me to be Joe so he can show someone how well he is surviving. *I'm fucking the shit out of this survival stuff aren't I, Hig?* He never told me another thing about his upbringing except that it wasn't what you think, but I imagine that his mother, if he had one, was pretty hard to impress.

Well. I guess. I say it to Jasper who has shifted so his head is hanging down off of *Valdez* but is still snoring. I put my hand on his ribs in the short fur and rub.

Let's go flying.

★

It's late afternoon, my favorite time after dawn. I fuel up. The pump runs off its own solar panel. Used to use a battery and inverter but the battery died so I wired it directly to the inverter and now can only fuel up if the sun is shining which it is. I have a hand pump if I need it, but it's a pain. I fill the tanks from a stepladder, through capped intakes at the top of each wing, and it's a real pain to be on the ground and pump and keep track of the fuel level which is checked by climbing up and looking straight down into the bladder through the fill hole. I can estimate and get it close, but it's way easier just to stand up there and pull the trigger on the pump hose and hear the

93

reassuring electric hum and the clicking of the numbers rolling on the meter like filling up a car used to be.

Used to. Plenty of gas still out in the world but problem is the auto gas went stale and bad a year or two after. 100 low lead, which I burn, is stable something like ten years. So I expect to lose it one of these days. I can add PRI and nurse it along for ten more years probably. Then I'll have to look for jet fuel which is kerosene and lasts for basically ever. I know where it is, the closest. I know that right now I'm the only one alive who knows, or at least knows how to get it out. But every time I land at Rocky Mountain Airport I feel vulnerable in a way I never do at my other stops. It's too big. A big old jetport with scores of buildings, hangars, sheds and the pumps and the steel fill plates out in the open.

When I have to, me and Bangley will pow wow. Maybe we'll have to break camp. Can't imagine. Or maybe I'll just have to take him with me to cover my back every time I fill up which would be a kind of party for him but would leave Erie wide open for at least half an hour.

Jasper is sitting up in his seat and I taxi past the rows of private aircraft still tied down. All have flat and rotted tires, many cracked windshields from hail. Some, the ropes frayed and wore and broke in big winds, and the planes upended or rolled into others across the ramp, or further. Last spring we had a gale and a Super Cub broke loose and ended up in the second story plate window of a fancy house across the runway, on Piper Lane, which was fitting. The green street sign like a pre-printed headstone.

Why don't I fly one of the Super Cubs or Huskies? Some narrow tandem (one seat in front, one in back), something more agile, that can swoop down and land short, can basically land and take off on a tennis court? Why do I fly my eighty year old Cessna four seater?

Because the seats are side by side. So Jasper can be my copilot. The real reason. The whole time I fly I talk to him, and it amuses me no end that the whole time he pretends not to listen.

We taxi between the rows. There are some beautiful old planes. The colored stripes, the blues and golds and reds are fading. The numbers. One I used to fly, a little home-built plane with a pull down bubble cockpit, stands nose down to the tarmac like a forlorn bird, the U.S. Air Force stars painted on the fuselage burned to washed splashes. It was built by a longtime friend of mine, Mike Gagler. An Alaska bush pilot who ended up flying jets for the airlines and built planes as a hobby. Never did anything like anyone else almost as a matter of principle. He died early with his family in a yellow house I can see from the open door of the hangar. He refused to go to the hospital, said they were just a way for the government to get the dead in one place. He was the last in his family to die, by force of will, so his wife and two daughters would have someone to hold them. I buried the four of them with the airport's backhoe when it still ran.

In the early days I took it out, Mike's RV-8, and wasted gas. Left Jasper sitting anxious and alone by the gas pumps and climbed straight into the sun and kept pulling the stick until the sky rolled down beneath me and the horizon came down over my head like the visor of a helmet. Big, slow, sickening backward loops and fast barrel rolls. I did it because I didn't know what else to do.

Then I'd buzz the runway at ten feet and see Jasper rooted on his haunches following me with his eyes, and even at that speed I knew he was worried, and grieving that I might leave him like everything else had done, so I stopped.

The wind sock midfield swings northward, puffing without urgency, so we turn south onto the taxiway, and I jam the throttle and we take off. One thing about everybody dying is that you don't have to use the designated runway.

Nothing is designated anymore. If it weren't for Bangley I'd forget my name.

★

I figure we'll fly the big circle then stop for a Coke. Scout the meadows below Nederland, below the peaks of the Divide, fly the spiral inward, check the roads and the two trails while there's good light, make sure Bangley is clear of visitors at least a day in the three directions, then land at the soda fountain and bring back a couple cases. Only eight minutes out to the northeast toward Greeley. A peace offering. Of bloated cans and plastic bottles. There's a stack of Dr. Pepper I can see with the headlamp in back of the semi, maybe now's the time to spring it on him like Christmas. Bangley seems like a Dr. Pepper man. One of Sprite for the families, land there one time, it's been a few weeks. As we bank left, north, the lowering sun spills through the glass like something molten.

Look straight down, the tract development north of the airport patterns itself in the head to toe lollipops of feeder and cul de sac, and if I squint, to blur the ones burned, I can imagine a normal late spring evening.

Continue the climbing bank west and level out at eight hundred feet and begin my scan.

★

Nothing. Nothing the whole way. Roads empty. Blessedly. Usually are. Had there been wanderers it would have fucked up everything, delayed our hunt. Then I would have swooped, cut the engine, played the tape. I have four songs on the CD

97

rigged to the amp and the speakers: they are titled

Turn Back North or Die
Turn Back South or Die
Turn Back East or Die
Turn Back West or Die

The words are easy to remember: just the title over and over. Followed by the exhortative: We know you are here. You will become dog food like many before you.

Bangley made me add that.

Fuck no, I said. That's unnecessary and disgusting.

Bangley just stared at me, his grin half formed.

It's true ain't it? Ain't it Hig?

Hit me like a punch.

Add it, he said. This isn't some debutante ball.

Mostly it works. Enough unknowns, enough survived that visitors can't be sure there isn't some phalanx of Mongols at the airport waiting to tear them apart. Which I guess we are. A phalanx of two. No, three. And they must think: These guys have an air force, a loudspeaker, a recording, what else have they got? We have Bangley, I think. You have no idea what that means. You better fucking turn back.

If they need more convincing I've gotten pretty good at shooting Bangley's Uzi machine pistol out my window on a left bank. I try not to hit anybody but sometimes I do.

I have been shot at fourteen times. Three went through the fuselage. Most people don't know how to shoot at airplanes. They never lead us enough.

Nobody now. Highway 7 is clear, 287, the interstate. Our trail west. Sun is pouring down Boulder Canyon brushing the tops of the Flatirons. Used to be our favorite day hike, the trail along the base of the slabs, when the when. To the north Mount Evans flushes with blood snow. Misjudged the time, no time to scout the hills if I am going on a beverage run. In truth I don't need to scout them anyway. I do it because it's beautiful to fly low over the foothills but we know where the deer are. If we are going to cut elk sign it will be on the ground. I bank east and beeline straight for the power plant on the St. Vrain SW of Greeley. It's a jackknifed double trailer semi half off the county road, half into a long farm driveway. I can see it five miles out. The dirty red and white sides catch the sun like a billboard. Hijacked for the potable water, I guess, the bottled water inside and all the pop. First time I saw the truck it probably wouldn't have occurred to me to land, but for the five bodies strewn around it. And one doubled out the driver's window. Tableaux of gunplay made me throttle back and circle.

I am not as quick as I once was, I am sure. Sometimes it is fog and shaggy horses. But the bodies spoke from the ground and the truck blazoned. Think, Hig. A gun battle around a Coke truck.

Which led to our monthly treat.

That first time, the farm pond east of the semi was slicked black in a crescent along the north bank, and wrinkled over the rest so I circled and landed on the yellow dotted line to the north, into the wind. I climbed down and turned for Jasper who waited bunched and excited on my seat, and I carried him to the ground. I dragged the men off into the grassy ditch by their boots so Jasper could—Discovered early on that it is easier that way than by the arms.

The doors of the rear trailer were padlocked, a simple brass U lock. I walked to the farmhouse and across a muddy yard and found the bolt cutters in the tractor shed.

Didn't occur to me til some months later that I could fly Bangley out there and he could drive the truck right to the airport. By then I enjoyed bringing back a few cases at a time. By then I figured to make it last the years of our lives. Little enough in our lives to celebrate.

Didn't occur to me either until much later that by then, by then if it were years, the cans might be utterly ruined by freeze and thaw. No matter. It was a good system now.

That first time I loaded three cases into the Beast and closed and latched the doors. I had the key turned in the mags to start the plane when I climbed out again and tied the strip of a man's red shirt to a mile marker for a wind indicator. Mile 4. I remember.

Riddled with three .22 bullet holes in a three inch group. Pretty good. Probably the farm boy practicing for prairie dogs.

Today it is again from the north. The wind. Shifted one eighty in less than an hour which is typical this time of year. This time of year I have seen the wind socks at either end of the runway at Erie facing in opposite directions, which makes for an interesting landing.

A line of telephone poles runs along the east edge of the road. Doesn't matter, they were set back far enough. The small reflector poles and mile markers easily pass under the wings. My first instructor told me that in an emergency landing a paved road was almost always wide enough if you landed dead center, almost always enough setback on any kind of pole or sign. What got dicey was a nice wide looking dirt road. The signpost you don't see could be the one that grabs a wing and cartwheels you.

Still, I bank left for a final approach into the wind, very high, and float down on full flaps, down the middle of the left lane sighting a spot on the road just short of a tall cottonwood, then at the horizon ahead, the road rising to meet me, floating downward, and then I smoothly pull the yoke, back back back to my chest and flare and settle one light bump while the stall horn blares. Still, after all these years, the thrill of a good landing. Have done it many times before from this direction and know I don't even need to lean on the brakes, just hold the nose up and let the plane roll out to the driveway and the truck.

One tap of the brakes, Jasper sitting his seat on his haunches on the thick quilt in copilot position, jerked forward just a little, resetting his front feet. Pull the red mixture knob and cut the engine. A prolonged sputter, the whirring prop becoming visible, slowing then silence.

Wind shudders the windscreen, shakes the plane. Windier than I thought. Gusty. Flattening the short grass in the field, intermittent like a breeze through a crew cut. Purple asters in the ditch nodding. The side window is open, I rest my elbow. Smell of damp earth rich with rot and newness. Heady with memory as only smell can be. Still a tang of ancient manure from the mud feedlot back of the sheds. Everything unstable this time of year.

Turn to Jasper.

Welcome to Old Coke City. Another On Time Arrival and perfect landing brought to you by the flight crew at Mongrel Air. Please remain seated until the aircraft has come to a complete stop. Careful opening the overhead bin.

Jasper deigns one glance, disapproving, and

continues staring straight ahead through the windshield, brow furrowed like any good copilot. He doesn't appreciate joking while on the job. He knows we're going to the truck so he watches the truck twenty yards ahead.

Then he growls. Short. A low huff that puffs the loose skin over his upper teeth.

Okay we *are* at a complete stop. There is no overhead bin. Don't be a stickler. Jeez.

His growl lower now, continuous. Hackles standing, hair on the rough behind smoothed flat over tight skin. Eyes fixed on the back of the Coke trailer. My hair, the small hairs on the back of my own neck, prickle and stand. Follow his eyes. The white painted latch back of the trailer angles out from the faded red door. A strip of black shadow between the two. Doors. The right one ajar. Barely. The smell coming north to south down the road. To us.

Without taking eyes off the truck I reach across for the AR. It's racked vertically, muzzle upwards in a bracket fixed to the front left side of Jasper's seat. Next to it the machine pistol. Thumb the latch of the chrome strapping and lift out the rifle. Courtesy of Bangley.

Okay, boy. Good one.

Whispering now, no reason.

Okay, c'mon.

No use to tell him to stay in the plane. He never will. Not in these gigs. Don't want him to sprain something jumping out. I unlatch my door. Two steps, wing strut to ground, half turn and gather him in one arm, the right, and lower him to the tarmac, his claws scrabbling for pavement.

Okay. Heel.

He knows. Has been through this before. Too many times.

We are sixty feet maybe fifty five. I fly with the rifle racked because it is too difficult to do in the air. Pull out the collapsable stock Bangley made me. Thumb the safety. Push the lever over, full auto to semi. The wind is light for a minute, warm in our faces, and rounded a little to the west carrying complex scents, earth, flower, even maybe salt. Of the sea. How far? Nine hundred miles at least. I listen. Just breeze catching in the whorl of my left ear. Jasper's growl has not ceased. I step. Wait. Step again. A kestrel flies over right to left, not high, a stooping, cantered flight. Step again. We cover half the distance and stop. Crouch and then go to one knee. Low as possible without going prone. Prone is best but prone is hard to move fast. Like this, if they fire out of the trailer, I am confident they will shoot high.

Bark of my own voice startles me.

You are dead men.

Wind.

You are dead men. You try to shoot your way out you are definitely dead men.

Jasper's growl. Sun warm on my left brow and cheek.

You are fish in a barrel. You hear me! You try to fight and this is your last minute on earth. Throw out your weapons come out. COME OUT! Hands where I can see them. If you do, do what I say I will not harm you. My word.

Wind. Sun. Bird. I am thinking, Do I mean that? No harm. I am not even sure. Whatever happens here I plan to live.

Three two one—OKAY YOU DIE!

I sight the iron sights. I know the last cases in the back are stacked to the roof. A third of the trailer emptied. Gives me enough angle not to shoot up the bottles and cans, probably. Two shots high—

No wait. A clank of steel, a scrape. Hand holding a crowbar snakes through the gap.

Steel bar, hand, forearm.

Drop it! Drop it! Drop it!

It drops. Hits the road with a clang.

STEP OUT, hands where I can see them.

They are big hands. Hair on the back dirty. Stuck through the gap they look like a thug trying to do a hand puppet show. Forearms in a blue ski jacket too short for his arms, greasy but new. Door pushed wider. Mallet head, wide blonde dreds, camo bush hat. Tangled beard. A huge man stepping down off the bumper, unwilling to turn his back.

There are two more.

Hoarse shout, the voice rolling through a half ton of gravel. Blinking back the sun.

A plane that runs. Where'd you get a plane that runs? Goddamn.

Shut the fuck up. Tell them. The same. Hands first.

Baseball bat, hands, arms in an oiled Australian duster, another Mongo stepping down. Long hair in a thick braid, eyes jittery: my face, the gun, the dog, the ditch. Wants to bolt. Jasper's growl a step lower.

You ain't got no bullets in that thing. World ran out of fucking bullets. Hear that Curtis? Calling back. Edging west. One step two.

Captain Pilot thinks he's gonna shoot us. Eyes skittered: the gun to the ditch.

Woulda done it already. Yes he would. Likes to talk this one.

Me thinking: So far he's been doing all the talking.

C'mon out Curtis. This is copasetic. Man's *kneeling* at thirty feet, got a gun but no bullets.

Him the closest one now three feet from the partly open door. I sight with both eyes open. Always have. Advantages. I can see the door. I can feel the evening pulling taut like a twisting wire. Dreds calling my coordinates like a mortar man. Heat. The heat of pure anger climbing into my neck, pure and clean like a white gas. My finger on the smooth cold curve of the trigger.

Door swings. Open. A shadow. Edge pulling back like a curtain, light following, lighting, lit the man in motion, swinging the bow across and down. I fire. Twice. Arrow like a hole torn in air, angry thwip of a vacuum high and wide, the man blown back, bow clattering, the front wall of Cokes toppling and spilling. Silence. One Dr. Pepper rolls out hits the road.

The two on the road half crouched and frozen, arms in reflex covering their heads. Tweedle Dum and Tweedle Dee.

The can of Dr. Pepper has rolled over, rested against Pony Tail's boot. A string of blood drips from trailer edge to the pavement where the can fell.

Look what you did. I am yelling. You fucking bonehead scum. Ruined it. Probably twenty cases of pop.

My chest, breath, vibrate with adrenalin and fury.

Killed your buddy too. Nice fucking try.

The men frozen, arms covering, crouched. This the last pathetic gesture before death. Fully expecting now to die. The gun already sighted on Dreds, finger already pressed on the trigger. Breathing hard. I hold there breathe. I will kill them.

Fuckers tried to kill me. For Coke. Well. For a not quite daily Coke. Twenty four in a case, once a month, I bring it back. The week going without—a contrived measure of want to make the next run a treat. For me and. To up my value with Bangley. Face it. Landing at the families' place with the Sprite like a god.

One is whimpering, the blonde one. Not bothering to beg.

Have to kill them. Leave them and they will empty the truck, hide it all in the ditches, windbreaks, no more monthly treat. These few things. Few enough things to look forward to. Plus they tried to kill me.

Dreds kneels, covers his eyes with his huge hands just like a kid playing peekaboo and crying. Pony Tail squeezing his head with forearms watching me in naked terror, half wincing, quivers, bracing for the shot.

Get up.

Get it over with! Dreds screams.

Get up. I'm not going to kill you.

The words like liquid nitrogen. A moment of complete freeze.

What you're gonna do is drag your buddy to the ditch and not say a word, not one fucking word while my dog has dinner.

The images colliding, conflicting in their terror shorn minds. Their own lives, the relief not even digested or believed, the horror of the feeding dog. Creates a vortex, a crosscurrent like the two flags at the airport facing each other in contrary winds. They both start to tremble. Hard.

I mean it. Not gonna shoot you. Like you said I would have already. Certainly would.

Hands down watching me. Kill them for a Coke. Not a staple, a luxury. The way before we killed for diamonds, for oil. Not. Not today.

You're gonna drag your buddy to the ditch and then you're gonna load twenty cases, fifteen of Coke, five of Sprite, and oh yeah two extra of Dr. Pepper, you're gonna load them in the back of the plane nice and neat and then I'm gonna climb in and fly away. And you can have the rest. Because I can't prevent it. Once I take off. Unless I kill you. Which I won't. Done too much of that. Go on.

The kestrel is over the field. The wind is in the short grass, the sun is almost on the Divide. He will hover and hunt until past dusk. Hover and swoop, hover and swoop. In his little helmet, hovering tireless, treading air. Hunting mice and voles.

I feel sick. Want to throw up on the road but won't. Sick of defending whatever it is I'm supposed to defend.

★

They loaded the cans. They dragged their compa to the ditch and I whistled once, turned my back. They carried four cases stacked at once, it went fast. I told them to load in the bow and quiver.

109

Pony Tail swung a long necklace of shriveled leather pieces when he bent over. Both of them smelled like death.

You're a dead man anyway, Pony Tail grumbled, passing me with a load.

What'd you say?

Nothin. Grunting the cases through the jump door.

What the fuck did you say?

He turned, passed. I stopped him with the barrel of the AR.

What was that about being a dead man?

Shoved the barrel into his ribs hard. His grunt.

The A-rabs. You can kill us but the A-rabs will kill you.

What d'you mean the A-rabs?

We heard it. In Pueblo. Ham radio. The A-rabs. They're here. Or coming. Kill us all.

He spat. Inches from my boot.

What is that? Shove.

What is what?

That. Your necklace.

He stood straight, swallowed. His eyes gold green in the last full sun. Mocking.

Them are cunts. Dried cunts.

I pulled the trigger. Tore him open. Without thought. Left him sprawled back on the road, guts spilled. The other, the Dreds dropped his load of cases and ran. South. South between two

green fields. Beneath a reef of clouds flushed
rose an antic figure diminishing to a dot.

★

Try to do the right thing. Circumstance intervenes.
What am I going to do with twenty cases of Coke?
Dole them out to Bangley?

V

When I told Bangley about the encounter at the Coke truck he took a can of snuff out of his vest pocket, a new can, and slid his sharp thumbnail around the coping of the lid and pried it off. I could smell it from the workbench, strong salty must like a shovelful of turned peat. He tucked it into his lower jaw, backed up two steps and spit out the hangar door, this one success in the domestic training of the man.

Thanks.

Hell Hig, once I learned this was going to be your kitchen and formal parlor, hell.

He leaned back against the high stool I put there for him near the door. So he could talk and twist and spit. He leaned, half standing, legs straight, arms crossed, never truly sat.

So you gave em a chance to live.

Turned, spat.

You were a Boy Scout.

Watching me. I imagined his mineral eyes when they shift make a dry sound like stirring gravel.

Ready to compromise an important source of caffeine. Not to mention carbonation. Not much carbonation in our lives, Hig. Effervescent we are not.

Couldn't help but smile at him. He turned, spat.

You were willing to sacrifice your own life too.

Twice. No, thrice. What's thrice for four? I can't even keep track.

He loosed a hand from under his crossed arms and winced down his eyes, scrunched his mouth, made to count. He had a three day beard, gray stubble like wire. Gave up.

Let's see: first mistake not working around to the side where you could shoot wide of the cargo and clear the back. You told me the trailer is two thirds full. Well. Plenty of room. And chances are the combatants are huddled up by the door. Got plenty of ammo. Anyway it would've flushed em. The guy with the bow could never have got set up.

Shook his head. Not amused.

Second time: when the guy called back to his buddy behind the door and basically gave your coordinates. Sighted you in, Hig. Gave his shooter angle and distance. Only thing I can figure for a move that bold is they knew they were dead anyway and thought to give this one desperate effort a chance. I mean, they knew they were dead with anyone else in the hemisphere but old Hig. They didn't count on that. Hig who must be trying to get to heaven.

Spat.

So they call out, Here's how to shoot this fucker, and you said you had them sighted. Now that would have been the time to pull off a shot or two. At least three. Kill the outside man first, that fast, the one closest to the shoulder where

113

he could turn the corner of the trailer, then the inside man, then the man who was obviously in the back of the trailer about to try to kill you. Bang bang bang.

Spat.

Nope. Not old Hig. Never fails to astound me. You wait til the door swings open and you see the guy with the drawn bow, and you wait til he looses off a shot just in case maybe he was hunting pheasant or something and didn't have your ass in mind—

Not like that.

He got off a shot or didn't he?

No use arguing. I leaned back against the workbench, crossed my own arms. I was embarrassed. I can say that.

Okay so you plug him. First right move all morning. But how many cases were ruined? If we had set up to the side like a good tactician, well. But okay. He's terminated. Threat neutralized. The other two are big pussies and freeze, stead of taking that opportunity to attack or retreat.

Shook his head.

They give the Hig one last golden opportunity. Far as you know. Present themselves as perfect targets. Practically begging you to end it.

Spat. Uncrossed arms, lifted the brim of the sweat stained camo cap and scratched his thinning scalp. Replaced the cap. Grin straight across.

But no. We are going to put ourselves in mortal

danger again. Fact we are going to *give* them the whole trailer of soda pop for their troubles. Which, by the way, Hig, you never told me it was a semi. Which we coulda drove over here anytime. I always figured a warehouse or something. Never even thought to ask.

Twisted, spat. Stayed half turned looking out into the sun across the ramp and the runway.

Turned back.

Well, your call. You found it. Stared at me.

Where were we? Oh yeah. I mean they tried their best to kill us, it's the best we can do. Give them all the Coke. Consolation prize. I guess. So we're gonna give it to em, but we'll give em another chance to kill us first. We'll get them to load us up with our own tiny consolation prize, and give them proximity while we're at it, you close enough you can touch em with the gun, them big and fast, perfect opportunity for another attack. One of you, two of them, the situation not controlled, not in the least, loading, unloading, the two at constantly moving spots, constantly changing angles, no restraints, not even tied together. Just like a work party, huh, Hig? Well.

Spat.

Well, might have been the best break you got all day. Because maybe it wasn't the smartest fucking move, but you are lucky Hig. That's one goddamn thing I'll say. Because then they gave you intel. Totally out of the blue. Un fucking prompted. Not even under duress. Not from Hig. We get the beta about the A-rabs.

Now he cursed for real. Under his breath. Now he didn't turn, he spat on the floor of the hangar.

We get the beta about A-rabs and what do you do? You plug the fucker. *NOW* you plug him. Finally realize he's not a Boy Scout like you, and you off him in cold blood. Before they could tell you what the fuck they meant. First intel about a possible *real* visitor, I mean a visitor with some fucking muscle, a possible goddamn *invasion,* and you terminate the conversation. Because you discover, oh surprise surprise, that the man is a rapist and a killer like every other survivor walking around this goddamn country. Holy shit. What a goddamn shock. God*damn.*

He was officially steamed. His neck, face were red. That one vein throbbing in his forehead. I felt the heat in my own face. He's right. That's what I thought. If I get caught short and killed one day it's because I'm too soft. Right? Is it worth living the other way? Bangley's way? Well, I'm an apprentice. Still. An acolyte in the School of Bangley. Just by living here. And not too great at it. Still.

Good job, he said. Happy hunting.

Stood up, unkinked his back, walked off.

Well, that didn't work out so well. I stopped at the truck to bring Bangley back a treat. Was thinking of him. Hunh. He didn't even take a Coke not a single one. He wouldn't take one while we were gone either. I knew the man. He might watch us in our sleep through a night scope but he would never touch a thing inside the hangar. Part of his Code. Anyway the Coke is tainted now. Tainted with incompetence. Here at what cost. Because even though I survived the encounter there is a cost. Statistical if nothing else. For Bangley, we only get so many fuckups before the jaws close, so the fight at the truck puts one more in my column which for better or worse is now his column. That's what steams him the most. He doesn't want to lose because he suffered some fool.

I blew the air out of my cheeks. Thought: The mountains will be good. Good to get up there. Breathe some fresh air. Thought: Strange. One other person but the families in a hundred square miles and I still need fresh air.

VI

Now we walk fast in the dark. Me and Jasper, the sled scraping behind. Cold. Good and cold. High stars nettle the black, no moon, crossing under the Milky Way like crossing a deep river. Never will get to the other side. We never do.

The argument with Bangley still rankles. Now just our breaths. Winter fat. Can feel it in my legs. Good to move, move fast.

I pull the sled on a lead with my right hand then switch. Pack is in the sled, rifle too. This time, Thanks Bangley, wearing a subcompact handgun, a plastic Glock weighs almost nothing. A sense of more survivors around, increasing traffic, don't know why.

Pass the tower on our right. Pass the Spot without a shudder. Thoughts come with the rhythm of the fast steps. Can get used to killing the way you can get used to a goat on the doorstep. Uncle Pete. With his bottle and cigarillos and stories. His living on a yacht with Louise. Their living in a trawler in Alaska. As if somehow being afloat could make a life more compelling. Never liked whiskey, he told me. But I drink it because it has a storied history.

The dead goats multiply. You can pull a goat off into the field, but a memory you can only haul into the sun and hope it desiccates. Dries to something crumbled and odorless.

We walk. We are half an hour from the first slopes, the first trees. The night is without weight: the dark weightless now in its immanent passing like a deer about to bolt. The morning light a thought that is just occurring. Still and quiet, high stars, no wind.

I think about the Plains tribes, the ones that lived here, that moved through. The Utes the Arapaho the Cheyenne. The Comanches came this far, the Sioux moving and hunting and raiding, the Kiowa, the occasional Apache. When I was a boy I read about the wars and raids between them and wondered why anyone would fight in a country this big. Why the landscape ever became a territory that needed division. Well. Bangley and I are two and sometimes our resource base seems cramped. Not because we don't have enough food, enough raw materials, enough quilts. It is ideological. Ideology that tears apart nations. Tore, past tense. What nations now? Whoever is left still fighting, scrapping over the leftovers. Maybe banding together like me and Bangley.

Still we are divided, there are cracks in the union. Over principle. His: Guilty until—until nothing. Shoot first ask later. Guilty, then dead. Versus what? Mine: Let a visitor live a minute longer until they prove themselves to be human? Because they always do. What Bangley said in the beginning: Never ever negotiate. You are negotiating your own death.

119

Me versus him. Follow Bangley's belief to its end and you get a ringing solitude. Everybody out for themselves, even to dealing death, and you come to a complete aloneness. You and the universe. The cold stars. Like these that are fading, silent as we walk. Believe in the possibility of connectedness and you get something else. A tattered union suit flying on a flagpole. Help asked and given. A smile across a dirt yard, a wave. Now the dawn not so lonely.

We are philosophers, huh, Jasper?

He's just happy to be moving. Together. He knows where we're going.

★

Follow the creek trail upwards. A trail long before we trod it, before the Arapaho, the aforementioned Cheyenne. Deer and elk, bighorn before. The coyotes who hunted them. Cougars. The wolves. The wolves again. Maybe mountain buffalo. Grizzlies occasionally, but mostly they are shy of trails, even game trails.

We move in and out of cottonwoods which make a deeper darkness. Thickets of willows. Up the grassy slopes going pale, into a short rock canyon echoing the spilling water. Then a ponderosa forest, smelled before seen, the scent carried downstream: redolent of vanilla, like a sweetshop. These still living. The sled scrapes over the trammeled roots, exposed rock. Clusters of deer scat long desiccated. I stop, let go the bridle, and hug a big tree, standing in a frieze of sweet sage that is also paler than the night, patches beneath the trees, fragrant also and tangy. Hug the thick rough bark, nose stuck in a resined crack, inhale vanilla strong as any small brown bottle, the tree pungent and sweet as butterscotch. A time when we entered shops that smelled like this. Staffed with high school kids in aprons struggling to scoop the hard ice cream. Seemed cruelly hard back then. Why keep it so cold? Thin girls blowing hair back and approaching each cone like a grudge match. Rum raisin my favorite. Melissa's pistachio. Or anything with chunks of toffee. But adored a butterscotch sundae. The saliva running in my mouth at the base of the tree. Would kill for it now maybe, not even a figure of speech.

Jasper is patient. He sits, then lies down. In other years he would have ranged ahead and swung out on our flanks, wide, crossing and recrossing the trail, following his nose, picking up game, irrepressible, but now he is happy to rest. Me too. We are in no hurry. There is plenty of stored food at the airport and Bangley can get along without me for a few days, though I hope not too well. Always the fear when we take to the mountains that he will learn to like it like this better. Alone. Though he is smart enough, a good enough tactician to know that long term his odds go down. Plus, he is not a farmer. Jasper has been through this before too many times and is polite enough not to be visibly embarrassed. The hugging a tree, the mutterings. Tonight—it is still night, though barely—I don't say a word, because tonight I am watching myself a little and I have always despised the sentimental, maybe because it is a familiar weakness. But the tree smells almost sweeter than anything in our world now and it smells like the past.

Apples used to be one of the sweetest things. In North America. Why they were such a treat, why the student currying favor left one on the teacher's desk. Honey and apples. Molasses. Maple sugar in the north woods. A candy cane at Christmas. Visions of sugarplums dancing in their heads. Sometimes in the fall on the way back from a patrol we land at an orchard north of Longmont. Acres and acres of apples, varieties I don't know the names of, most of the trees long dead for lack of water, those living along the still flowing old ditches gone scraggly, bristling with new shoots, reverting to some kind of wildness, the apples stunted and pecked, ravaged by caterpillars, but sweet. Sweeter than before. Whatever is left of whatever they distill is more concentrated in their complete and dangerous freedom.

I inhale deeply, arms stretched round, palms to the rough skin which is warmer somehow than the air, fingers holding the flaked corduroy of the bark with almost the same affinity, the same sense of arrival as they would hold to the swells of a woman.

These small what? Gratifications. And smell is always the smell itself and memory, too, don't know why.

We climb along the creek as the grainy gray seeps between the tall skeletal trees, the beetle kill ponderosa and lodgepole, the branches without needles, empty handed in death.

I still don't like it here. The dead forest. Which began to die in great swaths twenty years before. We climb. Step down to the stony bank, the cobbles rounded like eggs. To rest, drink, then climb again. Up into the spruce and fir which are still fragrant and thick with rich darkness yet.

Jasper. C'mon. You're lagging boy. Not feeling so good?

Run fingers through his thick short fur, up the bumpy ridge of his back, to the loose skin of his neck, and dig. Dig. He loves that. Turns his head away to stretch the skin. Have to bring aspirin next time. We have pounds of aspirin. Bangley says we should take it every day so we don't get Alzheimer's.

So we don't forget why the fuck we're here! he shouts, as close to glee as he gets.

So *you* don't forget. Seems to be more important to you than to me, Hig. To remember shit. Eat some goddamn aspirin.

Bangley perceptive in his own way, a judge of character.

We rest. I sit on a bench rock above a pool and Jasper lies over my feet. Does that when he's not feeling well. Morning now, the gray suffused with color. Barely. We rest until the sun filters straight through the trees with, I swear, a slight jangle as of loose banjo strings. The creek responding, a burble and lip.

Last fall I saw elk tracks. One set that wended down from the dark spruce, printed themselves in the silt where the creek ran in summer, and were lost again on the smooth dusty stones of the gravel bar. One. A large cow. A ghost. They, all of them, supposed to be gone.

A shriek. Kingfisher. Sometimes a kingfisher keeps us company. Lilts upstream ahead of us. The dipping flight reminds me of telephone wires weighted with ice, the same arc again and again and again. He perches on a dead limb over the creek, screams, flies again. Telling us, it seems, to keep up. For miles. Maybe lonely, shorn of company. Sometimes a dipper bobbing the stones at water's edge. Maybe once a year we see an osprey.

We like the birds, huh Jasp?

He opens his eyes a sec, doesn't lift his head off my boot. If I say another thing, I know him well enough: he'll lift his head to look at me to check if there is some subject that truly concerns him, that maybe I am asking for some consideration and he will hold the gaze on my face until he figures out what it is, or if it is nothing, so I don't say another word. Let him rest.

★

We rouse ourselves and climb. The ascent steep here, twisting up into the first bulwark of the hills.

We cross the old state highway at midday. Don't even touch the broken macadam, walk the big corrugated culvert beneath it, dry now since a flood washed the revenant and sent the creek around. Hollow in there. I think of Jonah and the belly of the whale. Used to shout and sing inside it to hear my compounding echo but don't anymore.

Jasper didn't like it.

We cross the highway and continue up the creek. I wait for Jasper to catch up. He looks stiff in the hips, his breath short, panting. First long walk this year, he is probably out of shape like I am, carrying a little winter fat.

★

Two wolves. Two sets of tracks in and out of the fine mud at the very edge of the water, moving fast. Catches Jasper's attention. For a minute.

Hackles rise but he quickly loses interest. Seems preoccupied with keeping up as if the walking is taking all his attention.

★

At what might be two, I decide to give us both a break. We are in no hurry. We are still some miles below where I saw the tracks but that means nothing.

Could be anywhere up here, huh, Jasper?

I pull the rod case out of the sled so he knows he is officially off duty.

★

A shallow run above a short rocky drop, just riffles. A fallen tree sieves the stream. Not quite canyon yet, but the big dark trees still living, the blue spruce and Norway, the doug fir, lean in close, their limbs strung with Spanish moss that tilts and moves in the wind. The moss I wonder how old. It is dry and light to the touch, almost crumbly, but in the trees it moves like sad pennants.

I assemble and string the rod and Jasper lies on a flat rock and watches me. It is the only one sunstruck and he watches me in a patch of warmer light, his own shadow thrown on the cobbles conforming to the round stones like thin water.

The stalks of last year's mullein stand on the bar like lightless candles. In the same sunlight I can see a hatch of tiny midges almost a mist.

I take off boots and pants, slip on the light, sticky soled sneakers I've used for years. When the rubber wears out I've got more. On the last trip to the parking lot at the box store I took five pairs my size. Not as light, but workable. Three years maybe a set so that should last me until until. I can't imagine. The pictures don't cohere in my head. To multiply the years and divide by the desire to live is a kind of false accounting. We'll keep track of this little rill. Of tying on fresh tippet and the tufty fly, and we'll blow on it for luck. Of this cast and the next and if we ourselves are lucky it will add up to nightfall.

And dinner. I want to yell that to Jasper but he is sleeping and he knows the word and would get too excited so I won't yell it until I catch a fish. The first one always goes to him.

★

I fished for a couple of hours. Cast and cast the caddis again and again. I walked to the top of the bend fishing the shallow water which turned silver as the sun came over the cut of the creek upstream. The current was silver and black twining, like mercury and oil. Then the sun moved over beyond the ridge and put us in cold shadow and the water reflected only the clear sky and I could see the stones again in the shallower runs. Green stones and water blue where it wrinkled and riffed. Somehow Jasper knows even in his sleep when I am walking more than a few steps and he roused himself and followed me and curled in a sand hollow between stones about fifty yards up. I left the fly on and tied a length of tippet to the hook and snugged on a beaded pheasant tail and caught four big carp in a few minutes. I let the bottom fly roll past the pool, the top caddis drifting easily, and it would stop, a small hitch, fleeting, not even a jerk, and then I knew a carp was mouthing the nymph below and I struck and set the hook. They fought without the vigor of a trout but with a sullen reluctance like a mule digging in its heels. They didn't charge upstream or wrap themselves in the branches of an old deadfall, they simply refused to budge which wasn't fun, but then there wasn't much fun anymore and I came to admire their stoicism. A stolid refusal to be yet consumed by the universe.

Like us.

So when I picked the fat torso up in two hands and thwacked the head on a rock I said Thanks bud knowing just what it feels like not to be ready.

I whistled. Jasper may be near deaf but something in the whistle tickles something in his head deeper than hearing and he uncurled and stood a little shakily and shook himself off and came trotting happily upstream and I gave him the first fish which could have weighed seven pounds. I filleted it, gave him the two slabs of gray meat, the head and the tail, and threw the bones back in the creek. The next one I caught I split and cleaned and the stomach was full of midges and a few big crawdads.

Already late. I'd been wading all afternoon and the current was cold where it pushed up against my knees and thighs but my feet were long numb with that kind of dead warmth. Starting to get chilled. I caught a fifth fish, smaller, cleaned it and pushed the butt end of a hooked stick through its gills and slid it down to the others on the stringer. Lay it in the sled. Rubbed my naked legs to get the blood going. The sun was gone, the creek now luminous in early dusk. I felt what? Happy. We were thinking of nothing but the creek, but dinner, but making a camp just upstream on a sandy bar I liked to visit. I slipped my pants back on, sat on a rock and put on my boots. Jasper was revived after the fish, watching me with his mouth open, smiling because he knew we weren't going far and there would be another fish or two, this time cooked and salted.

Okay, let's go.

We walked around a thicket of willow and alder not yet leafed out and found the path through a stand of green and living and venerable fir trees, the bark, the almost pumpkin orange they get when very old, and we found our fire pit in the sand a few rocky yards from the water and the smooth sleeping place beneath one of the big old trees.

I pulled some fallen limbs out of the denser woods that backed the camp and broke them up and lay them over a pillow of dried Spanish moss and quickly made a fire. So we could warm up. The wood was dry and full of resin and popped and cracked which was a domestic song above the syllabic murmur of the creek and the wind in the high boughs. Darkness was already in the forest, it filled the little canyon like a slow tide, and the flames deepened it but the sky was still bright with the thinnest blue and I could see two stars.

Jasper was happy too. He curled up close to the fire upwind and out of the smoke and lay his head on his paws and watched me cook our fish on a light long handled mountain frying pan which must have been made a hundred years ago. The handle was wrapped in a sheath of shiny tin to disperse heat and stamped with Simpson and Sons Ranchware. A hundred years ago when the ranchers ran their herds up in the mountains in summer on Forest Service leases and camped for days, rounding them up in the fall like a cowboy song. Those hardbitten riders squatting at just such a fire. What they could never have imagined. What we can't, cooking our fish here in the pan heavy with carp and spitting salvaged olive oil.

Spit and sizzle, pop of branches, the flutter of flames in a shifting wind, the same wind downstream carrying cold from the higher slopes and rushing in the limbs of the trees like the ghost of long ago surf.

Jasper is sitting up like a Sphinx now watching me closely. His moment. I salt the biggest fish, lay it on a flat stone and pull out the skeleton from the tail up, unzipping the bones.

Provecho.

He is up, tail wagging, first time today, and gobbles his dinner with quiet grunts.

I tie a taut line from the big tree standing sentinel on our camp back to a young alder and string up the tarp just to keep the dew off.

I cook a fish for me and kneel by the water on the rocks and drink and splash my face. In the smooth dark between stones with barely a current a waterskater slides away and a handful of stars shimmer.

I spread out our bed under the tree and lie down. Get up again, untie two corners of the tarp and slide it back to the tree. We'll get dewed on a little but I don't care, we can dry everything out by the fire in the morning. Tonight I want to see the sky. Lie down again and Jasper walks stiff to me almost a hobble, the hike today long, and licks my face all over until I am laughing and turn away. Then he curls against my side with his customary collapse and huff. We listen to wind high, water low. I tuck my arms under my head and watch the Dipper brighten. I feel clean. Clean and good.

★

In the morning I wake stiff. The sleeping bag and Jasper are covered in frost. So is my wool hat. Maybe not the best idea to sleep uncovered. It's okay, we'll start a fire in a minute.

You must be cold, boy. C'mere. I pull at his Whoville quilt to fold it over him. He is heavy, unmoving. Getting stiffer, the morning's harder.

C'mon, bud, this'll be better. Til I start a fire. C'mon.

He ignores me. I tug at the quilt and lay it over him brush his ear. My hand stops. His ear is frozen. I run my hand around to his muzzle, rub his eyes.

Jasper, you alright? Rub and rub. Rub and tug his ruff.

Hey, hey.

Pull on the scruff of his neck. Hey, wake up.

I push up to sitting and roll over, chest on his back, and cover him.

Hey, it's okay. Sleep for a while.

Sleep.

I pull him, stiff and curled, closer to me and lay the quilt over him and lie back. I breathe. I should have noticed. What a hard time he was having on the walk. The tears that weren't there yesterday flood. Break the dam and flood.

Now what am I going to do? Start a fire in a few minutes.

Jasper. Little brother. My heart.

I'll start a fire. Put sticks over moss and start. I'll cook the last two fish. I'll eat one. I'll.

★

We have traveled.
Now you will be the path
I will walk I will walk
Over you.

★

For the day I don't move. I keep adding wood to the fire. I leave him in his quilt wrapped and cozy just his nose sticking out. It is the sight of him there I don't want to leave.

He is the only one now. The only sight. Which. Tomorrow I'll. I don't know.

BOOK TWO

I

I don't. Don't do anything all day. Don't start the fire. Don't cook the fish. Leave them on the stringer hanging from a bough. Attractant to bear and cougar. Don't care. Get up to pee, drink a little water from the creek running colder from the icy night. Lower in its bed, the fallen tree propped on rocks upstream higher off the water. So. Retreat. Heart like the stream contracted too.

Go back to the sleeping bag and lie down next to him. Doze. Shove my leg over so I can feel his weight. Different now, wooden, but it is him. Drink in the afternoon. The day cool. The sun full on the creek, on the two of us, maybe three four hours then gone. Can smell the fish now. So.

Keep the tarp rolled back and wait for night. What was that song? *If I die before I wake, feed Jake, he's been a good dog . . .* Maybe better. But then he would have had to be the one to die of heartbreak. Better like this. Like the darkness pouring back into the canyon covering the stream covering us in a black shroud. Still. No resolution ever. None. Nothing decided, nothing finished. The Dipper wheels back into place. Just one turn. One turn of the wheel and we are different, never the same. Not ever. Not even those stars. Even they, they decay, collapse, coalesce, break apart. Close my eyes. It's what's inside. What's inside moving, swimming in the pain like a blind fish forever swimming. Is what lives what remains. Renews, renews the love and the pain. The love is the creek bed and the pain fills it. Fills it every day with tears.

Sometime in the night, sometime when the Twins are over the canyon, I think about the sled and the rifle inside it. What to do with it. I feel the weight of Jasper on my knee where I have wedged it beneath him and I think: He would not approve, no. He would say: what? He wouldn't say a thing. He never left his post ever, he would give me strength that way. We never leave our posts do we? This is just who we are.

Sometime under Gemini I fall asleep.

★

It is the third day. At daybreak I shift, feel him in the quilt and have a moment. A moment where I have forgotten and then a moment where I remember and still expect him to stir. Fully expect him to resurrect. Because he could. We have defied everything haven't we? Why not this?

And then I sob. Sob and sob. And rouse myself and carry him in the quilt curled, carry him just under the trees and begin to dig. With a stick, with a flat rock, with my fingers.

Most of the morning until it is deep enough to discourage a bear. Fitting. This was one of our favorite camps in the world. Year after year. If his spirit could look out. To the changing creek, season to season. I lay him in wrapped in the quilt and I say

Goodbye, bud. You are Jasper. My heart. We are never apart, not here, not there.

Then I scrape back in the dirt.

I spend the rest of the day gathering stones. Cobbles, eggs, heavy rocks. Smoothed and rounded by the stream. I build a mound as high as my chest. In the top I don't know what to put. I take off my old wool sweater. As much his smell as mine. I lay it over the top and pile on more rocks. To dissolve there like a prayer flag his smell and mine washing in the seasons. As if I could cover him.

Then I load up the sled and walk upstream.

★

Twenty times today I stopped and turned as if to call. Hey keep up. Twenty times I rolled my shoulders back into the hill. Put my head down, feet to the track.

Stopped once, turned my face full into the sun, eyes closed, let the light sear my tears.

139

Tipped my head back further, a coyote in full throat.

The creek on my right crashing over a ledge. The sun overwhelming eyelids, pouring down like heavy water.

If there is nothing else there is this: to be inundated, consumed.

★

It is not that there is nothing left. There is everything left that was before, minus a dog. Minus a wife. Minus the noise, the clamor of.

We think by talking and talking we can hold something off. Well. I couldn't, could I? You couldn't. You went along because you thought that was your job. Was I a fool? Were we both? To love is to take one side of the argument and hold it fast unto death. To land on one side with both feet. Or all four, huh, bud?

We fools going up the trail, two fools, now one.

★

There is a pain you can't think your way out of. You can't talk it away. If there were someone to talk to. You can walk. One foot the other foot. Breathe in breathe out. Drink from the stream. Piss. Eat the venison strips. Leave his venison in the trail for the coyotes the jays. And. You can't metabolize the loss. It is in the cells of your face, your chest, behind the eyes, in the twists of your gut. Muscle sinew bone. It is all of you.

When you walk you propel it forward. When you let go the sled and sit on a fallen log and. You imagine him curling beside you in the one patch of sun maybe lying over your feet. Not feeling so well. Then it sits with you, the Pain puts its arm over your shoulders. It is your closest friend. Steadfast. And at night you can't bear to hear your own breath unaccompanied by another and underneath the big stillness like a score is the roaring of the cataract of everything being and being torn away. Then. The Pain is lying beside your side, close. Does not bother you with the sound even of breathing.

★

That is some heavy shit, huh, Jasper? Getting all poetic on its ass when what it is is I miss you. I really fucking miss you.

★

I walked for three days. Barely ate or slept. The lying down in the bag was a pro forma kind of thing. I didn't feel like making a fire or sitting by it, I didn't feel like sleeping or not sleeping, I didn't know what else to do. Occasionally knelt on the stones and sipped from the creek. Walked west and then north. Straight into the Indian Peaks. When I am really hunting I leave the sled and pack at a base camp or landmark and continue quietly. I bring a smaller pack for the day with the down sweater, a liter bottle so I can take to the ridges or sit the day on some slope away from water. Matches, a game saw, a parka. Now I didn't. I hauled the sled scraping and bumping and made a racket and saw no game, only chipmunks, nuthatch, crows, alarmed squirrels raising chatter from the trees, letting the whole country know: Here comes Hig. Hig with his gun. But he's not serious, he's banging around with that contraption, he doesn't look so good, Where's his mutt? The squirrel on a limb, alarmed, tail curved forward over his back, alive and twitching, the chatter as piercing as an alpenhorn. Might as well just blow a whistle. Olly Olly Incomefree. Ready or not here I come. Even the crows alight, twist their heads, fix us, me, with a shiny eye, open beak, stretch throat and dredge a signal angry cry from croaky mutterings. I inspire them. To heights of outrage. That the hunter is careless. That he is slamming up the trail. That he is heedless, loud, unaware, bungling. That he is upsetting the Order. The chain of. The hunters and hunted. A lack of respect. Something is wrong with him. *CAWWREAACHH.*

Grief is an element. It has its own cycle like the

carbon cycle, the nitrogen. It never diminishes not ever. It passes in and out of everything.

The third evening it began to snow. A late spring snow but not heavy, not wet. The temperature dropped as suddenly as the passing of a cloud, cold, cold like midwinter and the wind dropped too. We were on the edge of a small basin above treeline and in the bottom were patches of old snow and a small lake recently cleared of ice. We. I. It is possible to continue together. Say what you like it felt that way to me. Walking behind, ranging to the side, the same but not apparent. Not as. A lake like a gem set in a bezel of tufted tundra and rough scree, the water green with the luminous unapologetic green of a semiprecious stone but textured with the wind. Then it wasn't. The surface stilled and glassed off, polishing itself in an instant, the water reflecting the dark clouds that massed and poured against the ridges like something molten and it was suddenly very cold and the snowflakes began to touch the surface. Ringless, silent, vanishing. I let go the sled's bridle. I was fifty yards from the water. The snow heavier. A white scrim that darkened the air, that hastened the dusk the way a fire deepens the night. I stood transfixed. Too cold for bare hands but my hands were bare. The flakes stuck in my eyelashes. They fell on my sleeves. Huge. Flowers and stars. They fell onto each other, held their shapes, became small piles of perfect asterisks and blooms tumbled together in their discrete geometries like children's blocks.

Something like laughter. That a flower could be this small, this fleeting, that a snowflake could be so large, so persistent. The improbable simplicity. I groaned. Why don't we have a word for the utterance between laughing and crying?

And I was suddenly very hungry. Took my eyes off of my left sleeve and looked around the col. The rock ridge and peak above me obscured. What the fuck are you doing here? Hig, what the fuck were you thinking? Why are you this high, this late in the day?

Shouldn't be. Benighted above treeline. Storms that move fast this time of year migrating like everything else. The cold. Exposed.

An old panic rose in my chest. The panic of nightfall, of storm, of being alone on open ground. Surprised the shit out of me.

Had to get down, get lower.

I mean the panic was familiar the way a dread nausea or hangover is familiar but so long absent I thought it banished. Like stuck between living and dying there is no use for panic. It wasn't. Banished I mean. Not a stranger at all. Panic close and familiar with its own smell, its own way of compressing the edges. I picked up the pull rope on the sled. Looked back at my own tracks over a field of crusted leftover snow. At the dark that thickened with the flakes. Too late to move. Fuck.

One thing is that Jasper always calmed me down. He didn't get too excited by much except maybe a wolf track, so I didn't either.

But it was calm. Without wind there was no danger. I could make a lean-to of the tarp against a boulder and snuggle into the bag and sleep. Tomorrow morning if the snow was not too deep I could head down and gain the shelter of the trees without trouble, I could fish the creek easy within half a day. A few hours down.

I had eaten all the jerked venison. A hunger deep, ravenous, alive. Had I not thrown out the other meat, Jasper's, I would have eaten it now. Who to judge? What matters if it is he or I, we are the same. But I had emptied the bags on the trail days ago.

Alright. There was water. There was a boulder pile on the other side, the slope side of the lake. I tugged on the sled and took a step and stopped.

There was a shadow on the ridge. All of this was very close: lake, slope, tumbled scree, sharp ridgeline behind it climbing out of the snowstorm and straight into the low lid of cloud. Just there on the razorback of the spur, just where it disappeared into cloud, a large dark shape. I rubbed the ice out of my eyelashes with the back of my arm and when I focused on the ridge again it was gone.

Made a slant roof of the blue tarp against a rock, tossed out the smaller stones to make a smooth

145

place to curl up, and covered myself and slept. Slept without dreams, without whelming grief, slept to wake in near absolute darkness to hear the ticking of the snow on the plastic sheeting to sleep again. Woke thinking the shape was large enough to be an elk. Thinking that I had seen no sign and wondering whether it was a good thing or a bad thing to wish for things that aren't there.

★

Tenth day out when I beeped Bangley on the walkie talkie. Early morning. I wasn't worried much about being covered for the few miles in the open, of being shot or followed out of the trees, but it was our ritual. Also it gave him a little time to readjust to me landing back in his world, maybe a couple of hours to remember how to be human. Maybe. Also if he was scoping the perimeter from the tower in the mansion which he would do every hour, it might save my butt from being fodder for friendly fire. How I go one way or the other never much concerned me but somehow that was one way I refused. I mean the thought of it: Bangley's mistake. Or maybe not. Maybe a half mistake, unacknowledged like poor old Francis Macomber. That was it. Didn't want to be him in the Short Happy Life. So I turned on the unit for the first time and squeezed the mike button twice.

Had two deer in the sled. They were smallish does, but there were two of them, enough maybe to justify the time gone, probably not. Didn't give a shit. He could say what he liked. Wasn't his rodeo anymore, wasn't mine really either, when I thought about it I knew less every day. Didn't know a goddamn thing.

One minute, less, then static, and

Well well. Prodigal Hig. Thought you'd croaked on me. I really did.

Hi Bruce.

Considered pause, kind of long. Stops him in his tracks every time. Reflex like pushing a button. Maybe his mom the only one who ever used the name. When she was mad.

Have some trouble?

No irony now. Which surprised me. Bangley almost sounded concerned. Hard to tell, though, over the walkie talkies.

A little.

Okay. Glad you're back in one piece.

Pause.

Are you? In one piece?

I held the hand radio out and looked at it. Bangley sounded like a frigging human being. Must be the reception, the static, something in the bending of the radio waves, some kind of solar flare kinda thing, distorting. What he meant was: Do you need help getting across?

Yup one piece. Legs arms, everything.

Okay give me ninety minutes.

10-4.

Hig?

Yuh?

You take a fucking vacation?

Ah, the old Bangley.

I keyed the mike. **Ninety minutes. Out.**

It was already light. I was squatting in my spot below a slope of ponderosas—a thicket of willows and poplars at the base of the first hills where the creek swung to the south and our trail continued straight east. Across open ground. If I'd had my ducks in a row I would have been set up hours before dawn and not make Bangley walk across to the tower in daylight. He carried the CheyTac .408 which was a light sniper rifle as light as something with that much power can be. His pride and joy, made for walking if you have to walk and still be able to shoot someone in the lungs a mile away.

I waited ninety minutes with the sun full in my face, which to tell the truth was not the best stratagem, to walk into it half blind, and I was glad to know he was up there in his tower, sun at his back with a clear view to the first trees in perfect light. Had had trouble three times. The one was the girl with the knife which was no trouble at all. I was thinking how trouble was really the last thing I expected, how warm at dawn, fresh with the smell of new grass and

148

early flowers, when I started to walk. I walked for more than an hour the load heavy on the level, both does quartered and piled in the sled, and I was more than halfway to the tower, laboring against the harness, pulling hard, when the radio strapped to my chest came alive.

Hig you got company. Urgency. A rare alarm.

Okay. Company.

I dropped the bridle and spun around. Back along the trail nothing. Tall sage, rabbit brush, gamma grass already knee high. Yellow and white asters blooming, fat bees already feeding, the trail smooth and empty behind me. Heart hammering.

Hig, they are stalking you. Quarter mile back. Read that? Quarter mile, a little more.

Okay. Okay. Got it.

Say 10-4. Repeat back the info. You're a pilot for chrissakes.

Jesus Bangley.

Trying to get you to calm down. Focus on the details. One at a time.

Mother of christ. Who spawned this guy?

Pause.

10 fucking 4. Quarter mile. I am focused.

Good. Okay, turn back around. Now. Turn back! Look at me. Grab a water bottle. Stretch. Make like you are taking a break. NOW!

Okay, okay, got it.

There is no way they can hear us, Hig. The wind is them to you. They are upwind. Look natural. Stretch. Drink. Key the mike like you are scratching your chest. You are all alone out here. As far as they are concerned, Hig, you are solo. Single prey.

Fucking great.

Where's your buddy?

My buddy? Oh, Jasper. Long story.

Short pause. Could almost hear the clicking, the slight recalibration of strategy.

Niner. Got that? Niner is the number. You got niner pursuers.

Niner? Holy shit.

Hig they know you are armed. They want your meat they want your weapon. They are not armed. Not with guns. Saw no guns. If they had guns you would be dead by now. Copy?

Yes, I fucking copy. Nine?

Hig listen. They have machetes. Looks like machetes or swords.

Swords? Fucking swords?

Hig, calm down. They are willing to take some losses. The way I see it. They really want your weapon.

Fucking Bangley. He was divining all this from two miles away. Standing in the tower leaning into the eyepiece of his spotting scope.

Great.

Willing to take some losses. Each one figuring

150

it'll be the other guy. They want to eat venison and they want the rifle. Read me?

Yes.

Say it Hig. Stay focused.

My heart was hammering. I almost laughed out loud. Right there with the sun at my back looking down the trail through the high brush with a frigging, practically a frigging division of visitors four hundred yards back.

Say it.

10-4.

Good. Settle your breathing.

Bangley, tell me what the fuck you want me to do? What should I do?

Breathe, I want you to breathe. They are stalking you Hig. They have all day. The way they see it. No rush. You are moving slow, they will close the distance. Little by little. Then they will charge you. They have done it before. They move like they have done this before. Copy?

Yes I fucking copy. 10-4.

Okay. You have the advantage. Advantage Hig. Right now you have the edge.

I do?

Fucking A, yes Hig. Listen to me.

I thought right then he sounded a little worried which didn't reassure me. Nine was a lot of fucking visitors who wanted to kill you. Me.

Listen to me. Up ahead, east, maybe eighty

151

yards, the trail drops into kind of a draw. Shallow, but deep enough. You stretch and pick up the rope like you are real fatigued and walk on ahead and down into that gully.

Bangley I *am* fucking fatigued.

Good Hig. That'll keep you calm. No espresso for Hig, not at the moment. Steady hand. We want your hands good and steady. Now walk. There is a large dense sage bush or something on the north side of the trail right in the bottom. Couple of bushes. Perfect. You drag the sled behind that brush and conceal it. Cut branches if you have to. You got two animals in there far as I can make out. Correct?

You're good Bruce. You're incredible.

Pause while he took that in. Not sure if I was being sarcastic or not, didn't even matter.

Glad that is dawning on you, Hig, I really am. The sled, the meat will be your cover. Case I am wrong about the guns. Case they have a weapon. A crossbow or something I can't see. They don't, but we want you covered. All exigencies.

He loved to say that. All exigencies. Well, it was the reason he was still frigging alive. I had to, I was handing it to him. Bangley.

You hide the sled and set up behind it. Got that?

Affirmative. Pause. Bangley?

Go ahead Hig.

My magazine holds five shots. One in the chamber. Six.

Pause. I could hear the breeze rattling the rabbit brush. Suddenly seemed really really quiet.

How am I gonna take out nine if they charge me? With six shots?

Radio crackle. Don't know when I was ever so glad to hear that. The sound of intervention, of calm in a firefight, the sound of tactical mastery. Bangley.

Okay listen, Hig. Breathe and listen. Stretch again. You got no clue, not a single inkling those fuckers are behind you. Wouldn't hurt to sing.

Sing?

Yeah, sing. Or whistle. Nothing more goddamn lulling than a whistle. Now listen, listen to me, Hig. When they come over the edge of that draw you wait. Plan your shots. You are going to be moving right to left. That's easier for you. Got that?

Yes.

Say it.

Right to left. 10-4.

Okay. Even if you aren't having your best goddamn morning you will drop two probably three. At least. You will also be firing from concealment. Those first shots will be a total fucking surprise, believe me. Total shock. They thought they had you. They thought you were

some poor exhausted deer hunting bastard on his clueless stroll home. Did not know they were walking into our fucking perimeter.

He was giving me a pep talk. It was working. Goddamn Bangley.

Hig?

Yuh?

You with me?

Okay. What the hell are they doing now?

Don't worry about them. They got all day, remember? Long as you're stopped, taking a break, they don't move. Okay, Hig, you drop two or three first go. Maybe four if it's your goddamn birthday. Now the rest are diving for cover and trying to locate you. They haven't had time to locate you. Now you have your ammo handy. Not all in your hand, you might drop the bullets. Line em out onetwothreefour five. Line out ten. Twelve is better if you're feeling generous. Right there on the sled. Ten.

Ten.

Good. You have a side load magazine. Never understood that fucking lever action hunk of nostalgia .308 of yours. What is that? Savage 99?

He knew exactly what it was.

Savage fucking 99. Goddamn Hig. Well I'm glad. Now I'm glad.

You are?

Fucking A. Side load magazine. That'll be a lot quicker than turning it over. Just thumb em in. One at a time, no hurry. If you have time lever it slow and quiet and feed in the sixth. Quiet cuz you don't want em to locate you if they haven't. And they haven't. Got it?

I took a deep breath. I was exhausted. I was suddenly really really happy to have Bangley as backup. Never been happier.

Got it. 10 motherfucking 4.

That's my Hig. Now there will be anywhere from seven to five left. You are in cover, concealed, and if they think it's worth their own worthless hide to keep coming, after you just dropped their buddies, they are more serious than I think they are. They probably won't. But they might be pissed, too. The pissed factor. Gotta give that some weight. The totally-apeshit you-just-killed-my-retarded-twin-brother factor. Which case you really got the edge.

I started laughing. Right there with the sun on my face, and the breeze coming off the mountains, carrying, probably, the scent *eau de marauder*, and my dog dead, I started laughing.

You laughing or crying?

He sounded seriously concerned.

Laughing, I'm laughing. Jasper died. In his sleep.

Sorry, Hig. I am. Now pull yourself together. Hig!

Okay okay. The totally-apeshit-retarded-brother factor. I'm with you, Bangley.

On task Hig. Stay on task. You got four to seven left. If they do charge you in anger just pot a couple more, we're all done here. Rest will back off, guaranteed. If they are smarter than they look, they will spread out first. They will try to flank you. That'd be serious but I have a good angle. Remember when you wanted to build the tower twenty feet high? Stop at twenty? And I said thirty and made you cranky for two weeks? Remember? And the porch? My double joisted reinforced porch? This is why. I can see em. Every one. They are gone to ground now, but when they move, even in a crouch, I got em. So stay put. If they spread out, just reload and I'll call em. You face the needle rock, due west, that's twelve o'clock and I'll call em from there. Direction and distance. Be like sporting clays.

Hig? You got that?

Sporting clays. Needle rock is twelve o'clock.

Good boy. You actually sound composed, Hig. Just thought of something. You packing your backup? Your Glock?

Yes.

In like Flynn. We do everything like I just said. All else fails, one gets too close, just draw that sucker and plug him. Make sure it's racked.

Wait til you get down out of sight and make sure it's racked. Got it?

Got—10-4.

Now pack up your water bottle, start whistling, pick up the rope and move.

That's what I did. I whistled. I put the harness over my forehead like a tump line, which was a way to relieve my shoulders, and I began to walk again. Real slow. I was suddenly tired to the bone, more tired than I could remember being. There was part of me that just wanted to lie down and sleep in the warm early sun, let them take the meat, the gun, my life. Get it all over with. But then another part wanted to work with Bangley. I mean I could tell he was excited by this challenge and I could tell the fucker actually believed in me. That I could pull this off. Weird, but I wanted to do it partly for him. Why I guess a team is usually stronger than the sum of individuals. I bent forward and dug in and tugged like a mule in harness and got the sled moving on the smooth trail which, once it was, it was easy to keep going. I got to the lip of the shallow draw and gathered the bridle in one hand, and backed up and picked up the sawed off kayak by the bow handle, and eased it over the edge. I controlled it by hand on the way down the little slope. At the bottom, while it was still sledding, I tugged as hard as I could and ran across. Sandy there, open in the bottom. Went as fast as I could. Once I had dropped out of sight they would be making up ground behind me, running themselves. I hustled the sled into the thick sage on the far side and levered it sideways to the trail. Almost the same movement I reached for the big Buck knife and started cutting thick branches. In less than a minute I had the sled well covered. Had been a green kayak, forest green, and I was suddenly very frigging glad I had had the foresight to pick something almost camo rather than something like bright fuchsia.

Fifty yards Hig. Fifty yards to the draw.

I worked the rifle out of its binding on the sled, the one box of shells, and lay down, lay the rifle over the flat hard hide of a hind quarter. Always quartered the animals hide-on, skinned them later which was more difficult but preserved the meat much better in transport. Glad I did now. The short fur made a good solid rest for the barrel of the .308.

Thirty yards. Thirty Hig.

Whispering now, close to it.

Slowing down. Single file on the easy trail. They don't have a clue, Hig. Got that? Advantage Hig. Just stay calm, wait for the bulk of em to come down into the bottom, and take em right to left, front to back. Reload. Do it again. You'll be fine. Gonna shut up now. Have fun.

He was out. Bangley. Such a weird thing to say:

Have fun. But the fucker meant it, that was the thing. It did something to my head. I was amped. Balanced the rifle on the deer hide, took the Glock out of the paddle holster on my belt and racked it, lay it on the fur to the right. Two feet over. Shook the red plastic bullet holders out of the box and worked each bullet out and lay it on the fur to the right of the rifle point forward, so I could thumb them in without changing their direction. My hands were shaking a little. Just a little. *Have fun.* Kind of changed everything. *You got exactly nothing to lose Hig.* That's what I told myself. So have fun. Heart thumping, but it was the almost happy anxious thump I remembered from playing soccer in high school. I was a goalie, the last stop, the last resort, the ultimate repository of the team's trust, and that's what it felt like now. Fuck up, you might as well crawl under a rock. But once it started it was all action, no thought, and the joy pushed up through the fear. That's almost how it felt now. Nothing to lose is very close to the Samurai *You are already dead.* That's what I told myself.

Lay thirteen brass shells out in a row. Lucky 13. I worked the lever and jacked a bullet into the chamber and thumbed the first into the magazine. Twelve left, a row of bright brass soldiers. Two full reloads. One deep breath and settled. Relaxed weight against the deer's thigh bone under the muscle and hide. Pressed into my chest.

Right hand around the receiver finger on the trigger and sighted both eyes open on the patch of dirt that was the trail where it dropped over the edge of the draw, the dirt almost polished with the passage of the sled, the passage of our years. Maybe a hundred and fifty feet. And

The first came over half crouched, neither fast nor slow, came over scanning and slowed, looking puzzled. But came. A very thin man in a full gray beard, bare arms covered in jailhouse tattoos, stars and crosses, carrying a sword. A frigging cavalry sword. Not seeing his prey, expecting to now, uncrouching reflexively to standing and walking down into the bottom and studying the slide of the sled in the sand. The one behind almost toppled him coming over fast, eager for a charge, a huge man, red bearded, also carrying a sword. All the thinking before stopped. Killers. They were killers. I wanted them. *Good goddamn, Hig, way to go boy.* Could hear Bangley's words like some kind of telepathic transmission. I don't know maybe my mouth actually watered. Pity the prey that fell before these men. Third was a long hair, wiry dirty hair to the waist, cleanshaven, in a black leather biker's vest—had a baseball bat bristled with screws. Long, maybe quarter inch screws with the heads sawed off and the shafts sharpened. Red and Screws barreled past the leader and trotted down the open bank in what could only be bloodlust, and they were just over a hundred feet before they stopped and began to scan. I had these three. Three others were coming over, a blur to me of animated mass. I had these. Front to back, Scrawny leader to Red to Screws was left to right, Oh well, I put the cross hairs on the leader, pulled. Familiar jump, the gun coming off the fur, lifting it just a little, levering and swinging right, I'd done this before scores of times to take two or three deer, swinging right to center mass, barrel now a fist's width off the rest, no problem, center Red and fire. *BANG!* Lever. No decision just fire. Barely conscious of the first two falling, the last, Screws, just beginning to crouch for a dive and *BANG,* the hit shoulder or side, him spinning and thrown and moving on the ground, then up, the mass at the lip uncoalescing, about to fragment, just aim for biggest object, two men together and pull, one arm back, thrown and falls. Lever. Four. Four! A surge of something, not joy not triumph but close. I was, we were, were a team, we nailed four—

Hig, move back! Run!

The radio loud now, urgent, almost insanely urgent

Run to me buddy! Now! The Glock! Pocket the Glock. Grab the bullets one hand the rifle run! RUN! To me!

Jesus. I did it. Something about the orders, the order, the sequence real clear, god bless him, I grabbed the Glock, shoved it in right pocket, scooped up handful of bullets, the gun, ran. Looked back. Just as I did the five came over the lip in a full tilt run, spread out. They were fast. Lean and fast, unencumbered but for the weapons in each hand. This image: five big men spread and charging. Sand would slow them, they'd be on me in thirty seconds. Just one, just one would kill me. Ran. Gun, bullets in hands, ran. Fast as I could. One more glance back, they were in the bottom now, in the open and closing—

WHROAAWMP

Concussion thrown rain of dirt dirt in mouth eyes

WROOOOAMP

Arms covering head jesus mother of god

WHRAWWWWWWWOMK

Shiver ground shake clawing dirt the dirt moving clods shower of clumps sand in a raining pebbles stalks wood thud a clod and

Silence. Ringing ears, ringing. Wet. Nose bleeding.

Hear out of it the ringing silence, the radio, **Hig? Hig? Hig! You alive? Hig!**

All the pieces. Hands claw back over ground. What? To head. Intact head intact. Ears ringing. Roll onto side, sleeve to nose, bleeding, not bad. Spit. Eyes. Clear eyes, blunt fingers, breathe. Intact

Hig! Godammit you're alive! Take a break, take a break. Nothing broken? All in one piece? Try standing. Slow. Hig!

Okay to knees. Stay there a while maybe a week. Hands and knees. Blood from nose dripping to dirt can see it, that's good, a good sign. Hands and knees breathe. Breathe. Okay I'm okay.

Hig, they're gone, scattered. See one, well parts of one, back a hundred feet. Maybe more casualties. Rest are off the radar. Gone, Hig. Hear me? When you can get it together, locate your weapon your rifle.

Hig? You're alright. Probably a little concussed is all. You still got the Glock? Hig? Check your pocket. Tell me you still have the Glock. Til we are absolutely sure the area is cleared. Tell me.

Hands and knees. Roll back to sitting. Blink in the sun. Talking to me. Bangley is talking to me. The radio. Reach hand to chest, hand stiff slow like slow motion, key the mike squeeze no strength

I. I

Hig you're okay. Thatta boy

I. I got the Glock

Oh man. That's good. Good man, Hig. Just stay put for a minute. Breathe.

Pause.

Bangley

Yes, Hig?

163

You're always telling me to breathe.

Laughter through the unit. Genuine relieved laughter. A draught of cold water.

Better than if you fucking don't, huh, Hig?

More laughter.

You did good, Hig. You did fucking great. You potted four at the start. Four! Way way past the line out of Vegas, man. We all had you at two tops, the sorta shaky way you sounded.

Laughter.

Thanks.

Pause.

What the fuck just happened? Bangley. What did you do?

Mortar. 81 mil British. Had to use the fuckers sometime. The porch on the tower I made you build? That's what it's for Hig. Save your ass. Wanted it to be a surprise sometime, kinda like a birthday present.

Crackle.

Surprised you, right Hig? It really did. Still have a bunch left. For when the shit really hits the fan.

Sat in the dirt in the sun while the blood in my nose dried to a crust and tried to digest the mortar thing. Fucking Bangley. Had a mortar tube hidden out by the tower all the frigging time. Good lord.

Crackle.

When I first saw the nine coming on you slow

I went down and fetched the fucker out of the brush where I had it stashed. Looked like you might really need some high powered help this time Hig.

Pause.

But you did really good. Might have made it without the mortars. Way you were shooting. Damn.

I saw my rifle knocked under a salt bush fifteen feet away. Tilted my head back like before: eyes closed, sun flooding, the ringing subsiding slowly like a vagrant wind. Laughed. Cried too. Laughed and cried at the same time, I don't know how long, just like a crazy man.

★

I flew that afternoon. Not in any shape to do it, but I did. To look for the other four, to see if they had designs on the families or on us and not a sign. Headed for the hills is what they did. The best thing. To fly. First time in years without Jasper. Still put his pheasant hunting quilt on the seat for luck, I guess, still took the turns more gingerly, the dives less sudden so as not to throw him—how I had trained myself to fly now. Flew the big circle and at the wave of the first hills west I looped back in and swooped low to look at the carnage, the three craters raw wounds in the brush, the bodies where we left them when Bangley walked out to help me bring in the sled.

I could barely pull it. Not that I didn't have the strength in my legs. My temples throbbed, an ache in the forehead, just couldn't seem to concentrate long enough to take five steps in a row with a sustained pull. Felt a little nauseous too. Bangley was patient and after sharing the harness he said

Hig take a break. I got this for a while. You've had a long day.

Are you going to tell me to breathe?

He took a sip from the plastic tube of his water pack and looked at me with fresh appraisal. He had a fleck of tobacco on his cheek that looked like a mole. The same exact place as Marilyn Monroe.

Hig?

Yuh.

Breathe only if you want to. You know, when you say that I am relieved. You are concussed Hig no doubt about it. Which I am truly sorry about. But. Better than being dead by a long shot. It's not as bad as it could be. Your eyes are facing the same direction and Hig hasn't lost his sense of humor.

He put the tump over his forehead leaned into it and walked.

Now from the plane I could see it all: the slide out of the sandy trail and the pile of brush where I had hidden the sled, a bit of red plastic in the dirt the little shell holder that came with the box, the spot I had probably gotten to when the first

166

bomb hit not eighty feet away. The four where I had dropped them, three in the sandy bottom one above, the birds, vulture crow raven magpie, lifting off in a scatter as I flew over. The one mangled by the mortar that could just as easily have been me. One arm, half a head gone. My head still ached and when I flew by low and saw him I leaned over and threw up out the window. Barely anything to throw up just the canned bean and venison salad Bangley made me in the hangar but still it spewed along the fuselage and I had to scrub it off next day. What it was, that might have been me. The mortar is not a precision weapon. Bangley said he had worked out the range the angle for five spots along the trail and was pretty sure about it but. What it was, it was a big gamble he saw me getting overwhelmed and.

I wiped my mouth with the back of my hand and flew south and east and scouted the approach roads to the families, and nothing. And when I came back around from the east I saw a dozen in the yard and the red union suit hanging limp off the pole and I landed. Bounced up the drive and shut her down. Climbed out stiff.

Aaron is a tall man, craggy, with a hooked beard, a beard like a scoop of carved wood. He was wasted by the blood disease as most of them were and moved slowly with deliberation like a man much older than he was. He waved his hand, huge on the end of the narrow wrist that stuck out of a patched flannel shirt.

I waved and walked and they all, mothers fathers kids, moved toward me in a ragged bunch and stopped and we faced off across the beaten mud of the yard. Fifteen feet. The unspoken irrevocable distance like an old Western movie where the mountain man meets the braves in some meadow. Or the homesteader confronts the landgrabbing rancher and his hired guns, the horses always pulling up to stand in a nearly taut line as if at a precipice. Always that bit of mutually respected demilitarized zone across which words can be flung followed maybe by bullets and arrows and death. That's what we called it, the DMZ. Awkward at first but not now. In this case we had decided without discussion or even any medical evidence that there was no way the sickness could infect from that far off. Probably not even from five feet, probably not even in a casual touch, but everybody, mostly me, felt better about this gap. If we needed to, we placed objects in the middle of it to be retrieved and that was okay too.

Aaron said Aren't you going to bring Jasper down?

I blinked at him, half turned back to the plane, then just stood. Couldn't breathe for a sec.

They were all watching me, I could feel it like a pressure. I hung my head down, watched a drop of salt water hit the dirt. Wiped it away.

Hig are you okay?

Aaron was bent forward, his thin back, his turkey neck, the beard. Land of the lost. Talk about being already dead. I straightened up.

He died Aaron. On the mountain. In his sleep. He was old.

I could almost see the wave of shock sway the little group. The last death here had been a child, Ben, a boy of eight or nine who got so excited, more than anyone when I landed the plane and carried Jasper to the ground. Many times he forgot the rules and bounded across the zone shrieking with glee and reached his arms out to the dog who stood up off his haunches and wagged and like the figures on the Grecian Urn he never got there, never attained his goal— always some long armed parent or aunt scooped him up with a mild scold.

I'm sorry Hig. We're all sorry.

The sincerity of it, the dignity. After what they had all lost and. It didn't matter. It was mine, my family. The second tear that spilled I wiped away and I told myself there wouldn't be another. Not in front of them.

Thanks.

A little girl stepped forward. Her name was Matilda. She had a handful of wild asters. She crossed to the middle of the Zone and lay it on the ground and smiled at me.

I picked them before, she said. For you.

Just as a present?

She nodded, looking up at me. She smiled, pretty, her skin waxy, dark rings around her eyes.

Thank you, I said. Thank you. And I broke down. Just stood there in front of them all and wept, wept uncontrollably, shuddering, and smiled at the girl through the tears. Her own smile faded and she looked scared and stepped back into the skirts of her mother and I felt bad but couldn't help myself. It was Jasper, not just. It was all of it. Was this hell? To love like this, to grieve from fifteen feet, an uncrossable distance?

I picked up the flowers but didn't step back. They were all little more than an arm's length away, two.

Thank you, I said to them all. Jasper loved coming here.

Which was true. I think the scent of children made him happy.

The flowers are beautiful. I sniffed them. Mmmmm. Wow.

Grinned. The girl smiled again from where she hung on the woman's skirts.

You put up the flag?

Aaron nodded. The last time was a week after the last Sprite. The solar water pump they used to draw from the creek to irrigate had died, just a bad fuse but they didn't have one and I did so the next morning I brought one. Now a tall

170

woman stepped through from the back. She was stunning, half her face. The disease had not yet claimed her vigor. Half her face had been burned horribly, some kind of gas explosion. When she talked she turned the burned half away and looked at you from the side and seemed to speak to air. Her name was Reba like the country singer of before and she could sing too, I had heard her. She held out a cracked plastic pickle bucket and I took it, hand to hand, the first time ever, and inside it brimmed with early baby lettuce.

We are having a bumper crop, Aaron said. I remember you saying you didn't grow it for some reason. We thought. He trailed off.

I smiled. I squatted down and reached out my hand to the little girl who had given me the flowers.

Go ahead her mother said.

She held out her little hand grubby with dirt and I took it and squeezed it lightly and smiled. I met her hazel eyes, a little bloodshot with the immune system war raging inside her, and held to her tiny fingers for a long moment, held to them like they were a rope and I was a man drowning.

★

The beans were already sprouting, showing the little curl just out of the turned dirt. The water was running in the furrows. I told Bangley I was heading out again.

We were in his shop which was the old sunken living room of a Mcmansion to the north of my hangar. It looked out of big double paned plate windows to the west, away from the runway to the mountains. It was a gunsmith shop plain and simple. Bangley made no excuses about knowing nothing about engines, wood, carpentry of any kind, agri-culture, especially agriculture, gardening, cooking, especially cooking, languages, history, math beyond arithmetic, fashion, leatherwork, gin rummy, sewing, or especially rhetoric—the decorum, the customs of a respectful rhetorical debate.

Spit it out Hig is what he liked to say in the last instance. Spit it out and don't pull any goddamn punches. It's just you and me here ha ha! No one else to impress.

But he knew guns, knew how to modify them, improve them, and he could build one from the ground up, from pipe and old flatware. In the box trailer he pulled behind his pickup on the afternoon he showed up at the airport he brought with him a heavy drill press, a welder, a generator, grinders, a band saw. When I pointed out that these skills—the welding, the soldering, the tempering—that they were applicable to all kinds of metalwork, he chuffed his gravel laugh.

172

Got no use for that is all he'd say.

He had also brought with him about fifty posters, all girls in bikinis or less holding various weapons and bannered with the great names in small armaments from Colt through Sig to Winchester. They were tacked up all over the walnut paneled walls where framed paintings used to hang, taped even to the edges of the windows. They were shooting submachine guns holding pistols in the low ready position like a fig leaf and sometimes not bothering to cover their total nakedness at all and the pain they caused me, I mean the sight of unclad women, actually constricted my throat so I kept my visits to the bare minimum so to speak. Ha. When I did go I hailed him from the yard and waited for a yell back, an invite maybe, trying to train him to do the same and stop giving me a heart attack at my hangar which I knew to be fruitless.

We got plenty of venison, Hig, he said straightening from a large pipe in a vise.

After our dustup the other day he announced that he was going to build a grenade launcher. He actually had one, an M203, but the range was inadequate to save my ass, he said, so he was going to rebuild it. More accurate he said.

Can't have the Hig getting concussed anymore, makes him too goddamn goofy.

Now he straightened and squinted at me while I tried not to look at the homicidal naked girls.

Weird: on a low table, by the leather couch he had decided to keep, was a framed picture of the family that had lived here: some ski vacation, three blonde kids in helmets, parkas, their parents standing behind holding skis and smiling broadly, teeth as white as the snowy mountains in the range behind them. Top of one of the mountains at Vail or somewhere. I never asked about it. I intuited that it was not as simple as being reminded of the filial warmth that once pervaded, but more likely some Bangley score keeping, like: Look you Yuppie motherfuckers, you had all that but who is here in your sunken living room today, healthy as a horse and crafting better weaponry so he can keep ahold of it like you couldn't.

Just a guess.

You thinking you need another fishing vacation? Last one wasn't exciting enough?

Shook my head. I'm flying.

Flying?

Grand Junction. Got a transmission from there a little while ago. From the tower.

His hands, which I thought of as paws they were so big and blunt looking, they let go the pipe, set down the file. He looked at me under the hanging gun rack he'd had me build for him in the beginning—he never did anything without a platoon's worth of firepower within reach.

Little while ago?

Three years.

His grin was straight across. He rubbed the stubble on his cheek and I could hear it rasping from across the room.

Three years.

He turned halfway back to look out the window west in the direction of Junction as if trying to gauge in spacetime the relationship between the distances and the passage of seasons. For just a second, for the first time, I saw him as a man getting old. He turned back.

Goddamn Hig. You weren't very good about returning phone calls were you?

I smiled at him.

Hig?

Yeah?

You having a midlife crisis?

Just behind him to the left on a wall panel beside the big window was a famous Czech model holding a short, wicked looking machine gun, something like an Uzi. She was weighting her left leg, her right hip cocked outward, and all the geometries led the eye from her green gaze to her mound which coyly peaked out of a very spare triangle of dark hair which could not hide the short line, the path to the promised land. It killed me. Breathing immediately constricted. It occurred to me that Bangley was a tactician to the bone. He read the layout of any situation instantly, and found the spring that wound the clock, the vulnerable entry. Was I having a midlife crisis?

Don't really believe in em, I said. Our whole frigging life is a crisis.

You think so?

No.

First the elk, now the control tower. Three hundred miles away. What's your Point of No Return?

He meant fuel. The point at which I wouldn't have enough to get back.

Two sixty.

Maybe you're chasing shadows Hig. You wanna kill us both?

I stood in the middle of the family's living room. There had been a big flatscreen, a surround sound stereo system, a player console on a side table with over ten thousand songs, a lot of country pop. Bangley had ripped it all out, hung up pegboard and the posters. There had been a game controller on the middle table. We had turned it on: *World at War VII.* I thought Bangley would like it. He turned away when I turned it on, and he visibly relaxed when I shut it off.

I know, I said.

He looked at me. His mineral eyes, his grin rigid.

I know it's a risk. Whoever was there who sent the transmission he had power. He was in a control tower so he had powerful radios. Maybe he knows something.

Knows something?

Some news.

News.

Like about the Arabs or something.

Bangley didn't move. Then he picked up the file and grasped the pipe with his paw and lowered his head.

Hig is a shark, he said. Gotta keep moving or die. Gotta do what he's gotta do.

I thought about that all night as I lay out at the base of the berm alone, Jasper's weight on my leg an aching absence. And watched the last of the winter constellations go under earth in the west. That was his way of giving me permission. Which I didn't need. Still.

★

Clear calm morning, early May, the wind sock by the gas pump hanging still, the sky over the mountains a ringing bowl of water-clear blue. Our resident redtail floats, riding the first thermal over the barely warming tarmac. Easy circles. His mate's nest is in a cottonwood at the edge of our fish pond and yesterday I heard the squalling cheeps of the chicks. Three I think. She stood, pumped her broad wings once and looked at me with a murderous acuity. Don't fuck with mama. Wouldn't dream of it I said aloud.

I turn on the pump and fill two six gallon gas jugs and load them behind my seat. Under seventy five pounds. Full tanks fifty five gallons usable. The extra gas will give me just under one more hour, not enough if I do any scouting along the way, not enough to get back, but I will take no more gas as I want to be able to land and take off short if I need to. Survival pack thirty pounds including ten days of jerky, dried tomatoes, corn, two jars olive oil. Five gallons water which I probably don't need as Grand Junction is so named for straddling the confluence of two big rivers. But it's a desert town and I don't know what will happen, how hard it will be to get to the river. Always carry water.

I keep Jasper's bird hunting quilt on the passenger seat. Lock the AR and the machine pistol into the vertical rack at the front of his seat.

What is the plan, Hig? Fly there.

Then what? Contact the natives.

Then what? Swap news.

You have no news.

I have what I have.

Then what? Fly home?

Good question.

Refuel.

Good luck.

Me and Me talking. Bangley is nowhere in

sight. Climb the ladder, top off the Beast. Enough direct sun to run the pump, enjoy the old analog clicking of the numbers rolling in the pump's window. The light warm breeze on my left cheek, the single skeining scream of the hawk. Roughed at the edges like his wings. The old excitement of a trip, a real trip, meaning new country. Surge of optimism don't know why. Bangley is right. The odds of any useful news are low, the odds of the man in the tower being a skeleton high. And what news is useful? I've asked myself that every day in the week since. What is news? We eat we sleep we secure the perimeter we defend ourselves I go up into the mountains some-times to get the news of the creeks and the trees. From the Beast the news of wind. What else is there?

Had to show Bangley how to water the garden for the first time, how to direct the flow from the header into the different marks, how to clean the furrows, show him what is and what is not a weed. He was ornery. He confessed that he'd sworn that he would never on this earth be a farmer, that the only dirt he'd ever dig in his life would be the dirt of a grave.

The hair stood up on the back of my neck when he said that. To know him this long and still be surprised.

My father was a farmer he said.

In Oklahoma?

He stared at me, the double ought spade in his hand looking nothing if not at home.

Okay so you've done this before.

He stared at me. He pursed his lips, looked at the blade of the shovel smeared with clay and half covered in the smoothly flowing current of a mark.

This is your show, he said finally. Were me I would've used the gated pipe stacked in the yard of that place to the north.

Now it was my turn to stare.

You're a farmer, I said.

Nothing. He winced down his eyes and looked off west into the sun. Vagrant breeze moved the hair sticking out under the back of his cap. The flow of irrigation water captured from the creek made a cold ripple and burble. It pushed against clods fallen from the edges, flowed over them in smooth humps that fell into tiny riffles behind them. Eddied along the edges. If I stared long enough I could magnify the furrow in my head, build a perfect trout stream from any straight line of water. I always irrigated barefoot and my feet were numb. I loved the sensation as I sat on Jasper's mound, the one he used to supervise from, and let the feeling come back tingling in the sun. Let them dry with heels propped on a piece of rag. Shook the dirt out of boots and socks before I put them back on.

I stared at him.

That's what it is, I said. In some previous Life of Bangley. That shovel. Looks like a goddamn part of you. Like you were born with it.

Turned his head and looked at me and the hair stood up again. Cold, icy as the water flowing over my right foot.

It's a spade, he said.

I nodded.

I know.

We looked at each other. What the hell, I was leaving in the morning.

You didn't like your father much, huh?

Hesitated, shook his head slow.

You hated the fucker.

Bangley's jaw working side to side.

You did everything. Jesus. A farmer. That's where you learned it. You could weld, blacksmith, shoe a horse, build a corral, a barn. Probably a better frigging carpenter than me. Holy fuck.

Crossed my arms over the handle of the spade and looked at the mountains. Gentle wind. A harrier, white rumped, beat the sage across the creek, fluttering and gliding just over the brush trying to scare up a rabbit. Two hawks, not the redtails, smaller, maybe Cooper's, gyred. A lot of songbirds vanished even before, but in this world the raptors seem to be doing fine. A hawk's world.

How long? Did you work the farm with him? Hating him?

We stood there. The water in the furrows conversed one to another in overlapping rills. No words and I knew with certainty that Bangley had killed his old man.

When you get back, he said finally. We'll make improvements. If you want. We could make it water a lot easier. But then I always thought Hig enjoyed working out here in the sun moving the dirt around.

That was considerate.

He scratched the blade of his cheekbone under his right eye. It was weird. I looked at him the way you might look if you'd just discovered your spouse was in the witness protection program. Had been a hit man or something. Or a senator.

Fuckin A.

Fuckin A.

I don't know whether to be mad or go hysterical busting a gut.

He smiled at me. Not the grim straight grin but the real half smile that was at once embarrassed at itself.

Personal choice, he said.

What?

Personal choice. Those are the toughest. When you have to think about shit like that.

You are fucking crazy. A crazy fucking farmer.

He was leaning on his crossed arms too and his grin went straight across again unsmiling and

I knew the conversation was over and that I probably shouldn't call him that anymore.

Now I was topping off the wing tanks. I moved the aluminum ladder around the nose, scraped it over the pavement to the left wing and climbed it with the heavy hose and nozzle over my shoulder. Click click click, the numbers unrolled, the fuel gurgled and hissed as it reached the sleeve of the cap. Seventeen point three gallons. Even now with all that it meant I still got a mild kick out of free gas. Free until. The sun was two fingers off the swells to the east, two fingers at arm's length meaning about half an hour meaning it was nearly six. Thirteen hundred Zulu. Greenwich Mean Time. Greenwich. Somewhere in England. Home of the Clock. Center of the Timed Universe. Used to be. Nobody much keeping track anymore was my guess.

When Uncle Pete died of what was probably cirrhosis hastened by cancer and he knew he had only a few months left he did something I thought was way out of character: he spent his days in his cabin organizing his slides. His vast collection of colored positives. He had grown up with film and had taken exclusively slides which he said were sharper. He put the yellow paper boxes, the white and blue plastic ones, each one a roll, in a foot high stack that mostly covered his kitchen table. In often intense pain, by the light of a small window by day and a standing lamp in the evenings, he unboxed them one roll at a time, slipping each mounted picture into a sleeve in a transparent binder sheet. He labeled them with a Sharpie: on the actual slide he put binder number/ slide number, on the page he put the same plus date taken and an up to three word description: Bone Fishing Keys. Beside the three ring binders, which held one to five years' worth depending on how prolific he had been with his camera, he kept another binder of lined paper with a keyed journal. This held longer descriptions, notes of particular pictures which sparked his memory. I visited him once during this time. While he catalogued, I cut and split the firewood for a long winter both of us knew he would not see. Three cords of maple beech ash yellow birch, cut from his woodlot on the side of a gentle hill, split and stacked along half of the front porch and around the side, the whole of which—me working while he sat inside—embarrassed him. At first I thought he was crazy. I mean he could have been sitting on his little porch watching the Vermont spring turn into a riotously green and sultry summer for the last time, watched the wrens and larks and owls in the lyrical commerce of breeding and nesting, leaf and air. Got bitten by black flies, gnats, then mosquitoes, on the last exquisite evenings. Why wasn't he out there on his Dartmouth rocker? Maybe picking on his beat up guitar?

But lying one night in my old bunk under a wide open window listening to a screech owl trying to terrify me with a woman's screams and only making me happy—the bittersweet cry of undigestible beauty and great impending loss—then it came to me: the obvious epiphany that he was reliving his life. Doh. Slide by slide, picture by picture. He was aggregating memory like a wall against extinction and the little boxes of slides were his bricks.

Up on the ladder in the soft morning, listening to the last pull of fuel gurgle into the wing tank and gauging the time by the sun. Something about that made me think of Pete and his albums leaning into the table in the dim close cabin that smelled of resin and woodsmoke and coffee. Like a man leaning into an incessant wind. Keeping track of things that have no use anymore except as a bulwark against oblivion. Against the darkness of total loss.

Well. I wasn't going to count the hours. I had a plane full of fuel and good weather and I was going to take off and fly west and see how far I got. I was tightening down the gas cap when I heard a scuff and saw Bangley walking across the ramp. He had a basket on his arm.

I grinned. It was like the old railroad song. Pete sang it. *Johnny's mother came to him with a basket on her arm / She said my darling son / Be careful how you run / Many a man has lost his life just trying to make lost time . . .*

It's not a pie, he said.

I grinned. Clicked down the cap cover and climbed down.

He handed me the basket, turned to the stepladder and chopped up on the locking struts so it half folded and carried it back to the pump. Inside the basket were six grenades.

Don't know why I never thought of it before, he said. Working on the launcher got me to thinking.

They lay inside like so many eggs inside a nest. The Egg of Death. Something in a fairy tale I once read and couldn't remember.

How many mags do you have for the AR?

Four. The big ones.

He nodded.

You got the hand pump?

He meant the pump with long hose I could use to get gas out of an underground tank or any tank. Aside from the extra fuel the thirty feet of hose was my heaviest item. I nodded.

What are you going to do when you run out of gas?

Land.

He nodded. He looked at the Beast, at the mountains. His hands were in his pockets. He was looking west into the light breeze, he said

You been a good partner Hig. A little goofy sometimes.

186

Oh fuck. My chest constricted thought I was going to—Well.

Like family he said.

I stood there rooted to the tarmac.

I'm not a easy man to get along with. Only ones ever got halfway there were my wife and son. And you. Big Hig.

I think my mouth actually hung open. I blinked at him.

Long story, he said. He smiled the half smile.

Keep your eyes rolling in your head Hig. Situational awareness. Don't get goofy thinking about the past and let some SOB blindside you. Try and come back.

I stared at him.

I'll keep the weeds down.

He walked away. I stared after him. Fuckin A. Fuckin A.

I hand cranked the heavy hose back on its roller and climbed into the Beast, latched the door. Hit the master switch, turned the key in the mags and pushed the starter.

★

Few sounds in the world as exciting as the exploding catch of a Continental engine firing to life. The first refractory turns of the prop. The roar smoothing out as the prop disappears in the speed of its rotation.

Go fast enough we disappear.

Bounced across the ramp through the lines of wrecked and disintegrating airplanes, turned straightacross the taxiway onto the strip and took off from midfield. Saw Bangley pushing into the door of the house that was his workshop, he didn't look up.

★

The Beast is hungry. Pulling at air like an excited horse. I look over: the empty right seat, just Bangley's egg basket and the quilt with the hunter aiming at the rising pheasant, over and over. Crumpled against the door. Even half deaf and stiff Jasper was a better copilot than most men. All men. That it has come to this: life distilled in a ratty blanket. The shot will never hit, the bird never fall but neither will that hunter ever miss. Or lose anything. His dog will never die.

The biggest hole torn by a mutt.

. . . *thinking about the past let some SOB blindside you . . .*

I fly over. Straight over the Divide. Boulder burned below, the triangular slabs of the Flatirons thrust against the greater mass of the mountains like blank headstones. *Prettiest town on earth couldn't sustain. Mark it.* The ski area El Dora scarred with old trails and slopes, the lines of the lifts just below us, can see the empty chairs swinging in the wind. A few bumps, the Beast more than compliant. Sail over the snow saddle. Close enough to see the tracks of a single large animal stringing the ridge. Not possible but. Too high. All of us caught out too high.

Winter Park and the Fraser Valley revealing itself on the other side as we go over. Scores of ski trails tender green against the rust of the dead forests. We used to ski there. The last time Melissa and I split up for a run and I rode next to a big man who said he was here for winter break with a church group from Nebraska. Nondenominational.

We just follow the Bible word for word he said. Word for word you can't go wrong. Shook his head nice smile. I'd be crazy to disbelieve him.

I thought of stones in a river, rock hopping. One rock to the next, nothing to think about. Word for word. Just follow them, man. Bread-crumbs right to God. Sitting the chair next to him, our skis dangling over sixty feet of air, I thought Maybe there is a different translation for *meek*. Maybe it's not the meek who inherit, maybe it is the simple. Not will *inherit* the earth, they already own it.

I told him I always got stuck at the Begats. I said I had just read Lamentations though and it seemed like *Mad Max*. I mean women eating their babies, everybody dying.

He didn't laugh.

He said, I try to stay on the Right Side of the

Bible. Left side was written by Jews. Some things to pay attention to, I guess, but if I were you I'd start with John.

We should have all paid more attention to the Left Side I am thinking now. The Wrong Side, the Side Where Shit Goes Really Really Wrong.

Drop down and follow the Fraser past Tabernash. Most of the valley burned except the firehouse and the discount liquor store which now stands alone at the edge of a field full of bighorn sheep. They rouse, swing and trot in a panic toward the blackened forest as I pass and I see four wolves standing out of the grass and they turn them back like sheepdogs. Fly on.

I know this country all of it. Doc Ammons, I can see his barn still standing in a hundred open acres this side of Granby. The house is gone but. His son Swift was my best friend in college and they were my second family. Three of us fished the Fraser often. Can see the log corrals, the ring where Becky trained her horses and riding students. Could probably find a stack of my old books in the log outbuilding where I used to sleep. Today I don't want the memories. I fly over.

Right through the gunsight slot of Gore Canyon wingtips up against rock both sides. Seems like. Fished here, too, the river dropping so fast, the rapids so loud, reverberating off the cliff—you had to be careful as you walked down the railroad tracks to look back often. More than one fisherman never heard or saw the train coming. Air over the water cold and heavy throwing up mist, the Beast loving it.

Do I? I used to love to fly like this. Twisting through a canyon fifty feet off the water.

Now I don't feel anything. I feel the way my unwadered legs felt after ten minutes in the snowmelt. Numb and glad to be. Glad to be numb.

The difference maybe between the living and the dead: the living often want to be numb the dead never do, if they never want anything.

Sunlight. Out the other end. The river quieting to black water, the rock folding back to hills, woods unburned. I can see duck smattering the pools. Herons out of the reeds, angular, spreading those huge wings at the sound of the plane. Color of smoke.

What do you want? Hig. What?

I want to be the color of smoke.

Then what?

Then. Then.

Pull back hard on the yoke and climb steeply out of the hole at State Bridge. Dry sheep hills, herds of antelope and deer scattered. In the flats along the Eagle River I can see the once swank Eagle Airport. Key the mike and call the tower. Ask for clearance to pass through their airspace. A hope and a habit. **Triple Three Alpha three to**

the east at niner thousand request transition your airspace en route—

Where am I en route to? Junction maybe. With a jog south to the Uncompahgre Plateau, the places I used to hunt. For no reason.

en route—

I want to say *En route to Something Completely Fucking Different.* I fly over.

II

Sudden lurch and buck. Again. Thrown to the left, left wing dipping. Hold tight to the yoke, correct and watch the altimeter. I love this. The yoke in my hands is neutral, the plane level and the altimeter needle is circling clockwise upwards. Updraft. The trees get smaller, pressure in the seat cushion like a great lifting hand. Late morning thermal, the still dark woods soaking the sun and throwing up this plume of warm air. The unasked lift is fast, heady, a little alarming.

Gain fifteen hundred feet with no work at all. Cross high over the Roaring Fork right over Carbondale, unburned, surrounded by rivers and green ranches. I blink. Looks like cattle there. Cattle of old. Black and red. Must be—nothing else that color. Damn. Cattle gone wild, sticking to home, miraculously out of the mouths of wolves. I'd drop to look but don't want to lose this height nor spend the gas to climb again for the next pass.

A ranch. Cattle. The spring river flowing by. A ranch house in the shade of leafing cottonwoods and globe willows. A cracked and broken road winding by. Squint and I can imagine someone in the yard. Someone leaning to bolt a spreader to the tractor. Someone thinking *Damn back, still stiff.* Smelling coffee from an open kitchen door.

Someone else hanging laundry in a bright patch. Each with a litany of troubles and having no clue how blessed. Squint and remake the world. To normalcy. But.

More normal the absences.

Huntsman's Ridge. Can see the long rockslide we used to ski, called it Endless. Seemed so then. Be perfect now: spring corn-snow compacted and stable. Zero avalanche danger.

Half the aspen forest still in leaf, still living. On our left the rugged wall of the Raggeds. I nod, fly over.

Now the country gets soft. It will be aspen forests for miles. I tap the fuel gauge.

Twenty nine point three gallons. Not enough gas to get home. As simple as that.

As simple as that we go over the edge.

★

I was wondering: Is this what it's like to die? To be this alone? To hold to a store of love and pass over?

★

We almost moved here. Paonia. Some misspelling of Peony. Melissa was tired of teaching, tired of the principal and the District, was itching to try something else. Organic farming maybe. Building was a lot slower over on this side of the state but I could've probably pieced it together with remodels, cabinets, the odd house. First time I saw it I thought it looked like a train set. Looks like a train set still. I let the Beast fall.

Cut power and glide down the south slope of Grand Mesa, the tops of the soft aspens a few feet under our belly. Still green, the pale trunks still startling, the ferns beneath them still a thick carpet no doubt harboring deer. Whoosh off a band of cliff. And the valley opens: a green river bottom backed by a high double mountain with a swooping saddle between. Orchards, the neat rows of tufted trees on either side of the river. Vineyards too. Tall cottonwoods marking the westward twisting course of the stream. In the west, where the river flows out of the valley into a dry desert scrubland, I can see the railroad tracks, the flat topped mesas and the massing uplift of the Plateau, purple in the morning haze. And the town, more a hamlet, clustered between the river and the hill with the white stone P.

Bought groceries here often, ammo, dog food. Used to wait seven minutes at the crossing while the coal train clattered by. Timed it once, resenting the loss of daylight. Look over at Jasper's seat.

You loved it here, huh, bud. Walk down to the river below the town park and throw the stick in the current. You weren't too good at stick. Or swimming. Loved it anyway. We should all be like that huh?

Bank downriver and aim for the high dry plateau. Guts in a knot.

★

I cannot live like this. Cannot live at all not really. What was I doing? Nine years of pretending.

★

The road we took crossed a green bridge. The canyon was called Dominguez. I am eight hundred feet above the ground. See the bridge. See the orchard pressed against the canyon walls, the dirt track. Follow it.

Sparse forest, piñons, junipers almost black and still living. Desert trees that don't grow up but grow gnarled and thick. Stunted and stubborn. Remind me of Bangley. They just refuse to die at any price. Some of these have been here since the so-named Spanish priest traveled through here with his god.

Never flown this. We always came here in a truck. The road is grown in. Overgrown track swings away from the smaller river to climb a ridge. Bank right to follow it into another drainage and the country I used to hunt. But. Off to the left in the path of the creek a flash of red rock, the upper wall of a canyon just revealed. Always amazed that such a small stream can leave such a landmark, that so much big country stays hidden in these clefts. I bank back to take a look.

As I near, the rim reveals the ruddy face of a high wall, deep red and waterstained in strips of black and ochre. Cut by ledges. Pale printed outline where a huge block came unglued. The cliff two hundred feet high if a foot.

It's a box canyon. I'll be damned. The exploding lime green tops of cottonwoods, a few bristled ponderosas. And. I circle tight. How could I have never seen it? Because I was following the road, if you call it that.

The split and riven little canyon widens into this boisterous green hole. Creek winds through. A meadow on the left bank. And. So shocked and curious I am descending in my gyre and I almost spiral into the high wall.

A stone hut against the cliff. Smoke wafting from. A stone bridge over the creek to the field. Cattle scattered on the watered grass. Half a dozen.

Cattle.

And.

A garden plot larger than ours. Fed by a ditch cut from an oxbow of the creek. And.

A figure in the garden bent.

And.

It's a woman.

Long dark hair tied back. Unbending to stand. Hand to forehead, shading to watch the plane.

A woman in shorts, man's shirt tied at the waist. Barefoot? Barefoot. Tall and lanky. Standing straight, tall, shielding her face and watching me. Mouth in a wide circle. Yelling? Yes.

A figure now out of the house if that's a house, a man with a gun. Old man. Old man with a gun raising it skyward and sighting. Jesus.

I don't hear the concussion but. Twang of bird shot, the tear of aluminum and a new hiss of air. Jesus. Then a pop, burn and sting, my face burning whole left side. Both hands grip the yoke. Pull straight back into a hard climb and roll right wing straight back over the rim almost brush the tops of the low junipers on the edge as I go over and lose sight of them. Bits of shattered glass roll into my collar. Hey. Hey. My window is gone. Left side window, what's left a mosaic of shattered tempered glass clinging to the frame.

Blood soaking my shirt. Air.

★

In that instant I knew what I had come for.

★

Not what you think: you are thinking Woman but that wasn't it. It was to be glad again to be alive.

The moment you realize nothing vital is broken inside you, nor in the Beast, that you are climbing, leveling out, that the engine is purring, the controls tight. That your trembling fingers come up to the side of your bloody face and touch, and touch gingerly, feel the four splinters of glass and that's it. A few shards. Fuck. And the roof of the cockpit is peppered with holes, just the liner, nothing all the way through metal. That close. The fucker almost took me out. If I hadn't been rolling away over the edge of the canyon all that bird shot would now be in my head. Damn. And in that moment I began to laugh.

My first glad instinct was to climb down there with the AR-15 and turn the old bastard into hash at close range. That felt good. It was feeling something, not morose. Hig, the SOB did you a favor. Woke your sorry ass up. Just was doing what you would have done to defend his hearth and home and woman.

Woman.

Was that his woman? The old badger. Who knew what arrangements were made in this world. First instinct was to climb down there and murder the fucker and take his woman. And. Why not?

Well, anyway Hig, whether you are a good man or a bad man, or just a pretty good man in a fucked up world, you are going to have to land the Beast first. Put her down in a rolling rocky country with one road that is no longer a road.

I banked around, went over the ridge away from the canyon and aimed the nose down into a sage meadow with the rutted track going straight south across it.

Double U-O-M-A-N. First sight of one viable, one tall, one without the blood sickness probably, and not frozen on a poster in Bangley's shop or spilled on the ground behind you, too young, with a kitchen knife in her hand—first sight and you are willing to forget everything. Like checking the landing.

Fuck Hig, get your shit together.

I pulled up. Circled low. The road was deeply rutted. Like it would bury the right main gear up to the strut. Nice one, Hig. Be a long walk back to anywhere.

That's not it. Just. I mean pussy whipped at a thousand feet. I realized, laughing, that it could've been men, or a hag. It was this new relationship to a person of any gender: that I was under no obligation to kill them. Or let Bangley kill them. I mean this was their house, not mine. I was the visitor.

Amazing how not having to kill someone frees up a relationship generally. Despite the fact that Gramps tried to kill *me*. Well. Bygones. I could walk down in there and shoot him or not, which was liberating. Or them. Could've been a whole platoon in the house or somewhere hidden just waiting for me. I circled low twice and mapped the rutted road carefully, where the ditch started, where ended, marked it with bushes and gaps. Could they hear me a mile away in the canyon? Probably. Probably right now they were lining up twelve gauge shells on the rock windowsill, probably she was shaking loose her hair, unbuttoning her shirt, and waiting to bait me in range like a Siren.

Hig!

Focus Hig, breathe. Say 10-4.

10-4.

Focus on the little things. Stay alive.

10 fucking 4.

I would've skipped the rutted track and put down right in the sage meadow but I did not have tundra tires and a rock hidden in the brush could snap a wheel off. Better the known danger etc. Made sure I could see a few feet either side of the ruts because I was going to have to put one wheel on the center hump and the other thwacking through the edge of the bushes. Then I decided to not be stingy. The landing was gonna have to be precise within inches. Better to know exactly how the wind was blowing.

I pulled up, gained three hundred feet, and dabbed the side of my face with a corner of Jasper's quilt. Then reached down between the seat to a little wood box I kept there and pulled the tab of a smoke bomb with my teeth and dropped it out the window. The thick orange plume boiled out of it and trailed after.

Landed twenty feet from the road and blew low and stiff east-northeast.

Damn, that was a bright idea. Good strong late morning crosswind could've messed with my plan. What else was I forgetting?

The reason Bangley was still alive was that he never forgot anything. Maybe he remembered a few too many things, a lot of redundancy, he didn't care. What else did he have to do with his day? It was just occurring to me that maybe the reason I was still alive was that Bangley never forgot anything. Bangley. Husband and father. Farmer. Damn.

Oh, I know. Hig, you forgot that trying to land on a deeply rutted basically a trail in rocky sage country you mostly can't see through—you forgot that it could clean your clock. Or clean the clock of the Beast which might be the same thing.

Okay, breathe. I came around a last time for final and pulled the bar up for half flaps and pushed down the nose, ruddered hard over for a full slip, and floated sideways into the field.

★

A bush landing has a way of waking you up. If you weren't already. Powered off, engine growl to idle, and kicked the Beast straight just before touch down, left wing down low into the wind and the left gear thwacked into the brush loud. I

202

struggled with the gusts. To keep the nose over the left edge of the ditch and not in it. Then the right main gear, the back right wheel hit the mounding dirt between the old wheel tracks and we jerked left. I struggled to keep that tire out of the rut. Must have, because I didn't feel anything break, just heard the loud rips and tumps and squeals as the thicker sage beat at the plane and held the nose off as long as I could and when it came down there was a merciful clear bald run of low rocks and chewed down grass, thanks bighorn, or whoever, and the Beast bumped and shook and I shuddered to a stop just before the piñons.

Whew. Breathe. First thought: My paint job. The beautiful Beast scoured with stick lines. Second was: That was way too close. That was fucking dumb. All of it was dumb. If I hadn't thrown the smoke bomb I would've wrecked. I looked at the digital fuel gauge before shutting her down. Just over twelve gallons left. Less than an hour. And less than an hour in the two jugs. Not even close to enough to get back. Dumb. But. I could get to Junction if I could take off with the same luck I had just landed.

★

Before I augured in the three stakes and tied her down facing into her takeoff, before I put two of Bangley's Eggs of Death in the pockets of my jacket, and slung the AR over my shoulder and walked away from the Beast, I did the first not dumb thing all morning. I took out the jugs and using the strut climbed over the wings and poured one each, the last fuel in each wing tank. Fuel up now. Better to fuel up before you get your undies in a bundle. And I took the key. Put it in my right jeans pocket and said

Hig. The key is in the right jeans pocket.

Never know how much of a hurry you might be in later.

III

Well she was not nude waiting for me by the creek, not even dressed out in the grass in front of the house singing, she was nowhere. Need not have tied myself to any mast. The smoke that had leaked from the chimney and billowed down-canyon was gone.

Place looked suddenly dead. Bucket kicked over in the yard, a dirty cooking spoon beside it. The cattle, a few sheep, were there heads down in the meadow all facing downstream. Ribbed thin, sharp hips, nearly starving. One big bird high up on the high wall gyring along the rock face. A peregrine. The ledge marked with a white ribbon of guano must be her nest. Circle out, circle back. Pity the ducks that angled down into this hole. No chickens. That occurred to me. Because of the falcon? No, the old coot had a shotgun. Because they would need a rooster then, or two, to maintain the flock—probably too loud every morning if you want to stay hidden, like letting the whole damn country know you're here. Smart.

I turned the scope upcanyon to where the creek spilled over the wall in a twenty foot falls. The top of the hole completely boxed off by this cliff. And two sides soaring. Pretty neat spot. A length of dead pine was propped against the rock beside the waterfall, limbs stubbed in a crude ladder.

Okay. If they went that way in flight they didn't pull up and hide the ladder, maybe only because it was too heavy or they didn't have time.

I was lying at the very rim, scrunched between two rocks looking straight down. Here my cliff was about a hundred feet high, maybe less. I was wedged tight and had to slide the holstered Glock around to my back so it wouldn't scrape.

Think like Bangley. That's what you need to do. Bangley's voice, I can hear it:

Goddamn, Hig. Old man and a scrawny girl got you all in a bundle. So far you got more firepower on your right hip than he's got by a factor of ten.

Yeah but what if there's more of them? Or if he's got more than the shotgun?

You see any sign of more? Stools in the yard, clothes hanging, bedding, old shoes?

Huh.

Good you're thinking like that, Hig, can't take that away. Ticking off the exigencies. Hig is an old dog but he learns shit little by little. But you gotta look at the intel staring you in the face. I'm not saying there aren't three more guys with weapons hidden in the trees. Good to plan for that, too. But you gotta act on what you believe. Plus you also got the rifle, you got the grenades. You got the grenades, right?

Yeah, two.

Hig?

Yeah?

What are you doing here?

Silence.

I mean what do you want? What the fuck do you want?

Silence.

You can't form a plan unless you got a mission. You can't have a mission if you don't know what the fuck you want. First rule. Have a clear mission, have an exit strategy.

I thought the first rule was Never Negotiate.

Negotiate, Hig, and you are negotiating your own life . . .

That's the first principle. Anyway what the fuck does it matter? You got a bigger problem to solve first. Which is: What the fuck, Hig, do you hope to accomplish?

The canyon darkened and I shivered. A cloud, a swollen cumulus tugged its shadow across the cut. Bearing away the last chill of a long winter. The shadow smelled like ponderosas. It passed over and the sun on the arms of my jacket smoothed out the goosebumps. It was comfortable snugged like this in the rocks. I could hear the buzz of a deerfly but it didn't bother me. In the moment I realized I could lay my head on my suntoasted arms and go to sleep no problem. My nose was inches from the ground. I watched an ant climb the stem of a small purple aster. Smelled good here. Like flinty dirt and new grass, mesquite.

Hig!

Uh, yeah. What?

Focus, goddammit. Get your dick outta your hand. Every minute you are lying out here not knowing what the fuck you are up to, you are vulnerable. So is the plane. Whoever was down there may be working their way to the rim to scout your sorry ass. Planning right now how to neutralize the threat that is Hig. What we would be doing and fast. Stead of just lying down there vulnerable, exposed, the way you are doing right now.

Huh.

Fuck. Hadn't thought of that. I blew out, nearly whistled. What is up with you? Are you completely out of it? Have you so totally lost your edge?

Did you ever have an edge?

Hig!

Uh what?

Know why you are sleepy? Why suddenly you could just stretch out and snooze til sundown?

Why?

Because you don't know what the fuck to do! I don't mean you wouldn't know what to do if you had a purpose. I've seen you, Hig. When you have a purpose like getting away from nine marauding motherfuckers and dusting their ass you're pretty goddamn good. Hig on wheels. But you don't have a clue what you're doing here. You're acting like

208

a goddamn lost puppy. One look at a tall girl who maybe doesn't have the sickness and you're goddamn gaga.

That's not it.

Why'd you risk the plane then? I saw that little maneuver. Pretty fucking dicey. Risk everything for a closer look at a crack. What if she hates men? Ever think of that?

Bad enough to risk it all for Something Known is what you're saying.

Then I thought: We're more likely to risk it all for something unknown. For some perverse reason.

I told you, Hig: Get all philosophical in a tactical situation and you're toast.

Toast.

That sounded good. Two pieces of lightly browned toast with butter and jam. Hadn't had butter in nine years hadn't had milk. I bet those cows gave sweet warm milk every day. One or two. I shifted the scope down into the meadow to scan for a swollen udder and I saw them. Pure dumb luck. He must have had at least two guns, which made sense to have a hunting rifle as well as a shotgun, because this was the flashing glint off his scope. A bare instant. Enough to let me place him in a thicket of cattails, at the edge of the creek, on the meadow side, away from the house. A large sandstone block about the size of a car had tumbled there and he was hard against it.

209

Right where I would've sat. Same basic strategy as we used at the airport: the house would be the draw. He sat where he, or they, could sight the open ground between the creek and the little stone house. All of that within shotgun range. Could take care of most passing threats with the two shots from the double barrel. And he, they, had the rifle too for long shots, or for after. They. Once I placed him I could just see the barrel of his rifle, darker, straighter than the reeds, and I could see her shift a mass of dark hair. She had the other gun. Shotgun. And he was not looking across the yard he was sighting straight up at me. Fuck.

The blast blew chips of sandstone from my snug rock all over the right side of my face. I jerked back. The second twanged in air just over my head. Fuck.

Blinked. Stone dust in my eyes. Right side of my face now stinging too. Hand to temple. No blood this time. Fucking Gramps. That's twice. Old bastard had my head bracketed. If I wasn't more goddamn careful the next shot would be dead center.

I could hear Bangley laughing. As if he were three feet away. Laughing out of the ether, like a not totally benign ghost.

Pickle, huh Hig? A quandary. All you want to do is make friends and now you might have to shoot somebody. Laughter loud and long.

★

Had a point, old Bangley, my tactical superego. The old bastard down below was a wicked good shot. Like professional good, like Bangley. He had nearly taken me out with a shotgun, like the Beast and I were just one big blue winged teal. Pretty good.

Why was I so giddy? Somehow the pickle I was in made me very glad. I mean, it wasn't a pickle. I could walk away. But. I had an image of a white rag tied at the end of a stick stuck over the edge of that cliff. Waving it like some Hollywood cliché. No one ever tried that with us back at the airport because A) it was always night, and B) we, mostly Bangley, shot them dead before they knew what was happening. If someone had tried that back there, then what? Never negotiate. Bangley would have gained maximum tactical advantage, called to them, *Okay come out in peace* and then he would've blown their heads off. Good old Bangley.

Yup, that was going to take some depth of faith and trust and even then it was a flip of a coin, and plus I didn't have anything white.

I scrambled back a bit, stood up, stretched. Refreshed almost like I'd had a nap. Then I trotted back to the Beast. I kept a stack of Xerox paper in the back seat pocket and a couple of crayons. Also a few palm sized stones and rubber bands. This so if I needed to drop a note mostly to the families I could. But a couple of times I dropped notes on wanderers camped out on the roads too close to the airport who didn't seem to understand my catchy NorthSouthEastWest song: *Turn back north or die etc.* Nor a stick of dynamite. These messages, the ones wrapped around the stones and dropped from the Beast, were very succinct and graphic and they always worked. Power of the pen. I was always very proud of myself when I crafted four lines that got a refractory band of pirates to pack up and scurry back up a road. I picked up half a dozen sheets and a black crayon and gathered up Jasper's quilt and trotted back across the park.

I was grinning. I could feel it stretching my smarting cheeks. I hunkered back down by the edge of the canyon and wrote on one sheet vertically as big as it would go: *I*

The satisfaction of composing. Remembered that Dylan Thomas sometimes would set down one word of a new poem then walk down to the pub and get shitfaced in celebration. For breaking the void of silence.

Well. Let's see how this goes over before I waste any more sheets.

Crept, wriggled to the edge of the clifftop which for my purposes was auspiciously formed in a real lip, sharp and dropping to a vertical, if not overhanging, face of sandstone. Keeping my precious splintered head well back, I reached out pushed and shook the quilt off the edge, unfurling it like a flag. Made sure the hunter and the flushing pheasant and the dog were right side up from the bottom's point of view and made sure my fingers did not go past the lip.

Most fun I'd had in years except maybe fishing and I think it's because it was a lot *like* fishing, except there were people at the other end of this line. Catch and release.

Soon as the quilt reached air another shot. Creased air right over my hands, head.

You hear bullets make the sound they always do in Westerns and war stories and guess what? They do. They make a *phhhht* like someone opening a poisonous can of soda. The Soda of Death. Like a vacuum following itself at the speed of a diving duck. Followed almost simultaneously by a little hum, a musical exclamation point.

Okay shoot at my quilt if you want. I have needle and thread.

Then silence. Quizzical. That's what it felt like.

Often fishing you can feel right away the spirit of the fish on the other end of the line. That connection. I mean you know right away: is it fierce, scared, experienced, young and dumb, wily, panicked, resigned, confident, mischievous. Any of it in a rapid tugging and zing of line. I often thought of the silence between people in the same way.

I unfurled the quilt and the shot blasted at nearly the same instant and then silence. A puzzled silence. I grinned. I knew Gramps was scoping the blanket, studying the repeating pattern, thinking, *What the fuck?* I knew from that distance with his scope he would be able to make out the scene. I scrabbled the ground for two heavy stones and weighted the top of the quilt and let it hang.

I let him puzzle it out, maybe discuss it. Then I took the paper, stuck it on the point of a four foot broken limb and pushed it over the edge: *I. BANG!* Swish. Complete miss. Ha! Not going for the paper going for my head, where it would be if I was just a little tiny bit closer.

Silence. I hung the paper on the stick vertically so he could read it. He could. They were really fucking close. I mean if I wanted to be really mean I could maybe just shove a boulder over the edge. Or spit.

I pulled the stick back. If I was chuckling it was the first time in maybe nine years. Chuckling— that word. It's not a word for the End of Times. I unpeeled the paper off the crayon with my teeth and wrote on the second paper again vertically, *AM.*

Why didn't I just shout down there? Well, conversations can get so crosswise so quick. What I've found. First time I met Melissa was in a coffee shop and I was too shy to speak so I wooed her with a note. Works. One wrong tone of voice and that's it. Nah, this was better. Plus the creek was pouring, plus wind, plus there was no way on earth I was going to stick my mouth over that edge.

Stuck *AM* on the stick hung it over. Now no shot. Silence. Sonofabitch was getting the hang of it. *I AM*. Existential enough. Shit, I could stop right there, just let them chew on that a while. Picked up the crayon, wrote *NOT*. Pulled in my stick, stuck it on. Let that flap in the wind.

The philosophical implications of going from the penultimate assertion to the last were profound. I mean Hamlet had nothing on this. The unfolding dialectic. Dang.

Then *A*. I wrote *A* covering one whole page stuck it out. *A. A.* Flap, rustle.

Then I sharpened the crayon on the rock turned the page sideways and wrote as big as I could fit: *PHEASANT.*

Hung it out there. Weighted the stick down with another rock and lay back face to the sun, arms crossed under my poor abused head, and let the warmth cover me and the sun work on the cuts.

They weren't going anywhere, neither was I.

★

If this were a Western I would now put my hat on a stick. I was wearing a hat. A sweatstained fray-brimmed baseball cap that said Cherry Hills

Golf Club. I took it off a visitor one night and I liked it maybe because it carried a message of consolation: the End of Everything meant the End maybe for all time, maybe in all the universe, of Golf.

I had nothing against golf.

Anyway there were probably Scotsmen in Scotland who somehow survived the pandemic and after and were now strolling over the heath playing the old game—no irrigation but mist and rain, no lawnmowers but herds of wild sheep. Thwacking their drives into the fog. That was a nice idea.

Maybe Gramps hated golf. Doubt if he could read lettering that small but if he had say a ten power scope, well, he might. I put it on the stick anyway, for fun, shoved it out there to the edge. Nothing. The old crust wasn't buying it. He was gonna wait til he saw an eye, an ear. Hmph. Now what? I could just stand up, walk to the edge and shout. Hey! I come in peace! In friendship! And. If they subscribed to the First Principles of Bruce Bangley I was a dead man. Curiously, for the first time it seemed in a while I wasn't ready to die. Not just this minute. I mean I had more than a casual interest in staying alive. For some reason.

Okay. I had an idea.

I walked back to the Beast got another stack of paper. Had all the time in the world: none of us seemed to be going anywhere. Unless they bolted for the tree ladder which they wouldn't as I could pot them as easy as the German officers in that awful Hemingway vignette that I loved. *It was absolutely topping. They tried to get over it, and we potted them from forty yards. They rushed it, and officers came out alone and worked on it. It was an absolutely perfect obstacle.* I mean if that's what I had been here to do.

I hunkered down by my rock in the sun, well behind it, and wrote out more words. Put them on the stick one after the other and held them over the lip as before. Deep silence while the fish on the other end thought about it.

I-COULD-BLOW-YOU-TO-SMITHER-EENS-BUT-I-WON'T—PEACE

Lucky I had half a ream of paper.

Then I took an Egg of Death out of my pocket pulled the pin which was pretty stiff and tossed it over the edge.

I threw it well upstream into what in my mind's eye I saw as the top of the meadow—well away from the cows and the cobwebbed sonofabitch and his girl.

The explosion was deeply satisfying. Thank you Bangley. I had the other pages ready and while they were still rattled and pinching their limbs to see if they weren't dead I pushed them out:

217

SEE?-NEXT-ONE-MIGHT-HURT

Long pause.

DON'T-MAKE-ME-RUN-OUT-OF-PAPER

Pause.

STAND-UP

I can admit I was really enjoying myself. For the first time in what seemed years my head seemed clear. Not like the thoughts were standing out in a meadow like those shaggy Norwegian horses and wondering what they were doing here. Not like one might wander off into the trees.

Just for good measure I crept the cap out to the edge again. Nothing. Maybe we were coming to an understanding. I crawled to the edge and peered over. They were both standing up in the cattails holding their guns out to the side. He was tall, fit, not that old, maybe early sixties, in a ratty fawn cowboy hat. She was taller than he and I'd have to say handsome. Skinny but strong jawed, high cheeked, dark eyebrows, long dark hair twisted into a braid. Can't say why but she looked smart from three hundred feet. I reached back for the AR and put the scope on them. If a man can spark he was sparking: mouth compressed in rage and his eyes which were gray were throwing off glints of fury. His face had the deep lines of a man who had earned them out in the elements. Her eyes were wideset and what? Violet? Something between blue and black. Her cheeks were inflamed scarlet and she looked scared but also something else: mildly amused. Was that it? She looked to be about thirty five.

Can you fall in love through a rifle scope? Damn. I pulled my head away and looked down with naked eye. Well proportioned, wide hipped, tall. Maybe too skinny. I brought my eye to the gun again and nudged the barrel and let the scope travel down. I admit. Her legs were scratched and inflamed and maybe too thin but they were long and tapered.

Breathe Hig. Say 10-4. Ten four.

Came up to one knee, still aiming, both eyes open. I yelled.

Hi!

He blinked. I nudged the scope over to her face and they both looked like they might be crazy or maybe in a bad dream.

Hi!

Kept the scope on her. She smiled. Actually smiled. It was subtle, small, but at ten power I could see the damn thing.

How should we do this? Yelling.

Silence.

Gramps! Relax! If I wanted to kill and rape and plunder you'd be dead by now!

Pause while he took that in.

I forgive you! I yelled.

I mean for trying to kill me more than twice! Nearly wrecking my plane. Nothing personal. I know. Would've done the same thing myself.

My shouts trailed off on the breeze. But I could see that they could hear me. I mean something was registering. I could also see when I lifted my head back and looked downcanyon that all the cows and a few sheep were huddling terrified against a tall woven brush fence across the bottom of the box.

Sorry for scaring your cows!

They stood there, arms out. I played the scope over both of them. He was chewing his cheek trying to make out what the hell was going on. And her. I wasn't sure. I could see gears turning and I thought something not unpleasant was dawning on her. That was my fantasy. I knew, I *knew* that I was addled somehow, but also that I was as clear as I had been in my adult life.

Okay you can keep your guns. I'm coming down.

Okay?

Okay?

He nodded. Finally. Pulled the gun back in to his body and stood again like a man in command of his world. I'll say this: there was something about the codger that was dignified and proud. He was a fucking good shot, I knew that. I got the feeling that everything the prickly bastard did he did with that amount of confidence. Just an impression from the bleachers.

If you decide to kill me you'll feel really bad later! I promise you'll deprive yourself of the best part of your day!

She smiled. Oh man. I was gone. I thought Maybe, maybe he is her dad. What a fool.

In purgatory there is really nothing else to be. I lowered the gun, stepped back fast and walked back to the Beast.

Just for luck and respect I put another grenade in my jacket pocket to make two and grabbed some venison jerky for a peace offering, then I slung the AR over my shoulder and trotted across the sage meadow. I worked myself upcanyon through the piñons until the cleft shallowed out and I found a game trail down to the creek.

IV

My heart was booming like a bongo but not from the effort. The ground was rough, yes, the way into the creek steep and strewn with boulders. I placed a hand on their warm shoulders as I hopped and pivoted around them, slid on loose dirt following the path of deer. Their droppings lay among the long brown needles of ponderosas and the sun mixed the scents which were strangely close to the musky scent of a living deer close by in pines. So that the hunter in me was roused. But that wasn't it either. My heart was hammering because I felt like I was heading to my first date.

That one, Hig's actual first date—I was so nervous it was a disaster. We went to see *Avatar* in 3D. I kept having to duck away and pee. Every time I brought back more popcorn or candy. She must have thought I was some sort of diabetic or bulimic or something. I didn't kiss her at the end nor try and she was clearly flushed and upset, and I'll never know if it was because she thought I was a geek and couldn't wait to get rid of me or—this only occurred to me months later—maybe she was as nervous as I and kinda liked me but didn't know how to ask and felt rejected when I left so abruptly. My first realization that someone else might be anxious for *my* approval, that they could be scared of *me*. Before the end of the world that was a profound insight. Now I pretty much took it for granted: everybody was scared of me.

Which is a weird way to head out on a date. Poor Hig, poor Frankenstein.

Not her. She smiled. She smiled.

I'd charmed em hadn't I? Charmed em right out of Kill Mode. Right out of their knickers. Hadn't I?

I stopped dead. Squinted down to the creek, took one more careful step into the shade of a pine. Maybe not.

The cute thing with the quilt. Codger had no patience. He placed a high value on his time his attention. While I was lying back in the sun enjoying myself, letting them think about things, he was forced to hunker down in the wet cattails, his blood boiling, fearing too—for life, for his gal—thinking, I'm gonna kill that smug son-ofabitch. First chance. Thinks he's so goddamn cute, how cute will it be when I make him watch his own balls roasting on the fire.

Like that.

I went on. Nevertheless. With the hair kinda standing up on my neck.

When I got to the stream I turned down it and followed an easy trail along the bank. Tall grass here, tiny white asters like daisies, Indian paintbrush. Wild strawberry, penstemon. Huge ponderosas, the smell of cold wet stone and vanilla. White moths circling each other over a gravel bar. Mating. The first date thing: that was history. My heart was still racing but not for that. I saw the moths flitting, three then two, in and out of sunlight, and thought: Hig, mating is probably not in the cards not this round. Not ever probably.

When you get to the short cliff at the top of the meadow, the one with the waterfall, when you swing down onto that tree ladder and put your back to Gramps, he is gonna shoot you dead with a delicious grunt. So there. Think this is a game, punk? You-are-not-a-pheasant-Correct:-you-are-a-dead-man. Write that on your little sheets. Bang. You just wouldn't leave us alone. Bang. Stop twitching will ya? Bang.

Bangley: *I-told-you-Hig:-never-ever—fuck-you-know-damn-well-what.-R.I.P.*

Hmph. Whatever quandary I was in before I was just as much in now. That's what I saw as I moved fast down the stream. Another thing: he, they, could've climbed up the tree ladder into the upper creek in two minutes flat and could now be waiting for me in the willows behind any tree and ambush me at leisure. I froze.

Did not want to die. Not now.

I could be in his sights as we speak. Goose-bumps again this time not from the chill.

Scanned down the creek. A box elder at water's edge, leaves the color of limes. A few cotton-woods below. When the wind pulsed, their leaves turned back, brightening like the palm of a hand held up in sunlight. Stop. They could be crouched behind those thick shaggy trunks.

Stop, Hig, Stop. Reconsider the folly of mere human connection. Listen to a tree.

When you fished, that's what you were seeking huh? Connection. Think of the cost to the fish. The fish did not want your connection and if a trout could have killed you with one gulp he would have. Gramps is that fish. He can swallow you.

Huh.

I backed up, got my body flat behind a tree. The creek was about thirty feet below me, the current already running clear and shallow enough to wade across. Low water for this early in the season, maybe thigh deep at the deepest. Scanned up the opposite bank. It was a slope, steep, of new grass and flowering weeds running up under an open glade of ponderosas. Toward the top of the ridge, crumbling rimrock broke through like moldering ruins, walls and parapets.

Perfect hiding place. Them. I mean a perfect spot to ride out the end. From here, upstream, you'd never have a clue that the stream would open up into such a wide deep hole, such a meadow. No reason ever to come down here, to follow the water. It wasn't the easiest going and the old track above, the road I'd landed on, would take you more quickly north and east. To places where the road crossed the little river without effort. From ground level at the top you couldn't see the hole, the canyon, at all til you were right on it, right on the edge. And I bet that the way up from downstream was beset by waterfalls and cliffs. It was perfect. A hideout. Outlaws of old would covet.

How did they get the cows in there? Only way in was the ladder. That occurred to me.

Why when I was in the most critical spots did my mind wander to curiosities? Bangley would not approve. Bangley would say *Get down. That ambush idea that's a good one. Hunker down and think about things.*

I did. Backed up the slope ten paces into the cover of a thick juniper that grew to the ground like a shaggy bush. Snuggled in behind it, pushed in to where I could sit and see through branches down the slope. Stiff twigs brushed my scabbing face stung. The scent was heady. It was like being inside one of those sachets. Why did she do that? Dusty blue juniper berries rained to the ground. Think this is what they made gin out of. Really?

Now what? I was safe. So what have you gained?

Crouched in a mass of prickly twigs. I was a troll who lived at the base of a tree. Looked at the world through a scratchy scrim of needles and branches. Lived on rain, on bits of song and memory.

I lay the rifle on the ground, hugged my knees, leaned into the thicker branches.

Exhausted. To the bone. The untethering that took such an effort. The flight over already seemed like another life. And the airport seemed like a dream. If the airport was a dream, then Jasper was a dream behind a dream, and before before was a dream behind that. Within and within. Dreaming. How we gentle our losses into paler ghosts.

Wait til nightfall that's what. In the dark I can walk downstream. Watch them. Climb down the ladder in safety. One benefit of so many nights fishing, fishing obsessively into the dark: I know how to trust feet to find the way.

A trout could see the smallest fly on the surface in the darkest night. The sky always luminous, luminous to a trout and the bug silhouetted against it. I loved catching fish in the dark. Often just the sound in a quiet pool, the blip, the tiny hyphenated splash then the tug. I loved it.

Darkness. Nothing. Sharp smell of warming needles. Sleep. Okay a few minutes. Sleep.

★

Up.

Huh?

Up. Back out. Touch that rifle you're a dead man.

Hard and sharp hard sharp thing against back of neck. Stick. Yup a stick. A long pole. At the other end a man with a gun. Fuck. Fuck. Good one Hig.

Hands on ground. Back out. Crawl.

Crawl. Slow. Now flat, lie flat. Hands behind head. Now!

Knee in back hard. Hand roughly pushing under jacket relieving me of the belted Glock. Hand running down my back, up again, down legs, expert, swift.

Roll over.

Same with the front, fast frisk, relieving me of the grenades. Into the pockets of his own barn coat.

Younger than. Or not. Leaner. White haired. Hard like shoe leather. Creases. Creased lines deep from cheeks down. Grimace lines. Spray of creases from corners of the eyes, outside corners. Gray eyes sparking. Used to sparking back at the naked sun. No bullshit at all. Every movement sure and swift.

Not sure why: up close I felt less afraid. Didn't feel panicked at all. Which was probably dumb right now. Gramps was not the least afraid of me, not a shred. Somehow I reciprocated.

Over again. Roll over.

Knee hard in back, sharp needles stinging right side of my face. Watched him from the corner of my eye. Shrugged a circle of coiled rope off his

228

left shoulder, shook it out one handed, bound my hands tight. One handed.

Must be a rancher, I said. Can tell by your hat.

Shut up.

Ten-four. Kinda nice not to make idle conversation.

Didn't say that, didn't say anything.

Knee hard down on the knobs of my spine, hurt as he yanked up, tightened the knot.

You shoulda kept on. Nobody bothers us here.

I did, I can tell.

Shut up.

Knee grinding ribs. He stepped back, five steps sideways, uncoiling rope, reached down, picked the AR out of the tree and slung it.

Now stand.

Didn't even give me a chance. One jerk hard on the rope yanked me to my feet, about ripped out my shoulders.

Walk.

I walked. And.

A relief to do what someone said. Someone who knew exactly what he was doing. Just follow orders. It occurred to me as I stumbled down the hill that if he had wanted me dead I'd be dead. Just like me before when I was on the rim and they were cowering below. Reciprocating. He was reciprocating now. A perfectly reciprocal relationship. Damn.

I'd been closer than I thought. Maybe two

hundred yards to where the creek went over the lip, poured over the twenty foot falls. I could see the top of their tree ladder sticking up to the left of the current. I could hear the cascade hitting the pool at the bottom. It sent up spray and the spray in the sunlight shimmered with a shifting shred of rainbow.

From this angle through the mist the little box canyon looked like Eden. Green and bounded, waterfed, remote from death. How was I going to get down that? Was he going to lower me by my bound arms—up behind me and tear out both shoulders? Or just shove me over the edge, hope the pool is a few feet deep? Break an ankle or legs, cripple me, all the better.

The whistle pierced, I jumped. Jerked around. Could've been the peregrine but right in my goddamn ear. She came out of the stone hut. She carried the scoped rifle. Bolt action. Also a small blanket. She sat at a wood slab table, rolled the blanket, propped the barrel on it like a sandbag, sighted upwards, thought better of it, lifted the gun and pulled down a bipod, two legs at the front of the barrel, sighted again. Better angle. On me. She'd done this before, that was clear.

She's very good. I taught her. You screw up just a little, you die.

He stepped forward and with one tug freed the knot on one wrist, left one tied to the end of his rope.

Climb down.

One handed? I'm afraid of heights.

Which was true. Flying is different.

He kicked me in the ass. No shit. A swift boot. Toe in the buttocks which lurched me forward, almost sent me over the edge. That hurt. Like a bastard. Kinda hurt my feelings. What if I had stumbled over? First time since he woke me up I really wanted to hit him.

Use two hands.

I crouched, clutched the tree with both hands swung down.

★

My name is Hig.

I was born in the Year of the Rat.

I have no serial number but my pilot's license number is 135-271.

I am an Aquarius.

My mother loved me. She really really loved me. My father. Absent but. Well. I had an uncle that taught me to fish.

I wrote thirty poems after college, twenty three of which were for my wife.

Jasper was my dog.

No kids. My wife was pregnant.

My favorite books are: *Shane. Infinite Jest.*

I can cook. Pretty well for a guy.

Profession: contractor. I don't like it. I hated it.

I should have been a high school English teacher or something. A pet groomer. I am free of disease, as far as I know I am healthy. I visit families with the blood sickness about twice a month.

My favorite poem was written by Li Shang-Yin in the ninth century.

Maybe it wasn't my favorite poem before before but it is now.

I have always been particularly attuned to loss. I guess. Got a bumper crop now.

May I have some water?

★

He tied me to a post in the yard. Facing the sun. Sat me on one of the stools, hands behind me. Tight. They stood and studied me. I squinted, tried to make them out. Thought of something.

My right jacket pocket.

He stepped forward reached in, dug around, pulled out two fresh cans of Copenhagen. Nine or ten years old, expired, but still. I'd brought them as gifts, so. He stepped to my side so I could see him bent, his head down, looking at me sideways, close. Then he opened one of the cans with that expert tear of the thumbnail, creasing the paper around the tin lid, the quarter twist and pry. He stuck his nose in, breathed. I could smell it. Salt and dirt. The tobacco was dust dry, I knew from Bangley, but he pinched two fingers, stuck a small load in his upper lip. He was an upper lip man. Spat.

Three points.

That all? Two tins. I think six is fair.

He handed her the tins and I was surprised to see her take a dip. He pulled the second stool around to the side of me, sat.

Sun'll be out of your eyes in twenty minutes.

She stood stock still in front, still backlit. She was tall. I couldn't make out her face. Could feel the bore of her stare though.

Does she talk?

Whoops. Minus three. Back to zero. That's where you like to be. That's what I'm getting.

I like to travel light.

He nodded barely.

That's good. The dip. Been a while. I don't give a shit how you like to travel. You could be carrying around a dining room set for all I care. Looked around. We could use one.

If I say anything you're gonna dock me points right? I mean unprompted. Right?

He nodded. Minus one.

And then I lose my frequent flyer opportunities I'm guessing.

Minus two. Get to minus ten I shoot you dead. No appeal. On the spot. Mention her again I dock you five. Cause now you know better. Tell an untruth, that's ten points, you're dead. Shit your pants you're dead. Piss yourself that's up to you.

Suddenly I wasn't having any fun. I heard the thudding of the waterfall, rhythmic like a tribal drum, heard one of the sheep bleat and that's exactly how I felt. Plaintive and kind of traumatized.

I looked at him.

You know what?

I said that.

Know what? Fuck you. Fuck you and your points. I came here in peace and you tried to kill me twice. I came here looking for something, I don't know what. I don't know what, you got that? Not death, though. We had enough of that back at the airport. Enough death.

I sat tightly bound on the stool and I looked at him and I could feel tears streaming down my face, stinging the cuts on the left side.

I lost my dog a week ago. Jasper. I don't need you or your shit. I got nothing. Go ahead, subtract twenty fucking points, shoot me dead. I'll be fucking glad. Go ahead.

I could taste the salt of my tears.

Let him up Dad, she said. Enough. Let him up.

Her voice was husky. I blinked up at her straight into the sun. Felt his capable hands loose the rope.

★

I walked away from them to a cottonwood by the edge of the creek and pissed. I didn't care. I wasn't shy. The pour and burble of the stream covered my sobs. Cool in the deep shade. Sobbed so hard I gagged. Maybe they were watching, no, they were definitely watching, fuck them. I just let it finish, then breathed. Knelt and splashed my face, the cuts that were already rashing into a spray of scabs. Drank. Why the fuck was I crying all the time? I didn't give a shit, not really. I wasn't cracking up, it's just what I felt like doing. Nine years barely a drop, then Jasper, now this.

The world opens suddenly, opens into a narrow box canyon with four sheep, and we grieve. Two shepherds, maybe not in their right mind, and we grieve. The relief of company not Bangley, not the blood disease, we grieve. We grieve. That this was once the middle of nowhere and now it's not even that. And I am not even that. Before I could locate myself: I am a widower. I am fighting for survival. I am the keeper of something, not sure what, not the flame, maybe just Jasper. Now I couldn't. I didn't know what I was. So grieve.

I stood in the shade of the tree in the cool breath of the moving water and let the sound, the light breeze blow through me. I was a shell. Empty. Put me to your ear and you would hear the distant rush of a ghost ocean. Just nothing. The slightest pressure of current or tide could push and roll me. I would wash up. Here on this bank, dry out and bleach and the wind would scour and roughen me, strip away the thinnest layers until I was brittle and the thickness of paper. Until I crumbled into sand. That's how I felt. I'd say it was a relief to have at last nothing, nothing, but I was too hollow to register relief, too empty to carry it.

I really didn't give a shit what this old bastard did to me. Nothing to lose is so empty, so light, that the sand you crumble to at last blows away in a gust, so insubstantial it's carried upwards to shirr into the sandstorm of the stars. That's where we all get to. The rest is just wearing thin waiting for wind.

Certainly not a place to negotiate from. There is nothing to trade. I didn't even think, *I spared his life and his daughter's he owes me at least one. What? One thing. Twenty frigging points.*

Walked back.

I'm leaving. Back up that fucking tree. Pretty clear you prefer your own company.

I looked at her.

Could I please have a dip? Was never a habit, but right now it smells good. Thanks.

Took a big pinch. The nicotine hit as soon as I'd taken the first swallow and I felt dizzy for a second.

Damn. I forgot.

I spit.

Shoot me in the back on the way up and like I said I'm not sure you wouldn't be doing me a favor.

They stared at me. She had a dark stain on her throat like a bruise.

I'll need my Glock, my rifle. You keep the grenades. Housewarming.

He hesitated, picked the handgun off the table, handed it to me butt first. I holstered it. He lifted the rifle to muster, across his chest, passed it to me.

Thanks. Thanks for kicking me in the ass.

I hauled off and slugged him.

The one I'd been saving, a solid short right that connected to his left cheek. It knocked him off his feet clean and hard and he hit the dirt ass first. Knocked his hat off. Total surprise. He pushed up on his hands and blinked at me and only when I let my eyes travel over the whole picture did I see one hand filled with a handgun. Like magic. A heavy .45, officer issue.

You didn't have to kick me in the ass. Or play executioner. I would've gone anywhere you told me.

Who was I to talk?

I turned around and walked across the open ground upstream, my back as naked and ready for a bullet as for the fall and click of the next moment.

★

You, You, Hey.

What?

Higs, right? That's what you said.

Hig.

Hig. You want some lunch?

Stopped. She was probably half an inch taller than me. A sunburned scar parted her dark hair, her right eyebrow. Thin and sharp. The bruise at her throat.

Lunch? Do people still eat lunch.

We do.

Glanced back at the house. The old bastard was shoving the gun into the back of his waistband, adjusting his hat, watching us.

He really your dad?

Yes. On my father's side.

No apology for him. No small betrayal. I appreciated that. *On my father's side.* What a funny thing to say. She was smiling.

He may not want to have lunch with me.

I didn't invite him.

She hooked her thumbs in the pockets of her shorts and straightened her arms in a stretch. I did notice. How it lifted her breasts, how it exposed her waist above the waistband.

But I will, if you all promise not to punch or shoot each other.

You all. A country girl. Before. I stared at her. Honestly I didn't know if I wanted to have lunch with them or not. I had gotten kind of used to the idea of living on air, of blowing away. Some comfort in that.

Hig? Yes? Bangley's voice again, disembodied. I could imagine his rough laugh if he knew he was kinda my superego. Which I couldn't get rid of, just like a bad pop song. *The girl is inviting you to lunch. She feels bad you almost pissed your pants. Ha! Be polite.* Okay.

Okay I said.

Cimarron. She held out her hand.

Everybody calls me—

She stopped, looked around the canyon, smiled.

Cima.

★

Shepherd's pie with butter. Well salted. Ground beef. I thought I was going to die. Pops was right, the sun traveled over the rim of the canyon and we ate at the plank table in the shade. Close enough to the creek: a pleasant sift. It mixed with the breeze which also sounded like rushing water when it shirred the tops of the cottonwoods. Butter. Melting in glops over the mashed potato, puddling. Who would've thought something so unresistant and pale could mesmerize a man? She kept bringing it, I kept eating it. A steel pitcher of milk chilled in the creek which I emptied twice. Holy shit. Hig had you climbed that stupid tree and flown away or even been shot in the back you would've missed the meal of your life. I was so enchanted with the food I didn't even notice if Pops was giving me the Wolf Eye or Stink Eye or Shark Eye or whatever kind of eye you give to somebody who has just raised a welt on your face and was now eating your provisions nonstop.

To be offered cold milk. To have your blue enameled plate filled again. By a woman. To have her walk from an outside fire bearing your dish. To sit in the shade of a big old tree, not a metal hangar, and eat. To hear the bleat of a sheep come through the loud rustle of the leaves. To have an older man sitting across from you in silence, eating also, enemy or friend not sure, it doesn't matter. To be a guest. To break bread.

The pleasure almost split me like a baking stuffed tomato. Like my heart swelled and my skin got thinner and thinner in the heat of it. Of company.

Bangley and I ate together often, but it was different can't say how: it was like feeding time in a zoo of our own making. This was different. I was free to leave. They were free to disinvite me. The sense of privilege.

Nobody said much. I moaned, grunted. Hunched over the plate. Only realized it when I looked up and she was smiling. Her face was drawn too thin. Her huge eyes reminded me of a radar dish absorbing everything, unable not to. Like the squelch was set too low and much of what she absorbed was pain. Another bruise on her forearm, the one that handed me the plate. Glanced up once and she was rubbing the back of her neck with a wince. Clearly getting pleasure also from my famished devouring.

Don't get out much Pops said. You.

I stopped chewing.

No not really. Where I live most of the restaurants are too expensive.

Where do you live?

Denver. North of there.

They were both staring at me now. Hungry like me. In a different way.

I set my fork on the boards, took a long swallow of cold milk, wiped my mouth on the sleeve of my jacket.

It was bad, I said. Ninety nine point whatever. Mortality. Just about killed everyone.

Your family? she said.

I nodded.

Everyone. Infrastructure frayed then fell apart. Before the end it was. It was bad.

Reached for the cup of milk and drank as if it could cool.

It was a frenzy. Everyone clinging to some shred: that they might be the one who was immune. Because we had heard of that, too, the mysterious resistance that ran in families. Genetic.

They were staring at me. He opened a pocket knife, picked his teeth.

When my wife died I made my way to the country airport where I keep my plane. I hid out.

You defended it, he said, scanning my face.

I nodded.

With help.

He was reading my own capacity for hell, for death, for wreaking it.

We defended it. Me and Bangley. Who showed up one day with a trailer full of weapons.

Bangley? He grunted. He knew what he was about old Bangley. Didn't he?

He put an elbow on the table, stretched out his long legs, picked his teeth.

He brought you along. Kinda trained you up. Set a perimeter didn't he? He had no problem killing anything that crossed it. Young, old, men, women. But you did.

But you got over it.

Dad.

Ninety nine point whatever. What's left? Point whatever. One out of two hundred? Three hundred? We've seen what that is. It's not usually pretty is it? Is it Higs?

Hig.

Big Hig.

I stared at him.

Not pretty what's left, is it?

I stared at him. His eyes were alight with equal parts cold knowledge and warm mischief.

He spat a fleck of food off his tongue. You're a hunter. Deer, elk. Before.

Nodded. How—?

He waved it away.

The way you hold your rifle. Way you move down the creek. Looking at sign. Can't help yourself.

My mouth opened. I saw myself stepping in the suncrackled needles studying the piles of scat. He was watching. He could have had me any time he wanted.

Never in the service though.

I stared at him.

Fact you don't like killing anybody. Not even a bull elk I'd bet. If there was one to kill. Not even a trout. If there was one. Too bad. You love to fish too.

Who the fuck was this guy? How—?

I saw you studying the creek. You stood right where I would've stood so as not to spook the fish in the pool.

I stared.

But killing is something you can get used to. Isn't it, Hig?

No.

So you say.

He leaned forward and his eyes bore into mine. He aimed his gray eyes into mine and they sparked like he had lit the fuses.

I suggest you shrug out of your pissant self-righteousness. Like a rattler out of old skin. You'd move easier, smoother. Turned and spat. Nobody at this table is an innocent. That shit with the pheasant? Had you been close enough I would've slit your throat. Not thinking. Glad you weren't. That would've been a real dumbshit move.

The whole thing, the speech, the image, it shivered my insides like a cold and sudden night wind. Who the fuck was this guy? He could've slit my throat in the juniper. While I slept.

He stood up, stretched. He was in his sixties, I guessed, but he was long and lean and looked to be strung together with catgut. He moved easily in his skin. A life bent to work which he loved, was my guess if I were guessing. A rancher clearly, some sort of soldier along the way. I was tempted to play What's My Line with him, too, but it felt gauche. I mean I didn't need to get into a one-up deal with this dude, into any kind of pissing match. He'd just given me maybe the best meal of my life. Or she had.

He said, Thanks for lunch. Touched her shoulder. How's the throat?

She smiled. Been better.

He nodded once, picked a bow saw from a peg on the outside wall of the hut and walked downstream. Opened a gate in the brush fence and went through. I poured another cup of milk from the pitcher. Must have been my fourth or fifth.

You're not used to it. You're going to make yourself sick. You'll have wicked diarrhea at the least.

You a doctor as well as a chef?

Uh huh.

The cup stopped at my lips. I put it down.

What kind of doctor?

Internist. Public health.

Her mouth stretched into the form of a smile but her eyes weren't smiling. Not even ironic.

Epidemiology to tell the truth.

Everybody around here seemed to be very into telling the truth, the whole truth.

Where?

New York City.

Oh.

Fuck.

What happened to your throat?

He was mean but he didn't seem mean like that. But. He was the only other person around. Unless they had attack sheep.

It's not what happened to. I mean it's the result of damage to my blood vessels. I hemorrhage quite easily. My muscles get very sore as well. A type of fibromyalgia. You see I contracted the flu. I barely survived. One result of the prolonged fever was the systemic inflammation that resulted in these conditions. But I had some resistance which we understand to be inherited from my father.

Biological resistance or sheer orneriness.

That too. I'm sorry we scared you. You scared us.

Again she didn't defend him, didn't feel the need. She was squarely in his corner as it should be. Right?

We talked about it. Dad doesn't pull punches as you see.

She poured herself her own cup of milk, leaned into the table. The breeze played with wisps of curly hair that strayed to her temple, her eyebrow.

You kinda triggered our Plan. He thought we should talk about what we would do when one day we were overrun. When, not if. Or when we were outwitted or outgunned. When you showed up with grenades we thought it might be that time.

Damn.

I thought, Maybe that wasn't a smile I saw on her lips. Through the scope. Maybe that was the face you make when everything is over. Over over.

One of the cows lowed long and deep with a rising inflection the way cows do. Like a question. The cottonwood leaves overhead flitted and ticked.

You have a pact huh?

She nodded.

He shoots you.

The cow mooed again, this time one short note as if answering her own query. Simple country life. Question and answer.

How close were you?

Close. He had the .45 out. After you threw the grenade. But then he said, Let's play this out another step. He said it will be a risk: he—you— can shoot me as soon as we step out. But he said he had a hunch.

A hunch?

He said you were weak. He said, Let's play this out.

That stung. I felt myself flush. Or maybe it was all the lactose hitting my system.

You all aren't diplomatic in the least.

Seems like a world that's way past diplomacy.

Maybe. Bangley feels the same way. My partner.

Anyway he gave me the .45 just in case. In case you did plug him from the rim and try to take me.

Jesus.

That's the world. That was the world we left.

I nodded.

He said, You can handle him. If he kills me, you kill him when he gets close. But if there are more. Then.

She touched her throat unconsciously. I nodded. She probably would have handled me if it got to that. Don't take it hard, Hig. It's kind of a compliment. They read you from a hundred yards.

Why didn't he kill me then? In the creek? Instead you all serve me lunch.

I widened my eyes.

You all aren't trying to fatten me up? I mean you've got that taste for human flesh like a rogue shark?

Now she really smiled. She laughed. Leaned her head back, showing me the large bruise, and laughed high and husky.

247

Ow. Cupped her palm over the ribbed architecture of her trachea. Hurts a little not much. A rogue shark. No. Whew.

She poured herself another mug of milk, drank slowly. No. Finishing her last swallow. No, we need you.

Oh.

Suddenly I did feel nauseous. Funny, but the first image was some sort of forced breeding experiment. Why that would make me feel sick I'm not sure as she was very good looking, I'd say almost beautiful. Though scarred and very fragile. But the image was me screwing her on a stone bed like an altar while her father stood over us with a gun to my head.

★

I didn't ask. The way these people shared things, I knew I'd be told soon whether I liked it or not. Exhaustion again. It swept over me. Like some sort of mustard gas. What was wrong with me? It was like nine years of vigilance had suddenly caught up. I felt like crossing my arms on the rough wood of the table and laying my head down atop them and falling asleep. Right now.

You don't mind if I take a nap do you? I don't know if I can stay awake.

It's the milk probably. She stood and pointed

farther under the trees by the water. There's a sort of hammock under there. Be my guest.

Be my guest. Guest. For better or worse. I thanked her for the meal and lay down by the stream in a suspended blanket and hugged my coat around me and slept.

★

I dreamt a house in a field that should have been my own, I mean I was returning to a place I had built, the expectation of haven, of a home that was to shelter everything I loved, and as I approached across a field without a road I saw an addition built on the side, the right side as I faced it, an annex bigger than the house itself, and it had angles that were strange to me, to my sense of things—disturbing dormers too high on the roof, juttings where there shouldn't be, and I realized with a sinking heart and growing sense of doom that someone that I would hate lived inside my house and had some sort of squatter's rights, some rights vague to me now and bargained away in an awful negotiation I could barely recall and that I could stop and stay there but only in a capacity of confirmation: confirming this thing that felt exactly like a nightmare: or I could pass on and relinquish somehow everything I had loved, loved up to this excruciating point, and I was standing in the field unable to make the decision to go in or walk on and I woke up sobbing.

Never occurred to me to break in and take my house back.

All the choices we can't see. Every moment.

Lay in the hammock and oddly there were no sobs in this unreal world, no collar wet with tears, just the cottonwood leaves shifting and spinning above me, the creek slipping past. You could wake from one nightmare to the next to the next and never eat or piss and die of thirst.

★

When I opened my eyes she was working in the garden. I could see her there through the trees along the creek crouching, probably getting ahead of the weeds. He came through the brush gate carrying two poles of fir, must have been long seasoned because he carried them lightly. Light tufts of feathers blew out of the trees, the parachutes of cottonwood seeds. Didn't float very well. Closed my eyes heard the rhythmic sough of the saw like a raspy animal breathing hard. Later heard the tunk, the crack of splitting wood. A cottonwood seed landed on my eyelid.

★

After a while I roused, splashed my face in the creek, walked out to where she was weeding, now shaded by the cliff. I squatted down in the next row beside her and began to dig with fingers and pull. She glanced over, smiled.

We have one too, I said. A garden.

She nodded.

Silence. We worked. In silence. The comfort of that.

★

Next day after breakfast we weeded again. The sun climbed, pushed the shade against the wall.

Do you have kids? I said.

She sat back on her calves, pushed her hair with the back of her wrist.

We were waiting to have children. Until he was faculty full time. He is a musician.

I nodded. Go on.

He finished his dissertation, had passed his orals just as the first cases hit Newark. We lived in a walkup on Cranberry Street that's Brooklyn Heights just across the river from the Seaport the Financial District. We could see the world from our windows. That view you see in all the movies—skyline, bridge. We were always stressed out. I make myself remember that, but now it seems like the happiest life anyone could wish for. The egg and bacon bagel I got every morning and felt guilty about—you had to walk down three steps into this narrow train car practically of a deli on Montague Street, always a line, always others on the way to work, impatient, getting coffee in those blue and white Greek cups, sugar and milk in first. Just that. He called my cell as I waited on the platform. Could just get one bar of reception: What do you want me to bring home? Indian? Pasta? Ha. A life made up of small meals. To remember that. Two people waiting for their real future which I guess was the coming of children like two people waiting for a train. The happiest expectation. Maybe not so happy at the time but seems so now. He taught at Hunter, an adjunct, made squat, loved his students hated the department. Waiting to get the degree. Waiting. Time in its pod. Blown open and scattered.

★

She talked to me like that. I mostly listening. He worked. Passed me without a word. I never offered to help. Something about his look prohibitive. I hiked up to the Beast and got my sleeping bag. The nights were clear and cool, full of stars, the stream of stars framed by the rim of the canyon like the banks of a dark river, dark but swimming with light. Through the leaves of the big cotton-woods. I slept in the hammock with the leaves above me a rustling roof. They moved the stars around and gave them voice. The first night the hammock hurt my back but after that it didn't. The third day I climbed the tree ladder with my rifle and brought home a large buck. Dragged it down the creek and lowered it on a rope off the rim of the waterfall and we ate the heart and liver that night.

I did it again the next day and he and I didn't bother to hang the quarters but butchered them together on the board table and cut most into jerky strips. Working fast and easy with no words. They had salt. A twenty gallon barrel they brought with them. We soaked the meat in salt brine in buckets. He didn't miss a trick, which is a thing I made sure not to tell him.

★

Funny how you can live a whole life waiting and not know it.

She spoke as she lifted a pile of greens from a bowl of pea pods. We sat at the table, in the shade of the big trees.

Waiting for your real life to begin. Maybe the most real thing the end. To realize that when it's too late. I know now that I loved him more than anything on earth or off of it. More than God, the one in my Episcopal liturgy.

She snapped the early peas, her hair hanging in her face, the backs of her hands blotched purple with blood. Her fingertips worked gingerly as if sore. They rolled a particularly tough pod back up to the knuckles of thumb and forefinger.

He died calling for me, looking desperately around the ward calling my name. Confused. Very early on, before all the networks went down and my friend Joel the doctor who ran the wing called me. Before we knew what this was. My mother was dying and it was too late to fly back home to New York, too late and I made the decision to stay with her and Dad. Joel said he would cremate Tomas and hold the ashes. I was beyond grateful. It was apparent that my mother would not survive. I would fly home in a week or two and drive upstate and spread his ashes in John's Brook up in the mountains outside Keene Valley where we spent every weekend we could. I worked for the city in public health so I had weekends, you know, rare for an internist. I was never on call except in a public health emergency and that wasn't often. We stayed in a white clapboard cottage in the village with a view of Noonmark from the sleeping porch. That's a little Adirondack mountain that looks like a parody of a mountain, very peaky like the Matterhorn but tiny. The little mountain that could. We climbed it often on Saturdays after sleeping in. Trotted happily up the ledgy trail to a rocky top just out of the stunted firs. And in the long evening we'd take the two single gear bikes up the paved road to a stone pothole with a little sluicing waterfall, the water always freezing, and we'd strip and jump in. This was our ritual while we waited for our lives to truly begin and I think now that maybe true sweetness can only happen in limbo. I don't know why. Is it because we are so unsure, so tentative and waiting? Like it needs that much room, that much space to expand. The not knowing anything really, the hoping, the aching transience: This is not real, not really, and so we let it alone, let it unfold lightly. Those times that can fly. That's the way it seems now looking back. Like those pleasantly exhausted bike rides up the side of a country highway on a warm evening. To a bridge. To a little rootsnaked trail through heavy maples. Where we padded barefoot upstream to a swimming hole. Even getting poison ivy so badly one weekend I missed two days of work. Seems from here that that was the sweetest time ever vouchsafed to two people. Ever. On earth. While we waited for him to finish his degree, for me to have a child, to do the real work of living.

She looked up. We are fools, you know.

Oh fuck. One fucking thing I do know.

★

It hurts you? To snap the peas?

She shook her head her hair swinging over the bowl not looking up from under.

It does, doesn't it?

What is hurt? I get a little sore. More like if your hands get dry and you crack a fingertip.

I watched her hands closely after that. Moving the pods deftly up and down the fingers sometimes switching to the third or fourth finger spreading the pain. Working swiftly without complaint.

Don't, she said. Don't watch.

★

Once in passing she told me that she didn't expect to live past fifty or fifty five. From what she knew of the damage to organs caused by the fever. She also confessed that in an odd way she was happier here than she'd ever been. Even with all the loss. Happier *being* whatever that was. Than *waiting*.

★

I lost count. Of the days. Maybe it was five, maybe nine. Time expanding like an accordion making wheezy earnest music.

The weather dry and warming. Day after day. The creek a little lower, a little less push, less strength in its roar, the falls diminished, its white lash narrowing as it spilled over the stone lip. The creek like a mood. Less exuberant. I woke sometime in the middle of the night and lay in the hammock, wriggled my foot out of the sleeping bag into the chill and found the rough ground with my bare foot and rocked myself back and forth. And watched the stars swim against their mesh of leaves. Like fish nosing a net.

That is what we are, what we do: nose a net, push push, a net that never exists. The knots in the mesh as strong as our own believing. Our own fears.

Ha. Admit it: you don't have the slightest idea what you are doing, you never ever did. With all the nets in the world, real or unreal. You swam around in a flashing confused school following the tail of the fish in front. Pretty much. Nibbling at whatever passed, in whatever current you swam into.

Even the love of your life felt like luck, like she might vanish in the finning crowd at any moment. Which she did.

What are you doing?

I don't know.

Rock rock. Back and forth. Lull. Push. Release. Swing back. The stars, the leaves, even the sound of the creek throbbing back and forth. Of a boat. Of a hammock. Of a child's swing. Of a womb. Back and forth. Rock rock. Smell of cold current, of stone, manure, blossom. Sleep.

★

He put it to me in simple terms. Came at first light to the hammock with a steaming enamel cup. They'd long since run through coffees and teas, now concocted a brew of roasted pine nuts and Mormon tea which was bitter and smoky, not bad. He sat on the sawed stump I used as a side table. Half nod toward it for permission, moved the Glock, lay it on my pack and sat. Handed me the cup. I sat up, straddled the hanging blanket. Turned up the squelch on my brain, on the running current of images. I'd been dreaming of my house again, this time not in a field but my, our, actual house on its street on the west side of town, two blocks from the lake. But it did not look like our house, it was a low brick bunker with chimneys that I knew was a crematorium, and I was standing outside it confused again wondering where I was supposed to sleep, to feed Jasper.

I suppose I'd heard his footsteps over the creek. I woke from the dream confusion into the compounding loss, into the gentle light, but in a world that is all loss that's like waking into air from air.

What can a fish know of water? Plenty I guess.

I shut the dream down, took the cup. He didn't look like he ever slept. I mean none of his features ever blurred. They got sharper in anger but they were always sharp.

In a few weeks if it doesn't rain, which it won't, it'll be time to go.

I sat up straighter.

I told you I would leave anytime. Just say the word.

He shook his head.

You've been more than hospitable, I said seriously. I think I'm getting fat.

He didn't smile.

I don't mean you, I mean us. The three of us. You are going to fly us out of here.

I blinked. Lowered the cup to my lap.

Do you have any frigging idea what it's like out there? Do you? Why would you leave here? This little Eden? Where you and what's left of your family can live in peace?

That's what I was thinking. I said, Why?

Drought.

I glanced at the burbling stream, the green meadow.

Last summer the creek almost dried up. We had to dig in the streambed to pool enough water just to drink. Half our cattle died. Pretty much been getting worse every year. Getting warmer. Just like they said it would.

He drank from his own cup.

We knew we'd have to bail. Probably this spring. We weren't sure where to go. And there is the fear of traveling without water. If it's drying up here, what is happening off the mesa?

He unsnapped the breast pocket of his shirt and dug out the Copenhagen. Took a small plug handed me the tin.

Then you showed up in the plane. To think I almost killed you.

Yup this definitely calls for a chew. I pinched one, handed it back. The familiar pleasure of gripping it under top lip, the mild rush.

You want to come with me?

Not a matter of want, Higs.

Rhymes with Big, I said. The old bastard.

He winced at me.

You two want to fly back with me to Erie, to the airport? And live with us? With me and Bangley? Out on the Plains?

He leaned forward on the stump, spat. I *want* to stay here. To live out my years in peace with my daughter. Call it a draw. The whole damn episode.

Shook his head as if to clear it. This life that I knew when I came back. Came out of the service, when I came back to the ranch. I knew it would be so much different than it is. Call it a draw.

He puffed out his cheeks. His hand was shaking when he put the cup to his lips. He put the back of his wrist into the corner of his eye.

It was my grandfather's ranch. He ran cattle up here in the summer before there was even a goddamn BLM to lease it from.

It occurred to me that the death of his grazing land hurt him more, incomparably more than the death of the human race. I liked him a lot better in that moment.

Why'n't you dig a well?

He grimaced. Don't think I didn't try. Under-neath this whole canyon is ledge rock. Four feet down. Can't even dig a decent grave.

★

In the minutes we sat, the rough sanded gray of dawn suffused with a smoother, brighter light, like clear water running over wet gravel. The country may have been dying. I knew the snowpack was less every year on the Divide, the runoff earlier, the creeks lower, more bony in the fall. But right now I heard a canyon wren, the six seven eight paced notes whistling down a scale never used by man. Answered by another. I heard a meadowlark across the field and saw the dipping flight of the kingfisher I'd seen almost every morning. Moving fast up the stream. The bigger rivers like the Gunnison weren't drying up. Not yet.

His face was tight, he looked past me. Whoever he was, whatever he'd done, he loved his land, his daughter, with a fierceness as natural and unprompted as weather.

The immediate problem that presented itself was: could I take off from the short sage meadow with the extra weight. Not at all a given. Maybe not with both of them, maybe not with one.

I don't have enough fuel to get back, I said.

He twitched. His eyes shifted back to my face and hardened.

Don't bullshit me, Higs.

Hig. Rhymes with Big if you forget.

It occurred to me too just then that maybe I better be a bit more tactful. If I couldn't fly them out of here he might just shoot me. Damn. I was starting to feel used. Loved just for my air power. Like the United States before. First Bangley then this. What if I had no plane? What if I were just Big Hig, just making my way through the broken world offering what I could, some kindness, some compassion, some technical knowhow but no plane. Who are you kidding? *Bang.*

Ask the guys at the Coke truck.

What?

Sorry. Been so much alone I don't know sometimes when I'm talking to myself.

I turned toward the running stream and spat.

I'm not fucking with you. I flew past my point of no return. That was right around Colbran.

He scanned my face again. The emotion was hard to read but his eyes moved over my features like a mason taking the measure of a very old wall. There was a frank reassessment in his eyes that unnerved me.

Higs, you are gonna fly us out of here. You fly us to a town, a fortified compound, I don't give a shit, and I'll take care of getting fuel.

I shivered. I bet he would.

Auto gas won't work anymore.

What?

After three years none of it would. Even adding lead. Went stale. Not stable enough. Hundred low lead is far more stable. Still good but pushing its life nine years out. Anyone out here, their gas is long dead.

He chewed the inside of his cheek. Hadn't spit once, I guess he swallowed it.

At Erie I wasn't worried. I had a line on a warehouse in Commerce City full of PRI which "restores gas to refinery condition" according to the literature in each case. Like magic. Enough to last another decade at least. But. Out here who knows. Even avgas might not work. Depends on the condition of the tanks, mostly.

It was hard to look at him. I didn't feel like a stone wall anymore. I felt like a rabbit. Caught out in the open.

Why'd you come here? he said simply.

Didn't answer. Not defensive, not reticent, I just didn't know. Not really.

You got in your plane and flew past your point of no return. In a world maybe without any more good fuel. You left a safe haven, a partnership that worked. For a country that is not at all safe, where anyone you meet is most likely going to try to kill you. If not from outright predation then from disease. What the fuck were you thinking? Hig.

My dog died, I said.

★

I told him about the radio transmission I'd picked up three years ago. I told him about hunting and fishing and Jasper dying and killing the boy and others, and being at the end of all loss.

I didn't have another idea, I said.

★

He knew it all. He knew that a Cessna 182 of the Beast's vintage usually carried fifty five usable gallons. He knew the burn rate per hour would be about thirteen. He knew the approximate distances. He had figured it all. He had figured I was right at the PONR, no return. Figured I had carried a couple extra cans. What he had figured and figured wrong was that I knew what the hell I was doing.

★

We'll go to Junction. We'll check out what you wanted to check out. The tower, the airport. Then we'll get some avgas. Then we'll fly back to Bangley. And if he doesn't like that we'll convince him.

I don't know if I can take off with both of you. From that meadow.

Oh you will. If we have to cut your legs off

and prop you up. I can work the rudder pedals.

He smiled grim but I saw a shadow of worry cross the winter of his eyes.

★

No point in slaughtering the livestock and making more jerky. We had what must have been twenty pounds from the venison I'd shot and we couldn't take any more weight. Probably couldn't take that. Cima said the livestock, they would fend for themselves and God willing there would be enough rain this season to make it through.

She wanted to take two lambs, male and female.

They can't weigh more than twenty pounds apiece.

I tried to explain that a small plane was more like a kite than a truck. I told her about learning from Dave Harner in Montana, what he yelled at me the first few days as I tried to land the 172 at airports around the shores of Flathead Lake. As I came in on final and the plane swerved and veered like a sick duck he'd yell *Jeesus Hig! You drive a motorcycle?* Yes! *You drive a pickup?* Yes! *Thought so! Well this ain't either one! This is a bird! Slight adjustments slight adjustments! Christ! That was atrocious!*

She laughed.

Harner, my instructor, had been a logger. A big timber logger when there were still big trees in the

Northwest. He'd run up and down the steep mountains carrying a forty pound chainsaw with a fifty inch bar and cut more wood than anyone else in all that country. Kind of a living Paul Bunyan.

Remember him? Paul Bunyan?

Of course.

Just checking. For his birthday, his thirtieth, his friends gave Dave a demo lesson at the local airport. It was Kalispell. They said they wanted him to see for himself all the country he had clear-cut. Kind of touching when you think about it. So he climbed in with a kid named Billy, a still wet bush pilot, and took the controls for the taxi and got the feel of the rudders right away, little touches—not like me, I almost ran into a box store on my first taxi—and it was his airplane for the takeoff and they climbed out of Kalispell. He did just what Billy told him, every little thing, and he was remarkably, freakishly relaxed. After all, he told me, how freaky could it be after running up and down forty degree slopes with a vicious cutting blade screaming and a thousand tons of timber falling all around you? It was calm, he said. Just uncannily, almost divinely, calm. Not his exact words. He said, Hig it was like flying inside a photograph, one of those real beautiful ones of country you love, all quiet and still the way you want the world to be. What he was talking about was the disembodied detachment you get flying. Like the world is as perfect as a train set and nothing bad can touch you.

I get that.

Yeah. He fell in love right there. He went batso. It was almost the same for me except that he was a natural, I wasn't.

Were you ever a natural? At anything?

I thought, At loss. At losing shit. Seems to be my mission in life. Course I didn't say it, who am I to talk?

Fishing, I guess. Trout used to throw themselves at me. You?

She shook her head.

★

I spent some time at the Beast. Climbed the tree ladder, walked back up the creek and out of the canyon. Summer caught me off guard. I walked shade to shade in the sun, it was no longer pleasant. Hot by midmorning. The water lower perceptibly by the day. Creek bottom showing its ribs. Logs and debris propped on the rocks, the rocks more prominent. Scared me. The stream was dropping early and fast. It would dry up. Even the fish tolerant of warmer water, even they would die. Carp and catfish. Crawfish. Frogs.

The dry pine needles crackled and crunched beneath my boots. Reflected the sun in the shadeless places so there was no relief for the eyes in looking down. Two weeks now, something like it, and the flowers were mostly gone. The fastest spring ever.

In the old cycles the drought would break, the monsoon would come, the snows would sweep in, and the life would come back. How was a mystery. To me. The trout, the cutthroat that had been here longer than us, the leopard frogs and salamanders, somehow they would return the next year. From where? Maybe in the gullets of birds I don't know. Not now. Probably.

I climbed the switchbacking trail up through the archipelago, the islands of shadow made by the ponderosas. Smelled the toasting bark, the still moist ground drying out. Harried by the summer buzz of a deerfly. At the top the cedars were dense. Thick and gnarled in the trunks, twisting into the sunlight, cradling boulders like ugly consoling arms, ever slowgrowing these had never been cut. Some probably seedlings when Cortes was looking at his men with a wild surmise. I walked across the open meadow, patted the Beast on the nose.

Missed you.

Looked down the little park. Short. The piñon and juniper at the end weren't tall, twenty feet at the tallest, but pines set back were forty feet high maybe. We could cut those.

If it was the middle of winter. The heat would make a big difference. Cold air more dense, hot air cutting performance by a shocking amount. We'd leave in the dark, just after, safe enough to see but close to the coolest time.

Here's what I mean. I stuck my head inside, she smelled the same always. Smelled Jasper, smelled what was probably still the 1950s and pulled out the POH from the vinyl pocket behind my seat. It's the Pilot Operating Handbook, the original from 1956. Thin little sucker probably less than an eighth of an inch, eighty eight pages with an illustration on the cover of the plane. In the back are the performance tables. These are wonderful things—literal and invaluable. What these are is some test pilot got into this very model and took off again and again. From this altitude and this one. At this air temp and that one. Technicians in white coats and those thick framed black glasses recorded the data and plotted the beautiful, simple, unhurried curves. They went home to wives in beehives and drank Seagram's Seven on ice in faceted tumblers. The test pilots, what did they do? They were veteran fighter pilots from the war, World War II, who had firebombed Japan and strafed aerodromes in Austria and settled into the new suburbs like the characters James Dickey wrote about, and back in the little cockpit at the Cessna test center in Wichita, with the plane shuddering in the old familiar way of any prop plane, then the former wing commander was like any lifetime equestrian who swings onto any horse anywhere with that complex and simple feeling of being home and freed from the constraints of the mundane.

In the back of my slim owner's manual were pages of these tables and graphs. Takeoff and rollout distances. I flipped—carefully—I always handled the POH like an ancient and priceless artifact—to the page titled Take-Off Data. Ran my finger across the airfield elevations to seventy five hundred feet and down the columns of air temps in Fahrenheit. Takeoff distance at empty weight to clear a fifty foot obstacle at thirty two degrees with no headwind was nine hundred and fifty feet. See? Don't ask me. Air is less dense as it heats up. Then I did something I never do, hadn't done since my private pilot's license test: I took out the certified weight and balance sheet I kept folded in a pocket in the bulkhead by my knee. Every plane has one specific to the very aircraft. Weights and moments. I pulled a sheet of clean Xerox paper and worked out the problem. I put Pops in front at a hundred eighty pounds and Cima in the rear at one twenty with a bag of provisions weighing twenty. Five gallons of water at forty. No lambs. The full gas cans were gone as I'd put the fuel in the tanks. I figured in the fuel, the guns, two rifles, the shotgun, the handguns, four grenades. Period. Two quarts of oil.

I scratched a nub of pencil over the paper and worked the numbers. Then I left the paperwork on my seat, left the door open, there was no wind, and paced the track through the meadow.

★

One eighty one eighty one one eighty two. Counted my steps. Reminded me of counting the seconds waiting for Bangley in a firefight. Skirted the ruts. Plowed grass with my shins. Eyed the turkey vulture gyring to the north. And when I got to two hundred and saw how much clearing there was ahead of me I knew. It wasn't long enough. Six hundred forty feet at most. There was no way.

Lastly. I already knew but I double checked. I took a stout wooden paint stir stick out of the same seat pocket. It was ticked with a Sharpie at intervals along its length and marked 5 10 15 all the way up to 30. Gallons. I climbed up on the strut, untwisted the fuel cap at the top of the wing on the wing tank and lowered in the stick. Drew it out turned it away from full sunlight and noted the fast vanishing and pungent wetness. Did it to the other side.

★

The guys in the white coats. The fighter pilot in his flight suit. With the wife in the beehive. Humming, tapping his fingers on the yoke of the Cessna to Rock Around the Clock. In 1955. All of about to break open: the manic music, Hula loop, surf girls, Elvis, all now from this distance like some crazed compensation—for what? The Great Fear. Lurking. First time in human history maybe since the Ark that they contemplated the Very End. That some gross misunderstanding would buzz across the red phones, some shaking finger come down on the red button and it would all be over. All of it. That fast. In a ballooning of mushrooming dust and fire, the most horrible deaths. What that must have done to the psyche. The vibrations suddenly set in motion deeper than any tones before. Like a wind strong enough for the first time to move the heaviest chimes, the plates of rusted bronze hanging in the mountain passes. Listen: the deep terrifying slow tones. Moving into the entrails, the spaces between neurons, groaning of absolute death. What would you do? Move your hips, invent rock n roll.

The men at the Cessna test center compiling those numbers, those distances. Erecting them against the smallest accidents while the gut fear of the Big One gripped their dreams. Is that how it was? I don't know. I overdramatize. But given what has happened how can you? Can't really overdo anything. There is no hyperbole anymore just stark extinction mounting up. Nobody would believe it.

The test pilots were working in perfect conditions on smooth tarmac. A soft field knocked off a percentage of performance, and the rough track in this sage field was another story. We could fill in the ruts, smooth it out as best we could, but.

I uncoiled the hose and siphoned the twelve extra gallons back into the cans. We wouldn't need them to get to Junction and it would save us seventy two pounds. Then I thought, Don't cut it too close, and I climbed back on the strut and poured back what I judged to be about two gallons. I left one full can in the sage and emptied the other one out in the dirt and then nestled it, the empty can, back into the Beast. Then I went fishing. I took my rod case out of its bracket behind my seat and the light nylon daypack with flybox and tippet and walked back down into the canyon.

★

My calculations showed that the best way to have any chance at all of taking off, of clearing the trees, was to leave the old man.

I could imagine how well that was gonna wash. I could imagine the conversation. I could just about hear the snick of his big knife clearing the plastic sheath, my own peep as the point of the blade came to my throat. *Don't bullshit me Higs! I told you not to fucking bullshit me.*

I caught five carp. Rolled a pheasant tail along the bottom and yanked them out one after another.

273

he peregrine glided along the wall above and let
erself fall, flaring just over the trees above the
reek. I think she was watching me, curious. Do
eregrines eat fish? The carp were skinny fish,
ong and thin and I realized with a whomp of
adness that they were starving. The shift in water
emperatures was affecting them, too, or their
ood. I unhooked them with special care, the care
had always reserved for trout, and held them
gently while they finned in my cupped hand
against the current, until their gills filled and the
undulations of their tail strengthened and they
wriggled away. I gave up, didn't feel like fishing
anymore.

The trout are gone the elk the tigers the
elephants the suckers. If I wake up crying in the
middle of the night and I'm not saying I do it's
because even the carp are gone.

I pictured the conversation. I can take your
daughter, twenty pounds of jerky but not you.

But. The light bulb went off. Hig, you had what
they used to call an epiphany. When discovering
something, some intellectual connection, had a
value like gold. Eureka.

I'd bring the weight and balance sheet, the
pencil and worksheet, the fragile POH with its
disattached cover and its incontrovertible tables
and go through the numbers as if for the first time
and let everyone draw their own conclusions.

She had lunch on the table in the shade. Pitcher

of cold milk, salted meat, a salad of lamb's quarter and new lettuce, green onions. I sat down. Pops watched me. He followed me with his eyes, watched me while he chewed. She ate. She moved easier today, lighter. The bruises seemed to be fading, her mood brighter. She ate slowly, breathed deep as if smelling the creek, each new blossom.

Can you? he said at last. He put down his cup, wiped his mouth on his sleeve waited.

No.

She put down her fork. The pack was at my feet. I pulled up the slider, loosened the drawstring, drew out the manual, the sheets, took the stub of pencil out of the band of my cap.

Weight and balance, he said. I nodded. Takeoff distance, he said.

Yup.

He was no fool. I had scrawled only the formula, left the weights blank. At the top of the page in the right corner I had jotted down some weights: One gal. avgas=6 lbs. One gal. water=8 lbs. Presently in tanks: 14 gals.

I slid it over. I ate.

★

He was sharp. Whatever he did before on the ranch, in the service, he didn't waste time. He took the pencil and went to work. Didn't ask, Is this right? Is this how you do it? Been a while . . . nothing like that. A man without the habit of justifying himself, making excuses. Didn't ever say, Higs check my math, will you? Nope, the SOB looked once at the problem, began to multiply, fill in the blanks work the equation. I saw him make a list down the right side of the page of provisions, each with its weight estimated. He worked it three different ways and each time I saw him scratch two or three items off the list. Saw him reduce the water to three gallons. Scratch off the steel gas can.

Unh uh.

He looked up.

The gas can. The siphon hose. Ten pounds. Need them absolutely. What if we have to walk to get fuel?

He nodded, restored it to the list.

Then he siphoned out avgas, reduced the tanks to 10 from 14.

No.

I interrupted him again. Pencil stopped, eyebrow raised.

Fuel stays.

Thirty five miles to Grand Junction, tops. One twenty mph with a headwind. Point three hours thirteen gallons an hour. Ten is plenty.

Forget it. If we have to circle, check all the runways, taxiways, if we get fired on, if we have to find a road.

He nodded. Went at it again. Finally he put down the pencil, straightened his arms against the side of the table, sat back. Stared at me. Thought I saw hatred. Hard to tell with Pops.

You did it already didn't you?

I nodded.

I stay, she goes.

Nodded.

You already knew that.

Nodded. He stared. A mobile light moved over his features. Gave them a look of animation though I don't think anything moved. I'd say, Could've heard a pin drop, but. Not with the creek right there. He stared at me, nodded slowly.

Okay, he said.

Just like that. It was done. Now I really liked the old coot, have to admit. He took his medicine, no whining.

I smiled at him, maybe the first time.

That's why we need fourteen gallons, I said. One of the reasons.

He looked puzzled, winced, pushed his tongue up under his lip where I knew he kept his chew.

We need fourteen because we've gotta land and take off again. We'll pick you up out on the highway. Won't be a problem. There's a decent straight stretch right at the bridge turnoff. All the runway we want. It'll be no sweat.

He didn't let his face soften, nothing like that. Just that in his stare, in the winter of it, I thought I saw a slight thaw, a reassessing.

You can walk out a day early and we'll pick you up at daybreak.

Okay, he said again and that was it.

BOOK THREE

I

There was no hurry really. Plenty of water in the big rivers if we got stranded in Junction. We'd wait a couple of weeks, fatten up, let the season round out into full summer, ride it while we could. Let the creek drop. I decided to enjoy it. I treated it like a vacation, first one I'd had since.

Since I'd made the unexpected contingency plan, things around the homestead had lightened up a little. Surprised me, frankly, that it had surprised him, the notion of picking him up later. He was so sharp, such a tactician. Like Bangley that way, always thinking three moves ahead in a crisis, and cool.

Then it struck me that the option must have occurred to him immediately. And then I respected him even more. He knew.

It was obvious to him that we could take off without him and pick him up later, but he would keep his mouth shut. Two reasons I figured. One, he was the kind of dude who subscribed to *Never take what isn't offered freely*. And Two, he was conflicted about leaving. Part of him, maybe the bigger part, wanted to stay, to watch the creek dwindle, to help the livestock into the next world, to die with his ranch and molder there into the flinty ground.

For a man his age with his values that option

was in many ways preferable to the other. The journey to a strange land—because it was a Strange Land now in every sense. Also, it was the plains, not the mountains—the making of a new life, the having to adapt to new threats, new rules not his own. It was a sucky prospect. And if he had told her that this was his preference he would have hurt her badly, she would never have let him, she would go hysterical to the extent that a woman who had been through what she had been through could go hysterical. She would not forgive him.

So the fragile little Pilot Operating Handbook with the table of takeoff distances, the curve incontrovertible beyond which there was no new life anywhere, only a faltering aircraft struggling to rise over the small trees and snagging its landing gear, then wings, the big cartwheel . . . it was his ticket out. Out of the plan. Maybe why he didn't look more shocked. Why he had worked the weight and balance in front of her.

Thinking about it like that I almost felt sorry I had broached the option. If he wanted to die in place he was a big boy. But.

I swung in the hammock. I recited every poem I had ever half remembered. I went fishing upstream and down. I ate. Took the spade up top and filled in the ruts in our airstrip, knocked down the brush. Helped Cima harvest the garden, the early greens.

It was a good garden. The dirt was rich, a lot

richer than ours back at the airport. It was full of worms and black from year after year of spreading manure. The families gave me chicken manure, but it wasn't enough, it wasn't like this. In the early morning, in the shadow of the bigger trees, the dirt was cold and wet, the new plants covered in dew. That smell. The shadow edged back and I liked to strip to my boxers so that my knees were in the damp dirt and the full sun was hot on my back. The dirt encrusted basket beside us, between rows.

Why'd you go back east? I said.

I got a scholarship to Dartmouth.

My uncle went there. Were you an only child?

She shook her head.

Twin brother. He died when we were fifteen. Motorcycle.

Man.

I had good grades. Good test scores. I was going to be a vet, go to Colorado State, come back home and set up a large animal practice. All my life that was what I was going to do. We had a college counselor, Mr. Sykes. He had a very good placement record, but he controlled who went where so tightly all the kids called him Sucks. One day in English class my junior year there was a tap on the glass of the door and he came in and handed me a folded note. It said My office 12:45. During the lunch hour. I remember we were talking about *The Love Song of J. Alfred*

Prufrock. Do you know it? I loved that poem until they taught it to me in high school. Did you know there is a Hidden Meaning?

Really?

Yup. Sex, art and scholarship are all class weapons.

Hunh. Funny thing to teach aspiring scholars.

We weren't aspiring scholars. We were supposed to go to work for StorageTek or UPS. Or Coors.

The note. Sykes, I said.

Oh. My heart galloped. Every year Dartmouth gave one scholarship to a kid from Delta High. It was endowed by the man who built the fiberboard plant, an alum. I guess he felt bad for all the formaldehyde smoke which reeked in the winter when there was an inversion. Every fall one kid got a note from Sykes to see him at lunch hour. He controlled it, chose the kid. I don't think that was even legal but that's the way it was. His little fiefdom. Kept all the families, the whole town, kissing his ass all year. For the rest of the class nobody could concentrate, they were all watching me. And my head was rushing with the possibilities, images of a future I had no pictures for. They tumbled together: ivy covered bricks, handsome upperclassmen in argyle sweaters, taking them off to row crew. You know I didn't have a clue. My days consisted of throwing hay before daylight and running cross country after school, and then back home for more chores, mostly giving oats and medicine to horses, and mucking stalls, and homework.

I was beet red, I could tell. The more I tried to concentrate on the poem the more I felt the eyes on me and when I glanced up and snuck a look, they were. I could already feel the envy. Like a wind. By the end of the day I wasn't sure if any of this was a curse or a blessing. Anyway, I went to see Sykes. I couldn't eat anything in the cafeteria so I just went to the Girls' Room and sat on the toilet and tried to breathe. He said, Cima I think you have a good chance for the Ritter Scholarship. He was completely bald. I thought his head was the shape of an egg. I remember seeing tiny beads of sweat on the mottled pink dome of it as if it were he on the hot seat. He was from Illinois, outside of Chicago, I remember. He said, You will write the personal essay in your application about ranch life and losing Bo.

I was shocked. Almost as if I had hallucinated that last request. Well, it wasn't a request. Come again, I said. His hands were resting on the desk and he actually made a careful triangle out of his thumbs and forefingers and pursed his lips and looked into it as if it were some Masonic window into my destiny. He said, You will write about being a ranch girl and losing your brother who was your soulmate.

I stared at him. I had heard that he controlled the whole application process. But nobody had ever said anything like that to me before. I mean put their big fat foot, clomp clomp, into my most interior landscape. Bo to me was like a secret garden. A place only I could go. A source of both grief and great strength. He was smiling at me. He had the smallest mouth and only one side came up. I remember. The turmoil. Life had just opened up really wide and bright then suddenly the horror: that to go there I would be asked to forfeit my soul. Something like that. Terrifying. I know I was flushing to the roots and I couldn't seem to articulate anything. He kept smiling at me. He said, You don't have to thank anyone now, it's certainly momentous. *Deus ex machina.* That's what he said! As if he were God! My word. He thought I was overcome with gratitude and I was actually so furious. I felt violated. I was so mad I could've taken his egg head and crushed it. I just mumbled and ducked out.

Did you write about Bo?

Yes. I wrote about how my college counselor had demanded that I write about my dead twin. I wrote a long essay, twice as long as asked for, about a certain kind of tact that was part of ranch culture and why I thought it had developed and why it was important and how the fact that a ranch girl writing about her missing twin might appeal to the admissions people at the highest caliber Eastern college was another example of the disconnect between us. Eastern establishment and

Western land based people. We didn't want anybody's sympathy. I was so angry. Never been so mad I don't think. I sent the application off without letting Sykes review it, which was strictly against protocol. Nobody had ever done it. He tried to scuttle the application, he was such a vengeful little fuck, but it was too late. I guess they were so impressed with my ranch girl grit or something. I got in, of course. Early decision, full ride. The college pressured the high school and forced Sykes to retire. You know the part that still troubles me about all that is that I knew I would. Get accepted. I mean I flipped the emotional payoff they were looking for, didn't I? I mean I was truly furious, but I also knew somewhere inside that it would make my candidacy even stronger. I have prayed about it often. I mean apologizing to Bo for using him to get into college.

I shook the dirt off some Swiss chard and lay it in the basket.

You didn't use Bo. You wrote exactly what you were feeling.

Yeah, but I've often thought that the move with the most integrity would've been to blow off Dartmouth for having that kind of expectation, those values, and go to Northern State. I mean it's an ag school. Was.

You were what? Seventeen? You wanted to flex your muscles. You were an ass kicker like your dad. Nobody on earth is more righteous than a seventeen year old. And it wasn't the college, it was Mr. Sucks.

You know what I mean. He was right, after all. About the subject that would snare them. I don't know. I think of him sometimes, a middle aged, single man, humiliated out of the one job he was great at. What he did with the rest of his life, how it was for him when the flu hit. Lonely, alone, terrified. Funny the things that keep you up at night after all that has happened.

Amen, I said.

Silence. I pulled out some new meadow grass. Hands black with crumbled dirt like bear paws. She was way too tactful to ask me. Still the ranch girl.

You want to know what keeps me up at night?

She sat back on her haunches in the sun, straightened, blew the hair out of her face. She had a strong straight nose, wideset eyes. A long slender neck, now bruised.

I couldn't say: I put a pillow over my wife's face at the end. That I felt her struggle in the last seconds trying to push away the death she'd asked for. A reflex right? That I held tight and leaned in and kept the promise I'd just made. That was the right decision. Wasn't it?

Could I say that we murdered a young boy in the middle of the night? That we didn't make him into dog food. That we murdered a young girl in broad daylight who was running after me with a kitchen knife probably wanting my help. Or that the memories of fishing alone for trout in a mountain creek with Jasper lying on the bank were maybe my sweetest memories. That so much of that is a dream or might as well be. That I don't know the difference anymore between dream and memory. I wake from dream into dream and am not sure why I keep going. That I suspect only curiosity keeps me alive. That I'm not sure any longer if that is enough.

I smothered my wife with a pillow. At the end when she asked. Like putting down a dog. Other things. Worse.

Her hand was still holding a clump of loose chard. It tightened on the leaves. She nodded. Her eyes were warm and steady.

And I wish I could have been there to do that for Tomas. I wish I could have done it. Why didn't I stay to be with my husband? My mother had hers, she didn't need me as much he did. Well, he hadn't contracted it yet. He was coughing a bit but we weren't sure. No fever. A lot of people were coughing, only a few were confirmed. But I should have known. In my position with the first reports coming in I should have known.

She sat up straight on her haunches and she cried silently. I put my chard in the basket and went to weeding. I shook the dirt from the roots and put the worms back in the ground.

★

The deepest spot was just beneath the falls. Even at low water it was four or five feet deep and cold. Hard to imagine it drying up, but it would without enough snowpack, enough summer rain. Once the days turned really hot I bathed there every day. I went late in the afternoon when the sunlight still reached the bottom of the canyon. I liked the contrast, hot and cold. It was shielded by willows. I hung my shirt up on one of the branches like a ragged flag so they would know I was there and pushed into the little pool on a beaten path. The spray from the cascade reached the smooth stones on the bank, must've been ten degrees cooler in there. Grateful, as grateful as I was all day, I unbuttoned my pants and untied my boots, stripped. Sometimes just sat in the mist, the outer stones the warmest, and dangled my feet and calves in the water: cool billow on my chest, sun on my back, the contrasts. And watched the patch of rainbow shift around in the spray.

I wanted to ask her: What *did* you all know about the flu, about the coming pandemic. Did you? Did it really take everyone so by surprise? Why was it so fast? What was the blood disease that came right after and why did so many who survived contract it? Wanted to ask her all that since she first told me she was a doctor, that kind of doctor. But then she preempted with the story of her husband dying without her in the ward and I didn't want to reopen old wounds etc but now I was resolved. She had brought it up. But then she was crying. I would've cried too probably but to tell the truth I was cried out. Wrung out like a human rag.

Sitting bare assed on the stones dangling my feet in the water, feeling the push of moist air off the falls, hearing nothing but the roar of plunging water, hot sun burning the backs of my ears. Thinking of nothing. Grateful for that. My favorite time of day. I could say now: I am at peace. Here on the bank of the dying creek.

The afternoon of the morning we had picked chard, I walked up to the falls and pulled my sweaty dirt smeared shirt over my head and thought I'd better wash it. Which was just rinsing it and slapping it on the rocks and wringing it out. I thought, Another thing to be grateful for, Hig: no pile of work clothes to wash and hang on the line and fold and stuff into the cubbies in the closet which were too small. Melissa and I never had enough room for our stuff. You'd think a carpenter would take care of his own little remodels, but no. Just your shirt, your pants, your socks. One fleece undershirt. A favorite wool sweater darned and darned again. You thought you were leaving Erie for a few days.

So I took the shirt with me and pushed through the willows and she was standing naked in the fogged water, facing me, watching something up high on the wall. She was willowy thin. I could just see her ribs. Long legged, the curve of her hips sweet, her mound prominent, the touch of dark hair not fully hiding her. Her breasts smallish, but not small. Tight as apples. What do I mean? Firm, full. Collarbones, nice shoulders. Strong arms, slender but strong. A bruise on her upper right thigh. I must have stopped breathing. She was, I don't know. Perfect. My one dumb thought was: How on earth did you frigging hide all that? In a man's too large shirt? My eye must be out of practice! That's what I thought. All in a split second. Because reflexively I turned to look up at the wall and saw the peregrine land in the nest carrying a bird, a pretty damned big bird.

How do you think she'll divide it up? she said over the water.

What? None of this seemed real. I looked back at her and she was half turned away, the small of her back where it dimpled, her sweet butt making another perfect curve. I. The curve that kills me. Dead Man's Curve. I blinked. I thought, She is nothing, not a frigging thing like one of Bangley's posters. She is like a million times more lovely. I didn't say, Sorry to surprise you, or anything. I said, She'll tear it to pieces. I mean I yelled it over the falls and then I turned around and fled.

Big Hig. Pretty cool in a plane, pretty cool with visitors, reduced to babble.

A while later she found me in the shade. Your turn, she said smiling.

She was passing the hammock, leaning her head, wringing out her hair. Where I was lying in a kind of endocrine shock—trying at once to recall and push away every detail I had just seen. Startled again by the sight of her and sure she could read my mind. I grinned back, sheepish as a sixteen year old.

When are you gonna show me yours? she said.

I must've started, flushed. Her smile was broad now and guileless and I saw for an instant the high school runner, the ranch girl who liked to win a barrel race.

★

Checked on the Beast, topped off the oil, pumped up the tires with a bicycle pump I kept in back. Took naps. The dreams of the old house stopped. Now I dreamt of big cats, tigers and mountain lions flowing down through the rocks to the river at twilight, the unblinking eyes seeing everything. In the dream there was a sense of supreme grace and power and also intelligence. In these dreams I came face to face with the beasts very close and looked into their eyes and something was transmitted but nothing I could ever name. When I woke, though, I felt infused with something strong and frightening and maybe beautiful. I felt lucky.

I had one dream, lying out in the hammock on an almost windless afternoon, that Melissa and I were bow hunting. She never did that, but I did. If I had the time between jobs to go out earlier and take a longer season, I'd buy a bow tag. In the dream we weren't hunting the cats we were hunting one of those rare ibex deals that went dark way before before, somewhere up in the foothills of the Himalayas, and when she had her bow drawn on a big buck, very close, I cried NO! and the animal leapt and ran and she turned to me and her face was bright with fury and betrayal. When I woke up I was gripping the rope side of the hammock and it took me a minute to realize where I was, that it was a dream, and then the near vertigo, thinking, This is a dream, and a little relieved I was in this one and not that one.

Cima's bruises lightened and vanished and new ones appeared. We seemed to talk nonstop. But I felt very comfortable in the silences that were never silent but filled with birds, wren and lark. With the flashing wingbars of nighthawks at dusk. Later there were bat squeaks, the bustle of leaves, the sough of the lowering stream. All kind of pastoral, a little strange given everything. I felt comfortable working beside her in the garden, cleaning vegetables in the shade of the board table. I'll tell you this: Once everything ends you are no more free. The more lovely this respite, the more some cagey animal inside of me refused to surrender. The more I dreamt of Jasper, of Melissa. The sadder I got. Weird, huh? Once shelling peas our hands touched over the pot and she let her fingers stay over mine. Just a second. I looked up and her eyes were steady, frank, more like the way a glass pond is tannin black, windless, serene, contained, waiting. Lovely. Waiting to reflect a cloud, to be swept by rain. I couldn't breathe.

The openness, the simple being-ness of those eyes struck me as brave and terrifying. I must have recoiled. She smiled inward and went back to shucking peas. I suppose as an internist you see all kinds of raw symptoms, nothing much surprises you.

We had enough venison, no reason to eat mutton or beef so we didn't. Pops thought some of the animals might survive here on their own if it rained later on, if the winter was as mild as last. When things get better we can come back, he said. Nobody else said a word. Pops was not in the habit of bullshitting himself but there it was, every man has his imaginary refuge.

Another week, two. Some inner wires began to loosen. Never know how tight we are until then. Pops was off cutting wood. I started a dinner fire for her in the outside pit and we sat on stumps and just watched it build. It swayed and whispered with the rhythm of the breeze. This time of day the wind came upstream as it did in all this country but something about the shape of the canyon made it eddy and blow around so there was never a safe spot by the fire away from smoke. We had already moved our seats twice. I was crying with smoke.

Smoke makes you cry and then you grieve, I said. Like cutting onions. Always made me sad.

She smiled.

I never been to New York. Did you like it?

I loved it. Just loved it. You know how some people say they wish they had two lives so they could be a cowboy in one and an actor in another? Or whatever? I wanted two lives so I could live in the Heights—Brooklyn Heights—in one and in the East Village say in another. I couldn't get enough of it. I wanted to go to Yankees games—Yanks not Mets—and to Off Off Broadway and poetry slams and get lost at the Met. Again. I went to every artist's retrospective there was. I could eat Sabrett's until I was sick.

Sabrett's?

Hot dogs. With kraut, grilled onions, mustard, no relish. Some evenings I walked Court Street down to Carroll Gardens and back. I got to know all the hawkers at all the folding tables selling scarves and children's books and phony watches. I thought, When we have kids we'll get their first books here. For two dollars! Probably stolen off trucks by the mob, huh?

Probably.

A world with a mob. That seemed quaint. The good old days. I said, What about the end? Did you see any of it?

She shook her head. She leaned down and pushed the butt of a stick into the fire and when she did her loose shirt swung away from her collarbones and I saw her breasts again fuller than they should have been, deep tanned and freckled on the top and milky below. I couldn't get away from them today. I guess that part of me just woke up. Probably been there all the time, Hig, and you were in the Fog.

The Fog of Being, I said.

What?

Sorry. I talk to myself sometimes.

I noticed.

Really?

She nodded. Do I?

Not that I've heard.

Silence.

I didn't see the collapse, the mass death. But I felt it coming. Like a pressure drop. The kind that is worse than bad weather. We had it a few times growing up at the ranch. A pressure shift you could feel in your pulse, your lungs. A darkening of the sky, a weird green tinged blackness. The cattle restless and upset beyond the usual omens of thunderstorm. That's the way it felt. Why I think I should have known.

Should have. This to myself. So many of those.

I could build houses out of them, burn them for fuel, fertilize the garden.

Do you know how it began? New Delhi?

She shook her head.

That's what the press reported. Mutation of a superbug, one of the ones they'd been watching for two decades. In the water supply etc. Combined with a bird flu. We called it the Africanized bird flu, after the killer bees. First cases in London and blamed on New Delhi. But that's probably not where it originated. We heard rumors that it originated at Livermore.

The national weapons lab?

She nodded. The rumor was that it was a simple trans-shipment. A courier on a military flight with a sample taking it to our friends in England. Supposedly the plane crashed in Brampton. Nobody will ever know—she looked around the box canyon and let the absurdity of those words trail off in the wind with the smoke.

I was wide awake now. She inhaled deeply and I could see—Hig! Her nipples against the thin fabric of her shirt. My god. Hig. You haven't heard any news, real news in almost a decade. It's making you horny!

Genetically modifying flu is an old business.

Right, I said.

Look me in the eyes when you say hello to me.

I shook myself. She was grinning at me through smoke.

Calmate, soldier, she said.
Never learned Spanish, I murmured.

★

We ate dinner I don't know what time, but sometime in the late evening when the sky was that luminescent blue that might hold a single star and the nighthawks flitted in the meadow and over the creek feasting on the latest hatch. They wintered in Mexico or somewhere and seemed to be doing alright. Shear winged and acrobatic as swallows. White wingbars blinking on a sudden shift in direction. Small peeps. A joy in watching the birds in their single hour of feeding.

I guess they ate then because the bugs were out. It was not cold as it would be later when truly dark and the ropy stars skeined together and you could feel the heat of the day radiating off the rock wall.

I took the few dishes to the creek and washed them with sand. They cooked outside most of the time in a firepit lined with river stones. On those nights father and daughter sat on two stumps and watched the wind rashed embers like TV. I set the wet dishes on the table and lay in the hammock and tried to see how long I could go without thinking about anything. I think my record was six Mississippi.

One night I fell asleep naked before I could

crawl into my bag and I woke in the dark with the weight of the cover settling over me.

Not alarmed, it seemed right. I made to sit up and a hand pushed me back. Shhh, she said. I came out to pee and thought you'd get cold that way.

I lay back.

Thanks.

She leaned over me I felt her hair brush my face, a touch of her breath, then she was lifting the quilt, stretching her length alongside, and she wriggled in her hips, her ribs in the margin of hammock tight against me and she said into my neck

There.

That's all. Then she fell asleep.

She was wearing the man's shirt. Nothing else. I could feel her mound against my leg. Mons pubis, right? The cradle of her pelvic bones. I lay there, heart hammering. I traced her body in my mind from her toes where they touched mine, kind of bony and cold, up her calves, thighs, to the inside of her knees, the kneecap where it burrowed into the crook of my own leg—you get the idea. My brain all on its own took the trip, followed the map, lingered at every place of interest, every scenic view. It was the novelty. My heart pounded and my dick uncurled and straightened and lengthened, and then it was almost pain. It throbbed, and my mind continued to travel. Up and down her length, every point of contact. At some point I must have exhausted myself, run out of gas, I slept.

★

The next morning I realized that it was the weight of another cramping your space in sleep, that it was hearing another's breathing. That simple. Jasper did that. Past that don't even go there. That was all she wanted or she would've asked.

★

The next day at breakfast which is cold meat and potatoes, in the garden, at the supper table, tending the fire, she is the same. The same calm eyes absorbing everything, the way a dark pond absorbs sunlight. The marvel of it. Women are like that. Pops is not, I'm not. He's no fool, probably expecting some similar development since Day One. Whatever development it is, maybe nothing. After all we are some of the few people left on earth just about. It's like one of those desert island jokes. The one about the hat. Be weirder if it didn't happen, right, Hig?

Not really. Doesn't feel like that. Feels frigging weird. Not weird, tumultuous. Momentous. Well, it's probably nothing. Probably doesn't mean a thing, I mean just an experiment to see how it felt after all those years. A sleep experiment.

His eyes rest on me a fraction of a second longer. That's all. Subtle but loud. I can't meet them. I look away. I get that Pops is a hard man where he needs to be hard, but beyond that he pretty much minds his own business and expects the same.

Does she want to be my girlfriend? What a stupid idiotic thought. Are you in goddamn high school? You are on the Beach man. Last man and woman left in what? Three counties probably. It's your patriotic duty to follow that through.

It is?

No.

What then?

Shrug.

Do what you want.

What do I want?

I want to be two people at once. One runs away.

★

The next night she came very late. I realized I'd been waiting most of the night without sleeping. Just waiting. Wondering what I would do, what she would. She lifted the quilt which I'd left unzipped and squeezed in and snuggled her mouth into my ear and murmured, Miss me. And fell asleep. It was an order and a question.

Pretty cramped. She lay in the crook of my arm which fell asleep, went numb. I felt her length, her thigh over mine, her breast against my side, the expansion of her breath. She smelled like smoke and something sweet, tangy the way sage is tangy. I got another bursting hard on. I lay there. You again? Becoming a regular are you? You are welcome, probably, pending good behavior. I lay there trying to make out constellations through the leaves, smelling her hair, listening to the relaxed concourse of her breath. In the middle of the night she found me, it. Slipped her hand down my belly and stroked. Lightly. Not a murmur, not a kiss, as if we were both asleep. We weren't. My body felt like an air base in one of those movies when the incoming siren goes off. Everybody scrambling toward the fighters from everywhere. Every cell awake pouring its attention toward my surprised dick. Felt really really good. Wonderful. Her hand slowed, paused, twitched twice, she was asleep. I was still hanging on a terrible edge. I lay there in a kind of suspended, excruciating wonder.

★

Pops and I took the spade, the machete up to the meadow, worked on the runway. Worked in silence, moving stones, leveling, tamping dirt, cutting brush. If there was any awkwardness it was mine. We were rooting out a mesquite bush in the middle of the track. He was prying with the spade, I was pulling on a rope we'd tied to the slender stump. I swung around the arc like on a tether to yank from a better direction, and pulled, and a stout root freed itself and kicked dirt into his face. He stopped, stood straight, blinded. Slowly cleared the dirt, spat. He held the shovel with both hands like a pike.

Hig, you're acting squirrely. More squirrely than usual.

He didn't say Higs. He blinked out more dirt, wiped his eyes with a knuckle.

Do you need my blessing or something? Like a corny movie?

Shocked me worse than if he'd slugged me. I held the end of the rope as if I weren't sure why, as if it were the tail of some beast I wasn't sure I wanted to be so intimate with.

At this stage in the game I got bigger fish to fry. I was never that kind of dad anyway. I never once said, Have her home by ten.

I looked down at my hand holding the rope, at the dirt all over his face and started to laugh. Christ. I laughed. The more I laughed the more funny it was. Shit, I don't know, maybe it was the pent up tension from the night before. Deadly sperm backup we used to call it. Maybe it was just the desert island cartoon thing, the protective father thing, the way that no one was acting like they were supposed to act. Was that it? Probably not. Probably simple relief that Pops hadn't killed me yet. Or that he was standing there with dirt all over his face and not mad. Or just that I hadn't laughed, really laughed, in way too long.

★

Must have been after mid-June. I lost count of the days. Probably not a good thing to do. I mean with no newspaper, no apparatus to tell you the date. Once you lose count, well it's gone forever.

We finished the venison, all but the jerky which we were saving for the trip, and we slaughtered a sheep and had been eating mutton for two days. Mutton and last summer's potatoes and new greens, lettuce, chard, peas. The days were hot and the creek a slow runnel and the nights warm. She came just a little while after dark, after I'd settled in with the flannel bag beneath me on the hammock sleeping only in my shirt. She was wearing a long man's shirt and her hand came to my face and passed over my cheek and she grabbed a tuft of my beard and pulled which made me laugh. There was a quarter moon like a ruddy lightship floating over the canyon and I could see her clearly. She was holding a blanket. She spread it on the dirt beside the hammock and lay down on her back, one arm propped under her head. She watched the moon, I watched her. I stuck my bare foot over the edge of the hammock and touched it to the wool of the blanket and pushed off and swung myself.

Playing hard to get? she murmured.

No.

I rocked. She unbuttoned the shirt. It parted. She pushed the far side of it off her breast with her free hand and still gazing at the sky she tucked her fingers under a button and pulled the rest of it to the side. It fell open. The rise and fall of her breath. The length of her. In the dark she radiated a soft light of her own like waves breaking at night. The smooth pale plain of her stomach. The—all of her.

Jesus Christ, Hig, don't turn away, don't close your eyes. Breathe, man! You are supposed to look, dumbass! It's not impolite. If you don't look you will insult her. Who the fuck do you think this is for, this is for you! She wasn't, like, just in the neighborhood.

All of that in my clamorous head. Telling myself to be respectful, act like a grownup. Soak up every detail. She has vouchsafed you some portion of pure luck. Be grateful.

The rusty moon painted her without shadow. My toes dug into the wool and I stopped swinging. I held still and watched her. A kind of suspended awe. The way I had watched a royal elk step out of aspen: what you are seeing, Hig, cannot be real, it is just too magnificent. Don't twitch a muscle or it will vanish.

She didn't vanish. She turned her head to me. I cleared my throat.

You were in the neighborhood, I said lamely. My voice came out kind of high like an adolescent who can't control the timbre.

She raised one eyebrow: maybe. She raised up on her elbows and shrugged the shirt down her arms. Then she rolled over and lay on her stomach, her head on her crossed hands. Offering another vista. The world can end but you are not immune oh no.

If you want, you can just look at me, she said. It's probably been a long time. I'm in no hurry.

She raised her sweet butt into the air.

Um, is it okay if we rush through that part.

Unh huh.

I got my ass out of the hammock, shucked my shirt and lay down beside her. I don't know why, but I thought of flying. How there is a checklist you tick down before starting the engine, before taxiing, before takeoff. How if you are flying every day all the motions are smooth, sequential, you barely look at the list, but if it's been a while you are halting, thinking through everything, taking each item one at a time, making sure. So you don't have a wreck.

I forget where to start, I said. I feel like a—

A fifteen year old wouldn't say that.

Yeah. I was thinking more like a pilot. A rusty pilot with a bunch of checklists. So we won't crash.

Touch my back, she said.

I did. I ran my fingers over her lightly. Her skin tightened and smoothed out under them. I thought of wind moving over a field of wheat. She whimpered.

Does it hurt?

No. God, no. She said it into her folded arms. It has to be light but it feels great.

My hand swept over the rise of her ass moved over her thighs the backs the insides.

Mmmm, she murmured. Maybe it's better when you forget.

She rocked up onto her side and her fingers found my hair, my beard, tangled into them, pulled my face into her. When her mouth found mine I disassembled. Not exploded like a bomb or anything, but came apart. A few pieces at a time. They floated away, went into a kind of orbit. A splintering galaxy. An extravagant slow motion annihilation. The only center was her mouth, her hair. It was her. A reconstitution around the core of her. Without thought. I rolled on top of her and she gasped in pain.

Wait—

Oh. Shit. Scrambling off.

It's okay, okay. Here. I'm not so fragile. She pushed me onto my back. She kissed me. Kissed and kissed her hair covering me. She kissed my eyes nose lips. With her mouth, then she lowered her breasts onto my face and kissed me, brushed with her nipples, eyes, nose, tongue. And then. Surprise. The shock of it. She lowered herself onto me. The first touch. Wet. Like her mouth. Resistance. That heat. Ever so slowly, and slip, surrender.

Oh god, don't move. All those pieces. She moved. Her moving over me called them called them. The way a thousand fish rock together with the swell. Back and forth. The way the stars in the leaves. I reached. In her, in the very center, somewhere the single only stillness where everything cohered. Nothing but reach.

And then I let go. From reaching the strain to what? Nothing. Relinquish. Fall. If I cried and I'm not saying I did. The bliss, the sheer loss of falling.

She keened and I exploded. Whatever constellation, whatever was achieved was riven by light and scattered to the dark and fuck, that's where it should have been all along. She lay on me shuddering her weight and all those bits of us rained down as soft and unapologetic as ash.

★

Whew, she whispered, her lips moving in my ear.

Yeah, whew.

We crashed, huh?

Yup. In a good way.

How you refill. Lying there. Something like happiness, just like water, pure and clear pouring in. So good you don't even welcome it, it runs through you in a bright stream, as if it has been there all along.

★

We lay as still as we could, heart pounding against heart, a sympathetic rhythm that ricocheted and bounced and went counter and synced again, both of us I think fascinated by the music of it and the sensation. After a while she rose up and pulled the flannel quilt over us and snuggled down beside me and we slept. Not like the other nights of confusion. A deep and relieved slumber. Real comfort, simple exhaustion.

Before dawn, to spare him embarrassment, I guess, she rose, buttoned her shirt and went back into the meadow to sleep in the blankets on the thick bed of ponderosa needles she used on warm nights. Out under the stars, she said, where she could see everything. But I think it was the comfort of the cattle breathing, the rhythmic tearing of grass, always two or three who grazed at night beside, around her. And he snored, she said. He came to the creek at first light as he always did, over the burble I could hear the splashing, the brushing teeth with the defunct flattened bristles, a few hawks and spits, a cough.

And she—I could hear her wishing him good morning, opened my eyes, saw her in the shirt but with pants now she must keep by her bed. The wonderful satisfaction of seeing her like that now, out in the world, as conscribed as it is. In knowing her now as I did. Closed my eyes to doze again. She always refused to let me start the morning fire. It's mine, she insisted. My ritual. Don't mess with my habits. They are how we get along around here. Relax. Sleep in. I did. When I got up she always had the mug of bitter tea ready. Welcome as much for the ritual of it I guess as for the puckering taste.

That morning I rose slowly, stretched, took an inventory: Hig, you have your arms? Check. Your legs? Check. You have not really been blown to pieces? Nope. You have your heart? Not a question you've asked before. Not after. Yes I do. A little joggled, a little fuller. Lighter and heavier, too, go figure.

They were at the fire. I smelled roasting meat. I splashed my face, chest, dunked my head, dried myself with the shirt, walked to the fire.

Morning.

Pops nodded. She was squatting, adding a chunk of split wood to the flames and the sunup breeze swirled the smoke around, wreathed her. She winced, grimaced, craned her face to the side, added the wood.

Morning, I said.

She was either too smoked out to hear me or couldn't answer. The grimace. She stood, stepped out of the smoke, put her knuckles to her teary eyes.

Morning, I said.

She wiped the tears, blinked at me out of irritated eyes. Saw her heave a breath. Didn't say a word. She lifted the steaming kettle off a stump, poured it, handed me my mug without looking at me.

Meat's gonna burn, she said. To her dad or to me or no one. Edge of frustration.

I'll get it, I said. I reached for the long fork but she pushed my hand away with her forearm, grabbed the fork, turned the chops on the wire grill.

Relax, she said.

My insides froze. Glanced at Pops who politely turned to the side on his seat, his expression blank. He studied the top of the far canyon wall, sipped his drink.

Again:

Just relax. I'll have chops in a minute.

I heaved a long breath, turned aside, too, studied the far wall with Pops. You have your arms? Hig? Hig? Yes, I do. Your legs? Yes. Stop there. Be grateful for that.

I could've cried. Stood in the billowing smoke and used it for cover. So this is how it is.

After a silent breakfast, silent chewing, I took

the dishes to the creek as I always did: three plates, three mugs, three folding knives, three forks, the long fork. Let the wire grill burn off. I spread the fine sand around on the enamel plates with my fingers, scraped at the grease. Focus on the task at hand, concentrate, Hig. The water. It seemed warm. Warmer. That was frigging sad. Sad. Dug the fork tines down into the gravel bottom, wiped them in my fingers. Fuck. I breathed. When I was done I lay them out to dry on the board table. Pops passed me. He was carrying the rifle, shoulder slung, and the spade.

I'm going to scout the highway, he said. I don't want to walk out there on the big day and find a beat up useless piece of road.

That made sense. We didn't have enough fuel to circle while he filled and packed some potholes.

He took a step, then glanced back at me.

Everybody's been through a lot, he said.

I loved him then.

For the first time I felt him as some kind of family. As much as you could construct from blowdown and debris.

Yeah.

He nodded, walked on downcanyon toward the brush fence.

She was sweeping the packed dirt around the fire with a twig broom. She did it every morning to beat back the crumbs and keep ants and mice away from the kitchen.

As I approached, she swept. No pause. Focused on the dirt ahead of the broom.

Want me to pick some greens for lunch, I said.

My guts were gripped. She kept sweeping.

If you want, she murmured. Swept.

Cima?

Sweep. The harsh twiggy scrape.

I caught her arm. She went rigid.

Ow!

I dropped it like a hot grill. She stared at me.

That's gonna bruise, she said. No modulation.

Cima. Jesus. I'm sorry.

I stood rooted to the dirt. Sheer panic. Couldn't even see straight. Against all will my chest began to heave and then I felt tears running off my chin. Completely paralyzed. She stared at me. A mask. Like a death mask but the eyes alive or gathering life. Her dark eyes still as coins, then somehow gathering light as eyes do and registering, softening. She stood there trembling and studying my face and then I saw the tears well in her eyes and they were hers again, the dark pools. We stood like two trees. Swaying. What was left of the fire's smoke puffed and wisped.

Last night she said. After we fell asleep. I dreamt of Tomas. Dreamt and dreamt of him.

Her lips shivered and her mask crumbled.

He was calling me. He was dying on his cot and calling me, bleating just like an animal that knows it's going to slaughter. Just like an animal, Hig!

314

And I stood against the wall unwilling to help him. My husband. My best friend.

She was sobbing with a hypoxic violence.

My love was frozen. Like a winter pond. I must have dreamt that for hours. In the end I couldn't take it and I picked up my skinning knife and walked over and slit his throat. Oh god!

She collapsed. I stepped forward and caught her. I thought of two trees nearly unrooted and leaning against each other.

I don't know if I can do this, she said. I thought I could.

★

Pops reported that the highway was good and straight for at least a thousand feet. Good enough, no big holes. He had left a bandana tied to a mile marker for a wind sock. Cima was warm enough, but more withdrawn. She came out to the hammock but not every night nor every other night. We didn't make love again for days. Five. Can't pretend I didn't count. And when we did, when we were about to—I mean we lay on the blanket naked, holding each other, not kissing, not talking, but just our noses exploring ears and necks, and hands reconnoitering a territory made brand new by these new reckonings of loss— when it seemed to be time to consummate or at least somehow celebrate this new vulnerability, I

315

pulled her on top of me and she was not wet and I had trouble entering and I could feel that it hurt her, and for some reason I thought of Tomas— the dream Tomas, bleeding—and a wave of panic overcame me and I lost my erection.

Damn the dream world. His ghost was wading through it and ruining what only a few days ago had been as euphoric as any love affair I'd known.

She gave my wanger a consolatory double squeeze which made me feel worse. Sighed heavily—I read Disappointment—and rolled off to the side. Her arms came around me gently. Lying on the blanket, arm in arm, in an unconsummated paralysis. I felt lonelier then than I had felt before the canyon. The hearts thudded and ricocheted against each other, but the spirit did not. I could not stroke her more than absently, or kiss her, or even talk with authenticity. As if failing in consummating love had robbed me of all legitimacy as a lover. Had stripped my license to love or even express affection. It was awful.

It occurred to me as I lay next to her on my side and tried to catalogue this new dread—the dread of separateness when love was so near—it occurred to me that what may have been transmitted at the critical moment the moment of truth, of penetration, was her own memory of the dream. I mean we communicate without speech of course. I thought that in all likelihood that blood curdling image of the dead had passed through her at the same instant or just before. Which meant that none of us was ready. Okay, Hig, I thought. Reason it any way you want. Make yourself feel better any way you can, but you can't rewrite it. It sucks. Can't make it better. I can't, I can't move. Can hardly breathe.

Hig.

She whispered the word, a wind eddying in my ear.

Huh?

Will you give me oral pleasure?

She said it in a French accent and I knew she was referencing that old classic, *Pulp Fiction*.

I chuffed, a soundless laugh without mirth.

Really? You don't want that.

She nodded, her head against my chest.

Okay. Big exhale. Duty calls.

I did. I kissed down between her breasts, her little innie belly button, the shallow horns of her pelvis, the lower plain of her concave belly, the patch of tight curls, the little lips, the smooth kernel, inhaled her, and then I went to work. Like a job. What works? What works best?

For a little while it was like that. And then she was lifting her hips and rolling herself under my lips and tongue and whimpering. And then she moaned, and then I was encouraging, then cheerleading with teeth, lips, tongue. Then tugging and releasing. I was flying her like a kite, that's what it felt like, and then I forgot all my bullshit self and the kite was very very high and tugging harder and the blood reasserted and she was coming. She was arched and coming and I was inside her and she was clutching and clawing my back. I realized I must be hurting her with my weight. I hastily rolled off and spewed in the air and we lay and breathed without thought and we were almost happy again. Almost without reserve.

Go figure.

And then it was three more nights because she was so bruised up. But the mood around camp was better. And I could feel a gathering of momentum toward departure.

II

Pops left before full light. Without ceremony or sentiment. Took one look around the canyon, the last pairs of cows and calves, the sheep and lambs, hefted a light pack, his rifle, and without a word walked downstream and out the brush fence.

Left the only life he had ever given himself to. The life of his own lineage, his father and mother, his father's father. It was in his blood truly and he latched the gate and walked out of the canyon.

I weighed everything again. Made a balance scale with a liter bottle, a five gallon pail, a stick and a rope. Hung it from a low limb by the stream. Five gallons is forty pounds half of it twenty, the liter bottle about two. I weighed the AR-15 rifle, Cima's pack, mine, the hose and hand pump.

How much does a lamb weigh?

The little mixed herd moved in the tall grass heads down. Three lambs shook their heads, their ears, went back to feeding. One butted his mother in the ribs to nurse. Their lives were about to change. If any survived the winter it would be a miracle.

I dunno, maybe twenty?

Let's see. You have a girl and a boy?

She smiled. A ram and a ewe? Yes.

Like the Ark. Here we go.

We wrapped one of the little guys in a sling

made of a shirt and weighed him against the bucket. He swung under the branch his ears flopping, his legs splayed extended his tiny perfect shining black hooves, a look of sheer bewilderment on his little face. I emptied the pail until they balanced. About seventeen pounds.

Okay, we can take them. Without your dad on takeoff we should be okay.

Should be?

It's a crap shoot anyway. We smoothed the runway, cut the tall trees at the end. The book says we need a hundred more feet. But they never met the Beast.

Short nod. Cima looked across the meadow, the canyon. If I were a painter—she was that beautiful. Maybe not her alone, but the moment. The green reflected darkly in her violet eyes, and I thought, If we crash and burn tomorrow morning, well.

★

Made a last fire in the dark, watched the flames lean and light the rock wall for the last time. Ate venison and potatoes, greens, drank the tea. Doused the fire with a hiss, a billow of steam. Heard the low of a cow, the rustle of the leaves.

Had loaded everything yesterday afternoon but the lambs. Cima slept in the fields with her animals, listening to them graze around her. Now we led the two lambs on strings of twine upstream, carried them up the tree ladder beside the trickle of waterfall. They squirmed, bleated. Two moms answered, followed the cries to the top of the field, confused. The sadness of our world, it underlies everything like a water. Set the lambs down foursquare on their feet and they stood tall and stiff, reassessing life from this height. And trundled after us.

Walking a lamb on a string is not at all like walking a dog on a leash. It was a constant conversation, an argument. Full of debate, concessions, sudden capitulations, obstinacy in the face of reason. They balked we tugged. They gamboled ahead, no shit, we ran after. There is no way not to laugh. It was the perfect distraction from the emotions of leaving such a place and all that it meant. Finally I picked up my lamb and carried him.

At the Beast Cima expertly hogtied the little guys and we set them on our packs behind the seats. We climbed in, pulled the seat belt harnesses over our shoulders and clipped the steel buckles at our waists. I handed her the clipboard with the checklists.

You be the copilot. Haven't had one in a while.

I primed the motor, pulled the stiff knob from the dash, listened for the spray of gas filling the carburetor and shoved it in. Repeat. Flipped on the master switch. The revving whir of the gyroscope.

Turned the key in the mags, inched the throttle forward a half inch, set my boots against the brakes and pushed the starter.

Two coughs, two half spins of the prop and I shoved the throttle forward and she caught and roared and shuddered. We all did, me, Cima, the lambs. A small plane coming to life is emotional. It's like a whole auditorium standing for an ovation. It's grand and a little frightening. I pulled the throttle back to an even idle which was quieter, less momentous, less shake and more tremble. Let the engine warm a little, watched the dial of the oil pressure gauge ease down into the green.

Okay, I yelled. Go down the Before Takeoff list.

Had to yell. Didn't carry an extra headset with me anymore. What would have been the point? Jasper didn't need it.

Trim wheel to neutral!

Check!

Align heading indicator.

Check!

Run up to 1700.

Check!

Mags.

Carb heat.

Primer set and locked.

Check!

All of it gathering its own momentum as the motor warmed, the digital columns for each cylinder on the engine analyzer climbed, the oil pressure fell—all while the motor roared, the plane shivered, all heading for the critical moment of takeoff. I loved this. It was this—the anticipation of being finally airborne as much as the flying itself that had kept me coming back again and again whenever I could.

Outside thermometer read fifty two degrees. Good. Nice and cool. Heavier air. Eased off the brakes and she began to roll. Jostled her through the sage into the newly cleaned track using the brakes to steer, turned her down to the east end and spun her in the circle we had cleared. She pointed west. Sun behind us made long shadows of the brush. High desert daybreak pungent and cool. Straight ahead across the meadow the cedar woods that were our limit, our raised bar.

She gave me a thumbs up. I checked the trim wheel one last time, shoved the throttle forward to the panel, glanced at the oil pressure, the Beast roared, shook I yelled, *God is great!* Released the brakes.

I don't know why I yelled that. It might have been the last thing I said in this life. I wasn't thinking Jihad I was thinking Hig, those Cessna guys in the white coats never tested this. They maybe never imagined a world eighty years hence when their plane would be a Noah's Ark for sheep. She rolled, broke inertia, almost balking at first, way too slow, and the thought flashed No way!

And then she bounded, gathered the runway, reeled it in, the trees at the end came, grew dark, larger, maybe halfway to them I felt her break ground, the airborne moment and I pushed the nose down hard, pressure, she wanted to lift off, climb, but I held her down, held her three feet off the track hard in the ground effect where she could gain the most speed. We hurtled like that barely off the dirt and then I heard Cima scream, the first trees billboarding right in our face, and I jerked up the Johnson bar and pulled the yoke, not pulled it but released to my chest and the Beast flared, the nose leapt, the plane reared, it seemed straight into sky, the single prayer Don't fucking stall, the stall horn blaring, airspeed dial, the needle hovering at sixty, the horn, the lambs chiming in, the weird thoughts you have when it all teeters: the lambs are the same fucking key. The same key as the stall horn. Sounds like their mom.

Not Cima. She just screamed. Once. I shoved the yoke forward again, swung down the nose to near level, prayed for speed for speed, soon enough the Beast took it, accelerated like a swallow that swoops after veering upwards for a bug and we flew level at sixty five, I looked down at the trees, thought, If we cleared them by two feet.

Not a regulation takeoff. Not in the book even for a short soft field. This is what our vector from the meadow probably looked like:

Well I must've been glad to be alive. I loosed a yell. The junipers rushed beneath us. The Beast rolled over the next ridge fifty feet over the trees, it seemed on her own volition, like a magic carpet. Coastered down the other side. One way to enter the next dream. She was beaming the way a small kid beams after surviving the magic mountain log flume at Six Flags. She reached over and pinched my arm.

We're alive see? Nice work.

We're awake.

You say the strangest things.

Even the lambs had caught the mood. They no longer cried, they lifted their heads off the packs and followed the conversation, floppy eared and guileless attendants. As far as they knew, all this represented the next stage in the normal life cycle of a sheep.

We crossed the big river and Pops was sitting on

his pack like any hitchhiker on a shadeless stretch of desert highway. Something in his attitude at once resolute and refractory, pinned to his long shadow, the rifle standing between his knees like the staff of an acolyte. Which he was: bent to the mission, devoted now to a new life. If we could get there. The bandana fluttered on the mile post, barely registering the breeze of a calm summer morning. I banked left and landed and tapped the brakes to a full stop right across from where he sat.

He climbed in behind his daughter. Noah's Ark, he said glancing at the lambs. That was all. Cima pulled the door shut, latched it and we took off to the west toward Grand Junction.

★

Something was not right. I won't say wrong because how it registered wasn't anything so definitive. Ten miles to the east I had made the first call. We had cleared the far cliffs of Grand Mesa, the great flattopped butte that looked like it must have been a peninsula in some shallow, plesiosaur haunted sea. A sixty mile long outcrop risen against the sky. It was banded with purple cliffs and covered with aspen forests. In summer they were waist deep with ferns and strung with dark lakes and beaver ponds. Melissa and I had shared some of our best camping trips up there, once tenting for a week on the edge of a lake with no road for miles and the trout just about jumping into our frying pan.

We had flown past it, beneath the rim, staying low to save fuel, the warm wind pouring through the empty frame where Pops had shot out my window, and there was Grand Junction, straddling the two rivers and sprawling over the desert hills. A vast gritty town that stretched all the way to the Book Cliffs to the north.

There were the highways, the streets, the developments, the cul de sacs, the flat blank roofs of the box stores, the vast parking lots. There was the industrial section along the Colorado River, the train tracks, the phalanx of warehouses. The city was threaded with cottonwoods. Many of the old trees that lined the streets and depended on watering were skeletal and dead but many were rooted deep enough and punctuated the thorough-fares with dashes and clumps of violent green like some Morse code.

The canopies of cottonwoods still shaded the river parks, some of the oldest and biggest fighting the drought just half dead, still clothed with leaves on one side. And fire. Not a corner of the city untouched. As if it had been fire not flu that had swept death through the town. The cars, every one it seemed, scorched. Where they were parked in the side streets in their rows, in mall parking lots, out on the highways, where they lay in such a chaos, such absence of pattern some giant might have thrown them like pick up sticks. Whole neighborhoods were burned to the ground. Others looked as if torched just to melting and left to cool the way a pastry chef glazes a brûlée. The sweet black smell of embered wood cloyed in my nostrils and I'm not sure if we could really smell the town a thousand feet up or if the sight produced it. And if there were skeletal trees there were human bones. I saw them. Not true skeletons as the connective tissue was gone, but the bones of the dead were everywhere gathered into heaps by some predator and scattered by scavengers. Heaps so big we could see them from here.

Cima vomited. Just the sight of the ruined town. Hurriedly she pushed open the side window and stuck her mouth in the gap and sprayed the glass behind her. This was the city where they did their big shopping, Costco and auto parts, farm equipment. This is where they came for a weekend movie when the one in Delta didn't interest them. The two towns being almost equidistant from the ranch. She had not seen it end. She and Pops left just as it was getting really bad. When there was still TV news, when the newscasters appeared more exhausted by the day, then scared and exhausted, then terrified as their colleagues dropped away to the hospitals and makeshift flu wards, or were just not heard from, assumed ill or dead, and the last TV anchors stood in, and the field correspondents taped themselves using tripods, the reports more frantic. And were finally cut short by mayhem. I remembered that. Because they had nothing else to do at the end: broadcast, courageous, the way the band played on the deck of the sinking ship, either that or go home and die.

Sometime in there Pops and Cima decided to leave the ranch and they loaded up the gooseneck cattle trailer and towed a little trailer for the four wheeler behind that, and they drove out to the highway in the middle of the night. With a dozen cattle, as many sheep, two saddled horses, two Australian shepherds, and provisions. And Pops had to fight his way through three barricaded ambushes in just the fifteen miles to the creek road, and shoot three crazy fuckers further on in the cedar hills, all of which he was pretty much expecting and didn't have much problem executing with his guns. But they shot one of the horses and two of the sheep inside the trailer, which made it less easy to pretend the next day that they were driving cows up onto their summer lease as they would on any normal morning in early May. He rode horseback and she drove the ATV, which pulled a small trailer of gear and supplies, the twelve miles into the canyon. She would have preferred to ride, she was never comfortable on four wheelers, but he was skilled at hazing and herding the livestock on horseback and the dogs were, too, and they were used to taking orders from him in the saddle.

The next morning they walked back downstream and he blew the one ford that crossed the creek with dynamite, and made the track impassable except on foot or horseback, and then only at low water.

They swept their tracks as best they could and obliterated them thoroughly for two miles before they left the rough road for the creek trail and the canyon. It took them all day. And then, thank god, two days later it poured rain.

All this she had told me over the last three weeks. So I understood the shock of seeing Grand Junction. It was one thing to lose the whole world as you knew it, another to see, to maybe smell your old neighborhood as charnel house and killing field.

She had made it out the window, streaked the rearward glass, but the plane still reeked. I handed her the water bottle I always kept between the seats and stole a look back at Pops to see if he would be triggered by the smell or the sights below him. It happens that way on boats and planes, the passengers already queasy and one throws up and it's a chain reaction. But he sat like a Buddha with a lamb in his lap, one strong claw on her shoulder, his face impassive and hard, leaning to the window taking it all in.

This is what you left, I thought. The vindication

of the choice you made to leave that night. Vindication and horror. Sometimes being right isn't all it's cracked up to be: how many times in the last few years I thought about bitter fruit, how when what you are right about is—well you can't even look at it.

But it wasn't the burned and devastated city, the pockets of virid trees, that were somehow wrong or simply not quite right. I was now six miles out. I was nine hundred feet off the ground and aiming for the airport, for the tower, where three years ago I had gotten the signal, the beginning of a message. I dialed the frequency—it was still there in my GPS—and made the second call.

Grand Junction Tower, Cessna Six Three Three Three Alpha six southeast at five thousand eight hundred inbound for landing.

Said it again. Then miracle: static. A loud burst of aural snow. I twisted up the squelch excited and called again.

Cessna Six Triple Three Alpha—

It wasn't crystal clear but it was. It was! A woman's voice. Maybe older, a little raspy. Slightly humored, kind.

Cessna Six Triple Three Alpha, wind two four zero at five, make a straight in approach, cleared to land runway two niner.

All formal, all perfect, by the book, just like before before. Said with a straight face. Like a normal business day at the old airport. Can't fully describe what that harkening back to normalcy did to my spirit. As if in pretending that this were airport operations as usual I could also pretend that my wife lived and my dog, that she was in her seventh month and they were back on the Front Range and I was about to touch down after a three hour flight away from them, not one that had taken nine years and on which there was no true return.

What wasn't right was not even that. It was the beacon. Almost every paved airport, has, had, a rotating beacon green and white. And I had seen it flash from ten miles out, and thought nothing of it. And then at six miles I saw it flashing again, pulsing like the heartbeat of a living enterprise and the dissonance—the burned out city at the end of the known world, and the living, pulsing light, the voice of the controller transmitting everyday commands—finally caught my attention and the hair on the back of my neck stood up. Can't tell you why except to say that it was odd to say the least: that they had power. Or: why shouldn't they? We had it at Erie. More and more airports had been supplementing with solar and wind. Or that the beacon shouldn't be on in daylight in clear, VFR conditions. Don't know why, except to say that something put me on edge.

I lined up. I banked twenty degrees left and straightened out for final and there was the long east-west strip built for jets stretching out in front of us like a vision. Smooth too. Looked it from here. Didn't have the buckled, cracked, potholed look of every strip on the east side of the mountains. Somebody had maintained it. Least it seemed that way from a mile out and descending. Backed off the throttle, set twenty degrees of flaps and let her float down at five hundred feet per, the Beast seeming to breathe relief at this reversion to past protocol. I swear she has an animus or a mind or something.

And as we came down slowly and the strip grew wider and longer and rose to meet us, we could see the rows of hangars, some caved in, some roofs blown half off by wind. We could see the control tower on our left, the cantilevered, green tinted, bulletproof windows. We could see wrecks of planes, a few on either side of the runway, a big jet at the end. As there were at every airport—the tied down craft battered by weather, eventually pulling loose and tumbling, but. That's when it hit me. Like a frigging bullet.

I was maybe thirty feet off the ground. I had cut power, topped the prop, done all the things you do in the final moments, and was getting ready to pull back the yoke and flare for a soft touchdown and. And it hit me.

The beacon, the tower: the wrecks on the field were scorched like the cars. Can't say I thought anything, nothing reasoned, articulated, there wasn't time. It was just the shock of the image: the burned and crumpled planes. Different from Erie. Different from Denver, from Centennial, the old planes ripped from their moorings and cart-wheeled over the airfield by wind. These were crashes. Live-engine wrecks. I did pull back the yoke, but not for a flare. I jerked it back and slammed the throttle to the panel and the engine caught and screamed and my palm slammed the carb heat knob back in and we lurched, reared skyward. We jumped off the field maybe steeper even than our takeoff half an hour before from the meadow. And the lambs wailed.

I looked out the low side window, the bowl of plexiglas, and in the same instant the cable came up. Sprung taut, probably missed my wheels by ten feet. Sprung like a trap. Which is what it was.

Holy fuck.

Hig, you are a cool bastard. That was Bangley talking. Giving me the rare Bangley thumbs up. And in that moment too I glanced at the fuel flow gauge and saw we had two gallons left. Ten minutes at most. Fuck.

I banked left to come around for a look and tensed for gunfire from the ground.

Goddamn. It was Pops. A *taut line.* He had moved the lamb and he had his gun up and he was scanning the hangars, the wreckage.

The cable stretched across the runway about a third of the way down and ten feet off the pavement, held taut by two sprung arms welded from T-bar steel. The arms were articulated downward like the bills of evil herons. The cable was painted black like the tarmac but I could clearly see its shadow and then the evil thread of it. No gunfire. I craned around.

Pops?

That was it, he yelled. Their one big trick.

Want to? I called back.

Get em? Fuck yeah.

Cima?

She looked confused, still sick, unable to appreciate the implications of what had just happened. She nodded.

We don't have much choice, I yelled. We're about out of gas.

I tightened the bank and swooped for another final, this time without checklists, without any thought at all except That motherfucker that motherfucker. I'm coming to get you. And the gut-punch feeling of betrayal. All those years, thinking about that radio call. The hope it had engendered. It drove me wild.

Everything was on automatic. I banked tight and swooped and touched down a hundred feet past the cable. Pops leaned forward and said:

Taxi past. There. Park behind that building, the second west of the tower.

I kept her rolling fast. The radio crackled on. **Nice landing** said the voice and it didn't sound like Aunt Bee now. It sounded frayed and hard. Then laughter. Laughter like hanging metal scraping over pavement, loud and sustained. **Congratulations. You're the first.**

I didn't call back. I turned left onto a broad taxiway and found cover where Pops said and shut her down. We were in the cool shadow of Big River Flight School and Authorized Cessna Service Center and we were close enough to the wall that we couldn't see the top of the tower and they couldn't get a bead on us, whoever they were. Climbed out moved the seat forward for Pops so he could squeeze out. A cricket chirped loudly from the base of the wall. Cima sat. Hadn't unbuckled. I didn't know what to say, I had never seen her like this. She seemed in shock. She was in shock. I walked around to her door opened it. Her long hand pressed against the panel over the oil pressure gauge and a new bruise spread along her forearm. She turned. Her eyes were bleary.

It's not just the meanness of it. The trap. That too. It's the city.

I nodded. She and Pops had retired early from the world before it had fired into full conflagration. They had seen enough, enough to flee but not the full demise. Not what I had seen every day from the air. What Bangley and I had known in the middle of our nights. The charred town and all that it implied.

You want to stay here?

Nodded.

Okay.

I walked back around, reached across my seat and unclipped the Uzi from its rack and held it out to her.

If someone shows up that doesn't look like me or your dad, plug em. It's charged.

She hesitated, nodded, took the gun.

I unsnapped the AR. Also took the handheld radio. Turned it on and dialed in 118.1, the tower. Sometimes it's a good idea to talk to your enemy. Not usually. Bangley had taught me that—the value of reticence. Also the value of over-whelming firepower. I reached back under one of the lambs and pried out the stuff sack that held the grenades, nodded at Pops, and we moved around the south corner of the building. I followed him. He hugged the wall so that we were still out of sight of the tower. Before we cleared the next corner and crossed the open ramp where small planes had once tied down, and came into full view of whoever was up there, we pulled up. It was about fifty yards to the next building, a single story brick, the offices of the FBO, a hangar adjacent and behind. We could see the back of it: a row of dark windows still mostly intact, and a metal door toward the rear.

Hig that old lady up there sounded just like my grandma.

And?

We're gonna clean her clock and whoever else. No questions asked. He looked at me.

I nodded.

Those cocksuckers invited you out here under false pretenses. Did you see all those goddamn wrecks? How many planes you think they did like that?

A lot. Scores. It's the biggest runway on the way to L.A. between Denver and Phoenix.

He leaned against the bricks.

Why? he said.

Why do they do it?

I mean not for the fuel. Half those wrecks burned. Not for the damn *meat*. Unless you like charcoal.

There'd be survivors. Some maybe not badly injured. And sometimes they didn't burn. Not all the way, sometimes not at all. There'd be supplies, food, weapons. Lambs. *Bahhh.*

Okay so what did they do with the pissed off survivors?

Silence. He stepped around the corner and the shot cracked. Blew brick dust into my face. I thought he was cooked. He fell back. I grabbed at him blindly, hugged him to me.

Fuck. Losing my edge, Hig. Thanks.

He was fine. He was breathing hard. I wiped my eyes.

That's what they do, Hig. Pick em off one by

one. Come out of the wreck injured, dazed not even sure what hit em and bang. Or use em for whatever they use em for. Okay now I'm really pissed.

He unbuttoned his patched flannel shirt, scanned the ground behind us and picked up a two foot piece of rusty rebar. Hung the shirt on it.

Stick this out past the edge when I say. Up here like this. We get into that next building we're made. Do NOT move from here until I tell you. He slid the bolt back, checked for a chambered bullet, crouched. Three two one, go!

I shoved out the shirt, the shot cracked, zinged, he was gone. He was sprinting toward that back door running like a halfback, feinting and zagging and two more shots exploded up pavement behind and ahead of him. He made it to the sight shadow of the building, to the spot where he could no longer be seen from above, and walked the rest of the way to the door. Turned, gave me a thumbs up before he tugged it open and disappeared inside. Fucking Pops. Hope I can run like that when I'm—what?—my age. I could never run like that. Damn. I pulled back the shirt. There was a neat hole halfway down, repeated in three folds. Gut shot. Ouch. I waited. One minute, two, began to count like I did for Bangley. At two hundred I wondered what was going on. At two twenty three: one shot. It rang over the airport like a bell. A single toll. Echoed and died. It was Pops's .308.

I knew the sound. Half a minute later the door in the back of the FBO scraped open and Pops waved me over. I ran. He held up his hand patted the air like *Take your time, relax.*

What the fuck? What happened?

A fool, that's what. Those windows up in the tower are thick bulletproof. Been like that since 9/11. But they have to shoot out somewhere. They have gunports. Like an old fort. I knew once I was inside, I'd have all the time I needed to set up the shot.

I stared at him.

You nailed the shooter through a gunport? Like through his scope?

Shook his head. Nah. Turns out they have two ports—a higher one, maybe chest level, for the long shot, one for the angle directly down to cover the base of the tower. He was looking out the upper one and I shot through the lower. You wanna blow the door, go up and pay a visit?

Damn, Pops.

He had shot whoever it was right up their skirts. Through like a four inch hole.

Oh yeah. We walked across. The door at the base of the tower was heavy metal painted green. He unzipped a greasy belt pack took out two sticks of dynamite taped them together with duct tape.

Been saving these. Seems like a good time.

He taped them to the heavy metal door on the

340

hinge side, close to the ground, lit them and jogged back. We ducked inside the Jet Center for good measure. It blew. Small bits of pavement rained against the windows. Reminded me of passing a truck on a gravel road. We jogged back. The door hung cattywampus off the top hinge, swung a sad metronome in drifting smoke. Pops stood in the doorway like a hesitant messenger.

Give me your gun, he said. You mind?

I handed it to him, he gave me his.

This'll be a little better for what we're doing.

Reflex: he tugged back the charging handle, checked that a shell was chambered, and went into commando mode. Not as if he hadn't before. Couldn't wait for him to meet Bangley. That's what I was thinking, even amused imagining the introductions as Pops covered the first flight of stairs and went up gun to his shoulder sighting up the stairwell both eyes open. The treads were concrete laid over steel and they beat a dull *tong tong* as we ran up. There were five levels. At each one he told me to stay in the well and cover it and he went through the door. He cleared each floor swiftly and we moved up. Leaned into my ear breathing in rasps.

You're gonna love the decorations in this place.

I could imagine. The top door, the door to the control room was locked. Of course. He shot the lock out, pushed through. The smell. A barrier. I gagged and spit. Cats everywhere. Freaked by the shooting, running over the radar keyboards, the comm panels, arched bristled and hissing against the dead black flatscreens. Calicoes and blacks, blue eyed Siamese.

The air reeked of cat piss and swam with light from the tinted windows, infused with green like an aquarium. On the west side, the side we had come from, where I knew the shooter would be slumped on his side beneath the cantilevered windows, was a man choking and crying. He was holding his guts which were spilled onto the floor. Blood seeped from his back, pooled in reservoir and ran across the floor in a sinuous ribbon like a creek.

He was an old man, older than Pops. His beard was white, his grizzled hair uncut, matted now and soaked in blood from the painted steel floor. The one who had first called, the one I had heard years before, must've been. He wore suspenders. His cap had been thrown into the middle of the open room. It was printed with yellow lettering, Peoria Jet Center "Service in the Heartland." Over the nausea, a wave of goosebumps. Fucker. The heartland had come west looking for a safe haven from the flu and hit this bastard's cable. Probably. His rifle lay a few feet from the cap. An AR-10 with a long barrel. Cats drawled in the loud panicked mews of a vet's waiting room. The old man gagged, gurgled, sobbed. One of the bolder cats was already lapping at the crimson creek.

Samuel! Cold shriek. *Sammy my Sammy my Sammy!*

I jumped. In the corner—there was no corner it was all corners, octagonal—on the east side was an old woman with her hair, no shit, in a bun. It was Aunt Bee. She stood next to a spotting scope on a tripod and wore, no shit again, a calico dress printed in blue cornflowers. She wore wire rimmed round glasses. Could have been your school librarian, your doting grandma, the face on the pancake syrup label. She was at once backed up straight against a nav screen and paralyzed mid lunge toward the shooter who must have been her husband, her hands clawing the air in front of her chest, and her mouth open in a scream. Pops shot her. Middle of the forehead. Twenty cats did hot laps around the tower, then froze in various poses of arched terror. Dropped the decibel level in the reverberant room by half. Now just cats and the old man.

Pops stepped to him, crouched.

Finish Gramps choked. His eyes swum up. They were filmed like poached eggs. *Shoot.* He begged.

Pops said How'd you spring the cable.

Wha—? He gurgled up a gobbet of blood.

The cable. How'd you spring it?

Bucko

Backhoe?

Gramps vomited affirmative.

Fuel? Where's the fuel? You have hundred low lead?

Shoot plea—

Where is it?

Ea tak

East tank?

Yu

Pops tugged on a bunch of keys clipped to the man's belt.

This the key?

Oauuuua

Is this the key?

Yu

Go to hell.

Pops shot him. I gagged.

★

Looked out the window once before fleeing the cats, the stench. Roof of the Jet Center covered in solar panels. Like Erie. How they pumped their water, fuel, powered the radios and beacon. East gas pumps right below not a hundred yards. Easy shot from here, how they protected it. The survivors? From any of the wrecks? Could have picked them off at distance, or Aunt Bee could have gone to her blocked spot like an actor, waved like a concerned grandma, gestured them urgently over. Easy enough. Damn.

Before we left the tower Pops invited me to the third floor apartment. I said I didn't want to see. He said, You are going to want to see. Cats were already venturing down the stairs. I followed him.

Ever been in a retiree's RV? The one they sold their house for? How spotless and neat, the bed made with a patch quilt, maybe a pattern of sunflowers smoothed taut, a plush bear on the pillow? Silk rose in a velcroed cutglass vase on the veneer booth table? It was like that. Single small bedroom, no window, immaculate plush wall to wall carpet, no cats. Except. In the room that would have been the living room where the TV might have been, one wall was pegged and on a hundred pegs were caps, mostly baseball caps with the logos of FBOs, aircraft service centers, aviation specialists of all types—cylinders, props, skins—from every corner of the country. The rest of the walls were covered with shelves. On the shelves, alternating, were pairs of spectacles—sunglasses, reading glasses, bifocals, everything—and crudely stuffed birds of every type. They were lumpy, dullcolored birds stuffed with some filler without benefit of armatures, eyes sewed shut without skill—owls, bluebirds, magpies, sparrows, ducks. And bird guides: antique Petersen, Golden, National Geo,

Sibley's. Seemed every one that had ever been published in the last century.

Hobbies still going strong, Pops said. That's a relief.

Fuckin A.

★

We gassed up almost like before, just flipped the lever and heard the electric pump and watched the numbers roll out the gallons. I checked the color, and for water and particulates with a clear plastic tube I carried. We found six more five gallon gas cans and filled them too. Fired the engine. She ran smooth so the gas was good. We took off. Pops said On the ground! Two o'clock. I banked over. Three bison grazed at the end of the strip, hides still patched and ragged from winter.

★

The buffalo are moving down to their old range, the wolves, the bighorn too. The trout are gone, the elk, but. I've seen osprey up on Jasper's creek, and bald eagles. Plenty of mice in the world, plenty of hawks. Plenty of crows. In winter the trees are full of them. Who needs Christmas tree decorations? Miles and miles of dead forest but the spruce are coming back, the fir and the aspen.

346

We flew over. The wind buffeted and rushed where my window had been. At Kremmling, in the hills beneath the Gore Range, was a vast fire. New since. Some lightning strike. Trees on the edge caught and exploded. We saw deer running downhill.

Look! she said.

Behind the deer was a grizzly bear. She loped, coming down hard on her short front legs, putting on the brakes, wheeling trying to herd two terrified cubs. Herd them down and down.

In the river, in the flat stretch above the canyon, deer were swimming.

★

I thought of a painting I had seen at the natural history museum in Denver. A bunch of mixed dinosaurs, I remember triceratops, fleeing across a sparse plain pursued by fire, and volcanoes erupting in the background. I wonder if they could run as fast as a mama grizzly or a deer.

★

The chairs swung on the chairlifts at Winter Park. New trees came almost to the seats. We had just enough fuel to make it to Erie, but just enough. I wanted to land and put in at least one extra can. In case. Of what? Just in case. We circled back to a clear stretch of highway on the west side of the ski town. Landed, jostled to a stop close to the buildings at the town limit. Stretched, poured in the cans of fuel. Stood on the strut, Pops handed them up. Edge of town seventy yards away, a rec center, a Sinclair station, a gaudy darkwood chalet: Helga's German Food and Spirits. Miraculously untorched, the town.

Cima stood in the road, hands in the pockets of her jeans, staring. Still seemed in some kind of shock. The world beyond their canyon. The empty burning world. The intact buildings the scariest. For me. Because they looked almost normal, because they echoed. They do whatever it is a struck bell does long after the sound fades.

I want to go in, she said. Pointing like a tourist at the German restaurant.

There?

Yes.

Quicker we load up and take off, safer we'll be. Empty, but. You never know.

I want to go in.

I shrugged. Pops was in his own reverie watching the Gore Range, the burning Never Summers from that distance, kind of transfixed. You can get used to a lot but maybe not this. All of a sudden. I whistled to him that we'd be back in a few minutes grabbed the AR and we walked up the frost heaved highway. Tufts of grass and sage, little poplars grew up out of the cracks. Small lizards skittered. We walked straight into the sun which hung over the snows of the Divide. Still snow up there, anyway.

Did you like German food?

I felt like we were on a date, which was weird. The canyon had been insulated from more than this whistling vacancy.

Hated it, pretty much.

Hunh.

She reached across, grabbed my hand. I'm not going anywhere, Hig, she said. Where would I go?

Lots of places, I thought but I didn't say anything. To the other side for one. Or way way inside. A lot of places someone else can never follow.

I kept my mouth shut. The door was open, there was no door. Maybe they'd burned it in the hearth along with the furniture. The windows were boarded up. Someone had been planning for the end of a bad patch, planning to protect the business, their life savings. Those signs of hope that were so quaint now, even perverse. We stepped inside.

They hadn't burned the furniture: all the tables, the heavy wood chairs, bulked in the dimness, attendant and stolid. There was a hearth in the center, a round fireplace, stone bordered, the requisite centerpiece of every dimwitted après ski designer. Probably fondue pots in the kitchen. Near the front, where rain and snow had blown in, the wood was stained and warped, but further back there was only dry dust and the tracks and shit of mice. Heavy oak bar in the back, tall wood stools, a smoky mirror unbroken. Reflected the light from the doorway like a molten pool on a creek near nightfall. She hesitated, then advanced and stood in front of the bar, looking into the big mirror. Back a few feet, stock still, arms out from her sides, and I thought of a child at a dance recital who has forgotten the next steps. Gone blank. Or a ranch girl at a new bar, a girl from the hills, overwhelmed, who didn't know what to order, how to ask. She looked at herself and she burst into tears.

★

Who was that ragged, burly, bearded man who held her? Is that you, Hig? You look all patched and tufted and threadbare like those winterworn bison. You're missing a tooth. You look like a homeless hockey player.

★

Didn't know. A little nervous about coming over the final hump. Over the Rocks, they used to say at the airpark like it was a big deal. Not for me, never was. I mean it was high, it was the Continental Divide, there was almost always snow, a shitty place to lose an engine under any circumstances, a long way down to the first clearings in the lodgepole, the long dead pines. On either side, Winter Park or Nederland. I always left two thousand feet of clearance, flying so high I got a little spaced out once in a while, and it was always okay. But. Now it *was* a big deal. How would it be? I aimed for the low spot in the pass where the old Jeep road went over the rocks and patchy snow, watched the low country rise up behind the ridge, the way it does when you are making it over, watched it lift and unfurl like one of those bannered flags they used to have at the Olympics, and saw there beyond the final buttress of foothills: old Erie, the airstrip itself soon visible south of the radio tower that no longer blinks, the ribbon of tarmac rolled out like a welcome mat just for me. Nervous about seeing Bangley again, that's what. It had been, by my best reckoning, just over six weeks.

★

Now we descended over the foothills, and I pointed the Beast toward Erie by rote. I aimed for the dirt escarpment that stood out like a billboard on the other side of the interstate, still fifteen miles off my aiming point from the west that would put me right over midfield. Seeing it, I flashed on the summer I was eighteen: returning home to Mom's little house in Hotchkiss. Surprising her. On walking up the switchback mesa road at dusk. The excitement of returning home, the fear of having it be nothing like I expected. My heart drummed. Could feel it in there trying to compete with the throb of the engine, the lower roar and vibration as I pulled back the throttle to descend.

To our eight miles of prairie. Over the last trees, the very last living pines wandering out onto the plain like disoriented sentinels, our perimeter, our margin of safety, and then I could see the tower, the one we'd built together. Bangley's sniper deck, the porch where he fired his stash of mortars—and then I was over the place and didn't look down too closely to see the bones, the bodies left unburied and scattered by now by wolves and coyotes, and whatever else. Could have seen, if I looked closely, the white bleat of a rib's arch or skull. And I felt a surge of—what? Of something for Bangley who I realized in that moment had become my family. Because it was to him, like to my mother twenty two years ago, I was returning home. Not my wife, my child, my mother, not anything but Bangley with his gravel voice. For whom it was a matter of pride to be a stubborn dickhead all the time. And I felt a twinge of fear, of recoil. What if he was straight up mad at me?

The warring emotions. And then I felt the fear full bore. When I dropped to six thousand feet and flew over the glinting river which was low, but running, and came in straight for the south end of the runway and saw the charred husks of the houses, saw foundations, saw one half of my hangar ripped open as if by a tornado and burned.

III

Bangley's house, a hundred yards north, the one with his gunsmith shop in the sunken living room and the photo of the blonde family skiing—it was standing, but the windows were shot out and there were scorch marks around the second floor dormer which was splintered, and next to it was a gaping hole in the roof. Oh fuck. Fuck fuck fuck.

Pops was straight up and alert on his pack, I glanced back, he knew it was all wrong, and Cima squeezed my thigh and couldn't keep herself away from the window, from pressing her face to it like a kid at the shark tank.

Before I landed I came in low and took a pass over the garden. It was still there, undisturbed. The water was still running across the head of the marks at the top of the plot, and there was water running in half the furrows.

But. Even from two hundred feet I could see the weeds. They filled the unwatered marks and climbed and crowned the ridges of banked earth.

I jammed the throttle and pulled up and came around again higher. Banked left and aimed for midfield and landed long and taxied straight to Bangley's house. Mixture, mags, master switch.

Off. Shut down. The Beast had barely stopped

rolling when I shoved open the sticky door and jumped out and ran to the house.

The front door was open, swinging slightly in the light wind.

Bangley! Bangley! Hey! You in here! BANGLEY!

I was surprised by the force of my shout. Sounded like a stranger.

Bounded down into the workshop. Oddly the big plate window looking to the mountains was intact but there was a string of bullet holes running diagonally up the wall over the hearth. The picture of the skiing family sat unmolested on the side table. Bangley's tools lay where he left them, the barrel and receiver of a Sig Sauer .308, one of his favorite guns, suspended over the worktable in two vises.

Jesus.

Pops behind me.

Your buddy, he said. I knew from our first interview that he would be a badass, else how could a guy like you—

Stopped himself.

Never imagined this.

Bangley!

Desperate. For the first time I felt it claw over me, the desperation like a bad odor. Weird. Never know how you feel about someone until their house is torn open.

Flinched. Pops's hand on my shoulder.

They caught him in here. He was working. It was during the day. Never expected a daytime assault like that. They came in from the front and he survived the first burst and he fought them off. He fought them to a retreat, then went upstairs where he could get a better view, better angle, and fought them from there. Probably only a couple of them had guns.

I bounded up the stairs. Heart gripped. What would I see? Had never been up there, never. The hallway lined with photos of the blonde family. Skiing, sailing, in a bamboo bungalow, palm trees, a yellow lab in a flowerfilled field. Saw all that at speed, taking the hall in running bounds on thick carpet, stopping once to orient myself toward the front of the house where the dormer would be. This room here. Shove open the partially closed door.

A child's room, the boy's. Poster of Linu Linu in a bikini over the bed, the bed covered in a quilt patterned with cowboys on bucking broncos. Butterflies pinned in frames on the wall and an electric guitar in the corner. Also slalom skis. Surfboard, a shortboard mounted on the angled ceiling, bright green graphic of the serpent in the apple tree and a naked Eve standing half turned away, her breast barely covered by the curls of her hair: SIN SURFBOARDS. A signed NASCAR poster. Car number 13.

Two hunting arrows, real ones, were stuck in

the poster and the wall above it was torn with bullet holes.

Two tubs of Copenhagen and a Folgers coffee can spittoon on the floor by the bed. Night vision binocs and two Glocks hanging in their holsters from a hat stand. Jesus. It was the son's room and it was Bangley's. This is where he lived. Fucking A. Preserved like a room in one of those historic museums. I flashed on Bangley's father, the one he had hated—and I thought, He never had a room like this I bet. He was healing himself or following some instinct of compensation or maybe something more weird, who knew, living in this museum, this play set of a room. And there was sunlight coming through the roof. A hole two feet across. No sign of an explosion, how did it get there? Oh. Almost stepped through an equal sized hole in the floor. The questions racing through my head and colliding in a NASCAR pileup. And the window burned. And sandbags stacked to the sill and up the sides. And no sign of Bangley which was at this point a good thing.

I stood in the middle of the room gulping air, catching my breath. Went to the windowless window and looked down at our encampment, our airport, and couldn't help burping up a bubble of stricken laughter.

He could see just about everything: over the low berm across the runway where I slept with

Jasper, right to the dumpster we had dragged away from my house, my house that was a decoy. He could see the porch and front door of that house, down along the line of rusted plane hulks, two sides of the FBO building, the doorway to my hangar. Not much he could not cover from here, which is of course why he had chosen it. Had never occurred to me, don't know why. Or that when I beeped him in the night with an intruder alarm that he could scope the whole scene from here. He would have known how many were stacked behind the dumpster, what they were carrying, how many more were maybe hanging back, knew it all before he sauntered up to our berm in the dark, had probably already planned who he would shoot first and how. Why he never seemed surprised, always seemed way too relaxed to me. Fuck. And the sandbags. He could have probably made the shots with one of his sniper rifles right from here. Fucking Bangley. How far was it? Three hundred yards, maybe. Easy. For him. And I felt standing there rising up in me the revulsion and admiration and I have to say—what? Love, maybe, that I had grown to feel for that certain fucked up individual.

He was good at one thing, really good at it, and the rest he muddled through with unyielding orneriness. One strategy, I guess. And he backed me up. Unfailingly, unhesitant. And, what?

Generously. I mean above and beyond, right? Never even let me know just how in hand he had the whole operation. And so when I left, he knew exactly the increase in threat, in danger. Could probably calibrate it to an exact and lethal degree, the way he would calibrate windage and elevation for one of his long shots from the tower, knew with chilling precision just how in danger he would be living here alone without me and Jasper, then just me, as a warning system. I mean the symbiosis, the extent to which I hadn't even been aware. And that somehow made the surly and ultimately brief resistance to me leaving even more touching. The basket of grenades. Telling me I was family. Telling me in my own way to have a good one, to be safe, not for him, but for me.

And those other trips. The fishing and hunting which he knew were recreational more than anything, or psychological, understood R&R, and which put him at deadly risk. His never once objecting.

This was his room. Kinda touching. Kinda peculiar.

I turned. Pops in the doorway his gray eyes moving over the child's objects, the guns.

That's Bangley in a nutshell, I said.

Well.

Pops's eyes traveling to the sandbagged window.

He didn't die here.

Pops stepped across to the singed hole that used to be the dormer window. Scanned downward, across.

He was wounded here. Pops touched a shredded curtain.

Knew he couldn't stay here, they would burn him out. Knew he had to move, hurt as he was. Had to move and attack. He was a good soldier.

Was?

Pops shrugged.

We both stood there. I couldn't move. I felt frozen.

And then we heard the double shot and the scream.

And then we were running down the hall, down the stairs, through the selectively trashed ground floor, out into the painful sunlight.

The Beast was yards away on the ramp that served as taxiway for these houses on the north. Cima was crouched beside it under the wing trying to make herself as small as the wheel.

Pops stopped short and I bumped into him, almost knocked him to the ground.

Wait.

He shielded his eyes and scanned. She by the plane was crouched and pointing. Toward my hangar which was closed. I mean the part that was still intact. She was okay, had been the sound of the shots that flattened her.

And then Pops was moving.

It's him, he said.

I overtook and passed him in three steps. Never know how you feel about someone until they die and come back. I shoved the hangar door, the one a person uses to walk through, the one cut into the main door which lifts, I hit it so hard I fell into my old digs. Stumbled across the big floor which I had covered in all manner of fine Persians from the other houses, stumbled so hard and headlong I wrenched my back, fuck, and hyperextended a knee, ow, pulled myself erect and stopped and stood like a tree and squinted getting used to the dimness.

There were two corrugated pale translucent panels in the roof that served as lowrent skylights and sort of lit the place with natural daylight when the doors were closed. And saw our couch, the *Valdez*, Jasper's easy chair, the workbench, the stool, the counter in the back where I cooked, and the red linoleum table where we often had our gourmet meals. Nothing else. But heard. Slight scraping like a mouse in the wall. Metallic.

I had a tool chest, rolling drawers, massive red steel, six feet wide. It was beautiful. Took me and Bangley most of a morning to roll it over from the service center hangar, to get it past the frost heaves and potholes, bridging the bad places with planking. It had a place of honor middle of the north wall. Bangley called it Red Square. I need a ratcheting flat wrench, quarter inch, he'd say. Can you get off your butt and go to Red Square and find me one? Please. The scraping came from the chest and the chest was gapped away from the wall. Bangley's steel toed work boot stuck out from behind it. Next to it, against the wall, his grenade launcher, the one he had been working on.

He was covered in dried blood. Looked like someone had dumped a bucket of it down the lower half of him. His eyes were swollen near shut, a white crust of dried mucus or vomit on the side of his face that lay on his arm. His left leg was bent at a weird angle. He lay on his favorite assault rifle, the M4, and his bloody left hand lay over the trigger guard.

A croak guttered from his cracked lips. The words came in the faintest grit of a whisper.

Fuckin Hig.

That's all. And his hand came up stiff as a claw and touched my beard.

★

Touch and go. For two weeks. More. If he died it would be from dehydration, blood loss. He didn't. Tough old bastard. We knew that. Cima didn't want to move him. Set him up on the couch. She set and splinted his leg which was shattered from a bullet in the thigh. She cleaned and sewed shut the hole in his left side which had broken a rib and missed his stomach. The hangar was hot in the afternoon but not too bad with the door up and the hole in the west wall. Took him four days to register my face again. For a few seconds. Lapsed into kind of a coma in between. She got water and Sprite into him with a turkey baster. On the sixth day he opened his eyes while she fed him and stared.

Mrs. Hig, he said.

She said she burst out laughing. Something about his expression, even that: the facial expression of a man half dead. She said it was like a challenge, daring her to deny it, and not devoid of self awareness, something like humor.

Doctor Hig to you, she said. She told me he held her eyes for a significant moment, nodded barely, and went back to sleep.

★

Pops got less tense by the day. I took him up with me in the Beast and flew the circuit. Pointed out the landmarks like a tour guide. Found him a headset and explained as we went. The tower, the river, the distances, which he could see. The high cutbank which formed our moat, the only decent ford across it, the berm. The thirty mile radius to clear the roads, the families.

When we flew over they ran from the garden, the houses, the sheds, a tattered and ragamuffin welcome, waving. The kids jumped up and down. I counted the children: seven. One less, not sure who. Circled, waved, held out a finger. I'll be back.

Cima said Bangley was essentially ICU, needed someone monitoring him 24/7. We took turns. Something about her. Something over the week had grown and flowered, something hibernating in the canyon had come out into the sunlight and liked what it saw. Hard to explain.

In the role of doctor, no doubt there was expertise, an easy competence that needed no thought, a return to a hard won usefulness that made her to me seem bigger. I don't know, taller, broader, a planet with more gravity than it had before. That was part of it. Watch anyone enter their arena of real mastery and you see it, the growing bigger than themselves. Love that. But it was something more too. As if the arrival at this half ravaged airfield on the plains, as alien as it was from anyplace she had lived before—New York, certainly, the mountains and mesas of her upbringing—as if it were an arrival she had been preparing for. For a long time without knowing it. Maybe. I don't know. Seemed that way to me. As if part of her relaxed, as if there were a shucking of some old skin. A husk of herself that had been a barrier I hadn't even been aware of. And in the sloughing off, she opened and flowered. Corny, huh? Not really. Magical. I mean to watch a person let go of something and flower.

I wouldn't know what it is she let go of.

I loved to watch her sitting on the stool which I cut down to couch height, watch her lean over Bangley and talk to him softly, not like doctor to patient, or saintly minister, but with respect, with humor, like two friends. I loved to watch her check the splint, rewrap bandages, her movements more assured even than when she tended the garden with me—the difference between a half grudging second nature and the assurance of pride, of skill hard won and tempered. I loved to watch her push the dark curls out of her face, tie them back with a string or stretch her long arms and wander out into the blaze of summer sun and walk across the ramp to where the lambs were tethered inside a fence Pops had built in the shade of a globe willow. I loved to watch her undress and dive into the pond by the river and stand as she stood in the spray that first evening and beckon me in. She was simply the most beautiful being Big Hig had ever seen.

We slept in the open on the ground where I had always slept. With Jasper. But we made a willow screen, and we opened two of the flannel sleeping bags and spread them on a double mattress we hauled out of my house, the one with the porch, and I slept as I never had, not since. We slept often holding each other in a tangle of arms and legs which I had never been able to do, not with anyone. I woke in the middle of the night as I used to do and propped my head on my arms and watched the stars and counted constellations and made up others, but now I did it with the pressure of her elbow in my cheek—move it gently over—her hair in my mouth, her thigh over mine and with a sense of having been spared and having been blessed.

Still, some nights I grieved. I grieved as much at what I knew must be the fleeting nature of my present happiness as any loss, any past. We lived on some edge, if we ever lived on a rolling plain. Who knew what attack, what illness. That doubleness again. Like flying: the stillness and speed, serenity and danger. The way we could gobble up space in the Beast and seem to barely move, that sense of being in a painting.

We made love as if the whole thing were new somehow. Maybe because we had to do it so gently, so slowly. Sometimes she moved onto me and took me ever so gently inside and straddled me and we lay still so still the stars moved behind her and we moved infinitesimally and it was somehow like a conversation and it filled me with a happiness, a welling joy I can't come close to reckoning.

Pops took a house next to Bangley's, took an

upstairs room with a view down the airfield, ever the tactician, the two like peas in a pod in some way. And sandbagged the one window and introduced himself to Bangley one morning and asked deferentially if he could borrow one of Bangley's rifles, the Sig Sauer. Bangley was well enough by then, it was the tenth or eleventh day, well enough to sit up on the couch and look Pops over, to speak through his sewed up lip.

The other old guy, Bangley croaked. That was the first thing he said.

Pops cracked a half grin and it went straight across, and I thought Fuckin A, they almost smile the same. Bangley's hands were bandaged and Pops reached over and touched his forearm. The gesture was touching and respectful.

That was a fight you put up.

Bangley looked at him steadily out of those eyes that could fragment, go kaleidoscopic. Didn't say anything.

Ten or twelve huh? Maybe three armed.

Fourteen, Bangley rasped. Fourteen and four.

Pops nodded.

What went through the roof?

Rock. Or some damn thing. Had a goddamn light cannon.

They picked up their dead.

Bangley made his best simulacrum of a shrug.

I guess, he croaked. After a silence he said, They bunched once.

His throat caught and he cleared it.

Thought I was dead. In the house. I hit them with the grenade launcher. Took two more on the way here. That was enough. For them.

Bangley studied what he must have been surmising was his new friend.

Who were you with? he said finally.

Navy SEALs, Pops said. Afghanistan. Other places.

Bangley nodded, barely.

Dressed like goddamn Mongols. Six of them female. Had bows. Knew how . . .

He trailed off, his eyes turning, coalescing around some memory. The slightest tremor running through his body.

Pops waited. If anyone knew.

I wondered, he said finally. I took the house just to the northeast. Wondered if I could borrow that Sig for a while. While you're in the hospital.

Bangley took a while to refocus. When he did he half nodded. That your daughter? Was his answer.

★

I took her to see the families. She wanted to go as soon as I landed with Pops. She took her medic bag. We landed on the drive and they came from everywhere, some running, some barely able to walk, mustered like some ragtag company along their quarantine line in the yard. We got out and I watched their expressions change as Cima approached. The dark ringed eyes widened in surprise, the lantern jaws fell open, the little ones like curious and half frightened deer, the heads coming forward. If they'd had swiveling ears they would have swiveled, the looks back to their mothers, the excitement.

Cima stepped right across the DMZ, and as one they fell back half a step, almost cringing, and opened a cove of space before her. She held up a long, strong, bruised hand.

It's okay. I'm a doctor.

As if that explained anything. She smiled. Realized how absurd and archaic.

Hi, I'm Cima.

It may have been her bruises, a subtle sense of frailty, of having survived a terrible sickness. I watched their faces. A few waved, nodded to me, smiled, but. They were studying her with a fascination, a curiosity that almost overcame fear, some kindred welcoming. Of a being maybe that was somehow like them, they weren't sure how. And different, too, different enough to kindle a fierce wonder. Well. They were Mennonites. A visitation was in their ken. And I thought I was the descending angel. I stood there in the yard for the first time ever not knowing what to do with my big hands, feeling like chopped liver and laughing in surprised and uncomfortable guffs.

And. She was a doctor. But.

Cima—I called.

She half turned.

They—

They. Of course she knew they were contagious. We had talked about it minutes before.

She held up a hand, a gesture of All Okay, and also a little of dismissal, and I had to laugh again. How times change. They had closed the cove around her into a circle and I knew that she had already seduced them or won them, that they loved her as I had loved her, I knew from the first moments.

The children reached out, clung to her skirt, one little girl, I think her name was Lily, Lily held her leg like a bear cub hugs a tree.

Hi! I heard Cima say. Hi. You *are* pretty. What's your name? And you? And this handsome little guy.

The wonder of being touched by a stranger. No longer untouchable.

I was worried but. Almost worth whatever would come just to see that scene.

She set up in a room in the old farmhouse what would have then been quaintly called the parlor, and she examined them all. She put on latex gloves. I could see them on her hands as she opened the door to the kitchen and called in the next. Gently. Must have had a stash in her bag. She sewed up bad cuts, dressed wounds, called for buckets of warm water. She counseled a young woman six or seven months pregnant. Consoled, I knew, an older man whose weeping could be heard from outside the screen kitchen door. She told me it was okay for me to come across, to mingle, it was a misperception. Like Hep C, she said. Like HIV used to be. Fluid transfer, blood. Otherwise—

The misperception that had saved their lives. The big signs along the fences at the edge of their fields THE BLOOD. The terror that evoked. The truth of it for anyone with a pair of binoculars to see: the wasted figures bent as if into a stiff wind, the exhausted movements, the hollow eyes. Kept them away, all attackers, preserved their lives as it killed them.

We flew back in silence despite the good headsets.

That night we lay out by the berm, lay close together. Both on our backs, both studying reefs of luminous clouds that tore off from banks over the mountains. They were rinsed by a half moon, and shuddered from within with heat lightning. I watched them fly over and hoped a big rain would send us running into the hangar to be Bangley's roommates. The country could use some rain. She said

There were studies at the end. A few convincing reports.

On the blood?

Mm hm.

I waited.

They suggested that the onset of the auto-immune disease was speeded by a breakdown in the body's ability to make its own vitamin D. Really a curious mechanism. Like AIDS with T cells. I mean if there is any known analog.

She paused, watched the clouds.

I love it when you talk like that.

She elbowed my ear.

There was no evidence that the converse is true. Hadn't gotten that far yet. All so new.

That vitamin D could slow the process?

Yes.

Maybe we'll have to make a run to Walmart.

She was quiet. We watched the clouds. They tore off but never thickened. Not over us. The rain, if there was rain, stayed on the peaks.

Hey, I murmured, wanna hear my favorite poem? It was written in the ninth century, in China.

I thought she was thinking medical thoughts, but then I felt her twitch against me. Not the nightmare twitches Jasper sometimes had but the twitch of falling, of letting go.

★

On or about. The best I can say now. Bangley had checked off the calendar in my hangar until the

372

attack which I thought especially thoughtful. But. So we knew that happened on June 19th. But he never could say afterward how many days he had been lying behind Red Square. At least a week he thought.

On or about the 4th of July I was working in the garden. Killing potato bugs one at a time. Cima was with the families. I had dropped her off in the morning and she said to pick her up for dinner, she wanted to be there all day. She was dispensing a vitamin D infusion, but I knew it was for the children. She couldn't stay away from them.

I was working in the garden. She was away. Bangley was playing chess with Pops. That's what they did. They sat on the porch of my house in the creaking chairs and played chess like it was a country store in some apocalyptic parody of Norman Rockwell. Bangley's cane against the rail. He was better at chess, but his mind wandered and then Pops could beat him.

I was squashing potato bugs between my fingers and I heard a sound that I had heard so often I didn't look up. But. It had been a long time. I craned my head, wincing eyes past the sun and there: two vapor trails. Parallel but one behind. And the distant dopplered rush of receding engines.

Not dreaming, no.

I hadn't run so fast. In years. Got to the Beast

and hit the master switch and flipped on the radio. I had a Narco scanner which ran the digits, the frequencies up through the silence and nothing. Static. Around and around went the numbers. Stopped like a roulette wheel. A break, a fraying of the grayness. A voice, words. Before I pushed the mike button I made myself listen and I couldn't understand. It was Arabic. Had to be. A conversation, laughter. Heading west at thirty thousand feet. Heading probably to California. From up there, we, our airport, would be indistinguishable from the rest of the landscape, the decaying infrastructure. I called and called. **The two jets, 747s, Erie, two 747s Erie. Boeing 747s who just overflew Denver, this is Erie.** I called and called. Until my voice was hoarse and the streamers of steam were a white memory, a mirage. I stared after them kind of stunned. Good or bad?

A week later, exactly, two more. About the same time. And the next week. The fourth week nothing. The four of us gathered on the porch at the afternoon hour like waiting for some fireworks or a dignitary. And nothing.

★

They could have immunity, she said. A race could have immunity. Or clusters of immunity. The Arab countries are tribal. An entire tribe could be immune.

In September, two more flew over. Never answered my calls.

★

We sleep outside into October. Maybe we will all winter. The way Jasper and I used to do. Piling on the quilts. Sleep some frosty nights with wool hats on, with just our noses sticking out. Head to head or butt to butt. We name the winter constellations and when we run out of the ones we know—Orion, Taurus, Pleiades, the Chariot—we make them up. Mine are almost always animals, hers almost always food—the Sourdough Pancake with Syrup, the Soft Shell Crab au Gratin. I name one for a scrappy, fish loving dog.

★

I still dream Jasper is alive. Before that my heart will not go.

★

My favorite poem, the one by Li Shang-Yin:

When Will I Be Home?

When will I be home? I don't know.
In the mountains, in the rainy night,
The Autumn lake is flooded.
Someday we will be back together again.
We will sit in the candlelight by the West
    window.
And I will tell you how I remembered you
Tonight on the stormy mountain.

Acknowledgments

Many friends and family have contributed insight and energy to the making of this book. To my first readers, Kim Yan Heller, Lisa Jones, Jay Heinrichs, Rebecca Rowe, Helen Thorpe, John Heller, Pete Beveridge, and Caro Heller I am deeply indebted. I cannot thank you enough. Lisa, as always, was a fearless and invaluable reader and guide. Helen's words came at the perfect time. John and Caro, my parents, have been the bravest, most creative role models.

For their close reading and expert knowledge, huge thanks to Jason Hicks; Jeff Streeter; Donna Gershten; Mike Gugeler; Kirk Johnson; and Jason Elliott, Navy SEAL. Thanks to Janis Hallowell, Nathan Fischer, Mark Lough, Ted Steinway, and David Grinspoon for more help.

Carlton Cuse was a source of great inspiration. Bobby Reedy put me on a special creek with a fly rod years ago. And thanks to Bobby and Jason Elliott for initiating me into the fearsome power of a sniper rifle.

Thanks to Brad Wieners for the first flying story and all the others.

David Halpern has been a friend and champion for many years. Without him, this book would not have been realized. I am profoundly grateful. Thanks to Kathy Robbins for everything. To Louise Quayle for such fine work. And to Charlotte Mendelson for her discernment and enthusiasm.

To my brilliant editor Jenny Jackson, I raise a glass.

And to Dave Hoerner, one of the greatest bush pilots who ever flew, thanks for teaching me to fly.

A Note About the Author

Peter Heller holds an MFA from the Iowa Writers' Workshop in both fiction and poetry. An award-winning adventure writer and longtime contributor to NPR, Heller is a contributing editor at *Outside* magazine, *Men's Journal*, and *National Geographic Adventure*, and a regular contributor to *Bloomberg Businessweek*. He is also the author of several nonfiction books, including *Kook*, *The Whale Warriors*, and *Hell or High Water: Surviving Tibet's Tsangpo River*. He lives in Denver, Colorado.

copyright information continued from page 4:

Excerpt from "'When Will I Be Home?' by Li Shang Yin" from *One Hundred More Poems from the Chinese* by Kenneth Rexroth.
Copyright © 1970 by Kenneth Rexroth. Reprinted by permission of New Directions Publishing Corp.

Excerpt from "Farms on the Great Plains" from *The Way It Is: New and Selected Poems* by William Stafford. Copyright © 1959, 1998 by William Stafford and the Estate of William Stafford. Reprinted by permission of The Permissions Company, Inc., on behalf of Graywolf Press, Minneapolis, Minnesota, www.graywolfpress.org.

Center Point Large Print
600 Brooks Road / PO Box 1
Thorndike ME 04986-0001 USA

(207) 568-3717

US & Canada:
1 800 929-9108
www.centerpointlargeprint.com

MONSTER
MISSION

Eva Ibbotson

CF KS2

CITY OF YORK

2 0 NOV 2009

LIBRARIES

440

First published in 1999
by Macmillan Children's Books
This Large Print edition published by
BBC Audiobooks Ltd
by arrangement with
Macmillan Children's Books
2005

ISBN 1 4056 6057 0

Text copyright © 1999 Eva Ibbotson

The right of Eva Ibbotson to be
identified as the author of this work
has been asserted by her in accordance
with the Copyright, Designs and
Patents Act 1988

All rights reserved

British Library Cataloguing in Publication Data

Ibbotson, Eva
 Monster mission.—Large print ed.
 1. Kidnapping—Juvenile fiction 2. Fantasy fiction
 3. Children's stories 4. Large type books
 I. Title
 823.9'14[J]

ISBN-10: 1-4056-6057-0

Printed and bound in Great Britain by
Antony Rowe Ltd., Chippenham, Wiltshire

To my husband, who really cared about unusual creatures

CHAPTER ONE

Kidnapping children is not a good idea. All the same, sometimes it has to be done.

Aunt Etta and Aunt Coral and Aunt Myrtle were not natural kidnappers. For one thing, they were getting old and kidnapping is hard work; for another, though they looked a little odd, they were very caring people. They cared for their ancient father and for their shrivelled cousin Sybil who lived in a cave and tried to foretell the future—and most particularly they cared for the animals on the island on which they lived, many of which were quite unusual.

Some of the creatures that made their way to the Island had come far across the ocean to be looked after, and lately the aunts had felt that they could not go on much longer without help. And 'help' didn't mean grown-ups who were set in their ways. Help meant children who were young and strong and willing to learn.

So on a cool blustery day in April the three aunts gathered round the kitchen table and decided to go ahead. Some children had to be found and they had to be brought to the island, and kidnapping seemed the only sensible way to do it.

'That way we can choose the ones that are suitable,' said Aunt Etta. She was the eldest; a tall, bony woman who did fifty press-ups before breakfast and had a small but not at all unpleasant moustache on her upper lip.

The others looked out of the window at the soft green turf, the sparkling sea, and sighed, thinking of what had to be done. The sleeping powders, the drugged hamburgers, the bags and sacks and cello cases they would need to carry the children away in . . .

'Will they scream and wriggle, do you suppose?' asked Aunt Myrtle, who was the youngest. She suffered from headaches and hated noise.

'No, of course not. They'll be unconscious,' said Aunt Etta. 'Flat out. I don't like it any more than you do,' she went on, 'but you saw the programme on TV last week.'

The others nodded. When they first came to the Island they hadn't had any electricity, but after his hundredth birthday their father's toes had started to

2

turn blue because not enough blood got to his feet and they had ordered a generator so that he could have an electric blanket. After that they thought they might as well have an electric kettle, and then a TV.

But the TV had been a mistake because of the nature programmes. Nature programmes always end badly. First you see the hairy-nosed wombats frisking about with their babies and then five minutes before the end you hear that there are only twelve breeding pairs left in the whole of Australia. Or there are pictures of the harlequin frogs of Costa Rica croaking away on their lily leaves and the next minute you are told that they're doomed because their swamps are being drained. Worst of all are the rainforests. The aunts could never see a programme about the rainforests without crying, and last week there had been a particularly bad one with wicked people burning and slashing the trees, and pictures of the monkeys and the jaguars rushing away in terror.

'What if *we* became extinct?' Aunt Coral had wondered, blowing her nose. 'Not just the wombats and the harlequin frogs and the jaguars, but *us*.'

The others had seen the point at once. If a whole rainforest can become extinct why not three elderly ladies? And if they became extinct what would happen to their work and who would care for the creatures that came to the Island in search of comfort and of care?

There was another thing which bothered the aunts. Lately the animals that came to the Island simply wouldn't go away again. Long after they were healed they stayed on—it was almost as if they knew something—and that made more and more work for the aunts. There was no doubt about it, help had to be brought in, and quickly.

So now they were deciding what to do.

'How do we find the *right* children?' asked Myrtle as she looked longingly out at the point where the seals were resting. One of the seals, Herbert, was her special friend and she would very much rather have been out there playing her cello to him and singing her songs.

'We shall become *Aunts*,' said Etta firmly, settling her spectacles on her long nose.

The others looked at her in amazement. 'But we *are* aunts,' they said. 'How can we *become* them?'

4

This was true. There had been five sisters who had come to the Island with their father many years ago. They had found a ruined house and deserted beaches with only the footprints of sandpipers and dunlins on the sand, and barnacle geese resting on the way from Greenland, and the seals, quite unafraid, coming out of the water to have their pups.

They had started to repair the house, and planted a garden, and then one day they had found an oiled seabird washed up on a rock . . . Only it turned out not to be an oiled seabird. It was oiled all right, but it was something quite different—and after that they realized that they had been called to the Island by a Higher Power and that they had found their life's work.

But one of the sisters, Betty, had not cared for the Island. She hated the wind and the rain and the fish scales in her tea and the eider ducklings nesting in her bedroom slippers and she had gone away and got married to a tax inspector in Newcastle upon Tyne and now she lived in a house with three kinds of toilet freshener in the loo, and sprays to make her armpits smell nice, and not a fish scale in sight.

5

But the point was that she had two children. They were horrible, but they were children. She called the boy Boo-Boo and the girl Little One (though they had proper names of course). But horrible though they were, they were children and because of this her sisters had become aunts since all you have to do to become an aunt is have nephews and nieces.

Which is why now the sisters looked so surprised and said: 'But we *are* aunts.'

'Not that kind,' said Etta impatiently. 'I mean the kind that live in an office or an agency and call themselves things like *Useful Aunts* or *Universal Aunts* or *Aunts Inc.*—the kind that parents pay to take their children to school and to the dentist, or to sit with them when they are ill.'

'Why don't the parents do it themselves?' asked Myrtle.

'Because they're too busy. People used to have real aunts and grandmothers and cousins to do it all, but now families are too small and real aunts go to dances and have boyfriends,' said Etta, snorting.

Coral nodded her head. She was the arty one, a large plump person who fed the chickens in a feather boa and interesting jewellery, and at night by the light of the moon she danced the tango.

'It's a good idea,' she said. 'You would be able to pick and choose the children—you don't want to end up with a Boo-Boo or a Little One.'

'Yes, but if the parents are truly fond of the children we shouldn't do it,' said Myrtle, pushing back her long grey hair.

'Well of course not,' said Etta. 'We don't want a hue and cry.'

'But if the children are nice the parents *would* be fond of them,' said Myrtle. 'And if they aren't we don't want them either.'

Etta sniffed. 'You'd be surprised. There are children all over the place whose parents don't know how lucky they are.'

They went on talking for a long time but no one could think of anything better than Etta's plan—not if the position of the Island was to be kept secret, and there was nothing more important than that.

There was one more aunt who would have been useful—not the one with the three kinds of toilet freshener, who was no use for anything—but Aunt Dorothy, who was next in age to Etta and would have been just the sort of person to have on a kidnapping expedition. But Dorothy

7

was in prison in Hong Kong. She had gone out there to stop a restaurant owner from serving pangolin steaks—pangolins are beautiful creatures and are getting rare and should never be eaten—and Dorothy had got annoyed and hit the restaurant owner on the head with his own wok, and they had put her in prison. She was due out in a month but in the meantime only the three of them could go on the mission and they weren't at all sure about Myrtle because she was not very good out in the world and when she was away she always pined for Herbert.

'Are you sure you wouldn't rather stay behind, Myrtle?' said Coral now. But Myrtle had decided to be brave and said she thought that she should come along and do her bit.

'Only we won't say anything to Daddy,' said Etta. 'After all, kidnapping is a crime and he might worry.'

Captain Harper lived upstairs in a big bed with a telescope, looking out to sea. They had mostly given up telling him things. For one thing, he was stone deaf so that explaining anything took a very long time, and for another, as soon as he saw anybody he started telling them stories about what life had been like when he was a boy. They were good stories but every single aunt had heard them about three hundred times so they didn't hang around if they could help it.

But they did go and tell the Sybil. She was the old cousin who had come to the Island soon after them. Sybil was bookish and one day she had read a book about Greek mythology and about a person called *the* Sybil (not just Sybil) who was a prophetess and could foretell the future. So she had started prophesying about the weather, mumbling on about depressions over Iceland and the wind-chill factor and really she didn't get it wrong much more often than the weathermen on the telly. Then she had gone on to other things, and had gone to live in a cave with bats because that was where prophetesses were supposed to live, and had stopped washing because she said washing would weaken her powers, so that she was another person one did not visit for too long.

When the aunts told her that they were going to the mainland to kidnap some children the Sybil got quite excited. Her face turned blue and her hair began to stand on end and for a moment they hoped that she was going to tell them something important about the journey.

But it turned out that what she was foreseeing was squally showers, and what she said was 'take seasick pills', which they had decided to do anyway for the boat.

They still had to make sure that their cook, who was called Art, knew exactly what to do while they were away on their mission. Art was an escaped convict who had been washed up in a rowing boat on their shore. He had killed a man when he was young, and now he wouldn't kill anything with arms or legs or eyes—not even a shrimp—but he made excellent porridge. Then they gathered together all the things they would need: chloroform and sleeping powders and anaesthetizing darts which they used for stunning animals that were injured so that they could set their limbs. All of them had things to carry the children away in: Aunt Etta had a canvas holdall and Aunt Coral had a tin trunk with holes bored into it and Aunt Myrtle had her cello case. As they waited for the wind to change so that they could sail the *Peggoty* to the next island and catch the steamer, they were terribly excited.

It was a long and difficult journey—

many years ago the army had tried to use the Island for experiments in radio signals and so as to keep its position secret they had changed the maps and forbidden boats to come near it. In the end they hadn't used it after all but it was still a forgotten place and the aunts meant to see that it stayed that way.

'Of course it won't be a real kidnap because we shan't ask the parents for a ransom,' said Etta.

'It'll be more of a child snatch,' Coral agreed.

But whether it was a kidnap or a child snatch, it was still dangerous and wicked, and as they waved goodbye to the Island their hearts were beating very fast.

CHAPTER TWO

By the time she was ten years old Minette had made the journey between London and Edinburgh forty-seven times. Forty-seven station buffet sandwiches; forty-seven visits to the be on the train and forty-seven stomach-aches because changing families always churned up her insides.

Minette's father lived in Edinburgh in a tall grey house and was a Professor of Grammar. Minette's mother lived in a flat in London and was an actress—at least she would have been if anyone had given her any work. They had been separated since Minette was three years old and they hated each other with a bitter and deadly hatred.

'Tell that louse of a father of yours that he's late with his money again,' was the sort of message that Minette's mother usually sent as she took her daughter to King's Cross to put her on the train to Edinburgh. Or:

'No doubt your mother is still running a doss-house for drunken actors,' her father would say as he fetched her from the train.

Minette never gave her parents these messages. She made up polite friendly messages for them to send each other but neither her mother nor her father believed her when she delivered them. And on the journey, which took five hours when she first began to travel, Minette would look out of the window searching for houses where she and her mother and her father would live together one day like an ordinary family with a cat

12

and a canary and a dog. For it went on hurting her, hurting and hurting—not that her parents were separated; lots of children she knew had separated parents—but that they hated each other so much.

On these journeys Minette was usually put in the charge of an aunt. The aunt came from an office called *Useful Aunts* and what she was like was important because if she talked all the time or wanted to play silly games, Minette couldn't give her mind to finding houses for her parents to live in, or imagining beautiful scenes where she was run over and taken to hospital and her mother and father rushed to her bedside and looked at each other over their daughter's bleeding body and found that they loved each other after all.

Then as she got up to go on her forty-eighth journey, Minette suddenly realized that it didn't matter *what* kind of aunt they sent to take her because she had given up hope. Her parents would always hate each other and she would spend the rest of her life travelling from London to Edinburgh and back again, never quite knowing which was her home or where she properly belonged.

And as though someone Up There had heard her, they sent her that day a quite extraordinary aunt.

She was so unlike the other aunts she had travelled with that both Minette and her mother stopped dead as they came up to where she waited, by the bookstall on Platform One of King's Cross Station.

'Are you . . . ?' began Mrs Danby.

The woman nodded. She was very tall with a small moustache and carried a large holdall which smelled slightly of fish.

'I am your aunt,' she said in a deep voice and pointed to her lapel on which there was a label saying *Unusual Aunts* and above that the words 'My name is Etta'.

If Minette's mother hadn't been in a hurry to go to the cinema with her latest boyfriend she might have asked more questions. After all an *Unusual Aunt is* not quite the same as a *Useful* one, but as it was she handed over the money for the tickets and Minette's lunch, took the cigarette out of her mouth long enough to kiss her daughter, and went away.

And presently Minette and the aunt sat opposite each other in one of those old-fashioned compartments which have no

14

corridor and watched the train make its way through the London suburbs.

Aunt Etta and her sisters had had a hard week in London. They found a boarding house full of people like themselves—aunt-like persons who had come to town to show their pug dogs at dog shows or go to meetings about setting up retirement homes for ancient donkeys. But they hated the noise and the traffic and the dirty air, and they did not find it easy to get taken on by an agency.

Even when Etta got her label and was sent out on jobs, the children she was given were unspeakable. She took a little boy on a trip down the river who spent the whole time stuffing himself with ice cream and popcorn and crisps and dropping the wrappers in the water. She was sent to take a small girl to have her teeth cleaned and saw her bite the dentist's hand, and she sat with a whining brat called Tarquin Sterndale-Fish who had the measles.

So by the time she met Minette on King's Cross Station, Etta had begun to think that this kidnapping idea was pretty stupid. The world seemed to be full of Boo-Boos and Little Ones and it was better to become extinct, like the

15

rainforests, than to bring such children to the Island.

Her first sight of Minette did not make her feel hopeful. The child had a crumpled, pinched sort of look; she was small for her age and very thin and looked as though she had been born tired. A wet and feeble child would be quite useless for the work that had to be done. She was also very stupidly dressed with a load of fluffy pom-poms in her long brown hair and a T-shirt which said *Pinch me and I'll squeal*—and a pink plastic handbag shaped like a heart dangled from her shoulder.

And if Aunt Etta did not like the look of Minette, Minette was not in the least keen on Aunt Etta.

For a while the two of them sat in silence. From time to time a drop of water fell from the canvas holdall that the aunt had put on the luggage rack on to her topknot of grey hair, but she did not seem to notice it.

'Is something leaking?' asked Minette.

The aunt looked up and shook her head. 'The canvas never seems to dry out properly. I use it to move seals about. Only pups of course; a full-grown seal would never fit inside.'

Minette began to be interested; her face lost its pinched and troubled look. 'Are you a vet, then?'

'Not exactly. But that does sort of come into it.'

There was another silence. Minette did not like to pry so she looked out of the window again. They were coming to the first of the dream houses which Minette had chosen to live in with her parents. It was an old station-master's house with hanging baskets of flowers and a little gable. And as though she read her thoughts, the aunt said: 'What a pleasant place to live in. There might be ghost trains going through at night with interesting spectres. That could liven things up.'

Minette stared at her. 'Do you believe in—'

'Of course,' said the aunt briskly. 'Certainly. I believe in almost everything, don't you?'

'My father says we mustn't believe anything we can't see or prove,' she said.

'Really?'

When they had been travelling for an hour, Minette opened her suitcase and became very busy. She had been wearing pink and orange socks with a border of

17

Mickey Mice. Now she took them off and put on plain white ones. Then she removed the T-shirt which said *Pinch me and I'll squeal* and put on a navy-blue one with long sleeves and no writing at all. And lastly she put the dangling handbag back in the suitcase and took out a practical leather purse.

The aunt said nothing, watching as Minette changed from a trendy little dresser to a sensible old-fashioned schoolgirl.

But Minette had not finished. She took out her brush and comb, propped a mirror on her knees, and began to plait her hair into two long, tight pigtails.

'I always change here,' she explained, 'because there's nothing interesting to look at out of the window. My father doesn't like clothes with writing on. Or funny socks. He thinks they're vulgar. And he hates untidy hair.'

'And when you come back you change back again—put on the pom-poms and unplait your hair?'

'Yes. My mother likes it loose.'

'And you? Which do you like?'

Minette sighed. 'I'd like it cut short.'

'Well I have some scissors here. Why don't we cut it?' She opened a very large

18

handbag and took out a pair of scissors.

'Oh no! I couldn't. Then *both* of them would be angry.'

Aunt Etta shrugged and dropped the scissors back into her bag. 'Actually long hair can be useful.'

'How can it?'

'Oh for polishing things . . . oyster shells and suchlike. And if you fell into the water it would be something to get hold of.'

They had come to the second of Minette's dream houses, a low white house on the bend of a river with a willow tree and a garden sloping down to the water. But this time Minette did not see her mother and father taking tea together on the lawn. She heard her father saying, 'That willow must come down, it cuts off all the light,'—and her mother saying, 'If you cut that tree down I'll have you put in a mental home.'

And suddenly, for no reason, she told this strange woman about her endless journeys from her mother's tiny flat with its smell of face powder and curry from the takeaway downstairs, and the tights dripping in the bathroom, to her father's cold, tidy, solemn house with its ticking grandfather clock. And about the silly

19

dreams she'd had of bringing them together and the hopelessness of it all.

'Do you think there might be a third place? Not my father's house or my mother's flat but somewhere else—by the sea perhaps? And that one day I might find it?'

She drew back, suddenly frightened, because the fierce aunt was looking at her far too intently.

But Aunt Etta was nodding. 'Of course,' she said. 'Of course there is a third place. There is one for everybody. But it's no good filling it up with people from your old life. If you want to find the third place you must find it alone.'

'But I'm a child. I can't go and live alone.'

'Perhaps not. Not exactly, but you might be able to make a new start just the same if you had the courage.'

'I don't have courage,' said Minette firmly. 'I'm a coward.' It was one of the few things on which her parents agreed. 'I'm frightened of the dark and of diving off the top board and of being bullied.'

The train stopped at York and the aunt bought sandwiches off a trolley. 'Now I suggest you go and wash your hands and freshen up,' she said, 'because it's time we had our lunch. Which of these sandwiches would you like—egg and cress or cheese and tomato?'

'Cheese and tomato, please.'

If Minette had known what was going to happen as soon as she had gone she would have been very scared indeed. For out of the pocket of her long navy-blue knickers the aunt took a little box with a brownish powder which she sprinkled carefully into the centre of the cheese and tomato sandwich. Then she unzipped the holdall and sat back in her seat with a very contented smile.

'My first one,' she murmured to herself. 'My very first one. Oh really, this is most exciting!' And then: 'I wonder how Coral is getting on?'

*   *   *

It had been much harder to get Coral to look like an Agency Aunt. She was the plump one who had been to art school when she was young, and she liked to stand out from the crowd, but she had done her best to look sensible. She only wore two necklaces and one pair of dangly earrings and the hand-painted squiggles on her robe and matching turban were *peaceful* squiggles, so that when she rang the bell of the big house in Mayfair she felt that she looked as aunt-like as she ever would.

The idea of fetching Hubert-Henry Mountjoy from his grandparents' London house and taking him back to his boarding school in Berkshire made Aunt Coral feel extremely glum.

Her first batch of children had been as bad as Etta's: a poisonous, podgy child who had tried to kick her shins, and a little boy who jumped on a beetle in the park. She was sure that Hubert-Henry Mountjoy would not be her cup of tea—a cold-eyed, snotty little aristo too big for his boots—and she had decided that if she caught him jumping on beetles she would wallop him hard and give up being an aunt and go home.

As she was shown into the Mountjoys' hall by a toffee-nosed maid, she felt worse than ever. The house was huge and dark and cold; there was a big brass gong in one corner; paintings of dead Mountjoys with handlebar moustaches hung on the walls. She waited for her first sight of Hubert-Henry in his school uniform with the deepest gloom.

The door of the drawing room opened.

A small boy came out, pushed forward by a tall, white-haired man who looked exactly like the men in the portraits except that he wasn't dead—and her mouth dropped very slightly open.

Hubert-Henry was small and lightly built with jet-black hair, olive skin and huge, very dark eyes. Something about the graceful way he moved and the wary look on his face reminded her of pictures she had seen of the children of South America who made their home among the vines and orchids and broad-leaved trees of the tropical forest.

The old man with the handlebar moustache now spoke. 'This is Hubert-Henry,' he said in a braying voice. 'As you see he was not born an English gentleman—but we mean to see that he becomes one, eh, Hubert?'

And as he dug the silent little boy in the ribs, Aunt Coral saw a look of such hatred pass over the child's face that she took a step backwards and hit her backside on the big brass gong. At which point Hubert-Henry threw back his head and laughed.

*   *   *

23

Half an hour later, they sat side by side in a large black car on the way to Hubert's school. The car was a closed limo and was the kind you hire for weddings and funerals, with a glass partition sealing off the chauffeur. It was a three-hour journey to Berkshire but the driver had refused to take Hubert-Henry by himself, so Aunt Coral was to deliver him to Greymarsh Towers and hand him over to the matron. The little boy, it seemed, had tried to jump from the train and run away the last time they took him back to his boarding school.

'Are you really called Hubert-Henry?' asked Aunt Coral as they began to leave London behind.

'No.'

'What are you called?'

'Fabio.'

He had a slight accent. Spanish, perhaps? Or Portuguese?

She hoped he would say more but he sat silent and sulky. Then: 'I said I'd bash the next aunt they fobbed me off with. Bash her really hard.'

'Oh, I wouldn't do that,' said Coral. 'I've got a kick like a mule. It's the hair, you see?'

'What hair?'

'The hair on my legs. We've all got hairy legs, me and my sisters. Hair gives you strength; it says so in the Bible. Samson and all that.'

But she wasn't really thinking about what she was saying. Aunt Coral was a little bit psychic, as artistic people so often are—which means that she sometimes knew things without knowing how she knew them—and now she dug into her basket, took out a pad and a piece or charcoal and began to draw.

Fabio, still sulky, turned his head away. When she had finished, she put the picture down on the seat between them. Presently she heard a little gasp. The boy had seized the paper and was devouring it with his eyes, and she saw a single tear run down his cheek.

'Is that what your home was like?' she asked gently.

Fabio nodded. 'The tree's right; it was a papaya, and the monkey . . . he was a capuchin and I tamed him. But there were three huts joined together, not just one—we lived in the end one closest to the river. The chickens were ours but the goat belonged to my uncle in the middle house. You've got the pig right, but his stomach was even bigger—it touched the ground.'

'So why did you leave, Fabio?' she asked. The homesick child was still staring at the picture she had drawn; the river, the great tree with fruit hanging from its branches and the fishing boat drawn up on the shore.

'I don't know *exactly*,' he said. But he told her what he knew and she pieced the rest together.

His father, Henry Mountjoy, had been an Englishman, rich, and the owner of a big house in the country; but he was a gambler. He got into debt and in the end he had gone off to South America to find gold.

Only of course he didn't find gold. He fell ill and Fabio's mother, who was a dancer in a nightclub, had found him half starving in Rio, and had nursed him, and after a while he married her.

But he'd ruined his health and he couldn't get work and soon after Fabio was born he went back to England. Since then Fabio had lived first with his mother in Rio and then, when she moved in with another man, upriver in the forest with his grand-parents and his uncle and his cousins. There were a lot of people in the three huts and very little money but

26

Fabio had been perfectly happy. His grandfather was an Amorian Indian and knew everything, and his grandmother had worked as a cook for a Portuguese planter and had told the most marvellous stories.

Then just over a year ago his mother had come with an Englishman in a silly suit who kept mopping his face all the time and wrinkled up his nose when he passed the pig. It turned out that Fabio's father had died and on his deathbed had begged his parents, the old Mountjoys, to bring Fabio to England and bring him up as an English gentleman.

That was the beginning of the nightmare. His mother had insisted that he went. Henry Mountjoy had talked so much about his grand house in England that she wanted her son to have his share. But the grand house had been sold to pay Henry's debts, and Henry's parents took one look at the wild little boy and shuddered.

Since the grandparents were too old to turn Fabio into an English gentleman, this odd thing was to be done in a boarding school. But boarding schools, according to the old Mountjoys, had gone soft. They had tried two from which Fabio

27

had returned much as before, only speaking better English.

Greymarsh Towers, though, was different. The headmaster believed not just in cold baths and stiff upper lips but in all sorts of things that one would have thought didn't happen any more, and the boys were vile.

'They call me "monkey" or "chopsticks" and try to tie me up. But I'm going to kill them this time. I'm going to kill them and I'm going to kill the headmaster and they can take me to prison and I don't care!'

But before he could get round to killing the headmaster, Fabio started being sick.

He was sick outside Slough, and on the far side of Maidenhead and in the entrance of a house called The Laurels in Reading, and the closer they got to Greymarsh Towers, the sicker Fabio became.

And when she saw Greymarsh Towers, Coral thought that she too would be sick if she had to return there. It was a huge bleak house with iron bars across the windows, and the stone walls looked slimy and cold.

It was now time to act. The chauffeur

was supposed to drop them at the school and she was to make her own way back by train.

'Will you please wait here, Fabio,' she said to the boy. 'Keep an eye on him, Mr Fowler. Don't let him run away.'

The boy, who had begun to trust her, cowered back in his seat and Coral marched up to the front door. The smell of Greymarsh would have been enough to put her off for life. Hospital disinfectant, tortured cabbage, lavatories . . .

As for Matron, as she came out of her office she would have made a very good camel: the nose was right, the sneering upper lip, and the distrustful muddy eyes. Except that camels can't help their expressions and people can.

'I am afraid I have bad news about Hubert-Henry Mountjoy,' said Aunt Coral. 'He has been laid low with a bad attack of Burry-Burry fever and can't come back to school at present.'

Matron pursed her mouth.

'Well, of course, that is what you expect from foreign children—he probably picked it up in his hut in the jungle.'

Since Aunt Coral had just invented Burry-Burry fever she only nodded and said she would let Matron know as soon

29

as the boy was better. She then returned to the car and said, 'I am sorry to tell you that there has been an outbreak of meningitis in the school. Everyone is in quarantine and Hubert can't go back at present.'

The little boy, who had been hunched against the cushions, now sat up and smiled. He had a very nice smile and Aunt Coral made up her mind.

'Well, I can't take him back,' said the surly driver. 'I'm going on to another job down in the West Country and I haven't a minute to waste.'

'That's all right,' said Coral. 'Just take us to the station. We'll make our own way back to London.'

Sitting on the station platform, Coral noticed the exact moment when Fabio's happiness at the thought of escaping school changed to misery at the thought of going back to his grandparents' dungeon of a house.

She hadn't had any real doubts but now she was certain. Should she use chloroform? Or the sleeping powder that Etta used?

Either way, thought Coral, Fabio was the one.

Etta and Coral had been right. Aunt Myrtle should never have been allowed to come on the kidnapping job. Almost as soon as she arrived in London she was so homesick that she thought she would die. She missed the sound of the waves on the rocks and the scent of the clover and the way the clouds raced across the high clean sky. But most of all she missed Herbert. She was used to sitting on the point every day and playing the cello to him, and now she began to worry in case he was missing her too.

Or *not* missing her, which would have been even worse.

So by the time she was sent to take Lambert Sprott to the zoo because his father was doing business in New York and his mother was buying clothes in Paris, Aunt Myrtle was in a bad way. Her hair kept falling down, she had a headache, and the map of the zoo looked complicated.

As for Lambert, he was a boy it was not easy to take to. He had pale distrustful eyes, a tight mouth, and carried a wallet full of money, a pocket calculator and his own mobile telephone so that he looked

31

like a shrunken bank manager, except that bank managers have learnt to be friendly and Lambert had not.

All the same she was determined to do her best, and to share with the boy the beauty of the animals they saw: the knock-kneed giraffes with their long black tongues, the dignified orang-utans with the tufts of red hair under their armpits, the Mississippi alligator, smiling as he steamed in his pool.

'Oh how fascinating animals are, are they not, Lambert!' she cried, getting carried away. 'Look at those bonteboks— the way they carry their heads. And over there, the dear dik-diks—so small but so fast when they run.'

Lambert yawned. 'They smell,' he said.

Myrtle was shocked. 'Well, they have their own scent, yes, but so do you. To a bontebok you would smell of human.'

'No, I wouldn't.'

Aunt Myrtle sighed, but she was determined not to give up. There must be a flicker of life somewhere in the boy. And there was: when something cost a lot of money Lambert became quite alert. He told Myrtle that you could get twenty thousand pounds for the horn of the white rhino, and that the Siberian tiger could

32

fetch double that because it was so rare.

'And so beautiful,' cried Myrtle. 'Look at the markings on its throat.'

Lambert yawned again—he was not at all interested in things being beautiful and he stopped to dial a friend on his mobile telephone, but the friend was out. 'I wouldn't mind going shopping,' he said. 'I've got my own account at Harrods.'

But Myrtle had not been told to take him shopping and, ignoring his whining, she led the way across a little stone bridge and stopped dead.

They had come to the seals. The females lay about like old armchairs, coughing and grunting, but there was one, a young bull seal, who seemed to be staring directly at her.

Tears of homesickness came into Myrtle's eyes; it could have been Herbert's brother lying there! 'Oh, Lambert, 'she said making a last attempt, 'look at the way his whiskers curve, and the shine on his skin. Did you ever see anything so lovely?'

'They aren't worth anything,' said Lambert in a bored voice. 'You can't get any money for seals. They're common.'

And then he opened his mouth and yawned once more. He yawned so that

Myrtle saw his unhealthy tongue, his tonsils, even the little flap of skin at the back of the throat that stops the food going down the wrong way—and something snapped inside her.

She wouldn't kidnap this loathsome child in a hundred years. The thought of waking up on the Island and knowing he was there made her blood run cold, and she could no more soil her cello case by stuffing the repulsive brat into it than she could fly. She would take Lambert back to his house and tell her sisters that she was a failure as a kidnapper, and she would go home.

Once she had decided this she felt better, but there was a long afternoon to get through still; one of the longest of her life, it seemed to Myrtle. Lambert lived in a large house bristling with burglar alarms and fitted with ankle-deep carpets, a private bar, a swimming pool, and a kitchen full of gadgets which hummed and pulsed and throbbed and which she had no idea how to use.

What Lambert's house didn't have in it was any people. His father was busy getting rich, and his mother was busy spending the money he made, so neither of them spent much time at home. Myrtle had been told to wait till the woman who gave Lambert his supper came, and hand him over.

Lambert sat down in front of an enormous telly and started zapping channels in a bored way, and Myrtle made her way to the bathroom to freshen up. She had decided to flush the chloroform down the loo; it bothered her having it when she had given up as a kidnapper, so she took the bottle and her bag of hairpins and made her way upstairs.

'What have you got there?' Lambert's suspicious voice made her turn round. He had put his telephone in his pocket and was glaring at her, narrowing his eyes. 'You're stealing something. What's in that bottle?'

He leant forward to try and snatch the bottle. Aunt Myrtle put it behind her back but Lambert kicked her hard in the shins, twisted her free arm and grabbed the bottle. Then he undid the stopper and put his nose to it.

'Don't!' cried Myrtle. 'Put it down, Lambert.'

But it was too late. The loathsome boy lay felled and quite unconscious on the floor.

35

CHAPTER THREE

Minette woke up in a strange bed with a lumpy mattress and brass knobs. She was in a big room; shabby, with a threadbare carpet and faded wall-paper covered in a pattern of parrots and swirling leaves. The curtains breathed slightly in the open windows. A high mewing noise came from outside.

Then she remembered what had happened and at once she was very frightened indeed.

She had been eating a sandwich, sitting opposite a strange fierce aunt who was supposed to be taking her to her father; and suddenly the compartment started going round and round and the face of the aunt came closer and then further away . . . and then nothing more. Blackness.

She had been drugged and kidnapped, she was sure of that. She could remember the way the dreadful aunt had peered at her as if she was looking into her soul. Minette knew all about fear but now she was more afraid than she had ever been. What dreadful fate lay in wait for her?

Would they cut off her ear and send it to her parents—or starve her till she did what they wanted?

And what *did* they want? Kidnapping was about getting money out of people and neither her mother nor her father was rich.

Moving in the bed, she found she was not tied up, but the windows would be barred and the door locked.

Pushing aside the bedclothes, she walked over to the window. She was wearing her own nightdress; the aunt must have kidnapped her suitcase as well. The window was open and as Minette looked out she gasped with surprise.

For she was looking at a most incredible view. Down below her was green, sheep-cropped turf studded with daisies and eyebright. A large goose with black legs walked across it, followed by six goslings with their necks stretched out. Beyond the turf the ground sloped to a bay of perfect white sand—and then came the sea.

Minette looked and looked and looked. The sea in the morning light was like a crystal mirror; she could hear the waves turning over quietly on the beach. There were three black rocks guarding the bay and on them she could make out the dark round heads of seals. White birds circled and mewed and the air smelled of seaweed and shellfish and wind. It smelled of the sea!

'Oh, it's beautiful,' she whispered.

But of course she would not be allowed to go outside. Kidnapped children were kept in dark cupboards and blindfolded. Any minute now someone would come and deal with her. She looked round the room. Old furniture, patchwork rugs, and by the bed—and this was odd—a nightlight. She had begged and begged for one at home but neither her father nor her mother had ever let her have one.

A small snuffling sound made her turn quickly. It had come from behind a screen covered in cutouts of animals in the corner of the room.

A fierce dog to guard her? But the noise had not been at all a fierce one.

Her heart pounding, she tiptoed to the screen and looked round it. On a camp bed lay a boy of about her own age. He had very dark hair and sticking-out ears and he was just waking up.

'Who are you?' he asked, staring at her with big round eyes.

'I'm Minette. And I think I've been

38

kidnapped by an aunt.'

The boy sat up. 'Me too.' He blinked. 'Yes, I'm sure. I was supposed to be going back to my grandparents. She gave me a hamburger.'

'Mine gave me a cheese and tomato sandwich.'

The boy got out of bed and stretched. He too was wearing his own pyjamas. 'We'll have to try and escape,' he said. 'We'll have to.'

'Yes. Only I think we're on an island. Come and look.'

She didn't know why, but she had had the feeling at once that the sea wasn't just in front of them but all around.

'Wow!' Fabio too was struck by the view. 'What a place.'

Minette had gone over to the door. 'Look, it isn't locked!'

'I'm going out,' said the boy. 'They don't seem to have taken our clothes away. They're crummy kidnappers.'

'Unless it's all a trap.' She thought of the films she had seen—holes suddenly opening in the ground with man-eating piranhas or sharks. 'Do you think they've kidnapped us to feed us to something?'

He shrugged. 'You'd think they'd choose fatter children than us. Come on, get dressed. I'm going out.'

There was no one in the corridor; there was no one on the stairs.

Then, from behind a door across the hallway, they heard a scream, followed by a thump, and then a second scream. Someone in there was being tortured— and it sounded like a child.

Minette leant back against the wall, white-faced and trembling.

'Come on—quick!' Fabio clutched her arm.

The children ran out across the turf, over the dunes, along the perfect crescent of sand. The tide was out; it was a shell beach; there were Venus shells and cowries and green stones polished like emeralds. No one stopped them; there was no one to be seen. It would have been like Paradise except for that ghastly scream.

'Look,' said Fabio.

A group of seals had swum towards the shore and were looking at them, swimming in a semicircle, snorting and blowing . . . With their round heads they looked like a group of Russian dolls.

The children were silent, looking at the seals, and the seals stared back at them. Then suddenly they turned and swam back into the deep water.

All except one, a bull seal with white markings on the throat, who came close to the shore, and closer, till he was in the shallows with his flippers resting in the sand.

'It's as if he's trying to tell us something.'

'He's got incredible eyes,' said Minette dreamily. 'He doesn't look like a seal at all. He looks as though inside he's a person.'

'Well, seals are persons. Everything that's alive is a person really.'

But that wasn't what she'd meant.

They took off their shoes and walked on the firm wet sand between the tidemarks towards a cliff covered with nesting kittiwakes and puffins and terns. The tide was still going out, leaving behind its treasures: pieces of driftwood as smooth as velvet, crimson crab shells, bleached cuttlefish bones, whiter than snow. There was no sign of any ship. They might have been alone in the universe.

'What's that noise?' asked Fabio, stopping suddenly.

A deep and mournful sound, a kind of honking, had come from somewhere inland.

'It must be a foghorn,' said Minette.

But there wasn't any fog, nor any lighthouse to give warning if there had been.

They listened for a few moments but the sound did not come again, and they ran on along the shore. It was a marvellous island; it seemed to have everything. To their left was a green hill; two hills, actually, with a dip between, the slopes covered with bracken and gorse. The far shore would be wilder, exposed to the wind.

'If we climbed up there we could see exactly where we are. There might be other islands or a causeway. If we're going to escape we're going to have to know,' said Minette.

They had to get away—that terrible scream still rang in their ears—but Minette couldn't help thinking of where she would be if she hadn't been kidnapped. In her father's dark sitting room trying to get interested in a book till he came back from the university.

Fabio seemed to be having the same sort of thoughts. 'I can't help wondering if my grand-parents will pay the ransom for me. They're horribly mean and they don't like me.'

Minette tried to think if her parents liked her enough to pay a lot of money to get her back but when she thought about her parents her stomach always started to lurch about so she said, 'There's a little path there to the top of the hill.'

They began to run towards the gap in the dunes, forgetting the lives they had left behind, forgetting even that awful tortured scream. The wind was in their backs; it was like flying. No one could imagine anything dangerous or dark.

And then it happened! From behind the hummock of sand that had hidden them, there arose suddenly the cruel figures of two enormous women.

It was the evil aunts!

The sinister kidnappers glared at the children, and the children, terrified, stared back. Here was the tall bony aunt with her fierce eyes who had drugged Minette's sandwich, and here was the plump mad person with her scarves flying in the wind who had given sleeping powders to a defenceless boy.

The children reached for each other's hands. Minette was shaking so much she could hardly stand. What punishment would they be given for escaping from their room?

It was the tall bony aunt, Etta, who spoke. 'You're late for breakfast,' she said in her fierce and booming voice.

The children continued to stare.

'Breakfast,' the other one went on. 'You've heard of that? We have it at seven and the cook gets ratty if he's kept waiting. Go and wash your hands first—the bathroom's at the top of the stairs.'

The children ran off, completely puzzled by this way of kidnapping people, and Etta and Coral followed. They were talking about Myrtle, who hadn't stopped crying since she came back.

'She's got to stop blaming herself,' said Coral. 'Mistakes can happen to anyone.'

'Yes. Mind you, Lambert is quite a mistake!'

Breakfast was laid in the dining room, a big room with shabby leather chairs, which faced the patch of green turf and the bay. All the windows in the L-shaped farmhouse had at least a glimpse of the sea. Even the bathroom, with its huge claw-footed bath and ancient geyser, looked out on the ledge of rock where the seals hauled out of the water to rest.

'Porridge or cereal?' asked Aunt Etta, as the children came in.

Minette blinked at her. 'Cereal,' she managed to say.

'Porridge,' said Fabio.

'Please,' said Etta briskly, picking up the ladle. 'Porridge, *please.*'

Fabio was the first to shake himself awake. 'This is a very odd kidnap,' he said crossly. 'And I won't eat anything drugged.'

Aunt Etta leant forward, scooped a spoonful of porridge from his plate and gulped it down.

'Satisfied?' she said.

Fabio waited to see if she yawned or became dopey. Then he began to eat. The porridge was delicious.

They were both on second helpings when the screams began again. This time they were even worse than before and were followed by sobs and wails and a low shuddering moan. Then the door opened and a woman they had never seen before ran into the room. She had long, reddish-grey hair down her back; a bloody scratch ran along one cheek and she seemed to be quite beside herself.

The children shrank back in their chairs, their fear returning. The woman looked every inch a torturer.

'Really, Myrtle,' said Aunt Etta, 'I've

told the children they mustn't be late for breakfast and now look at you.'

But no one could be cross with Myrtle for long, not even her bossy sister. The scratch on Myrtle's cheek had begun to bleed again, there were tooth marks on her wrist, and though she took a helping of porridge she was quite unable to swallow it.

And when she was introduced to Minette and Fabio, her tears began to flow again.

'Yours are so nice,' she sobbed. 'They look so intelligent and friendly.'

'That's as maybe,' said Etta. 'We haven't tried them out yet.' She frowned as more bangs and thumps came from across the corridor. 'He can't stay in the broom cupboard, Myrtle. What would happen if he goes for the Hoover? We'd never get the place cleaned up again.'

'It's just for now,' said Myrtle. 'I gave him my bedroom when he first came round but I was afraid, for the ducklings.'

Myrtle often had motherless ducklings keeping warm in her bed and her underclothes drawer.

'I suppose we shall have to *un*kidnap him,' said Coral. 'But how? No one's going to pay a ransom for Lambert

Sprott.'

'We could offer to *give* his father some money if he'll take Lambert away,' suggested Myrtle, blowing her nose.

'Don't be silly, Myrtle,' said Etta. 'For one thing we haven't got any money—and for another he'd tell everyone about the Island and photographers would come, and journalists.' She shuddered. Keeping the position of the Island secret was the most important thing of all.

'We could turn him round and round till he was completely giddy and leave him in a telephone kiosk somewhere on the mainland,' said Coral. But she did not sound very convinced by her idea.

Myrtle began to sob again. 'I should have left him on the floor,' she gulped. 'I should never have brought him. But it seemed so cruel just to leave him there unconscious.'

'Hush. What's done is done.'

But Myrtle couldn't be consoled. 'And my cello case smells of the awful child,' she wailed. 'He puts terrible stuff on his hair.'

'Perhaps he'll settle down when we've got some breakfast into him.'

Judging by the screams and thumps coming from across the corridor though,

47

this did not seem likely.

But Fabio was getting impatient. 'What about *us*? Are you going to unkidnap us?'

The aunts stared at him. 'Are you mad?' said Etta. 'After all the trouble we took. In any case, you haven't been kidnapped exactly. You've been *chosen*.'

Minette and Fabio stared. 'How?' asked Minette. 'What do you mean?' enquired Fabio.

Aunt Coral put down her coffee cup. 'It's time we explained. But first you'd better come and meet Daddy. He gets upset when things are kept from him.'

Captain Harper was a hundred and three years old and spent most of the day in bed looking at the Island through his telescope.

He was very deaf and very grumpy and what he saw through the window didn't please him. When he was young there had been far more geese coming from Greenland—hundreds and thousands of geese—and their feet had been yellower and their bottoms more feathery than the geese who came nowadays. The sheep had been fleecier when he was a boy and the flowers in the grass had been brighter and the seals on the rocks ten times larger and fatter.

'Huge, they were,' Captain Harper would say, throwing out his arms. 'Great big cow seals with big bosoms and eyes like cartwheels, and look at them now!'

No one liked to say that it was probably because he couldn't see or hear too well that things had changed, and when he told the same stories for the hundredth time, his daughters just smiled and tip-toed out of the room because they were fond of him and knew that being old is difficult.

'Here are the children, Father,' yelled Coral. 'The ones that have come to stay with us.'

The old man put down his telescope and stared at them.

'They're too small,' he said. 'They won't be a mite of use. You need ones with muscles. When I was their age I had muscles like footballs.'

He put out a skinny arm and flexed his biceps, and they could see a bump like a very small pea come up on his arm. 'We were all strong in those days. There was a boy in my class who could lift the teacher's desk with one hand. Freddie Boyle he was called. He was the one who put the grass snake down the teacher's trouser leg.'

The aunts let him tell the story about the grass snake and the teacher's trouser leg because it was a short one, but when he began on the one about Freddie Boyle's brother, who'd run over his own false teeth in a milk float, they shepherded the children out quietly.

'He won't notice,' they said.

When they went downstairs again they found Art, the cook, wiping porridge off his trouser leg. He had tried to give Lambert some breakfast and had it thrown in his face.

'Nasty little perisher you've got in there,' he said. 'Best drown him, I'd say. Shouldn't think his parents would want him back.'

Before he escaped and was washed up on the Island, Art had worked in the prison kitchens, which was why he made such good porridge. Because he'd killed a man once, Art didn't like the sight of blood and it was always the aunts who had to chop the heads off the fish before they went into the frying pan or get the chickens ready for the pot. Another thing Art didn't like to do was anything energetic.

'I don't know my own strength,' he would say, when there was anything messy or difficult to be done. 'I might forget myself and do someone an injury.'

This didn't seem likely—Art was a skinny person who hardly came up to Aunt Etta's shoulder—but he'd quickly locked the door on Lambert and, leaving him to scream for his mobile telephone, retreated to his kitchen.

But Aunt Etta and Aunt Coral now led the children into the garden behind the house. It was time to explain.

The garden was surrounded by grey walls to give shelter from the wind; but no walls on the Island were built so high that they shut out the view of the sea. Aunt Myrtle had gone down to play her cello to the seals. A bumblebee droned on a clump of thrift. It was very peaceful.

'Perhaps I'd better tell you a story,' said Etta. 'It's a true story and it begins with five girls coming to an island with their widowed father to look for a new life.

'They found a lovely and deserted place, but ruined, abandoned. All the people who had lived there had left long, long ago. Even the ghost in the old graveyard seemed to have gone away.'

Minette sat with her arms hugging her knees and her eyes closed. She loved stories.

'So the girls and their father repaired the house and planted a garden and learnt to fish and cut peat and do all the things the Islanders had done before they left. But of course the world outside was changing. Oil was spilled into the sea, and sewage, and trawlers started to use nets that caught even the smallest fish. The water became overheated by nuclear power stations. You'll have learnt all that at school.'

Minette nodded, but Fabio only scowled. Absolutely *nothing* useful had been taught at Greymarsh Towers.

'Soon the sisters and their father found themselves looking after things that came ashore. Oiled seabirds . . . stunned seals . . . poisoned squids . . . and other things . . .'

Etta paused and looked up at Coral who raised her eyebrows in a warning way. *Not yet*, said Coral's eyebrows. *Remember what we decided.*

Etta nodded and turned back to the children.

'The sisters worked from dawn to dusk. One of them was an idiot; she started shaving her legs and marrying tax inspectors, so she was no good . . . And one went off to foreign parts to stop

52

people eating rare animals. And the others got older and became aunts . . .

'And then one day they realized they might die before long—they might become extinct—and then what would happen to all the creatures? So they decided to find people to carry on after them. Sensible people. Young ones. People who knew how to work.'

There was a long pause. Then:

'Us?' said Fabio shyly.

Both aunts nodded.

'Yes,' said Aunt Ella. 'You.'

CHAPTER FOUR

So Fabio and Minette were set to work.

It was the hardest work they had ever done and it didn't stop from morning to night.

The day began with fifty press-ups on the grass behind the house. Etta was in charge of these, rising up and down on her elbows with her skirt tucked into her navy-blue knickers. She had thirty-one pairs of these, one for each day of the month. The children had seen seven of them on the washing line and she explained that it made it easier having things the same colour and the same shape so that one didn't have to think about things which didn't matter—like which of one's knickers were which.

Then they began on the chores. The aunts ran a smallholding; there were six goats and a cow, and two dozen chickens whose eggs needed to be collected, and fresh straw which needed to be put down.

There were buckets of mash to be taken to the eider ducklings whose mother had been fouled in a fishing net, and two seal pups who had to be hand-fed from a bottle. The children had thought feeding the seals might be fun, but it wasn't. The pups prodded and squealed when the milk didn't come fast enough; it was like being bashed into by two blubbery tanks.

A puffin with a splint on his leg lived behind the house, and in a tin bath with a wooden lid was an octopus with eye trouble.

And as they worked, the children were watched—*tested*, you could say—because anyone who was disgusted by a living thing, however odd, was no use on the island.

Minette was marched down to the

strand by Aunt Etta and shown a pile of pink and purple slime.

'These are stranded jellyfish,' said Etta. 'Put them back into the water. You'd better wear these.'

She handed Minette a pair of rubber gloves and stood over her while she carried the wobbling blobs back into the sea.

Fabio was taken to a big tank in the paddock and told to pick up an eel with a skin disease.

'Hold him behind the head while I scrub,' Coral ordered him. 'He's got scabies.'

When they were in bed at night, the children tried to think how to run away. Fabio now slept in a box room next to Minette and with the door open they could talk.

'We can't stay here and turn into slaves,' said Fabio.

'No. Except the aunts are slaves too. They work harder than us.'

This was true, but Fabio said it made no difference. 'We'll have to steal a boat.'

But their beds were warm; they had nightlights; the sea sighed softly beneath their open windows—and, before Minette could see even the smallest tiger on the ceiling, they were both asleep.

And while they slept the aunts discussed them.

'Well, so far so good,' said Etta. 'They haven't squealed or squirmed or wriggled. Yet. Or said "Ugh!" I can't bear people who say "Ugh!"'

'And they seem to be keeping to the rules,' said Coral.

The rules had been set out on the first day. 'You're not to go near the de-oiling shed in the cove,' Etta had said. 'Nor up to the top of the hill.'

'Nor to the loch between the hills.'

The children had grumbled about this.

'It's exactly like that fairy story about Bluebeard's Castle,' said Minette. 'You know . . . if you open the seventh door you'll have your head chopped off.'

But they had obeyed—even Fabio who had been so difficult to control in his grandparents' house. Nothing, though, could stop Fabio asking questions.

'What's that honking one hears sometimes? It sounds like a foghorn.'

'If it sounds like a foghorn I expect it *is* a foghorn,' said Etta, and that was the end of that.

But what of Lambert?

Lambert went on screaming and

kicking and wailing for his mobile telephone and Art (who did not know his own strength) just put down his tray and ran for it whenever he brought him his food. They had locked him in a room above the boathouse; it had been the Captain's study and the doors and windows were strong.

At mealtimes they tried to decide what to do with him. Coral thought they might set him adrift in a dinghy with enough food for a few days, and Fabio thought he should be dipped in boiling oil. But they never got very far because whenever they talked about Lambert, Aunt Myrtle always began to cry because she blamed herself for having kidnapped such an awful boy and brought him to the Island.

Then, on the fourth day, as they came down to breakfast, Fabio and Minette found all the aunts looking at them with a pleased expression. Their teachers at school had looked like that when they had passed an exam.

'Your work has been satisfactory,' said Etta.

'And your conduct,' said Coral, flicking her beads out of the sugar bowl.

'So we have decided that you may work in the de-oiling shed today.'

The children thought this was an odd kind of reward for being good; de-oiling seabirds is about the messiest job there is. But they kept quiet and presently they were following Aunt Etta along the cliff path and down to the cove on the far side of the bay.

The de-oiling shed was a wooden building set back into the cliff. At high tide the water came almost to the walls but now they could reach it by scrambling over low rocks covered in seaweed, and pools full of anemones and shrimps and tiny scuttling crabs. The children would have liked to linger and explore but Aunt Etta thrust them forward and knocked loudly on the door.

'Are you decent?' she called.

The children looked at each other. How could sea birds *not* be decent?

There was a scuttling noise, followed by a plopping sound—and then the door was opened from the inside.

The children had expected rough wooden walls; shelves, perhaps; a slatted floor. But the shed was more like the inside of a Turkish bath.

There were tiles on the walls; water gushed from a tap into a large, blue-painted sink decorated with seashells and into two tubs set under the high windows. Hairbrushes lay on a low table, and hand mirrors, and there were more mirrors on the wall.

But it was what was inside the sink or lying on the wet floor which held them speechless. You can read about such things as often as you like but seeing them is very different.

There were four mermaids in the shed. They wore knitted tops which Myrtle had made but their tails of course were free—no one would have worn one of Myrtle's knitted tops on their tails—and when she saw that the children, though pale, were not going to make a fuss, Aunt Etta introduced them.

'This is Ursula,' she said, leading them up to a very old lady who sat in the sink nearest the door. Her hair was full of broken pieces of shell and sticks; the egg case of a dogfish hung over one ear and she had only one tooth—a long one which came down over her lower lip.

But the girls who shared one of the tubs under the window were young. They were twins but they were not at all alike. Queenie was very pretty with golden ropes of hair and a pert look in her bright blue eyes; but Oona's hair was dark with a green sheen on it and her grey eyes were sad.

And, sprawled on the floor, trying to hide a piece of gum she had been chewing, was the girls' mother, Loreen. She was a fattish, blowzy person and looked as if she had given up on life. The knitted top she'd hastily put on was crooked and the flowers in her hair were very dead.

Aunt Etta frowned at the chewing gum, which Loreen had cadged from Art. 'A disgusting habit,' she said, glaring at the packet.

'It's my nerves,' said Loreen. 'I've got to have something for my nerves, with the state I'm in.'

She was certainly in a state. As well as a bruise on her cheek and a black eye, Loreen was very badly oiled. All of them were oiled but Loreen was really covered in the stuff.

'Have you been taking your tonic?' Etta asked.

'We've all been taking it. But we're not better. Oona's ears are still bad and Queenie's itching all over. We can't go home yet,' said Loreen firmly. 'Not for a long time.'

Etta ignored this. The way absolutely

nobody wanted to go away even when they were healed was beginning to annoy her.

'They're not very big,' complained the old crone, staring at Fabio and Minette. Everyone knew about the children and that they had been chosen and not kidnapped.

'We're strong though,' said Fabio, who was getting tired of this.

But there was one other person still to meet. In a washing-up bowl on the floor floated something pale and smooth which turned out to be a baby.

But not any baby. Probably the fattest baby in the universe. His wrists were lost in layers. and layers of fat; his neck was covered by a whole waterfall of chins; his small blue eyes were sunk in his swollen cheeks like currants in a pudding and he was bald. 'My youngest,' said Loreen. She looked tired rather than proud. 'His name's Walter.'

The children did not know what to say. Walter looked more like an overgrown maggot than a merbaby—but he was not oiled! When the oil slick came his mother had held him aloft and now Aunt Etta turned away from the washing-up bowl with pursed lips because Walter was exactly the kind of spoiled, pampered male of whom she particularly disapproved.

'Right,' she said to the children. 'Time to start work. The detergent's in that bottle—it gets diluted with three parts of water. And when you've finished put them under the hose—all of them. Oona gets three of these drops in each ear and remember, with anything fishy, scrub in the same direction as the scales or you'll be in trouble.'

The door closed behind her, and Queenie, the pretty pert twin, pulled a face.

'What's the matter with you?' she said cheekily. 'Cat got your tongue?'

'Now, Queenie,' said her mother wearily. 'Maybe they've never seen mermaids before.'

'As a matter of fact we haven't,' said Minette.

She picked up the roughest of the scrubbing brushes while Fabio poured out the detergent. Then they walked over to Queenie's sink, picked up her tail and began to scrub.

*   *   *

The mermaids had not had an easy time even before they were caught in the oil slick. Loreen's husband was a bully—mermen are often bad-tempered—and the bruise on her cheek came from him.

Then a bad thing happened to Oona, the younger of the twins. She was caught in a fishing net and dragged aboard a fishing boat, but the person who unwrapped her wasn't an ordinary sensible fisherman; it was a chinless wonder called Lord Terence Brasenott who thought catching a mermaid was a terribly good joke.

'I say, what jolly fun,' he kept saying. 'What a pretty little thing. I'll take you back with me,' he'd said and pawed her with his horrible hands and tried to kiss her.

Oona spent three days in his cabin, weeping piteously, and by the time she managed to free herself and dive overboard her voice had completely gone. This happens sometimes when people have a serious shock; it is bad for anyone, but for mermaids, who are famous for singing, it is particularly bad. Even now, Oona could only manage a whisper or a croak.

No sooner had they got over this

disaster than a French mermaid turned up from Calais and started making eyes at Loreen's husband. French mermaids have two tails and the whole thing went to the silly man's head and he turned his wife and children out of their cave and set up home with his new love. He even turned out his grandmother, Old Ursula, which was particularly hard on Loreen as she had to take her along. Being lumbered with your own grandmother can be difficult but when it's your husband's grandmother it can seem seriously unfair.

What happened next was Queenie's fault. She was pretty and she was headstrong and though everyone had warned her what ships were like nowadays, she insisted on sitting on a rock and singing to the captain of a cargo boat coming from the Middle East.

'Arabia's in the Middle East,' she said, 'so they'll be carrying gold and treasure like in the Arabian Nights; you'll see.'

Queenie had a good voice and she'd kept up to date with tunes and didn't waste time on 'Hey Nonny No' sort of songs, and it so happened that the captain was musical and a little drunk and when he heard her he got very excited and ran his ship on to the rocks.

But what came spilling out were not doubloons and pieces of silver which might have made the mermaids rich. What came out . . . was oil. Masses of thick, black, greasy oil straight from the oil wells of Saudi Arabia. It caught the whole family fair and square, half blinding them, weighing down their limbs. They just managed to reach the safety of the Island and land wearily on the shore—and there the aunts had found them.

The children learnt all this while they cleaned them up. It was incredibly hard work. The girls' tails were slippery and surprisingly heavy—and Queenie was ticklish so when they began to scrub she started giggling and thrashing about. By the time Aunt Etta returned, the children were soaked through and dirty and tired but she took no notice at all. They had to swill down the floor of the hut, and then the mermaids' tails were wrapped in clingfilm so they could be put into wheelbarrows and taken down to the bay without them drying out. Only Old Ursula stayed where she was and admitted that though the children might be small, they knew how to work.

When they had finished in the

mermaid shed, the children were taken to the house for a drink of fruit juice and a biscuit, and then they were sent to help Aunt Coral clean out the chicken house. Fabio's family had kept chickens in South America so he knew what to do, and he and Coral had an interesting conversation about the tango, which she was fond of dancing under the light of the moon.

'You don't happen to know the steps?' she asked him.

Fabio looked doubtful. 'I watched my mother when she danced in the cabaret.'

'Good,' said Aunt Coral. 'I've always wanted a partner.'

Fabio was not at all sure that he wanted to dance the tango with a very large aunt who had stuffed him in a tin trunk and kidnapped him. But he was too polite to refuse and he had noticed the night before that the moon was far from full so that he could only hope she would forget.

Then in the afternoon things got strange again because Aunt Myrtle took them down to the point to meet the seals.

They lay about by the edge of the water, the cows dozing while they waited for their pups to be born, the bulls jostling each other and shoving to test their strength.

But one seal was sitting quite alone on a rock. He had turned his back on the rough games of the other seals and was staring romantically out to sea. It was the seal who had come close to the shore on the first day; they would have known him anywhere.

'Herbert, I'd like you to meet Fabio and Minette,' said Myrtle, just as if she was introducing someone in a drawing room.

Herbert opened his eyes very wide and looked at them. It was an extraordinary look for a seal; both children stepped back a pace; they felt as though they had been weighed up and examined by a great intelligence.

'He can't be an ordinary seal,' said Fabio.

Aunt Myrtle looked at him gratefully. 'No, dear, you're absolutely right. Herbert *is* a seal but he's a very special kind of seal. He's a selkie.'

'What's a selkie?' asked Fabio.

Myrtle sighed. 'It's not easy to explain,' she said, 'because it's all to do with legends and beliefs. There aren't a lot of *facts.'*

'Tell us,' begged Minette.

Aunt Myrtle sat down on an outcrop of rock and the children came to sit beside her.

'All sorts of things are told about selkies,' she began. 'That they are the souls of drowned men . . . that they are a kind of faery and if someone sticks a knife in them they will turn back into humans.'

'*A knife!*' Minette was horrified. 'How could anyone do a thing like that?'

Aunt Myrtle shrugged. 'I certainly couldn't.' But she blushed, thinking of how she had sometimes wondered what would happen if she did get up the courage. Would Herbert really turn into a man, and if so, what *kind* of a man? Might he become a showing-off kind of man like a bullfighter, always trailing his cape about? Or a really boring person who thought about nothing except making money?

Herbert had come to the Island many years ago. His mother had brought him because he had a cough which wouldn't get better and it had got about that the Island was safe even for seals who were not well. The aunts had healed his cough and then Myrtle had played the cello to him and he had stayed.

They had known of course that he wasn't an ordinary seal. Herbert did not speak exactly, but he understood human speech and sometimes when he and his mother talked together in the selkie language, which is halfway between human speech and the language of the seals, Myrtle could make out . . . not the words exactly, but the sense of what they said.

'He had a very famous grandmother,' said Myrtle, dropping her voice. 'At least, we think she was his grandmother. She was called the Selkie of Rossay and there are stories told about her all over the islands.'

'Tell us,' begged Minette again. She could never get enough stories.

So Aunt Myrtle pushed her hair out of her eyes and began.

'The Selkie of Rossay was a female seal who lived about a hundred years ago. One night she came out of the sea and shed her sealskin and danced with nothing on by the light of the moon and a fisherman came and fell passionately in love with her.' Myrtle paused and gave a wistful sigh. 'You know how it is,' she said, 'when people are dancing by the light of the moon.'

69

The children nodded politely though they didn't really.

'So he hid her sealskin and brought her some clothes and married her and she stayed with him and had seven children and they were perfectly happy. Though when they sat down, even on dry days and in completely dry clothes, the children left a damp patch. Not . . . you know . . . anything to do with nappies. Nothing nasty—it was an absolutely *fresh* damp patch—but it showed they had seal blood.'

Herbert was listening most intently. He moved closer, he cleared his throat.

'Then one day when she was rummaging in a trunk, the selkie found her old sealskin and she put it on and the sea called to her—it called to her so strongly there was nothing she could do— and she dived back into the sea and after a while she married a seal and had seven seal children. But for the rest of her life she was in a terrible muddle, calling her sea children by the names of her land children and her land children by the names of her sea children and never really knowing where she belonged. At least, that is the story.'

Myrtle stopped and Herbert gave an

enormous sigh and rolled over on to his side. He might have forgotten how to speak like a human, but he had understood every word and the story Myrtle told was his own.

The Selkie of Rossay *had* been his grandmother. She had gone crazy in the end from not knowing whether it was better to be a woman or a seal, and Herbert's mother, the youngest of her seal children, had stayed with her till she died, seeing that she didn't starve even when her teeth fell out and her eyes filmed over.

Herbert's mother was still alive; she came ashore sometimes and nudged her son and tried to get him to make up his mind about what he wanted to be because she knew it didn't matter whether one was a man or a seal so long as one stuck to it.

But Herbert took after his grandmother. He couldn't decide. When Myrtle played the cello to him it seemed that being human was the best that he could hope for. But when he watched Art and saw what he would have to do if he was a man—wear trousers with braces or zips, and shoelaces and all that kind of thing—he would dive back into the water and turn over and over in the waves and think: This is my world; it is here that I belong.

When the children got back to the house, they found Art with a large piece of sticking plaster on his forehead. He had tried to give Lambert some lunch and Lambert had torn the plate out of his hand and hurled it across the room. Then he'd lain down on the floor and drummed his heels and screamed for his father and his mobile telephone.

'I'd have thumped him,' said Art now, 'but I daren't. I don't know my own strength. I might have pulped him into a jelly.'

Fabio didn't say anything but he was beginning to wonder about Art's great strength. Meanwhile Lambert was still in the room above the boathouse.

'But he can't stay there,' said Coral. 'The boy is a fiend. We've *got* to get rid of him.'

But though they discussed it for the rest of the day, none of the aunts could see how this could be done short of killing the child—which they would very much have liked to do, but which was not the kind of thing that happened on the Island.

CHAPTER FIVE

When the children came down to breakfast the next day they saw at once that the aunts were worried. Etta's moustache stood out dark against her pale face and her nose had sharpened to something you could have used to cut cheese.

'I really don't want to operate,' they heard her say, 'but it's serious. She's completely egg-bound.'

'Who's egg-bound?' asked Fabio.

Aunt Etta ignored him.

'I've tried massage; I've tried Vaseline; I've tried a steam kettle,' she said to her sisters.

'What about castor oil?' suggested Coral.

'It's worth a try, I suppose.'

'Can we help?' asked Minette.

'No.' Etta looked up briefly. 'Well, perhaps you can carry the buckets. We're going up the hill. And kindly fold your napkins properly when you leave the table. You left them in a disgusting heap yesterday.'

It was quite a procession which wound

its way up the hill. Etta carried an enormous bottle of castor oil, Fabio lugged a footstool and a primus stove, Minette had two buckets and a bundle of rags.

The path was steep and the morning was warm but Aunt Etta kept up a fierce pace. She also chose to give them a lecture as she went.

'Now I want to make it *absolutely* clear to you that I will *not* have favourites on this island. The unusual creatures you will be working with are *no more important* than the ordinary ones. A sick water flea needs help just as much as a mermaid. A flounder is *exactly* as important as a selkie. I hope you understand this because if you don't, you're not going to be any use doing your job.'

The children said, yes, they had understood it, but when they reached the top of the hill they were pleased they had been warned.

There were two hills, actually, with a dip in between which held a loch of dark, peaty water. On the far side of the loch was a great pile of brushwood and boulders and bracken. It looked like one of the stockades that the settlers in America used to build to protect themselves from the Indians.

But what stuck out over the top of the stockade was not an American settler. It was the head of an absolutely enormous bird.

The head was black but its beak was a bright yellow and made the children think of those great machines—crunchers or diggers or shovellers—that one sees looming over building sites. Its eyes were yellow too, huge and round and mad-looking, and as they stared they were blasted backwards by the deep honking noise they had heard on the first day.

'What is it?' stammered Fabio.

'It's a boobrie,' said Aunt Etta, striding round the edge of the loch. 'And I can tell you there aren't many of those left in the world. They're a sort of cousin of the dodo—people thought they were extinct but they weren't. They developed on a different island and the sailors didn't find them so they just grew and grew and grew. But then people started doing atomic tests and that kind of nonsense and the ones that were left managed to fly away.'

She led them round the other side of the stockade and they saw a short ladder propped against the side of the nest. Aunt

Etta climbed up it and beckoned to the children to follow but they hung back, thinking of the huge yellow eyes, the dreadful beak.

'Hurry up!' said Etta and, as they still hesitated, she turned round, took a deep breath, and let them have it. 'I have to tell you that kidnapping you was quite the most unpleasant experience any of us have had: that boarding house full of yacking women, and the London Underground with all those fumes. If you think we'd have gone to all that trouble just to let you get eaten by some bird, you need to have your heads examined. Anyway boobries are vegetarians, at least this kind are—more's the pity.'

So the children followed her up the ladder and jumped down into the nest which was trampled flat and lined with moss and feathers.

The boobrie was not really *so* enormous. She was smaller than an African elephant—more the size of an Indian one. It took a lot of courage to look up at her but when they did the children stopped being afraid. She *could* hurt you, of course, by stepping on your feet for example, but they could see that she was a bird with serious troubles of her

76

own.

The nest was ready for eggs but there were no eggs to be seen. The boobrie's chest looked sadly naked so that they knew it was her own feathers she had plucked out to make a warm lining, but a lining for what? Where were the eggs and where the chicks that would follow?

'I have to tell you that I am very worried about her,' said Aunt Etta. 'Being egg-bound is a most serious business.'

'You mean her eggs are stuck inside her? She can't get them out?' asked Minette.

'That's right. And she's too uncomfortable to go and look for something to eat.'

'Doesn't she have a mate to bring her food?' asked Fabio.

Aunt Etta snorted. 'She had but she's lost him.'

'You mean he's dead?'

'He may be, for all I know. Or he may have lost the way or forgotten all about her. You know what men are.'

This annoyed Fabio. 'I'm a man, or I will be, and I'll never leave my wife to starve in a nest. Never.'

'Why did you say it's a pity she's a vegetarian?' Minette wanted to know.

'Because it makes it hard for us to feed her. We could have thrown her a frozen side of beef, but to dredge up all those sludgy sea lettuces and sea noodles and gutweeds takes hours,' said Etta. She was stamping round the boobrie, batting her with a stick, thumping her. 'Get up, you stupid bird. I'm trying to help you.'

At first the boobrie wouldn't move; she sat hunched and shivering and from her throat came a single squawk which seemed to be her way of saying 'Ow!' But Etta was merciless. She thumped and scolded and prodded the bird till she struggled to her feet and stood there swaying and honking.

Then she climbed on to the footstool and peered into the boobrie's back end and there, sure enough, was a glimmer of white speckled with blue.

'You can make seventy-two omelettes from one boobrie's egg,' said Etta when the children had had a look.

But of course she didn't want seventy-two omelettes—she didn't care for omelettes anyway—she wanted living chicks. 'The next part is going to be messy,' she warned.

But the children stayed to help, dipping rags into the hot castor oil and handing them to her as she dabbed and swabbed at the opening.

'We'll just have to wait and see,' she said when she'd finished. 'But if this doesn't work . . .'

'Could she . . . die . . . ?' asked Minette in a quavery voice.

'Anyone can die,' said Etta snubbingly. 'Including you and me.'

But before she marched the children down again she took them up the further hill, which was the highest point of the Island.

The view was incredible. To the west, miles and miles of unbroken water with the sun making a golden path between the clouds, and to the east, a long way off but with their outlines sharp and clear, two islands; one hilly, one low and long.

And on a grassy ledge overhanging the wild northern shore was an ancient burial ground, with leaning and broken gravestones covered in lichen and battered by the rain.

'There's supposed to be a ghost here,' said Etta. 'But she only turns up every hundred years or so.'

'What sort of a ghost?'

'*A good* ghost. A kind of hermit. She was called Ethelgonda and she lived on the Island and looked after the creatures.'

'Like you,' said Minette.

'Not in the least like me,' said Aunt Etta crushingly.

'I didn't think good people became ghosts,' said Fabio.

'Well, a spirit then.'

The children spent the rest of the day collecting the special seaweeds that the boobrie ate and barrowing them up to her nest. Each time they watched anxiously for a sign of an egg but nothing seemed to be happening at all.

They were getting ready for bed that night when Myrtle came upstairs excitedly, her long hair flying.

'Come down for a minute,' she said. 'Herbert's mother has come and she wants to meet you.'

She hurried them down to the rocks and there, sure enough, sitting beside Herbert was a smaller seal, a cow with the same whitish mark on her throat as her son. Herbert's mother was old—there was something weary about the way she held her head—but she lumbered up to them, and snorted in a very welcoming way, while her son looked on proudly.

'This is a great honour, you know,' said Myrtle, hopping about like a young girl.

'She doesn't come out of the water often now; it tires her to be on land. Herbert will have told her about you.'

Since it is difficult to shake hands with a seal, they bowed their heads politely, and Herbert's mother came closer and said something, speaking in a low voice and in the selkie language. The children thought she was asking them to help Herbert make up his mind about whether to be a person or a seal and, when they were back in their rooms, Fabio had an idea. 'We could just cut him with a knife. Not hard. Just a nick—then he'd become human and that would be that.'

'Oh, we couldn't!'

'I don't see why not. Then Myrtle would have a friend. He could learn the piano and they could play duets.'

But when he thought about it, Fabio knew that Minette was right. He couldn't make even the smallest nick in that smooth and shining skin.

*   *   *

It was on the next afternoon that the children had a shock. They had taken yet another load of seaweed to the boobrie and were shovelling it into the nest when

81

the bird gave the loudest honk they had heard yet. For a moment they thought it might be an egg, for the honk was a welcoming one.

But it wasn't. The boobrie was looking at the loch.

The children turned to follow her gaze—and gasped.

A head had appeared in the middle of the lake.

But what a head! White and smooth and enormous . . . like the front end of a gigantic worm. After the head came a neck . . . also smooth . . . also white . . . a neck divided into rings of muscle and going on and on and on. It reared and waved above the surface of the water, and still more neck appeared . . . and more and more. Except that the neck was getting fatter, it couldn't all *be* neck—the bulgier part must be the body of the worm: a worm the size of a dozen boa constrictors.

The boobrie honked once more and the children clutched each other, unable to move.

The creature was still rising up in the water, still getting longer, still pale and glistening and utterly strange. Then it turned its head towards them and opened its eyes which were just two deep holes as black as its body was white.

'Whooo,' it began to say. 'Whooo'—and with every 'oo' the air filled with such a stench of rottenness and decay and . . . *old*ness . . . that the children reeled backwards. And then it began to slither out of the water . . . it slithered and slithered and slithered and still not all of it was out of the lake—and suddenly the children had had enough. Leaving their wheelbarrows where they were, they rushed down the hill to the house and almost fell into the sitting room where the aunts were having tea.

'I didn't expect you to knock,' said Aunt Etta, putting down her cup. 'One knocks at the doors of bedrooms but not of sitting rooms when one is staying in a house. But I do expect you to come in quietly like human beings, and not like hooligans.'

But the children were too frightened to be snubbed. 'We saw a thing . . . a worm . . .'

'As long as a train . . . Well, as long as a bus.'

'All naked and white and smooth and slippery . . .'

'It said "Whoo" and came at us, and its

83

breath . . .' Minette shuddered, just remembering. 'It came out of the lake and now it's coming after us and it'll coil round and round us and smother us and—'

'Unlikely,' said Aunt Etta. She passed the children a plate of scones and told them to sit down. 'It seems to be very difficult to get you to listen,' she said. 'I'm sure that all three of us have told you how unpleasant we found the whole business of kidnapping you.'

'Yes, indeed,' said Coral. 'That loathsome matron like a camel.'

'So it is not very likely that we would go to all that trouble to feed you to a stoorworm,' said Etta.

Being safe in the drawing room, eating a scone with strawberry jam, made Fabio feel very much braver.

'What *is* a stoorworm?'

'A wingless dragon. An Icelandic one; very unusual. Once the world was full of them, but you know how it is. Dragons with wings and fiery breaths in the skies. Dragons without wings and poisonous breaths in the water. The wingless ones were called worms. You must have heard of them: the Lambton Worm, the Laidly Worm, the Stoorworm.'

84

But the children hadn't.

'If his breath is poisonous . . . he breathed on us quite hard,' said Minette. 'He said "Whoooo" and blew at us. Does that mean we'll be ill or die?'

Aunt Coral shook her head. 'He's only poisonous to greenfly and things like that. We use him to spray the fruit trees. And he probably wasn't saying "Whoooo", he was saying "Who?"—meaning who are you? He talks like that; very slowly because he comes from Iceland and they have more time over there.'

But Minette was still alarmed. 'Look,' she said, staring through the window. 'Oh look, he's slithering down the hill . . . He's coming closer . . . He's coming here!'

Aunt Myrtle came to stand beside her. 'He'll be coming to visit Daddy,' she said.

'They're good friends,' explained Coral to the bewildered children. 'They think alike about the world—you know, that the old days were better.'

Standing by the open sitting room door, they watched bravely as the stoorworm slithered into the hall, slithered up the first flight of stairs, along the landing, up the second flight . . . In his bedroom they could hear the Captain shouting, 'Come along, my dear fellow,

85

come on in,' and the front end of the worm went through into the Captain's bedroom while the back end was still in the hall trying to lift its tail over the table.

Fabio had stopped feeling frightened but he was becoming very suspicious. 'Is there anything we have to do to the stoorworm?' he asked. If the mermaids needed scrubbing and the seals had to be given a bottle four times a day, and the boobrie's food had to be wheelbarrowed up a steep hill, it seemed likely that the stoorworm too would mean hard work.

And he was quite right. 'It's a question of seeing that he doesn't get tangled up,' said Aunt Etta. 'In the water he's all right but you will see a few trees we've stripped of lower branches—those are stoorworm trees and when he's on land we help him to coil himself round them neatly, otherwise he gets into knots. It's best to think of him as a kind of rope, or the flex of a Walkman.'

Fabio didn't say anything. He had already gathered that when Aunt Etta said 'we' she meant him and Minette— and she went on to explain that the worm was a person who liked to think about important things like *Where has yesterday gone?* or *Why hasn't God made sardines*

86

without bones?

'The trouble is he's so long that his thoughts don't easily get to the other end, and that upsets him,' said Etta. 'He wants to have an operation to make him shorter, but you must make it clear that we will *not* allow it. Plastic surgery,' said Aunt Etta, fiercely tapping her nose, 'is something we could never permit on the Island.'

'If you're bothered by his breath you can always give him a peppermint,' said Coral. 'Though why everyone in the world should smell of toothpaste is something I have never understood. And now you'd better go and fetch the barrows from the hill.'

CHAPTER SIX

'We must start to think seriously about running away,' said Fabio sleepily.

'Yes, we must,' agreed Minette, yawning.

They had gone on saying this each night—it was almost like saying their prayers—but they hadn't got much further. It wasn't just that they would have to steal the *Peggoty* from the boathouse, they would also have to know in which direction to sail her. And of course running away has two parts to it. There is running away *from* somewhere and there is running away to somewhere.

'It's all right for you,' Fabio said. 'You've got two proper parents. All I've got in this country is an awful school and awful grandparents.'

'Yes.' But Minette was doubtful. If she ran away to her father, her mother would be cross and if she ran away to her mother, her father would be cross. 'I'd just like to wait till the boobrie's laid her egg.'

And in the end, before they could make further plans, the children always fell asleep.

But as the days passed there was one thing that really annoyed Fabio, and that was Lambert.

Fabio didn't mind working hard. All the same, he and Minette both had blisters on their hands from trundling the wheelbarrows up and down to the loch; Minette had strained her wrist trying to get a comb through the old mermaid's tangled hair; and both of them were bruised by the young seals bumping and flopping against them as they gave them their bottles. And there was Lambert doing nothing—absolutely nothing—except kicking and screaming and throwing his food about.

'Why doesn't someone thump him?' said Fabio crossly.

But nobody did. Aunt Myrtle wasn't a thumper and the other aunts said that using force when training animals never worked. As for Art, he might have killed a man once but that was as far as it got. So each day Lambert was brought his food on a tray and each day he kicked and yelled for his father and his mobile telephone while Fabio and Minette did his share of the chores.

It was at the end of the first week that Fabio cracked, and it was because of the stoorworm.

The children had grown very fond of the worm. He ate the peppermints they gave him without fuss and the questions he asked were interesting, like *Why don't we think with our stomachs?* or *Why are we back to front in the mirror but not upside down?*

But wrapping him round a tree was an awful job. It wasn't just his thoughts that got stuck halfway down his body, it was all the messages which told his lower end what was happening, and on a day when they had spent a whole hour disentangling him from a bramble thicket, Fabio suddenly snapped.

Art was just making his way down to the boathouse with Lambert's lunch on a tray.

'I'll take that for you, Art,' said Fabio.

Art handed over the tray and Fabio opened the door.

Lambert looked up. Then he did what he always did when someone came into the room; he picked up whatever was closest to him and threw it hard. This time it was a sawn-off log ready to go on the fire.

Fabio ducked neatly. Then he threw the tray at Lambert. The tray contained a bowl of lentil soup, a slice of bread and butter, fried tomatoes on toast and a banana milkshake. All of these landed on Lambert except for the bread and butter which went slightly wide.

'Yow! Whee! Yuk!' Lambert spluttered and danced round the room, blinded by the tomatoes which were the large splodgy kind with a great many pips.

Fabio gave him a few moments to clean himself up. Then he said, 'Right. You're not getting anything more to eat till you come and work. Minette and I are sick of doing the jobs you ought to be doing.'

'I won't! I won't come and work!' Lambert tried to stamp his foot on the floor but stamped it into his soup bowl which split in half and skidded across the room. 'I won't stay here on this horrible island and I won't stay with these creepy women and I won't do anything. I want my father and I want my mobile telephone and I want to go home.'

Fabio waited. 'I don't care what you want,' he said. 'Minette and I want things too, but that doesn't mean we get them. From now on you're going to do your share and if you don't I'm going to thump you.'

Lambert had cleaned the tomato out of his eyes now. 'You'd better not,' he said. 'I'm bigger than you.'

This was true but it didn't bother Fabio. 'You may be bigger but you're weedier.'

Lambert was a coward, but Fabio was very small and slight. Lambert put up his fists and danced forward. He had never boxed but he had seen people do that on the telly.

Fabio on the other hand *had* boxed. He

didn't care for it but it was taught at Greymarsh Towers as part of making people into English gentlemen. He let fly with his right hand and landed a blow on Lambert's chin.

'Oow! Eeh! . . . You've bust my jaw. I'm going to tell my father. My father's rich and . . . Oowee . . .' Lambert was crouching down on the floor nursing his chin and moaning.

'Get up,' said Fabio.

'I won't.'

'Yes, you will. Get up or you'll be sorry.'

Lambert got slowly to his feet. The bruise on his chin blended nicely with the colour of the tomato smeared on his collar. Then suddenly he went for Fabio, tearing at his cheeks with his fingernails.

It hurt, but to Fabio it was a relief. He knew about fighting dirty. He had been doing it ever since he was three years old in the streets of Rio and if that was what Lambert wanted it was fine with him. Ignoring the blood streaming down his cheeks, he took hold of a handful of Lambert's hair and yanked the snivelling boy's head backwards, knocking it against the wall. Then he kicked him extremely hard on the shins.

'Ow!' moaned Lambert. 'Stop it!'

'I'll stop it as soon as you say you'll come and do your share of work.'

'I don't want to. I want my father. I want my mobile tele—'

Fabio yanked his head forward, then pushed it back again hard against the wall, and went on kicking.

'Are you going to come out and work or not?'

'No.'

Fabio kicked again—and suddenly Lambert crumpled up and collapsed on the floor.

'All right,' he blubbered. 'I'll work, but stop it.'

Fabio stopped at once. 'Come on, then,' he said. 'You can help me muck out the chicken house.'

The aunts saw the boys come. Fabio was carrying the remains of Lambert's lunch on the tray, including the broken soup bowl.

'You can take it out of my pocket money,' he said, handing them the pieces.

'What pocket money?' asked Aunt Etta.

'Even kidnapped children have to have pocket money,' said Fabio firmly.

93

So Lambert began to work. He worked badly and he worked slowly. He complained because the television was on the blink and whenever he could, he crept off to look for his mobile telephone which he was sure Myrtle had hidden somewhere. But when he stopped for too long, Fabio just looked at him and he picked up his tools once more.

Everyone agreed that such a tiresome, blathering boy had to be kept away from the unusual creatures—the selkies and the boobrie and the stoorworm—so they gave him jobs to do in the house or with the animals on the farm. But a couple of days after Fabio had beaten him up, Lambert crept down to the shore with a lemonade bottle he had stolen from the larder. Inside the lemonade bottle was a message he had written to his father telling him to come and rescue him, and he was going to throw the bottle into the sea.

But he never got as far as doing that. Instead he dropped the bottle, which smashed on the stones, leaving a dangerous mess of broken glass, and came back to the house blubbering and screaming at the top of his voice.

'I saw *a thing!* I saw a horrible creepy thing!' His whole body shook with terror. He looked as if he was going to have a fit.

'What sort of a thing?' asked Fabio.

He and Minette were sitting at the kitchen table, shelling peas for supper.

'A girl . . . all queer and horrible. She didn't have any legs—not any!' He sobbed and gulped again and a runnel of snot ran down his nose.

Minette handed him her handkerchief. 'What do you mean, Lambert?' she asked.

'The bottom end of her was a monster. She had a tail all covered in scales. It was growing from her body.' Lambert retched and turned his head away. 'I saw it. I *saw* it. I won't stay here, I won't!'

Minette and Fabio exchanged troubled glances. 'What was the top of her like?'

'I don't know . . . she had sort of green hair—and when I screamed she flopped her tail—I *heard* it flop . . .' He shuddered. 'And then she dived into the water.'

'It sounds like Oona,' said Minette in a low voice. 'Of course it would be her—she's been frightened enough already by that ridiculous Lord Brasenott. I'll go and comfort her. If only it had been Queenie, she'd have seen Lambert off.'

She slipped out and Fabio was left alone with the blubbering Lambert.

He had had an idea.

'Lambert,' he said. 'Listen to this, because it's important. When Minette and I first came, we saw all sorts of strange creatures—mermaids like you've seen and a long slithery worm and a giant bird—oh, all sorts of things—but then we realized they weren't real. They couldn't be real because creatures like that don't exist. I mean, there aren't any such things as mermaids, are there?'

Lambert had stopped crying. He was actually listening.

'No,' he said. 'There aren't.'

'So what has happened, Lambert, is that you're imagining them. It's like having a vision or a dream. And it's because of something that Art puts in the food. He uses a flour made of seaweed and it has a drug in it that makes you see things. He doesn't mean to harm us but it's the only kind of flour you can get here.'

'They aren't really there?' asked Lambert, sniffing the snot back into his nose. 'She wasn't there—that horrible girl and the awful tail that she flopped with—that wasn't there either?'

'No it wasn't. And anything else you see like that will just be a dream. You've heard of drugs that give you visions, haven't you? They're called halluci—' But here Fabio gave up, not sure of how to pronounce *hallucinogenic* or even if that was the word he meant. 'And it's best not to say anything to anyone—even if you think you see other things. Just don't take any notice, and if you get back to your father don't tell him, he'd only laugh at you.'

It worked. Lambert gave a few more gulps; he was still blotched, he was still hiccuping unpleasantly, but he was calm.

And from then on, if Lambert saw anything unusual he was sure it was because of something in the food.

The aunts weren't happy about Fabio telling lies, but it seemed safer than letting Lambert go screaming all over the Island and hurting the feelings of the creatures that he came upon.

And so the days passed. Minette and Fabio still talked about getting away but they always fell asleep before they could work out how to do it, and slowly the beauty of the place—the great wide skies, the flaming sunsets and the never-ending sound of the sea—seemed to be becoming a part of them.

But meanwhile in London all hell was breaking loose.

CHAPTER SEVEN

Eight days after Minette ate her drugged cheese and tomato sandwich, Minette's mother, Mrs Danby, rang Edinburgh to ask if Minette could stay with her father for an extra week. Minette's term had started but that was not the kind of thing that bothered Mrs Danby.

'I have the chance of a job filming in Paris,' she said.

This wasn't strictly true. What she did have was yet another boyfriend who said he'd take her to France for a bit of a 'jolly'.

Professor Danby, whom she'd interrupted as he was preparing an important lecture on 'The Use of the Semi-Colon', did not at first understand what she was saying.

'I can hardly keep Minette longer, when I haven't got her,' he said in his dry, irritable voice.

There was a pause at the other end while Mrs Danby fought down the slight fluttering in her stomach.

'Don't be silly, Philip. I sent Minette to you more than a week ago. She's been with you since the fifteenth.'

'No, you didn't. I had a telephone message to say you were keeping her with you and taking her to the seaside. I remember it quite clearly.'

The professor had in fact been rather pleased because the lecture he was giving was part of an important series—'The Use of the Semi-Colon', 'The Use of the Comma', 'The Use of the Paragraph' and so on—and he needed to get on with his work without being bothered by a child.

Now, though, he too began to feel as though his stomach was not quite where it should have been. But of course being the sort of people they were, the Danbys immediately began to blame each other.

'You must be mad, not letting me know she hadn't arrived.'

'I must be mad?' hissed the professor. '*You* must be mad. Any normal mother would ring up to see that her daughter had arrived safely.'

'And any normal father would ring and

find out why she wasn't being sent.'

'Are you accusing me of not being normal?' said the professor in a dangerously quiet voice. 'A woman who stubbed out her cigarette on a poached egg.'

'It wasn't a poached egg, it was a fried egg. And if you hadn't kept turning the lamps off because you were too mean to pay the electricity bill I'd have seen it wasn't an ashtray. And anyway, how a man who leaves a bath full of scum every time he—'

'Scum!' yelled the professor down the phone. 'Are you accusing *me* of leaving scum? Why I couldn't even get *into* the bath without wading through a heap of your unspeakable toenail clippings.'

They went on like this for some time but then they remembered that their only daughter was missing and pulled themselves together.

'Can she have run away?' wondered Mrs Danby.

'Why should she run away? She has two perfectly good homes.'

'Yes. But she's been looking a bit peaky. And she sees tigers on the ceiling. Perhaps I should have let her have a nightlight.'

'If every child who sees tigers on the ceiling ran away, there'd be very few children left in their homes,' said the professor.

But obviously the next thing to be done was to go to the police. So Professor Danby went to the police station in Edinburgh and Mrs Danby went to the police station in London. Then she rang her ex-husband and said that the police wanted them to come together and compare their stories exactly.

'You have to come down,' said Mrs Danby. 'And quick. They say there's no time to waste.'

So the professor took the train to London and the next day both of Minette's parents sat side by side in a taxi on the way to the Metropolitan Police Station.

The officer they saw this time was a high-ranking one, a detective chief superintendent who had a secretary sitting beside him to take everything down.

'Now, I understand that you have heard nothing since your daughter disappeared ten days ago?' he asked. 'No messages? No ransom demand?'

Both the Danbys shook their heads.

'I have very little money,' said the professor. 'I'm on the staff of the University and they pay abominably. It's a disgrace how little—'

'And I'm on the dole,' said Mrs Danby, unusually honest. 'So even if they asked us for money, it wouldn't help.'

The detective wrote this down. 'Now tell us, please, Mrs Danby, exactly where and when you last saw your daughter.'

'It was at two o'clock on the fifteenth of April. At King's Cross Station, Platform One. I handed her over to an aunt—'

'Wait a minute!' The superintendent's eyebrows drew together sharply. 'You mean *your* aunt . . . or *her* aunt . . . ?'

'No. *An* aunt. An aunt from an agency. Minette always travelled with aunts.'

The detective seemed to find this very interesting. 'Go and get me the file on the Mountjoy case,' he said to the secretary. 'Sergeant Harris has it.' He turned back to the Danbys. 'Now tell me from what agency you hired this aunt. It's an extremely important point.'

Mrs Danby frowned. 'Well, generally they came from an agency called *Useful Aunts.* I've used them for years—they're very reliable. But I think . . .' She rubbed her forehead. 'I'm not sure . . . I think this one may have been labelled *Unusual Aunts*. Yes, I think so. And there was some writing above that which said "My Name is Edna". Or maybe it was Etta.'

'If you hadn't rotted your brain with tobacco you might be able to remember,' said the professor under his breath.

But at that moment the secretary came back with a blue folder. 'Yes,' said the detective as he opened it. 'Yes. The two cases are extraordinarily similar.' He looked up at the Danbys. 'Another child disappeared on the same day as your daughter and he too was put in the charge of an aunt. I think we're getting somewhere at last!'

*　　*　　*

The old Mountjoys were always pleased when Hubert-Henry went back to boarding school. They hated having children about and they could never quite forgive their son for having married a foreign dancer in a nightclub and producing such an unsuitable grandson.

Then just a week after Hubert-Henry had left for Greymarsh Towers, a letter came from the headmaster which told old

Mr Mountjoy that even though Hubert was not at school because of Burry-Burry fever, the full fees for the term would still have to be paid.

That did it of course. Mr Mountjoy rang the headmaster and said what nonsense was this about Burry-Burry fever and where was the boy, who had been delivered to school on the first day of term?

And the headmaster said, no he hadn't, the aunt from the agency had told Matron that Hubert-Henry was ill.

So after the old Mountjoys had shouted down the telephone and threatened to sue the headmaster they went to the police. They might not be fond of Hubert-Henry but he was their grandson and their property and if anyone had taken him they wanted to know the reason why.

Which meant the police knew of two cases in which a child had vanished in the care of an aunt and it was now that the Great London Aunt Hunt began.

The police only knew about two aunts because Lambert's father was still in America, so that the boy had not yet been reported missing. But two aunts were enough to be going on with—and the newspapers and the police and the general public now went slightly mad.

Aunt Plague Menaces the City screamed the headlines, and *Monster Aunts on Killer Spree!*

Once people had been warned they saw these murdering women everywhere.

An aunt was caught outside a supermarket trying to impale a sweet little baby with a giant knitting needle while his mother shopped inside.

'I was only trying to spear a wasp,' she quavered, 'I didn't want it to sting the child.' But she was hauled off to the police station and it was only when they found the back end of the squashed insect in her knitting bag that she was set free.

An even more sinister aunt was seen in Hyde Park, kicking in the head of a little boy who lay in the grass.

'I seen her clear as daylight,' said a fat man who'd been walking his dog and sent for the police. 'Kicking like a maniac she was!'

And, 'Look how he's crying, the poor little fellow,' said the other dog owners who had crowded round—and it was true that the boy, holding on to his football, *was* crying. Anyone would cry, seeing their aunt bundled into a police van when she'd been showing them how to curl a penalty into the top right hand corner of the goal. She'd been a striker for the Wolverhampton Under-Eighteens and he thought the world of her.

There was talk in Parliament of a curfew for aunts, forcing them to be in bed by eight o'clock; the *Daily Echo* said aunts should be electronically tagged like prisoners—and an elderly lady was arrested in the shoe department of a department store for abusing her great-niece who was trying on shoes for a party.

'She was shouting and screaming at the child and her eyes were wild,' said the woman who had turned her in—and the aunt would probably have gone to prison, but while she was in the cells, the shop assistants downed tools and marched on the police station with banners, demanding that she should be freed.

'I wouldn't just have shouted at the girl, I'd have wrung her neck,' said a motherly shop assistant to the reporters standing round.

'The poisonous child had thirty-nine pairs of shoes out and she was throwing them round the floor,' said another shop girl. 'If you ask me, that aunt had the patience of a saint not to scream at her earlier.'

So the police let her go and then the newspapers said they were too soft and aunts should be flogged like in the good old days.

Meanwhile posters of Etta and Coral were stuck up in police stations and public libraries and bus shelters everywhere. These pictures had been drawn by an artist from the descriptions he had been given by the people who had seen them last, and they were extremely odd. Aunt Etta had a nose like a pickaxe, a blob of hair like a jelly bag on top of her head and a moustache she could have twirled, it was so big. Aunt Coral had a mad squint in one eye, seven pairs of earrings in each ear and absolutely no neck.

Have you seen these women? it said at the bottom of the posters.

But of course no one had, because women like that do not exist. And so the days passed and still the police had no clues to go on. The Aunts' Agency had closed down and it seemed as though the stolen children and their kidnappers had vanished off the face of the earth.

107

CHAPTER EIGHT

Aunt Etta woke and stretched and immediately felt very strange. Something had happened. And the something was important: perhaps the most important thing that had ever happened to her.

She got out of bed and went to the window. Her long grey pigtail hung down her back; her hairy legs and bony feet stuck out from under her flannel nightdress, but her mud-coloured eyes were as excited as a young girl's.

Yet there was nothing unusual to be seen. A flock of gulls were out fishing; the sun was just beginning to come up behind the two islands to the east.

'All the same, there is something,' thought Aunt Etta, and the excitement grew in her. 'Only what?'

Then she realized that the excitement was coming from her feet. It was being sent through her toe bones, and up her ankle bones and through her body.

For a moment she felt quite faint. Could it be . . . ? But no . . . that would be a miracle; she had done nothing to deserve anything as tremendous as that.

The sound of heavy breathing made her turn. It was Coral. She too was in her nightdress, folds of it wrapped round her like a bell tent, she too was barefoot and she too was panting with excitement.

'Oh, Etta; she gasped. 'I feel so strange.'

Coral's long hair, which she dyed an interesting gold, hung down her back; she looked like a mad goddess. 'I feel as though . . . only it can't be, can it? Not after a hundred years?'

'No . . . it can't.'

But they clutched each other's hands, because it hadn't stopped, the extraordinary, amazing . . . feeling.

'We must wake Myrtle. She's musical.'

But there was no need to wake Myrtle. Myrtle did not wear a nightdress; she wore pyjamas because she often went out before dawn to talk to the seals and she thought that pyjamas were more respectable. They were made of grey flannel so that she did not show up too much in the dusk and for a moment her sisters did not see her lying on the floor with her face pressed to the threadbare carpet.

'Myrtle, do you feel—' her sisters began.

But before she could answer, Myrtle lifted her head. They had never seen their sister look like that. 'Can it be?' began Coral.

'We must go up the hill,' said Myrtle and she spoke like someone in a dream. 'We must turn our faces to the north.'

'But dressed,' said Etta, coming to her senses for a moment. 'Not in our nightclothes. Not even if—'

But her sisters took no notice and Etta herself only had time to put on her dressing gown before there was a thumping noise from next door. It was the Captain's walking stick banging on the wall and it meant, 'Come at once.'

The sisters looked at each other anxiously. If he had heard it too it could strain his heart. So much excitement is bad for old people.

And when they first saw the Captain they were very worried. He was lying slumped on his pillows, his eyes shut, and he was trembling so much that the whole bed shook. But when they came up to him, they were amazed. Captain Harper was a hundred and three years old, but he looked for a moment like a boy.

'I've heard it,' he murmured. 'I've heard it and I've felt it. Even if that's all,

110

even if there's no more than that, I'll die happy now.'

'We're going on to the hill, Father,' said Etta. 'We'll tell you as soon as—'

The door burst open and Fabio and Minette came running into the room. They had tumbled straight out of bed, bewildered and still half asleep, and followed the sound of voices.

'Something's happened,' said Minette. She was wearing quite the silliest nightdress that even her mother could have bought, covered in patterns of dancing elephants and picnicking zebras, but with her dark hair wild about her shoulders and her bewildered eyes, she seemed to be listening to music from another land. 'We were woken . . .'

'It's a feeling . . . only it isn't only a feeling.' Fabio shook his head, trying to understand. 'It's a sound, except it's all through us. We're not making it up.'

The three aunts and the old Captain looked at the children, and nodded. It was a pleased nod, and it meant that the children were all right; they were proper ones, without a touch of a Boo-Boo or a Little One. Lambert, they were sure, would have heard and felt nothing.

'You'd better come with us. Get your

111

shoes on at least.'

*   *   *

Outside the feeling was stronger. Minette and Fabio, struggling for words to describe it, were lost. They followed the aunts on to the turf path which led to the hill. Minette wore Myrtle's shawl round her shoulders—no one had taken time to dress properly.

The 'feeling', whatever it was, was growing stronger. It came through the soles of their feet, but also now from above, from everywhere. If they'd been doubtful whether it meant anything, the creatures would have put them right at once. In the dawn light the birds wheeled round the cliff in a frenzy of agitation. The seals, usually drowsing on the point at this hour, were all in the water, swimming towards the northern strand—and in the lead was Herbert. Like all selkies he slept with one eye open: he had been the first to know that something incredibly important was going to happen and at once he had put aside his everyday worries. What did it matter now whether one was a man or a seal? He moved through the waves like a torpedo—and close behind Herbert came his mother.

The sky was changing. It was filled with strange colours which belonged neither to the dawn nor to the sunset; colours that the children had never seen and afterwards could not describe.

On her great nest, the boobrie honked with all her power . . . honked and stirred . . . and flapped her wings, trying to fly off after the others, but she couldn't, with the eggs so heavy and stuck inside her . . . and she pushed her muscles together, pressing and pressing as she tried to become airborne . . .

The stoorworm came out of the lake and slithered over the ground, following the aunts and the children. He was no longer the muddled creature who had lost control of his far end. He moved like a great serpent, controlled and lean and fast.

Down by the house the goats butted their horns against the walls of their sty, and broke free and went galloping along the shore like mad creatures.

The door of the mermaid shed opened and Loreen and her daughters slithered across the rocks and plunged into the water.

'To the north,' she shouted, holding

Walter in the crook of her arm, and they set off for the wild strand beneath the hill.

'Wait for me, wait for me,' shouted Old Ursula, but they had gone and she was left beating her tail furiously against the side of the sink.

The Sybil had come out of her cave. The mucky old prophetess was not talking about the weather now. She was writhing and moaning, her face had turned blue and her hair was standing on end. 'It's going to happen,' she said. 'It's going to happen.'

But the aunts did not wait for her to tell them what. They raced panting up the hill with the children beside them, and all the time the feeling was getting stronger, was going through every cell in their bodies.

They reached the top of the hill—and then they were certain. From all sides it came now, like the breath of the universe. Below them the sea boiled against the northern shore; the mermaids, their troubles forgotten, trod water and stared towards the horizon; the seals made a semicircle, and those who were more than seals, who had been human once, could be seen bowing their heads.

And to make everything certain, from

behind the largest of the tombstones with its strange carvings, there now rose a white, mysterious wraith, with rays of light coming from her face, and outstretched hands.

'It's Ethelgonda,' breathed Aunt Etta, 'Ethelgonda the Good!' And everyone fell to their knees, for this was a ghost who had not appeared for well over a hundred years.

The saintly hermit was smiling. She was totally happy; she enfolded them in her blessing.

'Yes,' she said, in a deep and beautiful voice. 'You have not been mistaken. What you have heard is most truly the Great Hum.'

Minette and Fabio, who had been spellbound by the apparition, heard the sound of the most heartfelt sobbing beside them and turned their heads. All three of the aunts were crying. Tears streamed down Aunt Etta's bony cheeks, tears made a path through Aunt Coral's nourishing night cream, tears dropped on to Aunt Myrtle's hands as she brought them to her face.

'It is the Hum,' repeated Aunt Etta, in a choking voice.

'It is the Hum,' nodded Aunt Coral.

And Myrtle too said, 'It is the Hum.'

'What is—' began Fabio but Minette frowned him down. She felt that this was not the moment for questions.

'So does that mean . . . ?' faltered Aunt Etta, and the children looked at her, amazed. They did not know that this fierce woman could sound so shy and uncertain and humble.

The hermit nodded. 'Yes, my dears,' she said in her melodious voice. 'It means that this place above all others has been chosen. You have been blessed.'

The aunts rose slowly to their feet. They could still not quite believe what they had heard, yet the Hum now was everywhere, filling the sky, coming up from the earth.

'So *he* is really coming? After a hundred years?'

The holy woman nodded.

The aunts did not ask *when* he was coming. They knew that one must not pry into mysteries, but accept them gratefully, and they were right.

'I can say no more,' said the saint. 'You must hold yourself in readiness.'

And then she vanished and they were left alone with their miracle.

'You heard what Ethelgonda said. We must hold ourselves in readiness. Readiness means cleaning. Readiness means tidying. Readiness means cooking and scrubbing and fettling. It always has and it always will,' said Aunt Etta.

She was almost her old brisk bossy self as she sent the children to scour out the goat sty and swill down the floor of the mermaid shed and pick up the litter washed ashore.

Almost, but not quite. None of the aunts were quite the same. Etta still hung her navy-blue knickers on the line each morning, but sometimes she patted her bun of hair like a young girl invited to a party. Coral's clothes got wilder and wilder; she was painting a great underwater mural on the back of the house in all the colours of the rainbow, and the tunes that Myrtle played on her cello had become very powerful and loud.

'If only Dorothy was here,' said Etta, who missed her sister badly. Hitting people on the head with their own woks was nothing to the excitement of what was to come.

The Captain insisted on clean pyjamas

every day so that he would not be caught short, and the old Sybil danced about in her cave in a frenzy of excitement. She still thought it was unwise to wash her face and hands but she decided bravely to wash her feet. This took a long time (mould had grown between her toes and mould can be interesting—the blue-green colours, the unusual shapes) but once one has heard the Great Hum life is never the same.

The creatures, in their own way, were as excited, and now the aunts understood why it had been so difficult to get anyone to go away. They must have known that something special was going to happen, even if they did not know exactly what.

Even the animals that never talked; even the herrings and the haddock and the flounders . . . even the lugworms buried in the sand seemed to be excited.

'How can a lugworm be excited?' Minette wanted to know, but when Aunt Etta dug one up for her, she saw that it might be so.

As for Art, he baked buns—hundreds and hundreds of buns which overflowed his cake tins and had to be stored in sealed bin bags in the larder. But the buns he baked were not ordinary buns, and nor were the omelettes they had for lunch and tea and supper ordinary omelettes.

Because something very wonderful had happened out there on the hill after Ethelgonda vanished. They were turning to go home when they heard a sound from the boobrie's nest which stopped them in their tracks.

It wasn't the mournful honking they were used to: it was a proud and cheerful clucking—a noise full of motherhood and joy. Pressing and pressing her muscles together to try and follow the others had not made the boobrie airborne, but it had done something else. And there it was; an enormous, blue-spotted and totally egg-shaped egg!

But the most touching thing happened the next day when they went up to congratulate the bird once more. For the egg she had laid when the Great Hum went through her body and she had pressed so hard, had been followed by three more. Four gigantic spotted eggs had rolled together and were keeping warm beneath her body, but when she saw the aunts and the children the boobrie moved aside, examined each egg very carefully—and then pushed one out towards them with her great yellow foot.

'Be careful, dear,' said Myrtle. 'It mustn't get cold.'

With difficulty, for the egg was heavier than a cannonball, they rolled it back . . . and the boobrie pushed it out again with her enormous foot.

The same thing was repeated three times—and then they understood.

'It's a present,' said Minette, awed. 'She wants us to have it.'

Minette was right. The boobrie wanted to *share*. There was nothing to be done except to fetch Art and load the egg on to a barrow—and since seventy-two omelettes are an awful lot of omelettes, the great bun bake began.

It was hard for the children to be patient during those days of waiting. They knew that when the time came they would find out what the Great Hum meant and who was coming. But on a day when Fabio was sent out for the third time to make sure that not so much as half a cigarette carton or a cotton reel had been washed up on the north shore, he dug in his heels.

'I think you should tell us,' he said. 'Me and Minette, I mean. We can keep secrets.'

'We will tell you when the time is ripe,'

said Aunt Etta, and they had to be content with that.

*　　*　　*

But what had been happening to Lambert?

The aunts were right. Lambert had slept through the beginning of the Hum and heard nothing.

When he did wake up at last, he realized that the house was empty. Doors stood open; there was no sign of Art in the kitchen. Everyone, though Lambert did not know it, was out on the hill.

'I want my breakfast,' said Lambert crossly, but there was no one to hear him.

By the time he was dressed he did hear a kind of thrumming noise, but to Lambert the magical sound seemed to be the kind of noise a generator might make, or some underground machinery.

But he was interested in the open bedroom doors. Since he had begun to work, Lambert had been allowed to come back into the house to sleep, but Myrtle and the others kept him firmly out of their rooms. Myrtle had not forgotten how he had frightened the ducklings when he first came.

Now, though, Myrtle's door stood open. Her bed was unmade and the ducklings had grown enough to manage out of doors.

Lambert crept in. His shifty eyes took in all Myrtle's little treasures and he sneered. Fancy bothering to pick up bits of driftwood and veined pebbles and arranging them on the bookcase as though they were ornaments. There wasn't a single thing in her room, as far as he could see, that was worth tuppence.

Then he stopped dead. Propped against the corner of the room was Myrtle's cello case. The cello wasn't inside it; he could see it leaning against another wall, half covered with a shawl, so the case would be empty.

Lambert crept closer. He knew he had been carried away in it though he could remember nothing. He had overheard Myrtle talking about it to her sisters.

And that meant that anything he had been holding when he was snatched might still be there!

Lambert's face was flushed with excitement, his thin lips were parted. If only the case wasn't locked!

And it wasn't! He tried the clasp, and it opened easily. The inside of the case was lined with blue velvet, faded and torn in places because it was so old.

At first there seemed to be nothing there except a crumpled silk scarf and a spare bow. Then as Lambert groped about in the back of the case, his hand found something dark and small which had been covered by the cloth.

Lambert's fingers closed round it with a cry. He had found it. He had found his mobile telephone!

He would get away now! He was safe. Hiding the telephone under his shirt, Lambert went back to his room and pulled the chest of drawers across the door. Then he crouched down like an animal with its prey and began to dial.

*   *   *

Three days after Lambert found his telephone, the children woke shortly after midnight to find Aunt Coral and Aunt Etta standing by their beds.

Fabio was so sleepy that he thought at first it was the full moon and he was expected to dance the tango with Aunt Coral, but it wasn't that.

'Put some clothes on,' said Aunt Etta. 'And clean your teeth.'

'We cleaned them before we went to bed,' said Minette.

'Well, clean them again. No one with gunge on their molars is worthy to hear what we have to tell.'

Still half asleep, the children stumbled up the hill after the two aunts. At the top they found Aunt Myrtle sitting over a fire she had made, ringed by stones, and it was by the flicker of the flames and to the sound of the sea sighing against the rocks below that the children learnt what they wanted to know.

'Mind you, what I'm going to say won't mean much to you unless you know your history, and I doubt if you know a lot of that,' said Aunt Etta. 'So let me start by asking you a question. What does the word *kraken* mean to you?'

Fabio was silent but Minette said shyly, 'Is it a sea monster? A very big one?'

Etta nodded. 'Yes. It is a sea monster, and it is bigger than anything you can imagine. But it has nothing to do with all the silly stories you hear. Nothing to do with rubbish about Giant Blobs or outsize cuttlefish or octopuses that pull people down to the ocean bed. No, the kraken is . . . or was . . . the Soul of the Sea. It is the greatest force for good the ocean has ever

124

known.'

Fabio and Minette looked at her surprised. This wasn't at all the way that Aunt Etta usually spoke.

So then she began to tell them the kraken's story. It took a long time to tell and the fire had burnt down and been rekindled many times before it was finished, but the children scarcely stirred.

*   *   *

'There was a time when everyone in the world knew about the kraken,' Aunt Etta began. 'They knew about his huge size and that when he rested, and his back was humped out of the water, he was taken for an island. They knew that when he reared up suddenly, the sea churned and boiled and no ship that was near him had the slightest hope of avoiding shipwreck.

'But they knew too that for all his size, the kraken was a gentle creature. His eyes were full of soul and when he opened his mouth one could see that instead of teeth he had rows and rows of tendrils which were the greeny-gold colour of a mermaid's hair. Through this forest of tendrils, the sea poured in, and it was the sea which nourished him: the tiny

125

invisible creatures which make up plankton were all that the kraken needed for food.

'They knew that the kraken came from the Far North and that the language he spoke best was Polar, though he understood other languages also. But mostly the kraken did not speak. The kraken sang. Or perhaps singing is not quite the right word. What the kraken did was to hum. It was a deep, slow sound and it was like no other sound in the world, for what the kraken hummed was the Song of the Sea. It was a healing song. If you like, it was the Breath of the Universe. Whales can hum too and Buddhist monks who spend their lives on high mountains trying to understand God . . . and small children when they are happy—but the sound they make is nothing compared to the sound made by the kraken.

'For many years the kraken swam quietly round the oceans of the world humming his hum and singing his song and stopping sometimes to rest. And when he stopped, people who did not know much said: goodness, surely there wasn't an island out in that bay before, but people who were wise and in touch with the things that mattered, smiled and felt honoured and proud. Because when the kraken came, they remembered what a splendid thing the sea was: so clean and beautiful when it was calm, so mighty and exciting and awe-inspiring when it was rough. It was as though the great creature was guarding the sea for them, or even as though somehow he was showing them what a treasure house it was.

'*Look!* the kraken seemed to be saying. *Behold . . . the sea!*

'In those days the kraken made it his business to circle the oceans of the world each year and whenever he appeared, people started to behave themselves. Fishermen stopped catching more fish than they needed and threw the little ones back into the sea, and people who were dumping their rubbish into the water thought better of it, seeing the kraken's large and wondrous eyes fixed on them. And when he went on again it was to leave the sea—and indeed the world—a better place.

'It was like a blessing, to have seen the kraken,' said Aunt Etta now. 'It brought you luck for the rest of your life.'

'Did you ever see him?' asked Minette.

Aunt Etta shook her head. She looked

very sad. 'No one living now has seen him. He hasn't been seen for a hundred years or more. He was dreadfully hurt once and he went into hiding.'

The hurt that was done to the kraken was not to his body. The skin of a kraken is a metre deep and no other animal can threaten him. No animal would want to— he travelled with a whole company of sharks and stingrays and killer whales who would have died rather than harm him.

But human beings are different. They always have been: interfering and bossy and mad for power. No one knew what kind of whaling boat had shot a harpoon into the kraken's throat. Was it a Japanese ship or one belonging to the British or the Danes? Did the whalers mistake the kraken for a humpback whale, or were they just terrified, seeing a dark shape bigger than anything they had ever seen rear up in front of them?

Whatever the reason, they let off the biggest of their harpoons and hit the kraken with terrible force in the softest part of his throat.

The kraken probably didn't believe it at first. No one had ever tried to harm him. Then he felt the pain and saw the dark dollops of his blood staining the sea.

When he understood what had happened, he began to thrash about, trying to rid himself of the harpoon—and the rope snapped. But the pain was still there and the kraken reared up, trying to dislodge the hooked horror in his neck. As he did so, the tidal wave made by his body tossed the whaling boat up, and drew it under the sea, and every one of the men was drowned, which was as well because the sea creatures who had travelled with the kraken would have torn them limb from limb.

And the kraken swam away to the north, the harpoon still in his throat. The pain died away and presently an old sea nymph came with her brood of children and cut the hook out of the kraken's flesh with razor shells and soon there was only a small scar left to show where it had been.

But the scar in the kraken's soul remained. He had travelled the world to sing the Song of the Sea and to heal the people who lived by it—and they had stabbed him in the throat. The kraken was two thousand years old, which is not old for a kraken, but now he felt tired. Let human beings look after themselves!

He swam still further north, and further still to where the wildness of the sea and the large number of humped islands made him invisible, and he turned his back on the world, and slept.

And while he slept, people forgot that there had been such a creature, and the stories about him got wilder and wilder until this healing monster was jumbled up in people's minds with Giant Blobs and vicious triffids and nonsense like that.

And the sea got muckier and muckier and more and more neglected.

But of course everyone did not forget. The sea creatures remembered—the seals and the selkies, the mermaids and the nixies, and the people who lived and worked on the islands and by the shore.

And the aunts remembered.

'Oh yes, we always remembered,' said Etta now. 'Our father told us about him and our grandfather told our father. We have always known, but we never dreamt—'

She fell silent, overcome by her feelings and the children gazed into the embers of the fire and thought about what they had heard.

Why am I not frightened, Minette wondered. Once she would have been terrified at the thought of a great sea monster swimming towards them, but now she felt only wonder. And something else: a longing to help and serve this creature she had never seen. She felt she would do anything for the kraken when he came. Which was silly, because how could an ordinary girl do anything for the mightiest monster in the world? But she didn't feel silly. She felt awed and uplifted as though some amazing task awaited her.

Fabio didn't feel quite like that. Fabio felt that the story he had heard needed a celebration. So he did something rather noble. He turned to Coral, sitting in her cloak beside him, and said:

'Aunt Coral, the moon is full—or very nearly. Would you like to dance the tango?'

CHAPTER NINE

Stanley Sprott, Lambert's father, had had a good time in America. He had bought three factories and a cinema and turned out a family living in a house next to the cinema so that he could bulldoze it and build a Fast Food restaurant. There had been a court case and a fuss because the family had a disabled child and a sick mother, but Mr Sprott had won. He always did win because he knew how to hire the best lawyers and now, as the chauffeur drove him in his Mercedes from the airport, he reckoned that his trip to the States would earn him a clear million dollars.

Beside him in the car sat his bodyguard, Des, a large man with small eyes and an even smaller brain. Des had only learned to read when he was 25 and he liked to show that he could do it, so as they stopped for the traffic lights he looked at the posters on the wall of the police station and said: 'There's some mad aunts been on the rampage, kidnapping children. They're offering a thousand pounds reward if anyone's got any info.'

Mr Sprott thought this was very funny.

'Aunts!' he snorted as the car moved on, leaving the pictures of Aunt Coral and Aunt Etta flapping in the breeze. 'Trust the police to be fooled by a bunch of aunts!'

Mr Sprott had a very low opinion of the police, who had tried to interfere with some of his enterprises and been thoroughly foiled.

Arriving in his house, he stood for a moment in the hallway and looked about him. He had the feeling that somebody who should have been in his house, was not.

But who? Who was it that was not there? While Des went to turn off the burglar alarms and look for letter bombs, Mr Sprott thought about this.

Well, for one thing his wife was not there. But there was nothing strange about that. His wife had faxed him from Paris to say she was going to go and buy some more clothes in Rome, and she had faxed him from Rome to say she was going to buy some more clothes in Madrid.

So it wasn't Josette Sprott who should have been there and wasn't, and it wasn't the housekeeper who always had two hours off in the afternoon.

Which meant that it was his son, Lambert. 'Lambert!' bellowed Mr Sprott, standing in the middle of the hallway.

No answer.

'Get him on the intercom,' Mr Sprott told Des.

But though all the rooms were connected electronically, Lambert did not appear.

Mr Sprott was not alarmed, but he was surprised. He had told Lambert when he was coming back and the boy, though an awful sniveller, was fond of his father.

Mr Sprott went to his study, sent out for a secretary, and was soon deep in his business affairs.

But when the housekeeper came back in the early evening, Mr Sprott was reminded of his son once more.

'Didn't you bring Lambert, sir?' she asked him. Her voice was hopeful. She really hated the boy.

'How could I bring Lambert? I haven't got him. I never had him—he's staying here with you.'

'No, he isn't. There was a message saying he was joining you in America. It was left by the aunt—she said there'd been a call.'

'The aunt? What aunt?'

'The aunt from the agency. She took Lambert to the zoo and when I got back the boy was gone.'

The flapping posters, the notice of the reward, ran through Mr Sprott's mind. They didn't seem so funny now.

'I'm sorry, sir, but—'

'Be quiet.' Mr Sprott was scowling. 'I'm

going to the police. Tell Merton to bring the car round.'

But at that moment, very faintly, a telephone rang upstairs.

It was his personal phone, or rather one of them. Mr Sprott bought mobiles like other people bought matches and now he couldn't remember which one it was or where he might have left it. Under his bed? On the lavatory cistern? In the cocktail cabinet?

'Find it,' he ordered, and the bodyguard and the secretary and the housekeeper ran all over the house trying to follow the sound.

It was Mr Sprott who reached it just as it was about to stop ringing. It was under a pile of monogrammed underpants in his chest of drawers.

'Hello!' he shouted. He was a man who always shouted into telephones. There were some strange noises; a sort of gulping sound followed by a gabble. 'Speak up, damn you. I can't hear you!'

'It's me, Daddy. It's Lambert. I've been kidnapped! You've got to come and get me!' More gulping, more tears. What a cry-baby the boy was!

'All right, Lambert. I'll come and get you, but where are you? Speak clearly.'

'I'm on an island. It's an awful place—'

'What island? Where is it?'

'It's in the sea.'

Stanley Sprott rolled his eyes. 'Yes, Lambert, islands are usually in the sea. But where? Which sea?'

'I dunno—they won't tell me—but it's cold. There aren't any coconuts. I've been phoning and phoning you every day.' He broke off, gulping again. 'My battery is running out.'

'Lambert, please think. Are there any other islands near by?'

'There's a couple on one side.'

'What side. East? West? North? South?'

'I dunno. The sun comes up behind them, I think. It's awful here—it's weird. There's these aunts; they're mad and they give me drugged food. You've got to come, you've got to! There's one after me now!'

The line went dead. Mr Sprott stood for a while thinking. An isolated island with two islands to the east of it. And—unbelievably—a posse of aunts.

He gave his orders. 'I want the *Hurricane* made ready. I'll pick her up at London docks. Get a couple of armed men aboard and see there's plenty of ammunition. Pick them carefully; this mission is secret!'

The *Hurricane* was his yacht—a converted patrol boat and his pride and joy.

It was only then that he went to the police. He would not trust them to find Lambert—that job he would do by himself without telling anybody—but he might as well find out if there were any other clues.

That evening a third picture appeared on the walls of the police station, and in bus shelters and public libraries. This was of Aunt Myrtle, as remembered by the housekeeper and the man who fed the seals in London Zoo. It was even more peculiar than the other two pictures. Aunt Myrtle seemed to be standing in a high wind with her mouth open, and once again no one came forward to say they had seen her.

But Stanley Sprott's team of researchers were already marking down all the islands in the North Sea and the Atlantic with two islands to the east of them. And the *Hurricane*, with a full complement of arms on board, lay ready at the docks.

CHAPTER TEN

He seemed to be swimming quite slowly and peacefully, though the swell he left as he moved through the water could be felt on shores a thousand miles away.

Above him, the air was filled with flocks of birds which circled him, and the sea creatures ringed him down below. The sky was a hazy gold and the sunsets were glorious and lingering, as though the sun could not bear to go down on such a sight, and the sea glittered and glistened.

As he swam, the kraken hummed, but not all the time. Sometimes he stopped and turned his head to speak to someone who was swimming close beside him and when he did that, the birds in the air fell silent and the underwater creatures moved their fins and flippers carefully, so as not to make a splash. Because the person who was swimming beside the kraken was important, and they wanted to make sure that he understood what the kraken was telling him.

Strange things happened as the kraken moved south from his Arctic hideout. He came level with an oil rig where men were working the night shift. The lights of the rig were only distant specks to the kraken but he paused and changed his Hum to a deeper one, and on the rig a man called Dave O'Hara said:

'I'm going to shut off the waste pipe.'

His mates put down their beer mugs and stared at him.

'Why? What's got into you? It's always on at night.'

This was true. The outlet pipe spilled its filthy sludge into the water night and day.

'I dunno,' said Dave, 'but I'm shutting it off.'

And he did so . . . and the kraken swam on.

*   *   *

On the Island, Herbert was the first to know.

His mother had come out of the sea a few days before and had tried to nag him again.

'You must make up your mind, Herbert,' she had said in the selkie language they spoke when they were alone. 'You're not young any more; and I won't be around for ever. If you're going

139

to stop being a seal and start being a man you must do it now.'

For a while, Herbert only looked at her. Then: 'Listen!' he said in his quiet and serious voice.

She had listened, and she had heard it because selkies are famous for the sharpness of their ears. Not the Great Hum with which the kraken sent out long-distance messages, but the quiet, thrumming noise he made when he was patrolling the ocean.

'This is not the time to be human, Mother. I shall greet him in the water, and proudly, as a seal.'

It was because of Herbert that Myrtle understood more quickly than the other aunts how near the kraken was. She had tried to play Herbert one of his favourite pieces—a minuet by Mozart. Usually he listened to this with his eyes closed, absolutely enchanted; Mozart was his favourite composer. But now he was restless, eagerly looking out to sea, and then he shook his head once as if to excuse himself and dived into the waves.

Soon it wasn't only Myrtle who guessed. Aunt Etta saw three snow geese—birds she had never seen on the Island before—and Coral came back from a shell hunt, dancing with excitement.

'The sea is changing colour,' she said. 'Only slightly, but it's changing.'

Then suddenly it seemed as though everyone knew that the time was coming and the last-minute preparations began.

In his bed, the old Captain sat with the telescope glued to his eyes and tried to be gloomy.

'Of course he won't be like the kraken was in the olden days. He'll be smaller, like the seals are smaller and the sheep, and the bosoms of the ladies. Maybe he won't be any bigger than a whale,' said Captain Harper. But if anyone tried to take the telescope away from him he became absolutely furious and, as the kraken came closer, he scarcely slept.

As for the aunts and the children, during those days they seemed to be welded together into one band of workers who thought of nothing except to make the best possible welcome for the kraken when he came. It was impossible to imagine that Fabio and Minette had been drugged and kidnapped against their will not three weeks before. There was no need to give them orders; they knew what needed doing almost as soon as the aunts and they, like the aunts, never spared themselves.

Then one day they too heard the Hum once more. It was the kraken's Daily Hum, his Working Hum, the Hum with which he cleaned and healed the sea, and it was getting closer, and closer . . .

There was only one thing which puzzled the aunts. Every so often the Hum stopped and they heard a low rumbling which might have been the kraken speaking. They couldn't understand the words from that great distance—and in any case none of the aunts spoke Polar—but they could understand the tone, and the feeling they had was that whoever the kraken was talking to was driving him a little mad.

But who could it be? The kraken had always been a loner.

They were soon to find out.

CHAPTER ELEVEN

The Great London Aunt Hunt was still going badly. The pictures of Etta and Coral and Myrtle went on flapping on the walls of police stations everywhere but the people who came to say they had seen one or other of them were obviously barmy. A man came and said a lollipop lady who was helping schoolchildren across the road in Kensington had a moustache and was certainly Aunt Etta, but she wasn't. Another man said he had seen Aunt Myrtle busking outside a cinema, but he hadn't. And anyone weighing over a hundred kilos and wearing jewellery was apt to be hauled off by the police in case she was Coral.

'Don't call me "aunt",' terrified women were begging their nephews and nieces all over London's streets and, by the time the children had been gone three weeks, the word had almost disappeared.

Minette's mother, as the days passed with no news, smoked three packets of cigarettes a day, couldn't sleep without slurping a full tumbler of whisky and allowed her flat to get into even more of a mess than before. Of course in some ways it was easier without Minette who kept trying to tidy up and open windows. All the same, Mrs Danby couldn't help wishing she had let her have a nightlight.

'And I should have taken her to the seaside—she always wanted to go,' she said to her latest boyfriend.

'You can take her when she comes back,' he said, dropping his empty lager can over the side of the sofa. 'Though I've never seen much point to the seaside myself. The water comes in, the water goes out—what's the sense in that?'

Professor Danby too wished he had done some things and hadn't done others. He had promised every time she came to take Minette to the ice rink and there'd never been time, and he'd known really that she didn't want an encyclopaedia without pictures for her birthday.

But when they telephoned each other for news of Minette, the Danbys quarrelled as much as ever. They had decided that she had run away, and of course they blamed each other.

'I'm surprised she lasted so long in that pigsty you live in,' the professor said.

'Well, really,' Mrs Danby would reply. 'Considering that your place would make an underground tomb on a rainy Sunday look like Disneyland, you've got a nerve!'

The Mountjoys were not sorry about anything they had done. They were sure that Fabio had had everything he needed in their house and that in sending him to Greymarsh Towers—and *paying* for it— they had treated him better than any poor

144

child from the back of beyond had a right to expect. But they did wonder whether they should tell Fabio's mother that he had disappeared, and his other grandparents in South America.

'I really can't face the thought of having a lot of foreigners coming here and waving their arms,' said Mrs Mountjoy. 'They probably paint their faces and don't wear shoes.'

Old Mr Mountjoy agreed. 'Still, she is the boy's mother. We'll give it a few more days and then if there's no news we'll have to let them know.'

Both the Mountjoys and the Danbys were angry with the police. 'You've gone cold on the case,' Mrs Danby accused the superintendent.

But she was very wrong. Discovering the third kidnap and the third aunt had given the police a new and important lead. Two days after Stanley Sprott came to report that his son was missing, an 'Aunt Myrtle' was seen in Putney swimming baths. She had long greyish hair and an open mouth, which is a silly thing to have in a swimming bath, so it had to be her.

The police wearily pulled her in and sent an officer to Mr Sprott's house to ask

145

the housekeeper to come and identify her—and learnt that Mr Sprott wasn't there.

So where was he, they wanted to know. He was supposed to be standing by in case there was news of Lambert.

At first no one would tell him, but when the policeman threatened to get a search warrant, the secretary admitted that he had gone away in his yacht.

'That'll be the *Hurricane*,' said the superintendent thoughtfully when the officer got back to the station.

They knew a bit about Mr Sprott's activities and his yacht.

'I think we'll see what he's up to. He may have got a lead on the boy.'

'What about the other parents—it's likely the children are all together. Should we tell them?'

'Not yet. If we find them we'll bring the parents out by helicopter. But we won't say anything yet.'

*   *   *

The team that Stanley Sprott had sent to the chart room at the British Museum, to look for lonely islands with two islands to the east of them, had found an ancient

146

map with three that seemed likely.

Now the *Hurricane* was steaming to the first of these—a place called Dooneray off the west coast of Scotland. It was a small island and there were no houses marked on it, but it seemed quite likely that the mad aunts who held his son were keeping him imprisoned in a cave.

As he paced the deck, Stanley Sprott was wondering about the ransom. Why had no one asked him for money in exchange for Lambert? Not that he'd have paid it—he'd have blown the kidnappers to hell before he wasted money like that—but it was odd. Everything was odd about this child snatch.

Though Mr Sprott was wearing a uniform—a navy cut reefer and a cap covered in gold braid—he never did any real work on the boat. He had a captain who sailed it, and two crew members to whom he kept shouting orders which they ignored. If they hadn't, they would have run aground many a time because Mr Sprott had no real knowledge or understanding of boats.

The *Hurricane* had all the silly things on board that one finds on boats that are rich men's toys: a jacuzzi with gold taps, a

147

vast bed covered with a leopard skin and a lounge with a built-in cocktail bar.

But the boat itself wasn't silly. She'd been a patrol boat belonging to Naval Intelligence and she had all the latest electronic aids to help her find her position. She also had something unusual; an outsize hold with reinforced sides in which Mr Sprott carried things he didn't want people to see.

And she was armed. A heavy calibre machine gun was fitted on the stern deck which Mr Sprott said he needed in case of robbers in the Indian Ocean. And though sometimes his passengers were pretty girls who sunbathed and did nothing except giggle and drink cocktails, sometimes his passengers were not silly at all. Like the two men now who were playing cards below deck. Their names were Boris and Casimir and they came from a country where a boy who didn't know how to use a gun by the time he was six years old wasn't too likely to grow up.

And always, whether the *Hurricane* was on a pleasure cruise or on serious business, Stanley Sprott took along his bodyguard, Des.

'There it is,' said the Captain, pointing to a low shape in the sea in front of them.

'That's Dooneray now.'

It was true that the island had no houses, but it had a whole rash of huts—new-looking, wooden ones. And moving round between the huts, and down on the shore, were people. Quite a lot of people.

'They're a funny colour,' said Des, screwing up his eyes.

Des was right. The people were . . . pink. Quite a bright pink which caught the light and glistened a little.

The *Hurricane* shut down her engines. There was no pier; they would have to drop the anchor and go ashore in the dinghy.

Some of the pink people looked up and waved.

'I'm not going ashore,' said the first mate. 'I'm not going if it costs me my job. Someone else can take the dinghy.'

'Nor me neither,' said Des. 'I'll do anything for you, boss, but I'm not going to land among that lot.'

'You'll do exactly what I tell you,' said Stanley Sprott. But he didn't speak with quite his usual venom. To tell the truth he too was looking a little sick.

*   *   *

No one could have been nicer than the leader of the pink people. He had a friendly smile and he introduced his wife, who was called Mabel, and his cousin, whose name was James.

But he wouldn't put on any clothes. None of them would put on any clothes.

'I'm afraid you must take us as you find us. This is a nudist colony; we believe most strongly that our Creator wants us to keep our bodies open to the air and light. In fact we would be grateful if you too would take off your clothes. It is a rule of the island that no one who comes here keeps his skin muffled in unhealthy garments.'

Behind him, in the dinghy, Casimir giggled and Mr Sprott turned to glare at him. Then: 'Rubbish!' he said. 'Now listen carefully: I've got you all covered.' He pointed to the two gunmen in the boat. 'And I want every man, woman and child to line up over there. I'm looking for a missing boy and I'm going to search every nook and cranny, so don't try to hide anything or I'll blow you all to hell.'

'We wouldn't dream of it,' said the leader politely. 'But can't we offer you some lunch?'

Mr Sprott shuddered. On a patch of

grass a group of people with nothing on were frying sausages over an open-air grill. He had never seen anything so dangerous.

A terrible hour followed. The pink people went on being polite and friendly but they still wouldn't put on any clothes. They let him go where he liked—into their sleeping huts, their communal dining room, their gym . . . Though he knew really that if Lambert had been held by mad aunts who were nudists he would have mentioned it on the telephone, Mr Sprott felt obliged to search every inch of the island, and made Des search with him.

When they left, the leader presented them with a bunch of sea thrift and an oyster.

'Go in peace, friends,' he said.

*   *   *

As they set a course for the second island on their list, Mr Sprott was not in a good temper. Mr Sprott in fact boiled and snorted and raged and swore that he would get the pink people arrested and deported and imprisoned, which was silly of him since the nudists had every right to be where they were. As for the policemen manning the fishing boat which was following the *Hurricane*, they laughed so much that they could hardly keep a straight course. They had watched Mr Sprott's landing through their binoculars and thought it was the funniest thing they had ever seen.

CHAPTER TWELVE

Minette woke early and immediately decided that she had to wash her hair. She didn't usually wash it before breakfast, but on this particular morning she knew it had to be done.

When she'd finished she draped a towel round her head and went in to see Fabio. He was polishing his shoes. Not the sneakers he'd worn ever since he came to the Island, but his smart shoes; the ones he'd been wearing when he was kidnapped.

He said nothing about her hair and she said nothing about his shoes and they went down to breakfast. Minette half expected Aunt Etta to be cross with her— Minette's long hair took ages to dry and when it was at all windy the aunts made her stay indoors till it was done. But Aunt Etta, sitting as usual behind the porridge pot, only said, 'Good morning'—and then both children found themselves staring at her in a way that was undoubtedly rude.

She was wearing her usual navy-blue jersey and her usual long navy-blue skirt and they were sure that underneath it she wore her usual navy-blue knickers.

But pinned to her jersey was a bow. The bow was made of pink velvet with white spots and after this amazing sight they knew that what they had felt when they got up was real.

What happened next was that Myrtle came in, looking windblown and agitated and said, 'Herbert's gone.'

Aunt Etta merely nodded. If it was true that the time had come, Herbert would have gone out to meet him at sea.

Then Coral appeared, wearing almost all her jewellery and a wreath of dried thongweed in her hair.

'There's a naak in the loch,' she said. 'A funny sort of fellow. The stoorworm won't be pleased.'

Naaks are Estonian; they are the ghosts of people who have drowned and are apt to be silent and grim. This one,

Coral said, was the ghost of a school-teacher.

'One of those strict ones with a cane, I should imagine,' she said, 'though it's not easy to tell underwater.'

The arrival of the naak all the way from Estonia made it certain. If the ghost of a drowned schoolteacher with a cane had come nearly a thousand miles to welcome the kraken, he must be coming very soon.

It was the strangest of days. Everyone was violently excited but they didn't dare to say aloud what they believed.

The stoorworm insisted on being wound round a tree by the north shore so that he could get a good view and, just when Fabio had fixed him up, he decided that the kraken would come straight into the bay by the house and asked to be unwound again.

'Wait for me, wait for me,' shouted Old Ursula to the other mermaids, and this time they did wait for the poor old thing and swam out to the rock they had chosen, holding Walter aloft, and sat there practising a song that Myrtle had taught them. It was a Lapp reindeer-herding song and not particularly suitable but it was the most Northern song that

Myrtle had been able to find.

In Art's kitchen, the iced buns he'd made from the boobrie's egg overflowed the larder, were stuffed into flour bins . . . and still they came from his oven.

The Sybil's face turned from blue to purple; her washed feet glistened in the light.

The Captain had pushed his bed right against the window and wouldn't take time off even to eat.

Only Lambert felt nothing and noticed nothing and spent the day crouched over his telephone trying to get through to his father, even though his battery was now completely flat.

By the late afternoon the shore was packed with creatures of every sort. Like people lining the route of a royal wedding or a funeral, they had come early to get a good place from which they could see. There were sea otters and jellyfish, there were anemones and starfish peering out of their pools; there were shoals of haddock and flounders and codlings . . . Some of the animals lined the north shore, others waited in the bay by the house; the birds and rabbits and mice and voles watched from the hill. The children could hardly eat their tea and the aunts

155

did not nag them. They too were having trouble with Art's boobrie buns.

The sun began to dip behind the horizon. The Hum, which had been steady all day, began to change its rhythm and every so often there was this strange gap filled with a kind of exasperated rumbling.

'Please don't make us go to bed,' begged Minette, and Fabio said he wasn't going to bed and if they tried to make him there'd be trouble.

But when darkness came and the old clock in the kitchen struck nine, and ten, and eleven, everyone lost hope. At midnight the children went to bed of their own accord; the lugworms and the water fleas and the starfish crawled back into the sand or burrowed under stones. On their rock, the mermaids stopped singing and the boobrie fell silent on her nest.

'We must have been mistaken,' said the aunts bleakly—and they too went to bed.

But when they woke in the morning, there was a new island out in the bay.

*　　　*　　　*

The island slept. It slept the sleep of the dead after the long journey—and round it

156

and on it and under it, the creatures who had come with it slept too.

The Hum had stopped. Only a slight sighing, a soft soughing, could be heard as he drew in breath and let it out.

For the watchers on the shore, this second welcome was different from the first. It seemed to have nothing to do with velvet bows and polished shoes. It came from somewhere deeper down.

Fabio and Minette stood side by side, half hidden by an old bent alder which grew by the brook where it ran into the sea. They couldn't find any words. There weren't any to find. The aunts, down on the shore, were holding hands like children.

On their rock, the mermaids were not singing and when Walter began to grizzle, Loreen shushed him angrily. For the kraken slept and the excited welcome they had planned had become a vigil. No one would wake the great beast: not the naak with his cane, not the boobrie on her nest; no one.

They waited for one hour, for two . . . The sunshine grew stronger. The sea was turning the most amazing colours, as if a rainbow was hidden underneath the waves, and the air as they breathed in

157

tasted like gorgeous fruit.

'It's like the beginning of the world,' whispered Minette.

And then the kraken sneezed!

*   *   *

Everything changed after that. The moles and the mice and the rabbits on the hill were blown backwards and righted themselves again; Aunt Etta's bun flew from its mooring of hairpins; the boobrie let out a startled squeal . . . and everybody laughed.

And the kraken lifted his head out of the water and began to swim very slowly, very carefully so as not to swamp the shore, towards the bay.

He was facing the house now, facing the aunts and the children.

Minette, and Fabio beside her, made exactly the same noise: a gasp of wonder and surprise. For in spite of all they had been told about the kraken—about his goodness, about his effect on the sea, about his healing powers—they had not been able to imagine anything very different from a gigantic whale.

But the kraken's eyes were not in the least like the eyes of a whale. They were

158

huge and round and golden: to gaze into them was like looking into a lamp which did not burn or dazzle but warmed and comforted. His nostrils were small and deep, but his mouth was large and generous, curving across his face like a bow, and tilted upwards at the corners.

As he moved towards them, the mermaids started to sing, croakily at first, then more strongly. Herbert swam beside the kraken's head, solemn and proud.

And now they saw that his body was not black as they had imagined but dappled in soft colours—the chestnut of a chaffinch's breast, the rose of a stippled trout, the blue grey of a moonstone—all were in his skin as it caught the light.

But he had stopped. He was looking at the aunts. He began to speak.

Unfortunately he spoke in Polar. It sounded like the rumbling and clashing of icebergs and no one understood a word.

Aunt Etta hurried into the house and fetched a megaphone. 'I'm sorry, we don't understand,' she shouted.

But the kraken had already gathered that. He tried again. This time he spoke Norwegian because Norway is further south than the Pole, and he tried only one word but still nobody understood.

'Could you try English?' shouted Aunt Etta through the megaphone.

There was a long pause while the kraken thought about this. Then he took a deep breath and said:

'Children?'

His accent was strange but they understood him perfectly and the relief was tremendous.

'What about children?' yelled Aunt Etta through her megaphone.

The kraken repeated the word.

'Children?' he asked. 'Are there . . . here . . . children?'

The aunts talked excitedly among themselves. Did that mean that the kraken wanted children, or that he didn't?

But anyway none of them were able to tell a lie. They moved over to the alder tree, pulled out Fabio and Minette and led them down to the sand. They didn't even think about Lambert who was still shut in his room. Lambert wasn't a child; he was a stunted adult.

There was a pause while the kraken looked at Fabio and Minette. Have we got it wrong? thought the children. Are we going to be eaten after all?

Then the kraken smiled. It was the

most amazing smile; his great mouth curved up and up and his eyes glowed with warmth.

And then he sank and the birds that had been resting on him flew upwards like a white cloud.

He was gone for a few minutes—and when he surfaced again there was someone on his back.

The someone was very small compared to the kraken; not much bigger than a mini car or a dolphin—but it was absolutely clear who he was. He had the same round eyes, the same wide mouth, the same rainbow-coloured skin . . .

But he was worried.

'Will I be all right, Father?' said the kraken's son, as he had said again and again on the journey.

'You will be all right,' said the kraken as he had said a hundred times. And then: 'Look—there are children to play with and care for you.'

They spoke in Polar but what they said was perfectly clear to everyone. In particular what was clear was the look the infant kraken gave to Fabio and Minette as they stood quietly on the shore.

And to the aunts there came a great thunderclap of understanding. When they had kidnapped the children they had done it because they wanted help, but even at the time it felt strange to find themselves behaving like criminals. Now they realized that there had been a Higher Purpose, as there so often is.

For they understood that the kraken was bringing his child to the Island to be cared for while he circled the oceans of the world, and that he wanted him to be with people of his own age, not elderly aunts.

'We are most truly blessed,' said Aunt Etta. She still had her megaphone to her mouth and the word 'blessed' echoed over the whole Island, and was taken up by all the watchers on the shore.

'Blessed,' nodded the stoorwom, and 'Blessed,' said the naak (but in Estonian) and 'Blessed,' cried the mermaids from the rocks.

Only Minette and Fabio were silent. Minette was remembering how she had wanted to serve the great beast when first she heard of him. Fabio, on the other hand, was wondering what infant krakens *ate*.

CHAPTER THIRTEEN

The kraken stayed for several days, resting after his long journey from the Arctic. Mostly he lay quietly in the bay keeping an eye on his child, but just having him there made everything flourish.

The children would run down to the shore barefoot every morning.

'It isn't just that the sand is more yellow,' said Minette. 'It's as if it feels more like itself. Like sand is meant to be.'

It was the same with everything while the kraken guarded them. The turf was greener and springier, the wheeling birds were whiter and the patterns they made in the sky were lovelier.

Everybody on the Island felt it— everyone except Lambert who stayed huddled in his room.

'Imagine we hadn't been kidnapped,' said Fabio. 'Imagine we'd never known there was such a thing as a kraken!'

If the kraken had been anyone else—if he'd been one of those saints whose feet people wanted to touch because they were so holy, or a pop star from whose head silly people tried to cut bits of hair—the aunts would have been worried because absolutely everyone wanted to be where he was. Art rowed out in the little dinghy very early one morning, and they could see him talking earnestly to the kraken's head, and when he came back he was different.

'I told him,' he said to the aunts. 'I never told no one else and I didn't tell you neither, but, well . . . when he opened those great eyes of his I saw it didn't matter, so I'll tell you now. All those years it's been on my mind but I was afraid to come clean.'

And then he told them that he hadn't killed a man at all. He'd been in prison for shoplifting but that didn't seem very exciting so he'd told the lie because he thought the aunts would think him more manly.

'But when I was with him, I reckoned you'd forgive me,' he said—and of course they did, and said that telling the truth was far more manly than killing people, which any creep could do if he set his mind to it and had the right tools.

The stoorworm swam out every day and slithered on to the kraken's back and they could hear the clatter and boom as they spoke together in Icelandic. No one knew what the kraken said to him but when he came back the worm was always calmer and never said anything about being too long for his ideas and needing to be made shorter by plastic surgery.

The mermaids too became different. They left the de-oiling shed and swam round the wonderful beast and sang—and though Oona was still croaky her voice came slowly back as she laid her head against the kraken's hide and the memory of the chinless Lord Brasenott became fainter and fainter.

As for the boobrie, she did something extraordinary. She plucked Aunt Coral's cloak from her shoulders and spread it over the eggs with her beak and then she flapped down to the bay and sat on the kraken's back and honked at him.

She honked for a whole hour and it was hard to believe that he understood her, but he did. She was telling him how sad she was without her husband and asking the kraken to look out for him when he swam on again in case he had lost the way.

'He was always a forgetful bird,' she said.

Herbert hardly came out of the water;

165

he was always close to the kraken in the bay. He had a new strength and dignity now that he knew he would spend his life as a seal, because there is nothing more calming than making up one's mind. Myrtle missed playing the cello to him very much, but she understood. As for Herbert's mother, who was very old now and very frail, she completely stopped nagging him, for she realized that if Herbert had decided to become a man with trousers and a zip he would only have been able get up to the kraken in a boat and speak to him through a megaphone and that would hardly be the same.

But it wasn't just the special creatures, those with a touch of magic in them, who wanted to see and talk to the kraken. Everything that moved or crawled or swam wanted to be with him. Processions of sludge worms, schools of pilchards and puffer fish, platoons of lobsters and countless moon snails, all made their way towards him.

'Is he getting enough rest?' Aunt Etta wondered.

But when she asked the kraken he only turned his marvellous eyes towards her and said (at least she thought he said—

his English was rather strange) that there was no living thing he did not welcome.

There were two people, though, who did *not* row out to the kraken and tell him their troubles. Minette did not ask him how to make her parents kind to each other, and Fabio did not ask him how to blow up the headmaster of Greymarsh Towers. This was partly because their past lives now seemed quite unreal to the children, but it was mostly because they were busier than they had ever been in their lives.

For the kraken wasn't just resting. He was watching. And what he was watching was his son. Or rather, he was watching how Fabio and Minette *coped* with his son.

*   *   *

It had been difficult for the kraken, deciding what to do with his child. At first he thought he would put off his healing journey round the world till his son was older. But baby krakens grow very slowly—he would have had to wait for more than a hundred years for the child to grow up, and when he realized what a mess the world was in, he knew he couldn't risk it.

Then he thought maybe he could leave his motherless infant in the Arctic among the walruses and polar bears and narwhals he was used to. But this plan had gone down badly with his son who wanted to travel with his father.

'You can't. It's too far,' the kraken had said.

It takes a year and a day to circle the oceans of the world and it was much too far. The baby swam slowly and often needed lifts on his father's back and no one can really give himself to healing the world when they are worried about their child.

The kraken had heard about the Island and the caring aunts as he heard about everything, and at last he had decided to see if it was a good place to leave his son. But he had not been quite happy. Aunts were fine things but these were aunts without children and the baby kraken needed people of his own age. Or rather people who were a bit older but could remember the troubles and the games and the tantrums of being very young.

Which was why the first word he said when he arrived was 'Children?' and why now he watched Fabio and Minette most carefully out of his golden eyes. If they were not suitable as childminders, he meant to give up his journey and go home. Once you have children nothing matters more than their safekeeping. Every parent in the world knows that.

*　　　*　　　*

The baby kraken was not at all like his father. He was still soft and blobby as though his body hadn't quite decided what was going to happen to it. Bulges came out of him sometimes, which were almost arms and legs but not the kind of arms you could do very much with, and not the kind of legs that were much use for walking. He would lose these later and become streamlined and suited to the sea, but at the moment he was rather like a large beanbag and one never knew what kind of shape he would decide to be.

And yet one could see that he was the mighty kraken's son. He had the same large wondrous eyes, the same wide mouth which smiled easily, the same interested nostrils which seemed to hoover up the scents of land and sea.

Like his father, he too could make the creatures of the sea come to him and

169

when he rested in a rockpool, the barnacles and whelks and brittlestars all seemed to glow with happiness and health.

But there was one thing he could not do.

'Can he *hum?*' Fabio asked on the first day.

They were having lunch. Lambert had bolted his food and rushed back to his room where he lay on his bed with the curtains drawn. He still believed that he was being drugged and that the strange creatures he was seeing were not really there, but seeing a whole *island* that wasn't really there was driving him a little crazy.

Aunt Etta shook her head. 'He's too young. A kraken humming is a bit like a boy's voice breaking; it just happens when he's ready. It's a pity, because that's how krakens speak to each other across distances.'

'Is there any way of teaching him to do it sooner?' asked Minette. 'Could his father ...?'

But Aunt Etta said, no—it would just happen when the time was right. She didn't add that his father was worried, knowing that there was no way his child could call him once he went away.

But if he couldn't hum, the kraken was beginning to speak. The trouble for Fabio and Minette was *what* he spoke. With his father he spoke Polar but other languages got mixed up with it, and when he started off in English he quickly wandered off into Norwegian or Swedish or even Finnish which the children did not understand at all.

But Fabio himself had needed to learn English not so long ago and he remembered that what he had learnt first was the name of things to eat.

After that it was easy. For the young kraken did not just feed on the plankton in seawater like his father—he was still growing and needed solid food which he ground up with his gums rather like an old man with no teeth.

'This is a sausage,' Fabio would say, holding up one of Art's bangers and the kraken would repeat 'Soss', or 'Spag' when it was spaghetti of which he was very fond, and of course he soon learn to say 'More' or *No!*' which all young creatures learn to say very early.

By now he was letting the children play with him in the water, throwing a ball or pretending to hide behind a rock. He would even follow them in the dinghy—but always after a short time he went back to his father and stayed very close to his side, for the bond between those two was very, very strong. And though the great kraken was more certain with every day that passed that he had found the right place to leave his son, his heart was heavy at the thought of the parting that must soon come.

CHAPTER FOURTEEN

The next island on which Stanley Sprott landed did not have any naked people on it. It did not have any people on it at all. What it had on it was sheep.

They came to it through driving sheets of rain. It was the wettest rain they had ever come across and it looked as though it must stop soon because the sky would have emptied itself, but it didn't. And on the low-lying, sodden island were hundreds—no, thousands—of soaking sheep.

'There's nowhere to land,' said the skipper.

But when they'd circled the island

twice they found a narrow inlet and, chugging up it, they saw a shingle bay where the dinghy could be beached.

No one had wanted to land among the pink nudists and no one wanted to land among the wet sheep.

'The boy won't be there,' said Des. 'No one could last on this dump.'

But Mr Sprott had a bee in his bonnet about a honeycomb of underground caves and tunnels full of mad aunts who were holding Lambert.

'They might have brought the sheep to put people off,' he said, 'or they might come up and shoot them for meat'—and he ordered the *Hurricane* to put down her anchor.

Leaving Casimir to guard the boat they rowed to the island and went ashore.

It was not a pleasant place. Sheep are not often cheerful once they are grown up and these sheep were the wettest, gloomiest sheep you could imagine. They stood pressed together, the water running down their noses, giving off a smell of wet wool and lanolin. Some of them had foot rot and though sheep-pats are not as squelchy as cow-pats, they are not agreeable to walk on in the rain.

'We must go round and round the

173

island in smaller and smaller circles; that way we won't miss any openings. It's like looking for a ball in a field,' said Stanley Sprott.

So they trudged round and round, the water dripping down their necks, slipping and sliding on the wet grass and on the wet other things, while the sheep huddled together, too miserable even to lift their heads, and occasionally made a gloomy bleating noise which did not sound much like *Baa* but more like the crying of doomed spirits in hell. If the mad aunts had brought them to put people off they hadn't done so badly.

'There won't be any caves,' said Des. 'The soil's wrong for caves.'

But Stanley Sprott only told him to keep his mouth shut.

Then, almost in the middle of the island, they did find an opening which led underground.

'Down you go,' said Mr Sprott, very excited. 'Make sure they know you're armed. We'll keep you covered.'

So Des went down into the hole and came back almost at once looking very sick.

'Well? What's down there?'

'More sheep,' said Des, rubbing his

behind. 'Rams. Two of them and as mad as hatters.' He turned round so that Mr Sprott could see the jagged holes in his trousers. 'Lucky they didn't get through to the flesh. It can give you rabies, being butted by rams.'

*   *   *

While Stanley Sprott had been pursuing his son among nudists and sheep, the police had been following in a fishing boat. Now, though, they ran into bad weather; fog came rolling in from the west and the skipper of the fishing boat found that his radar was jammed. He insisted on turning into the next port to get it fixed, and this meant that the *Hurricane* steamed on without being tailed.

There was only one island left that fitted Lambert's description. It was a long way away but it had to be the right one; it had to!

'Full steam ahead!' barked Mr Sprott to the skipper, who only raised an eyebrow. He'd had the *Hurricane* doing twelve knots ever since they'd seen the last sheep and he wasn't going any faster till the weather cleared.

175

Meanwhile in London, Minette's parents and Fabio's grandparents had called a meeting to complain about the police and the feeble way they were handling their case. The superintendent had told the Danbys and the Mountjoys that there was a possible lead on the children's whereabouts and having some hope again brought out all their disagreeableness.

The meeting took place in the Mountjoys' cold house with the brass gong in the hall and the portraits of dead Mountjoys on the wall. The Mountjoys didn't like the look of Mrs Danby, who was as usual chain-smoking and wearing a blouse which showed more than they thought was right. They liked Professor Danby a bit better because he was stern and gloomy like themselves. But the main point of the meeting wasn't to make friends, it was to complain.

'If you ask me, the police are too busy finding homes for dirty tramps and mollycoddling the unemployed to do their job properly,' said old Mr Mountjoy.

He had decided not to send for Hubert-Henry's family after all. His wife

176

had been having nightmares about Indians with poisoned arrows ambushing her in her bed, and her heart was not strong.

Professor Danby agreed. 'Even when they find the kidnappers I expect they'll just send them to prison. In the old days they'd have been hung, and rightly so.'

The Mountjoys nodded their heads. 'It is absolutely shocking the way this case has been dealt with. Outrageous.'

They decided to complain to their Member of Parliament, and Professor Danby said he would insist on a full inquiry.

Mr Mountjoy approved of that. 'And I shall write to the Minister for Law and Order. God knows what the country is coming to when three children can vanish off the face of the earth without anything being done about it!'

Mrs Danby stubbed out her cigarette and lit another one. 'I'm thinking we might sue the police,' she said thoughtfully. 'Get some money out of them. We might as well have something for the anxiety we've been through.'

Professor Danby was about to disagree with her. He always disagreed with his wife—but this time he didn't.

'It's an idea,' he admitted.

'We could give the kids a good time with the money we get,' said Mrs Danby. She'd buy Minette lots of new dresses and if there was any money over she could do with some new clothes herself. There was a lovely pink georgette with a black underskirt she'd seen at Adrienne's Boutique . . . and the sitting room carpet was getting really shabby.

Professor Danby too was thinking of how he could help Minette with some extra money to spend; her bedroom when she stayed with him could do with a proper writing desk so she could do her homework, and if there was any money to spare he needed the new three-hundred-volume *Grammar Scholastica.* He'd had his eyes on it for months but the cost was absurd.

Even the old Mountjoys thought that suing the police was a good idea. Hubert-Henry's fees at Greymarsh Towers were ridiculously high; any help would be welcome.

They were working out how best to do this when the parlourmaid came in with the tea things on a silver tray. She was the only one who had been fond of Fabio and now she asked whether there had been any news of him.

'No, there hasn't,' snapped Mrs Mountjoy and told her to bring some more hot water. What were servants coming to, sticking their noses into family business?

*　　　*　　　*

While the Danbys and the Mountjoys met to complain in London, something sad and serious happened in the city of Newcastle upon Tyne. The mother of Boo-Boo and the Little One tripped on a cracked paving stone and broke her hip.

Breaking a hip is a bad business. An ambulance came and rushed her off to hospital where they put a pin into the joint and told her she had to stay in for a week and be careful for a long time after that.

This left her husband, the tax inspector, with a problem. Being a tax inspector is very hard work. You have to go to an office every day and fill in lots and lots of forms and send rude letters to people who are trying not to pay their tax, and do a great many sums. Betty's husband, whose name was Ronald, was a very good tax inspector and he did not feel he could look after Boo-Boo and the Little One as well as doing his job.

But now something amazing happened. He was just wondering what on earth to do with his children when a tall, fierce-looking lady came striding up the path, carrying a suitcase and the kind of saucepan that people use to stir-fry things in. The tax inspector had never used one because his wife Betty did not cook foreign foods, but he knew it was a wok and once he had realized this, he knew who the lady was. It was Betty's sister Dorothy, who had been imprisoned in Hong Kong for hitting a restaurant owner on the head because he was serving pangolin steaks in his restaurant. She must have kept the wok as a memento and as she came closer he saw that he was right because there was a dent in the side which might well have been made by the restaurant owner's head.

'Where's Betty?' said Dorothy, putting down her case. She did not like her sister Betty, who shaved her legs and had three kinds of toilet freshener in her loo, but families are families and on her way home to the Island she had decided to call on her and see how she was.

She soon realized her mistake. Visiting

Betty in hospital was one thing, but being asked to look after Boo-Boo and the Little One was quite another.

'I can't stand children, you know that,' said Dorothy. She could have said, 'I can't stand *your* children,' but she didn't because of Betty being 'family'.

Betty began to cry. Her leg was in plaster and hitched up to something and she had a bruise on her face where she had fallen, so when she cried she looked very pathetic indeed.

'Please, Dotty—oh, please. Poor Ronald works so hard, and he can't give up his job.'

Dorothy didn't like being called Dotty and she didn't like Ronald and she really loathed Betty's house where everything was covered in little crocheted hats or frilly embroidered cloths or sprayed with some gooey scent which climbed into your nostrils and stayed there. Betty's chairs had chair covers and the chair covers had more covers to keep the covers clean, as though sitting down was a dangerous act, and the whole thing drove Dorothy round the bend. Also she was homesick for the Island and for Myrtle and Coral and in particular for Etta who was next to her in age and her closest friend.

But there was Betty looking absolutely miserable—and after all it wasn't her fault that she was an idiot and had two ridiculous children. Life isn't fair and never has been.

'I'll stay for a week,' Dorothy said. 'Till you're over the worst. But that's all.'

But after a few days Dorothy cracked. Boo-Boo (who was a boy) and the Little One (who was a girl) were the daftest children she had ever seen. They cried if their pyjama cases got mixed up, so that Boo-Boo's sleeping suit ended up in the skirts of the fairy doll and the Little One's nightdress was zipped into the stomach of a fluffy poodle. They cried if she handed them the wrong bath towel so that Boo-Boo had to dry himself on Big Ears and Noddy whereas the Little One was rubbed down in roller-skating Yogi Bears. They threw a tantrum if she brought the cereal packet to the table without its frilly cereal packet container, and they complained because she hadn't combed out the tassels on the lampshades.

'Right, this is it,' said Dorothy on the fifth day. 'I'm going home.'

But when she told Betty, who was still in hospital, her sister cried once more.

'What am I going to do?' she sobbed. 'None of my neighbours seem to want to look after my children.'

Dorothy opened her mouth to tell her why and closed it again. After all, Betty was ill and she was her sister and she wouldn't be able to shave her legs for weeks because of the plaster. On the other hand nothing now could stop Dorothy from going back to the Island.

'I suppose I could take the children with me. Just till you're better.'

As soon as she said it, she wished she hadn't, but it was too late. Betty looked at her gratefully. Usually she would have done anything to keep her darlings from that rough place where the animals wandered in and out of the house and nothing was done *nicely*, but now it was her only hope.

'Thank you, Dorothy,' she said. 'Perhaps the sea air will do them good.'

So the following week Dorothy took the train to catch the steamer to catch the second steamer to catch the ferry which would in the end get her to her home. She did not have a chance to let her sisters know whom she was bringing, which was as well. Even if they had been very badly oiled, Boo-Boo and the Little One would not have been welcome on the Island.

CHAPTER FIFTEEN

Minette sat on her bed beside the open
window, trying to brush her hair. Aunt
Etta insisted on a hundred strokes each
night, but now she put her brush down
and sighed.

'I'm never going to have children.
Never. It's awful.'

'Oh come on,' said Fabio, wandering in
from the bathroom. 'It isn't as bad as
that.'

But it had been very bad.

They had woken early and at once
known what had happened. Even before
they went to the window they had felt the
emptiness and the silence.

Downstairs the three aunts sat stiffly at
the breakfast table. Coral looked thinner
and Myrtle's blouse was on back to front.

'Go to him,' said Aunt Etta as soon as
the children had finished. 'You're excused
all your other duties.'

Outside it really hit them. Yet the
kraken had only been here just over a
week. How could the bay seem so empty,

so wrong? And how could such a great beast slip away so silently?

It was all very well for Aunt Etta to say, 'Go to him,' but where was he? Not by the shore, not in his favourite rockpool. The mermaids were guarding the entrance to the bay but the children knew he would not have tried to follow his father. He might be small but he knew what it was to keep a promise.

They found him in the end, half hidden under an overhanging rock. He was almost submerged but his head came up out of the water and he was staring at the open sea. When he saw them, he made the most pitiful sound they had ever heard, a heartbroken moan which ended in a whimper. Like a puppy told to 'stay', when his master leaves the room, the baby kraken waited . . . and looked as though he would wait to the end of time for his father to return.

'Come on,' said Fabio leaning down from the rock. 'It's time for breakfast. We'll go and see what Art has got for you.'

But the kraken only looked at him and then two tears welled out of his golden eyes and rolled into the sea.

He wouldn't eat and he wouldn't play.

'No ball,' he said when they fetched the beach ball and 'No hide an' see.' He wouldn't follow them in the boat, though when they moved away he moaned and shivered even more. In the end they got into the water with him and swam round him rubbing his back and telling him again and again that his father would be back, that they loved him, that he was the last of a great and mighty line of krakens and must try to be brave.

Everyone helped. The mermaids came and sang to him but he only closed his eyes and juddered with sighs. The stoorworm swam out and spoke into his ear.

'To go is to come,' said the worm in his solemn voice.

What he meant was that the earth was round so that the great kraken was on his way back as soon as he set off. But thoughts about the earth being round were too difficult for the kraken's son, whose tears went on flowing and making the seaweed and the little fish look larger and brighter wherever they fell.

'Do you think if Myrtle played the cello to him it would help?' asked Minette, but it didn't. Although Myrtle had just said goodbye to Herbert, who had gone off with the great kraken, she came at once, but you never know where you are with music. It can make you happy but it can also make you very, very sad.

The children did not dare to leave him alone; whenever they moved away he moaned even more pitifully. Art brought their lunch to the shore and they tried to share it with him but he only turned his head away.

'No boss,' he said when they offered him a sausage roll, and 'No cheeps,' when they handed him the chipped potatoes that had been his favourites.

By the end of the day the children were getting frantic.

'What if he just fades away and dies?' said Minette, close to tears.

'He won't,' said Fabio.

But his eyes were even blacker than usual. People *did* turn their faces to the wall and die; he had seen it in Brazil.

*   *   *

When he had been on his way for a few hours, the great kraken began his Healing Hum once more. Everything was as it had been when he was on the way to the Island. The sky was blue, the air was soft;

above him flew his escort of birds, below him the dolphins and seals circled him.

He drew level with a fishing boat a hundred miles away. The crew had pulled in three tons of tuna and were casting their nets once more to add to the pile of bloodied thrashing creatures on the deck when the captain straightened himself and rubbed his forehead.

'Enough,' he said suddenly. 'We've caught enough.'

His crew stared at him. He was the greediest fisherman in that part of the world; he'd been fined again and again for exceeding the quota.

'You heard me,' he said and the nets were pulled in and the boat turned and headed for home.

But though the kraken went on putting the sea to rights, as he had done before, his heart was heavy. There was an awful emptiness on his left side where his son had swum beside him, and at night his back felt strange without the small bump that had slept on it.

'You're to promise to stay and be good,' he had said to his son, and the child had understood, but it was best not to remember the look in his eyes.

After they had travelled for a day and a

night, Herbert came to the front of the kraken's head and said goodbye. It was hard for him to leave the kraken and return to the Island but his mother was getting very weak and he felt it was his duty.

It was even lonelier after Herbert left. Other seals swam with the kraken but they were ordinary seals, not selkies; they did not know his thoughts as Herbert had done.

On a great rock, after another day of swimming, the kraken saw something he had been looking out for. A huge black bird with a yellow beak and yellow feet, huddled up and muddled-looking. He paused and looked directly at the unfortunate bird and, as the kraken's eyes pierced his sadness, the boobrie came to himself again. He remembered that he had a wife who had been expecting eggs and that he had gone to look for food and got lost, and forgotten who he was and where he was going.

Now, as clear as daylight, the boobrie saw the Island and the nest by the loch and his partner waiting and waiting. Why, he might be a father by now . . . and he flapped his wings once and twice and a third time and then managed to lift himself off and to fly away.

And the kraken swam on.

*　　　*　　　*

By the third day Fabio and Minette were beginning to lose hope. They had tried everything they could think of to cheer up the little kraken. They used up all Art's washing-up liquid to blow bubbles for him, they invented underwater games, they sang to him and told him stories, but nothing helped. The only thing you could say was that when they left him even for a moment he was worse; moaning more pitifully and watering the sea with his tears.

What worried them most was that he wouldn't eat.

It wasn't just 'No boss; it was 'No spag,' though he had loved spaghetti, and 'No burgs,' even when Art soused the hamburgers with rich tomato sauce. They watched carefully to see if he was feeding himself from the seaweed and plants by the shore, but he wasn't.

'I can just see him getting thinner every minute,' said Minette, who wasn't looking exactly fat herself.

At teatime Aunt Etta came down to

the shore and said enough was enough.

'You're to go up to the house and have hot baths and have your tea in the dining room. You look like something the cat's brought in, both of you.'

'No, please. We can't leave him,' said Minette. 'We want to bring a tent down and spend the night on the beach.'

'Better not keep Art waiting,' was all Aunt Etta said.

So the children had their hot baths and went into the dining room. Art had laid out all their favourite things: sardines and cheese straws and chunks of pineapple on sticks.

And the cake tin was on the sideboard. Poor Art always put the cake tin on the sideboard. He put it out for breakfast and for lunch and for tea, hoping and hoping that someone would manage to eat another bun.

For if one can make seventy-two omelettes from one boobrie egg, it is quite amazing how many buns one can make. Art had made the buns look very beautiful: there were buns with pink icing and a cherry on top and buns with white icing and smarties on top and buns with brown icing and chocolate drops on top— but one by one the aunts and the children

191

had stopped eating them. Boobrie buns are very filling and they just couldn't get them down any more.

Now, as Fabio picked up the tin, Minette said 'No! Absolutely not. I couldn't!'

'I know,' said Fabio. 'I couldn't either. But I wonder . . .'

When they got back to the shore the children took no notice at all of the kraken. They sat down very close to the water's edge and opened the cake tin. Fabio held up a white bun and Minette held up a pink bun. They pretended to eat them, making loud chewing noises.

'Buns,' said Fabio, rubbing his stomach.

And: *'Buns,'* said Minette, sighing with pleasure. The kraken came closer and watched them. The children went on pretending to eat buns. The kraken edged closer still.

'No buns for you,' said Fabio. 'You don't like buns.'

An offended look spread over the kraken's face. He was not used to being left out. He was half out of the water now, his head on the sand.

'Buns?' said the kraken, trying out the word.

Fabio shrugged. 'Well, you can try one,

192

I suppose, but you won't like it.' He picked out a white bun with a big cherry on top and held it up. The kraken studied it . . . opened his mouth . . . shut it. For a moment, nothing happened. Then a glow came into his golden eyes.

'Buns,' said the baby kraken. 'Ah, *buns!*' and opened his mouth once more . . .

When he had eaten seven buns Fabio turned to see Minette crouching on the sand. Her hands covered her face but he could see the tears squeezing out between her fingers.

'Well, really,' he said crossly. 'You'd better *not* have children of your own if you're going to be as wet as that.'

CHAPTER SIXTEEN

'If you could go back now—if your parents came to fetch you away, what would you do?' asked Fabio the next day.

Minette felt the familiar crunching in her stomach. Only what was the crunching about? Was it about whether her parents loved her and loved each other, or was it about something else . . . ?

Was it about going away from the Island?

'How could we leave him?' she said. 'We'd have to stay till his father came back. It's only a year and a day—less now. We'd have to stay that long, wouldn't we?'

Fabio nodded. 'That's what I think. But if they find us . . .'

They had been playing ball with the little kraken in a rockpool, keeping a close watch because Walter was nearby and sometimes the kraken became muddled and thought the merbaby with his round bald head was a beach ball too.

'I'm not ever going back to my grandparents,' Fabio went on. 'The ones in London, I mean. Not ever. If I have to leave the Island I'm going back to South America. I don't know how, but I'm going.'

Minette nodded. He looked very small, sitting on a boulder with his hands round his knees, but she believed him. Both the children had changed since they came to the Island; they were stronger, and sunburnt, their hair thick and glossy with health.

'Isn't everything beautiful?' said Minette, looking out across the bay. 'Of course it was even before he came, but now . . .'

This was true. It was early summer now; the grass was studded with clover and ox-eye daisies; the rowan which sheltered the house was covered in new green leaves—but it was more than that. It was as though the great kraken's blessing stayed with them, and would stay, even though he himself was gone.

Everyone felt it—and even fewer people went away! The naak did not go back to Estonia; the mermaids, though they had lost all traces of oil, stayed where they were—and the Sybil went on washing her feet.

After the kraken left the Captain had sent for his daughters.

'I can die happy now,' he said, 'because I've seen him. So you can measure me up for my coffin.'

But when the aunts had gone away to cry and came back with a tape measure, they found him and the stoorworm taking tea together.

'If my head is upstairs and my tail is downstairs, where is *me?*' the stoorworm was asking, and it was clear that the old man had changed his mind about dying.

But down on the point, Herbert's mother really was coming to the end of her life. She had chosen the Island as her

Last Resting Place, which was a compliment because selkies are fussy about where they die.

'I'm ready to go, Herbert,' she said. 'I'm ready to give myself to the waves.'

And Herbert said: 'The time will come, Mother. Don't hurry it.' But he knew it would not be long now and that when the great kraken returned for his son, Herbert would be free to go away with him.

It was during these peaceful days that they were woken by a sound that was new to the Islanders: a proud and joyful squawking that sent the aunts and children running up the hill.

And there they were! Three chicks the size of bull terriers, their feathers still moist from the egg, their yellow beaks already open as they cheeped and wriggled for food.

'More wheelbarrowing,' was all Aunt Etta said, because with the male boobrie still away the mother would never manage to feed her chicks alone, but the aunts were almost as proud as the bird herself. Boobries have not bred where there are humans for hundreds of years.

Even Lambert had suddenly become almost nice and this was the most extraordinary thing of all. He did his work without grumbling, he ate his food—sometimes he even smiled.

'He too has been touched by the spirit of the great kraken,' said Myrtle, but Fabio disagreed.

'If that creep is being nice there'll be a reason,' he said.

And he was absolutely right.

*   *   *

The battery of Lambert's mobile had suddenly given a spurt of life and he had dialled his father's number. The *Hurricane* was now steaming towards the Island and it so happened that Stanley Sprott heard his phone ringing down in the cabin and answered it.

Mr Sprott knew better than to ask his son anything sensible, like 'What latitude and longitude are you on?' or 'Are there any submerged rocks near the entrance to the bay?'—but there was one question he did ask.

'Those women who are holding you prisoner—are they nudists?'

'Eh?' said Lambert, who did not know what nudists were.

'Are they wearing clothes?' Mr Sprott

wanted to know.

Lambert thought about this. 'Yes,' he said. 'They're wearing clothes.'

'And sheep? Are there a lot of sheep?'

Lambert said he didn't think so. 'Just a few on the hill.' Then his battery began to play up again and he said frantically: 'But you're coming, aren't you? You're coming to fetch me?'

'Yes, Lambert, I'm coming,' said Mr Sprott.

It was after he talked to his father that Lambert changed. Soon now the *Hurricane* would come and his father would blow everyone to hell: the creepy aunts, the horrible children and the foul monsters who weren't really there. When Lambert smiled now it was because that was what he was thinking about: all the people he hated lying dead in their own blood.

* * *

'I feel sick,' said Boo-Boo, leaning over the rail of the steamer.

'I feel sick too,' said the Little One. 'I feel sicker than you.'

Aunt Dorothy looked at them with loathing. What she really wanted to do was throw them into the sea and make her own way to the Island. Doing good is all right when you are beating up restaurant owners or thumping people who are trapping rare animals for their skins, but doing good by taking on your sister's horrible children is just stupid.

The steamer was hardly going up and down but now first Boo-Boo and then the Little One were sick and as soon as they'd finished they started worrying about whether they had messed up their clothes.

'Etta is going to kill me when she sees them,' thought Dorothy.

But though she would very much have liked to throw them both overboard she realized it could not be done so she took them down into the cabin and dabbed at the Little One's velvet coat collar and Boo-Boo's silly blazer, and told them to lie down till they landed.

But landing was only the beginning. After that they had to take a ferry to a smaller island and then they had to wait till the one fisherman who could be trusted not to gape or gawp or give away the secrets of the Island could take them across at night. There was no one else the aunts ever used—and just how sick these idiotic children would be in an open boat at night was anybody's guess.

* * *

The *Hurricane* came in quietly at noon. She anchored to the south of the Island, hidden from the house by a copse of windblown trees, and Mr Sprott took Des and one of the gunmen with him in the dinghy for a reconnaissance.

But even if she had come into the bay by the house no one would have seen her. Fabio and Minette had taken the kraken to the north shore with a picnic and the aunts were visiting the Sybil, which they did once a week to see that she was eating properly. Even the Captain was not looking through his telescope but dozing quietly in his bed.

Mr Sprott had at first meant to come in with his cannon firing but then he had thought better of it. After all, Lambert had to be got out safely first.

As the dinghy rounded the spur of rocks, with its row of slumbering seals, he saw a boy standing alone on the edge of the sea.

'It's Lambert!' said Des.

And it was!

Whatever plans Mr Sprott might have

made were set aside as his son waded towards him and threw himself weeping into his arms.

'Take me away, quick. Take me to the *Hurricane*. Oh hurry, please, Dad.'

Mr Sprott pulled himself out of Lambert's clinging arms and looked at his son. He looked well. In fact he looked better than he had ever seen him look; but that was neither here nor there. The boy was obviously terrified.

'It's an awful place. They feed you poisoned food and then you see things,' sobbed Lambert.

'What sort of things, Lambert?'

'Creepy crawly things . . . things that slither, and freaks with tails—only they're not really there.'

There was a sudden yell from Des. The bodyguard knew that it was as much as his life was worth to yell when they were trying to get into a place unseen but now he stood up in the dinghy and pointed with staring eyes at a rock sticking out of the water.

'My God,' he shouted. 'Look, guv'nor! It's a bloomin' mermaid!'

'No, it isn't,' cried Lambert. 'She isn't really there. It's because of what you've eaten. None of them are there, the other one isn't there and the old one isn't there and the long white worm isn't there. They're all because of what Art put in the—'

'Be quiet, Lambert,' said his father. Then to Des, 'Catch her.'

Des didn't need to be told twice. He slipped off his holster and dived into the sea.

The girl was Queenie, and she thought the whole thing very funny. She waited till the clumsy man was almost up to her— then she gave her silvery laugh and vanished underneath the waves.

'She isn't there, she isn't there,' Lambert went on yelling. 'It's what you've eaten—it's Art's seaweed flour.'

'Don't be silly, Lambert,' said his father. 'I haven't eaten any seaweed flour and I saw her quite clearly. Unless it was a trick. It must have been a trick, but if so it was a good one.'

Des was still thrashing about in the icy water. Now suddenly he dived down, grabbed at something—and missed. But when he swam back to the boat he had two things clutched in his hand. A silver fish scale and a golden hair.

Mr Sprott examined them. Then he turned to his son.

'Now then, Lambert,' he said. 'Just tell us what else you've seen on the Island.'

'I haven't seen it—it isn't—'

'All right, boy. Tell us what you *haven't* seen, then. Tell us carefully.'

By the time Lambert had finished babbling about old mermaids with no teeth and long white worms that sucked peppermints and outsize birds the size of elephants—all of which *weren't there*— Mr Sprott's face wore a look of eager cunning. Of course it was probably all rubbish, but if it wasn't, the money one could make! And those trees with the branches stripped off—the ones that Lambert called stoorworm trees—they were there all right.

'Go on, what else?' he prompted, digging his son roughly in the ribs.

But Lambert had said all he could. The sight of that island in the bay that hadn't been there at night and then *really* hadn't been there in the morning had frightened him so much that he couldn't say another word, nor about the small island that had broken off from the big one and was around somewhere.

'Please, Daddy, take me home,' he whined. 'Look, there they are; they're coming for me!'

Stanley Sprott looked up. The three dreaded women whose pictures were on the wall of every police station in London were coming towards them.

Aunt Myrtle was in the lead, which was unusual for her. She was carrying a brown paper parcel and she was very nervous—but in a way Lambert was *hers*, just as Fabio was Aunt Coral's, and Minette belonged to Etta, and she felt she had to hand him back herself.

'Good morning,' she said, bracing herself. 'I see you have come to fetch Lambert—he will be pleased to go home. I'm afraid he never quite fitted in.'

Mr Sprott stared at her. The cheek of the woman was unbelievable!

'I've washed and ironed his underclothes and his pyjamas. I wasn't able to take many of his clothes in the cello case but you'll find everything is there.'

Myrtle now felt she had done all she could and stepped back, leaving her sisters to take charge, which they did by asking Mr Sprott if he would care to stay to lunch.

As she spoke, Etta was looking warily over the bay. She had told everyone to stay out of sight as soon as the dinghy had rounded the point but one could never be sure, she thought, not realizing that it was already too late.

'No, don't,' begged Lambert. 'Don't eat anything in there—you'll think you'll see creepy-crawlies.'

'Be quiet, Lambert,' said his father—and told the aunts he would be delighted.

It was a strange lunch. The aunts had been well brought up and though they thought that Mr Sprott was just as nasty as one would expect from someone who was Lambert's father, they were most polite, passing him the salt and pepper and filling up his plate.

'Won't you try a brandy snap?' asked Aunt Coral. 'They were freshly made this morning.'

Mr Sprott took one and decided it was time to come to the point.

'Now, ladies,' he said, smiling his oily smile. 'I have a suggestion to make to you.' He leant forward, folding his hands on the tablecloth. 'I am getting on in years and I need somewhere to end my days—so I want you to sell me this island.'

There was a gasp from Myrtle, and Aunt Etta stared at him in amazement.

'Sell the Island?' said Coral.

'Sell the Island?' said Myrtle.

'*Sell* it!' thundered Aunt Etta.

'I take it it belongs to you, does it not? And Captain Harper?'

The sisters looked at each other. They had never thought of *owning* the Island. It was just there and they looked after it. But now they remembered that their father had in fact bought it from an old couple who could no longer do the work.

'I suppose it does,' said Etta now. 'But there's absolutely no question of selling it.'

'No question at all,' said Coral.

'Oh no, we couldn't do that,' said Myrtle bravely.

Mr Sprott leant back in his chair and smiled. They did not seem to realize that they were completely in his power.

'I'm prepared to offer ten thousand pounds,' he said. 'And that's generous for a miserable little island . . . I mean for a simple unspoilt island with only one house on it.'

He'd get the money back in a month, charging two hundred pounds for helicopter rides to the Island of Freaks. The pretty mermaid was worth a fortune on her own; he'd put her in an aquarium and people would have to pay extra to hear her sing and comb her hair. As for that creepy worm, he could just see the visitors clutching each other and screaming. He'd have to keep him in a cage with electric wire. It would be a cross between a zoo, a funfair and Disneyland.

'Very well, ladies. Twelve thousand pounds and that's my last word absolutely!'

But Etta had had enough of this unpleasant game. 'I'm afraid we wouldn't sell the island for a hundred million pounds,' she said. 'We regard it as a Sacred Trust. Now if you would care to take Lambert back with you, I will tell Art that he can clear the table.'

'Oh no you won't!'

Mr Sprott's voice had changed. He had become the dangerous bully that he was before. 'I think you have forgotten something, dear ladies. You have kidnapped three children. Abducted them by force. My son and two others. The penalty for kidnapping is life imprisonment—and it might even be hanging. They're thinking of bringing back the death penalty, I've heard. So I really think you'd better sell me the Island—or would you rather I turned you over to the police?'

There was a sudden scuffle at the door.

'You can't! You can't turn them over to the police because they didn't kidnap us.' Minette had run all the way from the North Shore. Her hair was tousled, her clothes were in a mess but what was strange was that she wasn't at all frightened. 'I *asked* if I could come. I asked Aunt Etta if there was a third place and she brought me here.'

Fabio, who had followed her into the room, caught on at once. 'And I wasn't kidnapped either! Aunt Coral saved me from a vile school where they tie you to pillars and try to set fire to your clothes. If anybody says I was kidnapped, I'll thump them!'

'And Lambert wasn't really kidnapped either.' Minette, who never lied, seemed to have gone crazy. 'He tried to steal Aunt Myrtle's chloroform and the fumes knocked him out and Aunt Myrtle brought him along because there was no one at home to look after him.'

Both children stood and glared at him like angry tigers.

What they were saying was rubbish, Mr Sprott knew that. The police would get the truth out of them in no time—but he had changed his mind. It had seemed worth a try to do everything the easy way—buy the island and then do what he wanted with it when they'd all gone. But there were other ways of getting what he wanted.

'Very well, it looks as though I was mistaken. Come along, Lambert, I'll take you home.'

He took the brown paper parcel with Lambert's pyjamas, shook hands politely, and left with his son.

Oh yes, there were other ways of getting his hands on those weird beasts, thought Stanley Sprott. Before he'd finished they would wish they *had* sold him the island, because what was going to happen now would not be pleasant at all!

CHAPTER SEVENTEEN

Meanwhile, in London, Minette's parents had found a better way of making money than suing the police.

Mrs Danby thought of it first and Professor Danby didn't hear about it till he saw a newspaper which the tea lady had brought into the University Common Room.

On the front page was a picture of Minette as a baby in her mother's arms. *Heartbreak Mother Mourns Lost Daughter* said the headline, and underneath the picture were some terribly sad things that Minette's mother had said, like there was no second of the day when she did not feel the pain of being without her daughter like a wound in her side. *She was a little angel* Mrs Danby had told the reporter, and she went on to say that a candle burnt night and day by Minette's bed and would go on burning till she was safely returned.

As soon as he saw the newspaper, Professor Danby rang his wife.

'How much did they pay you for that?' he wanted to know.

'Twenty thousand,' said Minette's mother, 'and no more than I deserve with what I've been through.'

'I don't know how you can bring yourself to talk to a filthy rag like the *Daily Screech*,' said the Professor and slammed down the phone.

But all day he was furious. Twenty thousand pounds! It wasn't as though he wasn't suffering just as much over his lost daughter. He didn't light candles by her bed because of the fire risk but the housekeeper, who was fond of Minette, had bought a bunch of flowers and put them in her room. Of course the *Daily Screech* was out of the question—he wouldn't be seen dead with his photograph in a rag like that—but if the *Morning Gazette* was interested he might say a few words about his sorrow and his loss. There was a photograph somewhere that the housekeeper had taken outside the university in which he was standing beside his daughter wearing his gown and hood. It had come out rather well and made it clear the kind of background that she came from.

Fabio's grandparents were too snobby to talk to any kind of newspaper, but they appeared on a late night television panel to bleat about the lack of discipline in modem life and the feebleness of the police who still hadn't returned their grandson.

And even as Minette's parents were getting rich and Fabio's grandparents were complaining, a helicopter was getting ready to take off from the Metropolitan Police pad outside London. It was a small machine manned only by one policeman and a policewoman—and their orders were clear.

'Remember, if you get a chance to land, it's the two children we want. The aunts can wait. And don't pick a fight with Sprott. We're after the boy and the girl right now, and nothing else.'

*   *   *

As soon as they opened the door of the mermaid shed, Fabio and Minette realized that something serious had happened.

Loreen lay on the tiled floor, chewing mouthfuls of gum and weeping. In her sink in the corner, Oona looked stricken and pale. Old Ursula was shaking her head and muttering.

'It's my fault,' Loreen wailed. 'I've been a rotten mother and I deserve all I get.'

'What is it?' the children asked. 'What's happened?'

Loreen hiccupped and tried to speak but what with her gum and her sorrow no one could make out what she was saying and it was Old Ursula who said: 'Queenie's eloped. She's swum off with that muscleman who came yesterday and tried to catch her.'

'What muscleman?'

212

'He came in the dinghy with Lambert's father and Queenie went up to sing to him. We didn't think she fancied him but she's gone.'

A low croak came from Oona as she tried to speak. 'She . . . *didn't* . . . fancy him. She . . . said his biceps were silly.'

But the other mermaids took no notice of Oona, who was trying to make out that Queenie hadn't gone of her own free will. Twins always stuck together and what had happened with Lord Brasenott made Oona think that all men were evil, which was silly.

'I spoiled her,' wailed Loreen. 'She always had the best shells and the prettiest pearls for her hair.'

'Now don't carry on so,' said Ursula. 'It isn't your fault Queenie turned out so flighty.'

'She didn't—' began Oona—but Loreen only put another piece of gum in her mouth and went on wailing. 'I've been a rotten mother, and it's all my fault,' she said again, and she picked Walter out of the washing-up bowl and slapped his tail though he hadn't done anything except grizzle and whine in his usual way.

'We must tell the aunts,' said Fabio.

'Oh dear, must we?' cried Loreen.

213

But Old Ursula said yes, it was best to own up. 'Get some wheelbarrows and we'll go up to the house,' she said.

So the children came back with three barrows and Art, because flopping about overland made the mermaids' tails sore, and no one took any notice of Oona who went on croaking that her sister had not *liked* the muscleman.

The aunts were very much upset. Not because Queenie was flighty, which they'd known all along, but because it meant that Mr Sprott now knew that there were mermaids on the Island—and maybe other things too.

'I wonder if he knew before he came to lunch,' said Coral. 'Do you think that was why he wanted to buy the Island?'

'Perhaps he'll come back with photographers?' faltered Myrtle.

Fabio and Minette looked at each other. They had lived in the world outside long enough to know that Mr Sprott might come back with something much more serious than that.

*   *   *

A day passed, and half a night, and then they heard the sound they had been

214

dreading: the noise of a boat coming into the bay. So Sprott was back already!

In an instant the aunts were out of bed. Etta ran for the Captain's blunderbuss, Coral fetched Art's catapult, Myrtle grabbed the long-handled brush she used to scrub her back.

Outside, the night was black and moonless but they could make out the boat nosing in beside the jetty. The engine died . . . the cargo was unloaded . . . and almost instantly the boat went into reverse and moved away.

The aunts, clutching their weapons, peered into the darkness. Then suddenly Etta broke the silence with a great shout and ran towards the jetty. And there, standing tall among her suitcases, was a woman in a long raincoat holding what seemed to be a frying pan.

'Dorothy! Oh my dear, how wonderful to see you!' She hugged her sister, unable to keep back her tears of happiness and relief.

It was only then, as the other aunts came forward, that Etta could make out two small figures standing behind the luggage.

'Good heavens, Dorothy, what have you got there?' she asked, shining her torch.

'You may well ask,' said Dorothy, and pushed Boo-Boo and the Little One forward into the light.

*   *   *

Having Betty's children to stay would have been bad at any time. Now with Queenie gone and everyone so jittery, it was a nightmare.

They were awful children. Not awful like Lambert but awful all the same. It wasn't their fault; they'd been brought up to behave like idiots. Boo-Boo (who was a boy called Alfred) wore a bow tie and kept asking Art for shoe polish.

'It's got to be *tan*, not brown,' he said to poor Art, who was trying to prepare mash for the boobrie chicks and take the Captain his meals and cope with the extra people to feed.

The Little One (who was a girl called Griselda) began to cry straight away because Dorothy had forgotten to pack the hankie with a picture of a flower fairy on it which she kept under her pillow, and both the children were terrified of germs. Fortunately they were so wrapped up in their silly fusses about which pyjama case was which that they didn't even notice the strange animals or the danger they might be in. They just went on dusting the chairs before they sat down in them and looking at themselves in mirrors and complaining because their underclothes hadn't been ironed, exactly as if they were still in Newcastle upon Tyne. If Fabio hadn't been so busy with the kraken his temper would certainly have got the better of him but as it was he hardly saw them.

But having Dorothy made up for everything.

Dorothy knew that there was evil in the world. She had met people like Stanley Sprott and she had seen some dreadful things abroad—'monsters' that were supposed to be mermaids kept pickled in jars, or deformed beasts put in cages for people to gawp at—but she was not afraid. It was Dorothy who filled the Captain's blunderbuss with carpet tacks and set up tripwires behind the house and showed them how to make a cosh.

But when at the end of the first day Etta took her sister down to see the kraken, the tough, hard-faced woman changed into someone very different.

'Oh Etta,' she breathed, looking down

at the little creature as he slept, 'that I should live to see this day!'

*   *   *

Queenie sat in Mr Sprott's bathroom on the *Hurricane* up to her waist in scented water. The bath was a jacuzzi, with water bubbling up from all sorts of places. The taps were gold and so were the shower fittings and on shelves all round were cut-glass bottles full of wonderful things: coloured crystals and glittering hair sprays and creams for making the body firm and more creams for making it soft once it was firm and more creams still for making it not just soft and firm but also pink.

The creams belonged to Mrs Sprott, but she wasn't there so Queenie had the bathroom to herself. It was exactly the kind of bathroom she had dreamt of when she heard stories about mermaids marrying princes and going to live in palaces, but as she splashed more water over her tail, the tears kept welling out of her eyes and she was shaken by terrible sobs. She had never in all her life been so unhappy and afraid.

For Oona had been right. Queenie had

not swum away to be with the muscleman. Queenie had been most cruelly caught by Mr Sprott's henchmen and this bathroom was as much her prison as any cell in a cold and dirty dungeon.

She had gone out for a moonlight swim and when she got to the end of the bay she found a net under the water stretched between two rocks. At first she thought the net had been put there by fishermen but as she tried to free herself it was pulled tighter and tighter still, and she was towed away behind the dinghy and hauled aboard the *Hurricane* like a slab of dead meat.

'Oh, why didn't I listen?' cried poor Queenie. 'My mother told me to stay out of the way of men.'

She would have given anything now to see Loreen chewing her gum or Old Ursula with her toothless smile; she even missed Walter. But the person she longed for most was Oona. She understood now how Oona had felt on board Lord Brasenott's yacht; no wonder the poor girl had lost her voice. The round window of the bathroom had a curtain but Des and the two horrible men who guarded the boat had pulled it aside and every so often their faces leered in at her.

'Oh, what is to become of me!' cried poor Queenie, and felt so sad that she wanted to die.

And while Queenie wept in the bath, Lambert snivelled in his father's cabin.

'I don't want a mermaid for a stepmother,' he whined. 'I don't want a mermaid for a stepmother *anyway* and I certainly don't want a mermaid for a stepmother who isn't really there.'

'Don't be silly, Lambert,' said Mr Sprott. 'One doesn't marry mermaids, and anyway your mother is still alive.'

But he sighed deeply as he said it for Queenie was much prettier than Mrs Sprott with her purple hair and her claw-like fingernails and her greedy eyes. Mrs Sprott was a kind of dung beetle, only instead of collecting balls of nice soft manure she collected clothes and shoes and jewels and furs and dumped them in his house before going out for more.

'They'll laugh at me at school if I have a mermaid for a stepmother and I don't like fish. Even half a fish I don't like . . . even a fish that isn't really there,' moaned Lambert.

'Oh be quiet, Lambert,' said Mr Sprott. 'No one's going to marry her. We're going to show her off in a tank and make a fortune out of her. But first she'll have to tell us where the other creepy-crawlies are to be found. I'm going to catch the lot of them and then—'

But he didn't finish what he was going to say. Lambert couldn't be trusted not to blab. Not till the weird beasts were on board and tied up and on their way across the Atlantic would he say anything. He had decided to set up his funfair on an island off the coast of Florida which belonged to a friend. Or rather to a business partner. A man like Stanley Sprott did not have friends.

But first he had to cross-examine Queenie and see how much of his son's babble was true. He found Des ogling the mermaid through the bathroom window, while Casimir and Boris grumbled that it was their turn.

'I found her,' Des was saying. 'So I get the longest turn. She's mine really and the old man ought to—'

He turned to see Mr Sprott standing behind him. 'If any of you lay a finger on this mermaid you'll go straight overboard,' he said, and told Des to board up the window. Then he opened the door and drew up a stool beside the bath.

'Now, dear,' he said, 'I've got a few questions to ask you. It's about your family. You're not alone, are you? You've got a mummy and a daddy?'

'I haven't got a daddy,' said Queenie, pulling Aunt Myrtle's bodice righter round her top.

'But a mummy . . . and little brothers and sisters?'

'Only one of each and my great-grandmother.'

Queenie was too frightened to realize that she was being trapped.

'And of course there are the other . . . unusual creatures on the Island. Lambert told me about a worm. White, isn't he?'

Queenie nodded. 'He's very clever,' she said.

'And what else is there on the Island?'

Now at last the mermaid saw where this was leading. 'Nothing,' she faltered. 'Just the aunts.'

'Oh, I think there are,' said Mr Sprott. 'Perhaps if I take the plug out of the bath it will help you to think.' 'No! Oh please, no!'

To take water from a mermaid is the most terrible thing you can do. But Mr Sprott had already pulled it out; the water was draining away. Now he picked up the

222

electric hairdryer.

'No!' she cried again, trying to protect her tail from the terrifying heat.

Mr Sprott turned it off.

'You've remembered something else?'

'There's a big bird . . . a boobrie.' Surely he wouldn't want the boobrie? What use would she be to him?

'And where is it to be found? Is there a nest?'

'No . . . I don't know . . . It's up on the hill. Oh please put the water back.'

But Mr Sprott did not put the water back—and now he put on the dryer again and let the ghastly heat play over her tail fill the freshness of the silver became dull and dead . . . Queenie's tail had been her pride and joy and now it looked as though it had been on a fishmonger's slab for a week.

She held out as long as she could. Then she said pitifully: 'There are some selkies. They're just seals really. There's nothing to them.'

But Mr Sprott wasn't to be fobbed off so easily.

'What sort of seals?' He had dropped the hairdryer. Instead he had taken a pair of scissors and was holding a hank of her golden hair, ready to chop it off. 'Go on—answer. Don't keep me waiting. I don't like to be kept waiting.'

'I don't know,' whispered poor Queenie. 'It's just stories. People say they can turn into humans if someone drops seven tears into the water or if they're touched with cold steel.'

Mr Sprott's eyes glittered. He saw the circus ring . . . a seal on a tub . . . then a sharp pronged fork in its backside and lo, a woman jumps down. A transformation scene, better than a pantomime.

'Go on—what else is there? What else?'

But though he threatened her again with the hairdryer Queenie kept silent about the little kraken. For she knew that the end of the kraken meant the end of the sea as she knew it—and thus the end of her world—and Mr Sprott did not dare to hurt her any more or she wouldn't be worth putting on show.

'I'll speak to you again tomorrow,' he said, turning the water on again. 'Don't think I've finished with you, because I haven't.'

But as he gave his orders—the hold to be cleared, reinforced nets and lifting gear to be got ready, and harpoon guns to stun the beasts before they were hauled aboard—he did not realize that the greatest prize on the Island was still unknown to him. Neither Queenie nor Lambert had mentioned the kraken's son.

CHAPTER EIGHTEEN

The great kraken had reached the warmer southern seas. The fishes who joined him were brilliantly coloured, with fan tails and exotic spikes, and from the islands flashing birds with crests of crimson and orange came to welcome him and perch on his back. The water was clear and calm and the corals on the sea bed were of every colour under the sun.

As he swam the great kraken hummed his Healing Hum, and the turtles who had lumbered out of the sea to lay their eggs on the sandbanks were left in peace, and the rich men who had come to slaughter the porpoises pulled in their harpoons as the swell made by the kraken's passing reached their boats.

Yet the kraken was not happy. The dolphins and seals that swam round him felt this and were puzzled. He was smiling less; his golden eyes sometimes had a clouded look.

But why? He did not know—only that somehow he felt uneasy. He was missing his son of course, but there could have been no safer place to leave him than the Island of Aunts.

'I must pull myself together,' thought the kraken. 'I do not belong to myself; I belong to the sea.'

And he put aside his vague and troubled thoughts and swam on.

*　　　*　　　*

Two days after Boo-Boo and the Little One came to the Island, Old Ursula disappeared. She had swum out to say goodbye to Herbert's mother and never came back.

The other mermaids were frantic.

'I should have been nicer to her,' wailed Loreen. 'I shouldn't have said her tail smelt. It did smell but I shouldn't have said it.' And Oona wept because time and again she'd left the old creature flapping in the sink instead of helping her.

As for the aunts, they now knew once and for all how great was the danger they were in. Great-grandmothers do fall in

226

love but they aren't often silly about it when they do. Old Ursula could not have eloped, she must have been snatched—and that meant that Queenie too had been taken by force. And sure enough, when they searched the bay, they found a net stretched between two rocks.

'We must have a Council of War,' said Etta, and made everybody do thirty press-ups so as to make the blood go to their heads and help them to think.

But even with all the blood in their heads, they knew that fighting off Sprott and his men would be almost impossible and that their only hope would be to get the animals to hide.

'The stoorworm must stay at the bottom of the loch—no coming up for chats,' said Coral.

'And Herbert and his mother should come closer to the house,' said Myrtle. 'They could have the pond in the vegetable garden.'

Art offered to guard the mermaid shed with the Captain's blunderbuss—secretly he still hoped he might have a chance to kill someone after all—and they decided that the Sybil must be brought indoors; she was far too loopy to be left on her own.

But it was easier to decide what should be done about the creatures than to get them to do it. The stoorworm pointed out that he was after all a wingless *dragon* and should be helping to guard the Island, not skulking about in the bottom of lakes, and Herbert wouldn't bring his mother any closer because she wanted to die beside the sea and not in somebody's Brussels sprouts.

But of course it was the kraken that they worried about most of all, and it was now that the aunts wished from the bottom of their hearts that they had never kidnapped Fabio and Minette.

They knew exactly where the little beast could be hidden. In a large underwater cave, a kind of grotto on the North Shore with only the smallest opening on to the strand. It was a beautiful place, with a pool of clear, deep water surrounded by gently shelving rock, and at the back of the grotto was an opening to the cliff which gave enough light to see by. The opening came out by Ethelgonda's burial ground and the naak had promised to keep watch up there.

But to keep the kraken in a cave when he was used to the freedom of the sea would not be easy. He would need people all the time. And people, to the kraken, were Fabio and Minette.

'There is no question of you staying alone with him through the night,' said Etta firmly. 'My sisters and I will take shifts.'

'Yes there is. We'll take a blanket and lots of food—but we're going to do it. It's our job,' said Minette.

'It's not your job to risk that kind of danger.'

But something odd was happening to Fabio and Minette. Perhaps it was from living on the Island among creatures that did not need to speak very much, but they seemed to know each other's thoughts.

'If you didn't want us to do our work you shouldn't have kidnapped us,' said Minette.

And Fabio, between gritted teeth, said, 'Nothing is going to stop us being with the kraken. Nothing.'

* * *

By nightfall, everyone was at their posts: Art guarding the mermaids, Coral crouched by the boobrie's nest, which they had ringed with barbed wire; the Sybil zooming round the house muttering about wind-chill factors and burning the Captain's semolina.

And the kraken hidden in his secret place beneath the cliff.

The children had lit candles and put them on the ledges, and the flames flickering on the stone lit up the colours of the rock.

'It's like Merlin's crystal cave,' said Minette dreamily, and she was right. Because the kraken was his father's son, all sorts of creatures came to be near him in the water: crimson crabs and clusters of pipefish and families of sea mice . . . But if it was beautiful in the cave, keeping the kraken quiet and happy was hard work. Fortunately he was learning English so fast that they could sing to him and tell him stories.

'More *Snow White*,' he would command, or 'More *Puss in Boots*.'

But the stories he liked best were the ones they made up about his father—about the great kraken and his adventures as he swam through the oceans of the world.

Where the sides of the grotto sloped to the water there was one place which was almost flat and it was there that the children had made a kind of camp. They had brought sleeping bags and plenty of food and of course the tin of boobrie buns. If the kraken got restless and swam too near the opening of the cave, they only had to bang with a wooden spoon on the tin and he would hurry back, his mouth already open for his treat.

Even so, the aunts were worried about them and, sometime in the small hours, Etta and Dorothy stopped patrolling the Island and went down to the grotto again, determined to make the children come up to the house and go to bed.

The kraken was asleep, his head just out of the water. And on either side of him, curled up on the ledge so that their arms were almost touching him, slept Fabio and Minette.

And the aunts turned back and said nothing, for it was clear that these three lived in a circle of friendship that nothing now could break.

*　　　*　　　*

There was no attack from Sprott's people that night, but just before dawn something did happen.

Down on the point, Herbert's mother slipped quietly from life. Her eyes filmed

231

over; she sighed deeply, her whiskers trembled . . . Then she spoke her son's name once—not in the selkie language but in proper human speech so that Myrtle too could understand.

'*Herbert*,' said Herbert's mother. She didn't say anything more but from the way she said it they knew that she thought Herbert had been a good son and she was thanking him. Then she hoisted herself slowly to the very edge of the rock, lifted her head once towards the sky—and gave herself to the sea.

It was a beautiful death—exactly the kind of death the old seal had chosen—but of course for Herbert it was a moment of great sadness, and when it was over, Myrtle would not leave him even to get her meals.

Her sisters were worried about this. Myrtle had always felt things too much. When she was small she had tried to bring a tin of sardines back to life by floating the headless fishes in a wash basin, and they did not think she should be out on the point on a night when there might be danger.

But Myrtle in her own way was obstinate.

'I can't leave Herbert alone with his

sorrow,' she said—and she wrapped her legs in an old grey blanket and settled down beside her friend.

*   *   *

There was a time when Queenie would have hated sharing a bath with old Ursula but now she was touchingly glad of her company. The old mermaid was as tough as old boots and she didn't give a fig for Mr Sprott's threats.

'He can't do anything to me. I'm old and I don't care,' she said.

Mr Sprott hated her. She spat at him and cursed him and tried to bite him with her single tooth, and when Des came anywhere near she screeched at him.

'Don't you dare ogle my great-granddaughter you plug-ugly,' she yelled.

'You can't put that old horror on show,' said Des. 'Nobody'll pay to see the likes of her!'

Mr Sprott shrugged. 'Maybe I'll sell her to medical science to be cut up,' he said. 'No one knows how a mermaid's tail is joined to her body.'

Seeing Ursula so angry and unafraid did Queenie good. But of course they both knew what danger they were in. And

233

sure enough, later that evening Boris and Casimir came in with blindfolds which they tied roughly round the mermaids' eyes. Then they were wrapped in coarse sacking and felt themselves raised up, swaying on steel hooks, and then lowered, still swaying horribly, into some deep cold place.

When they could see again, they found that they were sitting in a crude, rusty tank filled with water. The tank was in the corner of a large, dark, empty space, stuffy and evil-smelling. There were no windows and no lamps, and all they could hear was the slap of the water against the ship's sides.

They were in the hold of the *Hurricane* which Sprott had prepared, like a slave ship of old, for his prisoners.

'Don't worry, you won't be by yourselves much longer,' jeered Des. 'Lots of your little friends will be along soon.'

Then he climbed up the steel ladder, pulled it up after him, and shut the trapdoor, leaving them alone in the foul-smelling darkness.

*　　　*　　　*

There were five men in the launch: Stanley Sprott himself, Boris and Casimir, and the bodyguard, Des. Lambert had been left behind with the skipper—the poor boy was definitely going crazy—but Sprott had forced the mate of the *Hurricane* to come too.

The launch was towing two large inflatable rafts loaded with equipment, with which to net the creatures and stun them before they were floated out to the *Hurricane*.

All the men had guns and knives and whistles to blow if they wanted extra help and their orders were clear.

'Now remember, if you have to shoot, shoot the aunts, not the creatures. You can't get money for aunts. But don't shoot at all if you can help it. We want silence and we want speed.'

The launch slid on to the sand. The men got out.

Boris and Casimir set off up the hill; they were going for the boobrie and the stoorworm. Sprott himself and the mate made their way to the mermaid shed: Sprott liked the idea of carrying the wriggling, struggling mermaids over his shoulder.

And Des was to capture the selkies.

Des had grumbled about this. 'What do you want a couple of old seals for?' he asked Mr Sprott.

Sprott had not told anyone what Queenie had said about selkies; it was probably rubbish anyway. 'They're supposed to be able to sing,' was all he said.

So Des was not in a good mood as he climbed up the rocks towards the sleeping seals. Even if they could sing it didn't seem very exciting—lots of animals made noises in their throats—and how the devil was he supposed to pick out the selkies from the others?

'There's two of them, lying apart from the rest,' Lambert had said. 'They've got funny eyes.' And then he'd started to snivel and go on again about how they weren't really there.

But as he got closer, Des saw that Lambert was right. There *were* two seals lying apart from the rest. A big bull seal and a smaller one; a cow probably. He'd tackle the smaller one first and if things went wrong he could always skin the brutes. Sealskins fetched a good price.

Des crept closer. The big seal opened his eyes, and even in the dim moonlight, Des could see that his eyes were not quite like those of an ordinary seal.

But it was the smaller one he was after. She'd been asleep but now she stirred . . .

Really it was uncanny how human she looked. Her body was just a grey splodge and he couldn't see her flippers, but as she yawned and opened her eyes you could almost forget she was a seal.

Des shook himself. He was getting fanciful. Better get her netted and dragged away. It shouldn't be a problem; she was only half grown—he probably wouldn't even need the stunner.

He crept the last few metres, got to his feet—and threw the net.

And the selkie screamed. He had never heard such a scream coming from the throat of an animal. It was a completely human scream and it was all Des could do not to drop the net and run back to the ship.

But he didn't. He cursed and tried to tighten the net while the seal struggled and kicked—and then suddenly the screams had words to them! Proper human words.

'Leave me alone,' shrieked the selkie in her high-pitched voice. 'Let me go at once, you brute. Help! Oh, help!'

Up by the boobrie's nest, Coral got to

her feet, vaulted over the barbed wire—all sixteen stone of her—and began to run towards the point. Etta, who had been helping Art to guard the mermaid shed, seized the blunderbuss and did the same. Going to rescue Myrtle was something they did as naturally as they breathed.

But someone else was coming to Myrtle's rescue.

As Des straightened himself to pull the net tighter, something came at him: an enormous wet wall of grey muscle . . . a tank of solid blubber which sent him sprawling. He tried to get to his feet but the bull seal threw back his head and roared and then he opened his mouth and Des saw the evil-looking teeth and felt his hot breath. The creature was going for his throat . . . in a moment it would be all up with him.

Choking, struggling, Des tried to reach his knife but every time it was in his grasp, the seal charged again. Helpless, sprawled on the ground, he tried to cover his face, but the awful teeth were closing on his flesh . . .

Then when he thought his last moment had come, he found the knife, and lunged. The seal reared back and he almost missed . . . almost but not quite.

He'd made a nick in the animal's shoulder, nothing more . . . but, my God, what was happening now? It wasn't teeth that were fastening round his throat, it was hands, it was fingers . . .

With a blood-curdling shriek, Des managed to struggle to his feet—and then he ran . . . ran and ran, almost mad with horror . . . ran, with the spittle running out of his mouth, away and away across the Island, trying to escape from what he'd seen. Ran until he stumbled over a gorse bush, and found himself falling . . . falling down towards a pool of dark water far below.

CHAPTER NINETEEN

The stoorworm had always been worried about his thoughts getting stuck halfway down his body.

Now he didn't worry any more. The terrible sadness he felt as he lay curled up in the hold of the *Hurricane* had not got stuck anywhere. It went right down through every single segment to the tip of his tail. He was just a long tube of wretchedness and despair and shame.

239

It had all happened in a moment. He had heard the boobrie squawk in terror and come up from the bottom of the lake to see if he could help, and a man had shot something into his throat—a red hot needle it felt like . . . and then he remembered nothing more till he woke in a kind of snake pit in this ghastly place.

'I have failed my friends,' he thought, 'and I have failed myself.' And he felt so sad that he wanted to die.

From the rusty tank in the corner where the mermaids sat, came the sound of sobbing. Oona was sobbing because *men* kept coming down below to peer and pry—men that were worse even than Lord Brasenott—and she was terribly afraid. But the noisiest and most terrible tears came from Loreen.

'My baby!' she kept hiccupping. 'My little darling, where is he?'

When Sprott had overcome Art and broken open the door of the mermaid shed Walter had been asleep in his washing-up bowl and there had been no time for Loreen to grab him before she was thrown over Sprott's shoulder and carried towards the boat.

'Will someone find him?' gulped Loreen. And old Ursula said of course they would—but the trouble was, no one knew what was happening on the Island and who was left.

Perhaps the most heart-rending sight in that ghastly place were the boobrie chicks, penned in a wire cage, their yellow beaks bruised and blood-stained . . . and lying down, with her great yellow legs in the air like an outsize chicken ready for the pot, their mother. Lowering the struggling giant bird through the trapdoor had been so difficult that they had given her another injection and now the chicks climbed over her, peeping in bewilderment, not understanding why their mother was so still.

But Sprott's greatest prize was not in the hold. The kraken lay on the deck, tethered by ropes which bit so hard that he could not even turn his head, and every few minutes Sprott came up to look at him and rub his hands and gloat. He had no idea what it was that he had caught, only that it would make him very, very rich. For it could speak, this thing which they had caught when Des fell into its cave. It had said 'Father' once, when they nailed it down on to the deck, but now its eyes were closed and it spoke no more.

'Hurry up down there,' Sprott shouted to the crew who were fixing the starboard engine. They would have been gone long before but for the engine playing up. It was high time they got away across the Atlantic. He'd given orders to have the thing on the deck hosed down every ten minutes but it wasn't eating. None of the creatures were eating . . . they needed to be in proper cages.

For a moment he wondered if the little boy was dead—the one who'd tried to stop them in the cave. Probably not—the skulls of children were tougher than you'd think. All the same he'd be glad to be gone.

'I thought I told you to hurry,' Sprott shouted once again.

But still the *Hurricane* lay unmoving on the grey sea—and on her deck, the little kraken, his heart broken, prepared for death.

*　　　*　　　*

Minette sat on the floor of the boxroom, her hands round her knees, and waited for Fabio to wake.

She had been there for several hours and she would not move however much the aunts complained.

'You're not helping him,' said Etta. 'He'll come round when he's ready.'

But she did not speak in her usual brisk voice, and Minette took no notice. All the aunts were like wraiths since the kraken had gone.

So Minette watched and waited by her friend. Outside, in the bathroom, she could hear the high, stupid voices of Betty's children.

'There's something nasty in the washbasin. It smells fishy. You can't clean your teeth,' whined Boo-Boo.

'It's eaten my Tinkerbell toothpaste. I don't like it here. I want to go home!'

'I want to go home too. I want to go home *now*.'

Minette sighed. She could never get used to the awfulness of Boo-Boo and the Little One. What was in the washbasin was the merbaby, Walter. He was missing his mother, and chewed anything he could reach.

Fabio lay without moving on the bed; the bandage round his head stood out very white in the darkened room. What if he didn't come round at all?

But that was stupid. He was breathing. He had concussion, that was all.

Minette shut her eyes, remembering. They'd been in the cave, telling the kraken a story . . . trying to stop him going too near the entrance. Then suddenly something had hurtled down from the opening in the cliff above them and landed in the water. A man they had never seen before, gasping and struggling for breath.

They hadn't been frightened at first— not till he clambered out and stared at the kraken . . . stared and stared . . . Then he felt in his sodden clothes, and from an oilskin pouch he took out a whistle and blew three sharp shrill blasts.

They had understood then. Fabio charged at the man, trying to wrench the whistle away, but it was too late. More men came from the sea and the cave filled up with shouting and torchlight and the glint of weapons . . . Minette had gone to the kraken's head, slipping into the water with him, trying to calm him but the net came down over them both . . . He'd thought it was a game at first— cruelty was something he couldn't understand—and she'd half hoped they'd take her with him so that she could comfort him. But they had pulled her out roughly and thrown her back into the pool.

And as she climbed out she'd seen Fabio lying on the ledge of rock . . . and the blood seeping from his head . . .

Out in the corridor the Little One was whimpering again. 'They've given me the wrong sweeties. I've got blue sweeties and I'm a girl. Girls ought to have *pink* sweeties.'

It was another hour before Fabio stirred, but then he was awake at once.

'Have they got him? Has he gone?'

'Yes.'

Fabio put a hand to his head. 'Did they knock me out?'

'They kept thumping your head against the stone.' Minette's voice broke as she remembered Fabio's courage and the cruelty of the men.

'And the others? The storworm . . . the mermaids?'

'They've got everyone except Walter.'

Fabio had managed to sit up.

'Is the *Hurricane* still there?

'Yes. We don't know why but she is.'

'Then we must board her. We must rescue him. We must rescue everybody.'

Minette stared at him. 'You're mad. How could we? We've only got the *Peggoty*—and the aunts won't let us out of

245

their sight. We're really prisoners now because they blame themselves for you being hurt and because they left the creatures unguarded to help Myrtle. You've no idea what it's like down there. And Dorothy broke one of the thug's noses with her wok; they dragged him back to the boat but there's blood everywhere.'

Fabio took no notice. 'We have to. We have to get to him.'

'Even if we did, what could we—' began Minette and broke off. She felt like Fabio underneath. They had to try and help.

Fabio had pushed back the bedclothes. The room spun round, then steadied. He was just trying his feet on the floor when the unspeakable Boo-Boo came in.

'That's my teddy you've got there. I put him to sleep in your bed when you were in the cave and I want him because we're going to play Mummies and Daddies in the garden and he's my little boy.'

Fabio threw the stuffed animal across the room.

'Get out,' he said. And then: 'There must be someone who could help.'

Minette looked at him. He had had an awful blow to his head—would he be able to cope with any more strangeness?

But that was silly. Fabio could cope with anything.

'There is somebody,' she said.

* * *

Herbert sat quietly on the point and looked out to the sea which until yesterday had been his home. He wore a pair of Art's trousers, stripy socks and a sweater of the Captain's. The clothes felt prickly on his skin, and his soul felt prickly too. The tears of Myrtle, the despair of the aunts, buzzed round his head. It had been so quiet in the sea.

But what was done was done. He was a man now, not a seal, and it was as a man that he must try to help the kraken's son.

The *Peggoty* was in the boathouse. She was only an old fishing boat, not a tenth the size of the *Hurricane*, but if he could get alongside and get a grappling hook on to the deck he could climb up the rope and board her. Some selkies, when they changed shape, had trouble with their arms and legs, but his were strong.

He was checking the *Peggoty's* oars, when Fabio and Minette appeared in the doorway of the shed. Fabio had pulled a

247

woollen cap over his bandage.

'We want to go with you,' said Minette.

Fabio was silent. He had expected to find it a shock meeting someone who not twenty-four hours ago had been a seal, but now nothing mattered except to get to the *Hurricane*. Herbert had been a handsome seal and he was a handsome man but what was important was that he looked trustworthy and reliable—and strong. Some people who listen to music on the cello can be a little arty and vague, but not Herbert.

'Have you asked the aunts?' said Herbert, coiling a rope.

The children did not answer. Then:

'We have to go. The kraken was our job. We have to help him, and the others too. We have to try.'

Herbert straightened himself and looked at them. He was a man now but he was not a man like other men. He had a sense of all nature being one . . . of children being part of the universe and not creatures set apart. He knew that if the little kraken died the sea would never be the same again, and he remembered that the kraken had trusted these two as he had trusted no one.

All the same, knowing the danger, he

hesitated.

But it looked as though the matter would be taken out of his hands. For before he could speak all three of them heard the unmistakable drone of a helicopter coming towards the Island. The noise grew louder, the helicopter circled the Island once . . . then began the descent on to the level patch of grass behind the house.

Tears sprang to Minette's eyes and Fabio drew in a hissing breath. Now, just when they had a chance of reaching the kraken, they had been found and would be dragged back.

Frantically they looked about for somewhere to hide. But it was too late. A policeman was climbing out of the machine and hurrying towards the house; a policewoman followed.

The adventure was over.

CHAPTER TWENTY

King's Cross Station had not looked so smart since the Queen had arrived there at the time of her silver jubilee.

There were streamers all over the

station saying *Welcome Back!* and on Platform One where the train bringing the kidnapped children was due to arrive, was a party of schoolchildren carrying banners. The banners said things like *You are safe now* and *Your troubles are ended*, and the children who carried them had learnt a welcoming song which they would sing as soon as the snatched children stepped out of the train.

A chocolate firm had sent a bumper pack of sweets, and their prettiest salesgirl, dressed like a chocolate bar, was waiting to present it. A famous clothes shop had made up parcels of T-shirts, and a bicycle manufacturer had brought two mountain bikes to present to the children who had been snatched so cruelly by the kidnapping aunts. Everyone knew about the miracle which had made it possible for the police helicopter to swoop down and gather up the missing boy and girl in a single daring raid.

Mrs Danby, Minette's mother, was in the place of honour, standing on the strip of red carpet which had been put out for the children to walk on when they stepped out of their First Class Carriage. She wore a dazzling new outfit which she had bought with the money from the

Daily Screech: a shocking pink suit and a little pillbox hat with a veil. When she ran forward to hug Minette she would push the veil up so that people could see her tears. Professor Danby stood beside her, looking solemn. Whenever his wife took a step forward so as to be nearer to where the train would stop, he took one too. He wasn't going to be upstaged by that show-off he'd been fool enough to marry!

The old Mountjoys had been given special chairs so that they could wait for their grandson in comfort. They were of course very pleased that Fabio had been found, but they couldn't help wondering if all the work they had put into making him into an English gentleman had been wasted. The children had been discovered on some rough island in the middle of the Atlantic ocean and that could hardly be a good thing. Maybe they would come off the train with straw in their hair and mud on their shoes—if they wore shoes at all.

And of course as well as the schoolchildren and the relatives and the Lady Mayoress with her golden chain, the platform was full of cameramen and journalists and television crews with all their gear. The moment when the poor, snatched, little children got down from the train and ran into the arms of their loved ones would be shown not just all over England but all over the world. Even now the commentators were setting the scene, babbling excitedly into their microphones.

'Only five minutes to go, before the train bringing those frightened, wretched youngsters to safety will draw up just twenty metres from where I stand,' said the lady from ITV. 'Mrs Danby can hardly hold back her excitement—she has just run forward so as to get even closer to her missing daughter . . .'

This was true—Mrs Danby *had* run forward, but this was because her husband was up to his tricks again, trying to upstage her so that the camera picked him up as well as her and she wasn't having that.

'And the grandparents of the wild little boy who found shelter and kindliness in their home—what a touching couple they make, in the autumn of their years, waiting with joy for this great moment,' the commentator went on.

Up in Edinburgh, Professor Danby's housekeeper was glued to the telly. There'd be a row about which of the parents was to have the girl first, she thought, and hoped it would be the professor because she'd put flowers in Minette's room and polished her new writing desk.

Minette's mother's boyfriend was watching too, lying as usual with a can of lager on the sofa. He too hoped Minette would go to her father first. Not that he had anything against the kid but the flat was cramped and he'd got the sack again and needed somewhere to flake out in the day.

And in the hospital in Newcastle upon Tyne, Betty sat in the dayroom and watched, surrounded by other patients and those nurses who could spare a moment. She needed the treat because her hip was mending very slowly; she should have been out of hospital a week ago and there she still was.

'Only three more minutes now,' said one of the newscasters looking at the station clock, which was a silly thing to say. Since when have trains coming down from the North been on time, even trains full of police officers bringing kidnapped children back to safety?

The commentator described Mrs Danby's hat once more and told the viewers that old Mrs Mountjoy's face was full of longing.

The schoolchildren holding their banners shuffled their feet and cleared their throats, ready for their welcoming song.

The station clock ticked on.

And then at last they saw the train coming, curving round into the station, and a great cheer went up. The Lady Mayoress straightened her chain, the crowd that had gathered outside the platform gates waved, the television cameras whirred . . .

The train slowed down . . . stopped.

The door opened. A policewoman got down, and another . . . then they turned and held out their hands to the two children.

The girl was the first to come out. She was lifted down from the carriage and stood for a moment looking about her, smoothing down the velvet collar of her coat and patting her curls.

Then the boy was lifted down, and straightened his cap and dusted down his blazer.

'Where's my mummy?' said the little girl in a cross and whining voice. 'I want my mummy. You said you'd take us to her.'

'I want her too,' wailed the little boy. 'I want my mummy *now.*'

Mrs Danby's mouth fell open. The professor glared. 'Is this a joke?' snapped Mr Mountjoy.

And in the dayroom of the hospital in Newcastle upon Tyne, poor Betty gave a single high-pitched cry and fell back senseless in her chair.

CHAPTER TWENTY-ONE

Herbert was magnificent. In spite of the darkness and the choppy sea he sent the *Peggoty* sailing steadily towards the single light burning on the *Hurricane.* His hands on the tiller never faltered, he seemed to understand the old boat as he understood the sea.

Fabio and Minette sat very close together in the stern, not daring to speak. When the helicopter took off again and they realized what a wonderful mistake had been made, they had wasted no more time. While Herbert was filling petrol cans by the jetty, they had climbed aboard and down into the little cabin full of fishing hooks and ropes and tackle and pulled a tarpaulin over their heads. With luck, by the time they were found, they would be too far out to turn back.

But it wasn't Herbert who found them—it was Aunt Etta and Aunt Coral. It had never occurred to the children that the aunts would be part of the boarding party. Dorothy was staying behind because she had sprained her wrist when she bashed Casimir with her wok and Herbert had forbidden Myrtle to come.

'You have had a shock, Myrtle, and you must rest,' Herbert had said, and that was that. But not even Herbert had been able to stop Etta and Coral.

They had never seen the aunts so angry.

'Turn back at *once!*' commanded Etta. 'These children will *not* face any more danger! I forbid it!'—and Coral tried to get hold of the tiller and force the boat to change course.

But Herbert stood firm. He had sensed the change in the sea and knew what would happen to the ocean if the kraken's son perished. Even the children did not matter compared to that.

They glided silently alongside the *Hurricane.* No lights were burning in the cabins; no one expected an attack. With unbelievable strength Herbert threw the knotted rope and they heard the grappling iron fasten on the wooden boards.

Within seconds, Herbert had climbed the rope and was on deck. Etta and the children followed. Coral with her bulk took longer but she did it.

They stood in silence, listening. Herbert had his knife ready. If they could cut the kraken free and push him overboard, he could swim to safety.

They had almost reached him when it happened.

The door from below opened, a beam of light was thrown on to the deck—and Lambert, in his pyjamas stood there, blinking.

The poor boy was definitely going crazy. Since the *Hurricane* had filled up with creepy-crawlies that weren't really there, Lambert had been plagued by dreadful dreams. In this one he'd dreamt that Old Ursula had come to his school, sliding on her tail, and said she was his grandmother and all the boys had jeered at him and thrown him buckets of fish.

Now he came on to the deck, too afraid to wake his father, and saw a huddle of shapes creeping towards the tarpaulin where the thing that didn't exist was lying.

He gave a cry of terror and as Herbert turned, the knife in his hand, the klaxons began to blare and searchlights raked the deck.

Ten minutes later, the rescuers had joined the prisoners in the stench and darkness of the hold.

*   *   *

You couldn't really blame the police. When the helicopter landed on the Island, two little children had run straight into the arms of the policewoman and begged to be taken home.

'Take us away,' they had lisped pathetically. 'We hate it here. Take us home to our mummy.'

It was clear that the poor little scraps had been abominably treated. They had not been allowed to clean their teeth and been given sweets which tasted nasty— drugged ones, the policewoman was sure. All the way they had whimpered and complained and it was clear that the aunts who had held them were as evil and dangerous as everyone imagined.

But of course the muddle took some time to sort out. The tax inspector had to come from Newcastle upon Tyne to fetch his children and no one knew whether the T-shirts and the chocolate bars should be given to them or kept for when the other children came. And the whole business of capturing the vile kidnappers and the children that they were holding had still to be done.

But it couldn't be done at once because a great fog had come down, covering the Western coast and making it impossible for helicopters to take off, or ships to move.

*   *   *

The prisoners had been in the hold of the *Hurricane* for several hours when they heard the engine judder into life.

Soon they would be off, and then . . . Nobody put into words what would happen once they were out in the Atlantic, but all of them knew. Why should Sprott let them live to tell the world what he had done.

In a corner, Minette was talking quietly to Fabio.

'If I could get to the kraken . . . just for a few minutes?'

Fabio shrugged. 'How would it help?

We've nothing to cut him free with.'

'I've got an idea. It might not work, but we've got nothing to lose.'

'What sort of an idea?'

Minette looked round. The aunts were dozing, their backs against the wall; the worm was curled round himself like a piece of worn-out hosepipe . . .

She moved closer to Fabio and whispered in his ear.

Fabio looked doubtful. 'Remember what Aunt Etta said—that they can't do it till they're ready.'

'Yes, I know—but once or twice when he's been learning a song, I thought . . . And anything's better than nothing.'

'All right,' said Fabio. 'Let me think.'

He sat for a while with his head in his hands. Then he went over to speak to Herbert who nodded and went over to the mermaids' tank.

'I can't,' they heard poor Queenie say. 'I haven't the heart.'

But Herbert was firm: 'I'm afraid you must,' he said in his sensible voice.

An hour later Des came down the ladder with some bread and a bucketful of drinking water and as he did so, Queenie called to him.

'Des,' she trilled. 'Could you come here

a minute?'

He put down his bucket and sidled past Herbert. He could never be sure whether this was or wasn't the man who had tried to strangle him on the point—it had been too dark to see his face—but Herbert gave him the creeps.

'I've got ever such a painful place here in my bath,' Queenie went on. 'Would you come and look, please?'

Des bent over her and Queenie tossed her hair so that it fell over his face.

'No, not there,' she fluted. 'You show him, Oona.'

It was only thinking of the kraken that gave Oona the courage to come closer to the man with his horrible hot breath, but she did it, and she too tossed her long thick hair so that Des was completely covered in the mermaids' tresses.

'Where?' he kept saying. 'Where does it hurt?'

Only Boris was guarding the hatch—Casimir wasn't good for much since Dorothy had broken his nose—and Fabio now climbed up the ladder. 'Help,' he shouted. 'The mermaids are being pestered. Send someone down!'

Sprott heard him and was furious. He had forbidden the men to go near the twins.

'What's going on there?' he yelled and, as Boris turned, Fabio dodged round behind him running towards the deckhouse, while down below the mermaids began to scream.

The chase did not last long—Boris caught Fabio and almost threw him down into the hold. But Minette had been behind Fabio and managed to slip out unseen in the muddle and the fog, and make her way to where the captured kraken lay.

* * *

The kraken lay tethered and dangerously still. He still breathed but only just; his eyes were closed.

She tiptoed forward and laid her cheek against his head, and her tears fell on his face.

But Minette had not escaped from below deck to cry. She had only a few minutes to do what she had set herself to do.

'You mustn't give in like this,' she said into his ear. 'It's wrong. You're a brave and important person. You have to fight back.'

The kraken tried to turn his head but the ropes bit into his throat. She saw the look in his golden eyes and her heart sank. But she wouldn't seem to be sorry for him; that was not the way.

'You must remember who you are,' she said sternly.

The little kraken sniffed and was silent.

'You must think of your father,' she went on.

'Father,' said the kraken. He seemed a little stronger when he said that and she could see he was thinking of the mighty creature who had given him life.

'That's right.' Minette followed this up. 'What does your father do?'

The little kraken sighed. It was a heartbreaking sound, as though all the sorrow in the world was coming out of his throat.

'Go on. Think,' prompted Minette.

The kraken sighed again. He was not good at simply thinking. Then:

'Smiles,' he said.

'Yes. He smiles. He's got a lovely smile.' Minette saw the curve of the great beast's mouth as he swam into the bay. 'And what else does he do?'

There was another pause. Then: 'Swims,' said the little kraken. 'He swims.'

'That's right. He swims.' Minette nodded hard, giving encouragement. 'And what does he do when he swims?'

No answer.

'What does he do when he swims round the oceans of the world making everything better? Think.'

The little kraken thought. You could see him trying, but the ropes were beginning to cut into his flesh. He was too young to think through pain.

'Don't know,' he moaned.

But Minette would give him no chance to go under. 'Yes, you do. When he swims he does something else. What is it?'

Another sigh. Then: 'He hums,' said the little kraken.

'That's right.' She rubbed his head to give him encouragement. 'He hums, doesn't he? Humming is what krakens *do*.'

He tried to turn his head. His eyes were still bewildered.

'Humming is what krakens do,' repeated Minette. 'Isn't it?'

'Yes.' His voice was very weak but he was following her.

'And you're a kraken,' she insisted. 'Aren't you? A kraken is what you are.'

It didn't seem as though the poor

exhausted creature could speak again, but he took a weary breath and tried once more.

'I'm a kraken,' he repeated obediently. 'A kraken is what I *am*.'

* * *

At first she'd thought it was going to work. There had been a flash of pride in his eyes as he spoke; but almost at once he fell silent and turned away—and then Boris came and pushed her roughly down the ladder.

Now she sat beside Fabio, her head in her hands and knew that it was over. She had done all she could and she had failed.

In the darkness, the wan faces of the captives showed a wretchedness that was beyond tears. The two aunts sat with closed eyes trying to bear what they had done. Facing their own deaths was not so hard but what they had done to Fabio and Minette was not to be endured. Only Herbert was still upright, listening to the sound of the water against the sides of the ship.

Another hour passed . . . and another . . . The *Hurricane's* engine had been turned off while they waited for the fog to lift, but now they heard it start up again.

Unsteady at first, fainter than before . . . wavering . . . but gradually settling into a kind of thrumming rhythm.

Except that the engine hadn't sounded quite like that . . .

Fabio who had been dozing, sat up suddenly and dug Minette in the ribs.

Then slowly, wonderingly, the wretched prisoners looked at each other with a dawning hope.

*   *   *

The great kraken had reached the Islands of the Southern Reef. The turquoise water, the coral strands, were staggeringly beautiful.

There was little to do in this paradise. The people who lived there respected the sea and the creatures in it, and they came out to pay their respects to the great kraken, standing with bowed heads. They did not gawp or gape or stare; the legend of the kraken who healed the sea was in their stories and had been for generations.

'He does not smile,' said the old chief, whose great-grandmother had seen the kraken when he came before and told

266

him about the healer's mouth curving in a bow which made everyone joyous to watch.

'He is troubled,' said the chief's wife, who was a magic woman.

'How strangely his hum is sounding,' said a child. 'There are two hums, aren't there? A big hum and a little hum.'

'It must be an echo.'

But the kraken had stopped swimming. He was quite still in the water, resting. His head was tilted. Like the islanders he was listening . . . listening . . .

What was going on? His own hum was being interfered with. It was being disturbed. This had never happened before. Sometimes there had been an echo from his hum when he swam in a ford between mountains, and sometimes the whales joined in, but this was different. What he could hear was his own hum but it was smaller.

He fell silent, and all the creatures under the water came up to look at him and wonder what was happening.

But the silence was not complete. The small hum, the *underneath* hum, was still there. It was unsteady, quavery . . . but it was growing now in strength.

A great judder went through the

kraken, sending the resting birds up in a flutter from his back. He made himself absolutely quiet once more, but it was still there—this other fainter hum that wasn't his own hum . . . and yet was just exactly that.

Then the people on the bather reef saw a most extraordinary sight. The great kraken reared up out of the water—and now he did not hum. Instead he roared.

And then he turned.

CHAPTER TWENTY-TWO

'I don't want to watch! I don't *want* to!' shrieked Lambert. He tried to hold on to the cabin door but his father dragged him out so roughly that he fell forward on to the deck.

'You *will* watch, you namby-pamby little shirker. You'll watch them go overboard and you'll like it. It's time you learnt that you don't get something for nothing.'

Pushing and pulling, kicking Lambert's shins, Mr Sprott forced his son towards the rail.

He felt hard done by. If the aunts had

sold him the island as he wanted he wouldn't have to drown them now, and the children too. It was their own fault really. There was no way he could get his money-making schemes under way with people blathering and giving the game away. He was going to say that he'd found the creatures wild at sea and rescued them.

'Right, go and get them,' he ordered Des. And then, furiously, 'I thought I told you to stop the thing making that blasted noise!'

Des looked at the kraken, still tethered to the deck. 'I've tried, boss. I've kicked him and I've thumped him but you said I wasn't to do him in.'

Evil people cannot bear the sound of the hum. They feel it as a threat to all they stand for, and the kraken had been humming now for many hours.

Boris meanwhile had opened the hatch.

'Out,' he said. 'Up! Only the peoples.'

One by one they came out. Fabio, Minette, the aunts . . . Herbert.

On deck it was cold but marvellously fresh after the stuffiness of the hold. Gulls were flying above them; it all looked so normal—except for the look in

Sprott's eyes.

'I don't want to see them drown, I don't want to,' yelled Lambert, twisting in his father's grasp.

The children moved closer together. It was going to happen, then—and almost straight away.

Boris and Des had fetched the weights they were going to tie to their victims' ankles; not that there was much chance that they would be able to swim to safety. The *Hurricane* had been steaming steadily away from the Island.

The aunts had come to stand behind the children; Etta behind Minette, Coral behind Fabio as though by some miracle they could still protect them.

Fabio and Minette had linked hands. Everything inside them seemed to have turned to stone.

Don't let me make a fuss, Fabio was praying. Don't let me be like Lambert.

'We'll start with the fat one,' ordered Sprott. 'Take her to the rails and get the weights on.'

Des went over to Aunt Coral.

'Move,' he said, prodding her with the butt of his gun—and as he did so, Fabio went mad.

'How dare you!' he shouted and tried

270

to attack the bodyguard with his fists.

Sprott thought this was very funny. 'All right, you can go first then if you're so full of beans,' he said, and the two thugs pinned Fabio's arms behind his back and started to carry him to the side.

They were trying to fix weights on to his thrashing legs when the skipper put his head out of the wheelhouse.

'Better hurry,' he said. 'I don't like the look of the sky.'

There was nothing to like the look of. Not the sea, not the sky, not the surface of the water, not the clouds. Some dreadful weather was on the way.

The waves darkened, the water boiled; the sun vanished behind a mushroom cloud.

The gulls flew up screeching.

And on the deck of the *Hurricane*— someone began to scream.

*   *   *

'Hold on to me,' Fabio had shouted to Minette, but they were torn apart at once by the mountainous icy waves.

Minette had thought of herself as a good swimmer but this was nothing to do with swimming—she was being hurled up, then sucked down, rolled over . . .

And the cold was beyond belief.

All round her were broken planks and debris from the *Hurricane*. The ship had split in two the instant the great kraken had rammed her. She saw the roof of the boobrie's splintered cage bobbing close by; two of the chicks were clinging to the top of it—but where was the third?

A wave broke over her head and she went under again; the weight of the water pressed her down and down; her lungs were bursting. I'm going to die, she thought, as far as she could think at all.

Then with a last thrust of her legs she reached the surface. And as she did so, she saw someone quite close to her, swimming as masterfully and strongly as if he was in a millpond rather than the raging sea.

'Wait, I'm coming,' called Herbert, and she reached out for him, but then another wave took her and she went under yet again and was sure she was lost. Then she felt herself pulled up and up by her hair . . . and found that she was clinging on to Herbert's back and able to breathe once more.

'Hold on tight, but don't choke me,' called Herbert—and set off through the waves as calmly as he had done when he was still a seal.

'Fabio?' she managed to ask.

But Herbert had not seen Fabio.

They passed the stoorworm and saw something large gripped tightly in the coils of his tail. The worm's ancestors had come from the sea and Herbert wasted no time on him. He would get Aunt Coral to safety if anybody could.

A mattress swam past them, then the galley table with the third boobrie chick clinging on by his yellow feet.

'Keep still, Aunt Etta,' came Queenie's high-pitched voice above the sound of the waves. 'You mustn't wriggle.'

The twins were holding Aunt Etta up between them as she spluttered and kicked her feet.

Hanging on to Herbert's back took all Minette's strength, but she was still searching desperately for Fabio.

'Please, Herbert, we must find him.'

After he and Minette were torn apart, Fabio had sighted the lifeboat which had been thrown clear when the *Hurricane* sank. He managed to swim towards it . . . to get a hand on the gunnel . . . If the people inside it would help him he could pull himself up.

But the people inside it were Stanley Sprott and his crew.

Sprott looked over the side and saw the struggling boy. 'Get rid of him,' he said.

And as the small hand came up, Boris hit it with an oar and pushed the boy back into the water.

There was not much hope for Fabio after that. He was going down for the last time when Herbert found him.

'Hold on to my shoulder,' he ordered. 'And don't talk.'

Herbert was an amazing swimmer but he knew that to support two children all the long way back to the Island might be beyond his strength. Even a seal would not try to swim with two pups on his back.

Everyone was in difficulties. The raft on which the boobrie chicks balanced was sinking and above them the boobrie mother squawked in anguish, not knowing which of the two to pick up in her beak. The worm's tail muscles had gone into cramp from holding up the waterlogged Aunt Coral . . .

Herbert measured the long way to the Island and set his teeth.

'Come on, everybody, follow me,' he called manfully.

One could only do one's best.

The kraken had found his son. He cared for nothing else. He swam away from the shipwreck with the child on his back. Anger still coursed through his body. He was not the Healer of the Sea now. He was a father whose child had been hurt. Let everyone else beware for he and his son were on their way!

But after the first joy of being safe, the little kraken wriggled forward so that his mouth was right against his father's ear, and began to talk very fast in Polar. He was explaining what had happened and how the people on the Island had tried to keep him safe.

And then he said the word which the great kraken had spoken when he first swam into the bay.

'Children?' said the little kraken. And again, looking back at the wreckage: 'Children?'

But it was not really a question. It was an order. The little kraken was growing up.

And the great kraken sighed because he wanted above all to be away from the shrieks and the splintered wood of the

275

wreckage and be in the quietness of the sea. But he heeded his son—and he turned and swam back to the wreck and to the struggling creatures trying to hold each other up in the water.

Then Minette and Fabio felt something below them . . . the strong living island of muscle that was the kraken's back . . . and felt it rise and rise till everyone was safely gathered on it—the aunts and the creatures, the boobries in their cage . . . and they themselves, sliding off Herbert's weary shoulders to feel firm ground beneath their feet.

It was an incredible, magic journey that they took after the panic and terror they had been through—floating secure and safe on the great creature's back, until the Island was in sight, and there was no more danger and no more fear.

*   *   *

But the kraken had not saved everybody.

Stanley Sprott lay sprawled across the bottom of the battered, leaking lifeboat. Boris, only half conscious, was clinging to the gunnel. Des was hanging over the side, trying to be sick; he had been drinking seawater. Lambert was curled up like a baby between the skipper and the mate.

Casimir had drowned in the struggle to reach the lifeboat after the *Hurricane* was rammed.

They had been drifting for a long time. The sea was still strange; slate colour one minute; the colour of blood the next. No rescue ships were setting out in this awesome ocean.

In the lifeboat there was no more water and no more food. The men's lips were blistered. Their swollen tongues stuck to the roof of their mouths. Befuddled as they were, they tried to make sense of what had happened.

Only they couldn't. No one could make sense of it.

'An island?' muttered Sprott. He could see it, bigger than anyone could believe, moving towards them with the speed of a comet.

But how could it? How could an island move?

'It wasn't there,' said Lambert suddenly. Weakened by hunger and thirst, those were the only words he could still say.

Sprott's head was a jumble of pictures.

A mermaid holding up . . . an aunt. But

had there really been mermaids? And a great bird the size of an elephant flapping over the wreckage . . .

No, it was ridiculous. It was impossible. He fingered the bruise on his forehead. He must have concussion.

'Not . . . really there . . .' murmured Lambert. He wouldn't last much longer unless they were rescued soon.

I'm going mad, thought Sprott. I'll have to be careful. We'll all have to be careful or they'll put us in a loony bin if we're rescued. All that happened was that a storm came up and the *Hurricane* was wrecked. Everything else is nonsense.

'Not . . . there . . .' said Lambert faintly.

Sprott looked at his son. He had always despised Lambert but he was sorry now. Lambert was right. He had said all along that the . . . things . . . weren't really there and they weren't. How could they have been?

'Quite right, Lambert,' said Stanley Sprott, and leant back and closed his eyes.

If they were rescued he'd say nothing— and see that the others said nothing too. He wasn't going to be locked up as a loony, that was for sure . . .

The last days on the Island were strangely happy. The children knew they would soon be fetched away but they were able to enjoy each moment as it came and being in an adventure seemed to have done everybody good.

The stoorworm no longer complained about being too long for his thoughts.

'If I'd been any shorter I couldn't have held up Aunt Coral in the sea,' he said and stopped talking about plastic surgery once and for all.

As for Loreen, when Aunt Myrtle fetched Walter out of the washbasin and put him in his mother's arms she let out a shriek of joy.

'He's grown hair!' she cried.

'He's grown *a* hair,' said Queenie who was giving herself airs because she had saved Aunt Etta.

But the most exciting thing happened to the boobrie. After she waddled up to her nest with her three bedraggled chicks she found somebody sitting in it.

The boobrie paused, hissed . . . stretched out her neck. Who was it who *dared* to sit on *her* nest? Hooting, honking and complaining, she flapped her wings and prepared to attack.

Then suddenly she stopped. She lay down in front of the stranger, she clapped her beak against his . . . her eyes rolled with welcome and with love.

'My goodness,' said Fabio. 'It's her husband. He's come back!'

And he had. He didn't seem to be a very intelligent bird but knowing that there were two boobries now to look after the chicks was a great relief to everybody.

Herbert was of course a hero, but not at all conceited. He began straight away to tidy up the aunts' house and to label Art's storage jars and to show him how to cut the heads off fish.

But it was Myrtle who had been his special friend and he did everything he could to help her. He told her when her skirt was on back to front and he corrected her when she played a tune too fast on the cello, and he insisted that she had swimming lessons twice a day.

'Oh, Herbert, the water is so cold!' Myrtle would cry.

But Herbert said it was dangerous to live so close to the sea and not be able to swim, and every morning and every evening Myrtle had to get her rubber ring and put on her chill-proof vest and Aunt

Etta's navy-blue bloomers and go into the sea.

But the important thing—the thing that was on everybody's mind—was what was going to happen to the kraken.

After he had brought them safely to the shore the great kraken had moved a little way away to the mouth of the bay. He stayed submerged most of the time and out of sight and his son stayed with him.

'He's thinking,' said Aunt Etta and she was right.

He was thinking about what to do next. Should he give up his healing journey around the world and go back to the Arctic? Or should he find somewhere else to leave his son? For he knew without being told that things were going to be different on the Island.

Then one morning Ethelgonda appeared, shimmering above her tombstone, so they knew that it would be an important day.

And sure enough by noon the great kraken swam slowly into the bay with his son on his back. It was a most anxious moment. No one could blame the kraken if he turned his back on human beings once again and left the sea to spoil, and it

281

was as though all those who waited by the shore were holding their breath.

Then he began to talk. He talked in Polar and it was his son who translated.

'Although people deserve that I should leave them to their mess and their wickedness, I have decided to go on with my journey around the oceans of the world. But I shall not take one year and one day to make the journey. I shall take two years and two days . . . or even three years and three days, so that my son, who has been restored to me, can come also and be with me at my side.'

When he said that a great cheer went up and Fabio and Minette hugged each other because it was the closest to a happy ending they could hope for.

That evening when it was quiet, the little kraken came and said goodbye all by himself to the children who had cared for him. There was just one bun left in the boobrie tin but when Fabio gave it to the kraken he did not at once open his mouth. He said: '*Share!*'

So the children broke the bun into three parts and everybody had a piece. It was a most squashed and sorry-looking bun, with cracked icing and a wilting Smartie clinging to the top . . . but afterwards the children remembered it as tasting like a bun in Paradise.

The next morning the kraken and his son had gone.

And only a few hours later the noise they had been expecting was heard over the Island: the sound of a helicopter. But not one . . . three . . . and coming from them a whole posse of policemen with guns and handcuffs and body-armour—come to fetch back the children and arrest the aunts.

CHAPTER TWENTY-THREE

Aunt Etta and Aunt Coral had been in prison for several weeks before their trial for kidnapping came to the courts. The children were not allowed to visit them and so the first time they saw them was in the dock at the Old Bailey, handcuffed to the police-women who brought them up from the cells.

For Minette and Fabio, seeing them like that was like being kicked very hard in the stomach and Minette gave a gasp of distress which the people in the courtroom heard.

'Poor little thing—look how frightened she is,' they whispered—and it was true. Minette was very frightened and so was Fabio—frightened for the aunts and what might happen to them; very frightened indeed.

Etta had always been thin but now she was all bone, and Coral's bulk had gone so that her skin hung in folds. It wasn't the prison food or the other prisoners that had worn them down, it was waking up day after day to the grey walls which closed them in. It was their loss of freedom.

The courtroom was very dark and very old. The judge sat high above everyone else like God, and below him were men in gowns and wigs: a ferrety-looking man who was the prosecuting counsel and had to prove that the aunts were guilty, and a man with a round face like a Christmas pudding who was the defence counsel and had to try and show that the aunts were innocent. The jury—three women and nine men, sat on the judge's right. One of them, a lady with a large bosom and red hair, kept fanning herself with a piece of paper. Minette's parents sat on benches facing the judge, as far away from each other as possible, and the old Mountjoys were in the back row.

It was only Aunt Etta and Aunt Coral who were being tried. Myrtle had been allowed to return to the Island because Mr Sprott was in a clinic in America and too muddled to accuse anyone of kidnapping his son. Etta and Coral were glad of that. They thought that Myrtle would probably have died in prison.

The case had attracted a lot of attention. *Killer Aunts Brought to Justice* screamed the newspaper headlines and the strange pictures of Etta and Coral that had been on the walls of the police station were printed again, making everyone certain that these were the most evil women in the world.

'Will the prisoner stand,' said the clerk of the court—and the children drew in their breath for the prisoner was Etta.

The charge was read out.

'Do you plead guilty or not guilty?' she was asked.

'Not guilty,' said Etta, holding her head high.

Then the witnesses were called. Minette's mother came first, tripping towards the witness box and patting her hair. She was sorry the trial wasn't shown on the telly because her hat was

285

exactly right—serious and dark but very flattering—and because she had been an actress she swore to tell the whole truth and nothing but the truth in a very dramatic way.

'Is this the woman who met you at King's Cross Station?' asked the prosecuting counsel who looked like a ferret, pointing at Etta.

'Yes it is.'

'And did you think she was a fit person to have charge of your daughter?'

'Yes, I did, because she came from an agency. But I thought she had a sinister face.'

'Could you tell us what you mean by sinister . . . ?'

Minette's father was called next and described the false message he had had to say that Minette would not be travelling to Edinburgh.

Then it was Minette's turn.

There had been a lot of argument about whether Fabio and Minette were old enough to give evidence, but in the end it was decided that they could. So Minette too swore to tell the whole truth and nothing but the truth and then a footstool was fetched so that her head came over the edge of the witness box and the ferrety man began.

'Now, Minette, will you tell us what happened when you travelled with this person to Edinburgh,' he said. 'Just take your time,' he said, speaking very carefully, as though Minette was three years old.

'We talked about things,' said Minette.

'What sort of things?'

'Seals . . . and whether there were ghosts or not . . . and then I asked her if there was a third place.'

'Could you tell us what you mean by that?'

Minette bent her head, thinking. 'All my life I've kept going backwards and forwards between my parents . . . and when I got there they were always horrible about each other so I got . . . tired. And sad. And I asked Aunt Etta if there was a third place. A place that wasn't *either* or *or*—and she said there was, there was one for everybody. Only they had to be brave and want it.'

'And what happened then?'

'I fell asleep. And when I woke up I was there. In the third place.'

'I see. You woke up in a completely strange place. And were you frightened?'

Minette smiled—a slow, very sweet

smile which lit up the dark courtroom like a beacon. 'No. Not for long. I had a nightlight you see. I was frightened in London and in Edinburgh because of the dark and the cracks in the ceiling. I used to think I saw tigers . . . and my parents both thought I was silly. But there when I woke, the first thing I saw was this light.'

The ferrety man in the wig didn't like her answer. His job was to prove how wicked the aunts were and she wasn't helping. 'Are you telling me that you woke up in a completely strange place *having been kidnapped* and you weren't frightened?'

Minette lifted her chin.

'I wasn't kidnapped,' she said clearly. 'I was *chosen.*'

That evening the newspapers quoted her words. *'I wasn't kidnapped, I was chosen,' says child snatch victim,* and they all carried pictures of Minette.

The next morning it was Aunt Coral's turn and it was Fabio who went into the witness box and climbed on to the footstool. Again it was the ferrety prosecutor who asked the first questions.

'Now, my boy, will you tell us what happened on the way to Greymarsh Towers.'

'I was sick,' said Fabio.

'Is that because you were frightened?'

'Yes.'

'You were frightened of that lady there?' he asked, pointing to Aunt Coral.

'No. I was frightened of going back to school. It was a horrible place. They put my head down the toilet and kicked me and hung me out of the top-floor windows by my ankles because I came from Brazil and wasn't like them.'

There was a sympathetic murmur from the public gallery and the lady with orange hair stopped fanning herself and made a clucking noise.

'I don't think we need to hear about your school,' said the ferret, but the judge leant down and said Fabio should tell his story in his own way.

'So Aunt Coral went to talk to the matron and then she came back and said I couldn't go to school because they were in quarantine and I was terribly pleased. But then I realized it meant going back to my grandparents and that was almost as bad. They made me kneel on dried peas and they kept saying how vulgar my mother was. And then I realized that Aunt Coral knew how I felt because she was rather a magic person and I knew I

289

could trust her.'

'So you were drugged and kidnapped,' the prosecutor went on.

Minette at this point had smiled but Fabio didn't. He glared, but the words he said were the same.

'I wasn't kidnapped,' he said. 'I was *chosen*.'

By the next day the newspapers were writing rather differently about the trial and some strange things were happening. Those children who were old enough to hear about the trial began to ask their parents for different bedtime stories: stories about magical aunts who came and took children away to islands where they didn't have to go to school.

Of course the aunts were guilty, everyone knew that. They would go to prison, probably for the rest of their lives, but there wasn't so much glee about, and the people who stood outside the courtroom holding up banners saying *Hanging is too good for them* stopped yelling and went home.

The third day of the trial was the last and the ferret started his questions again.

'What exactly did you do on the Island?' he wanted to know.

'We worked,' said the children. 'We

helped to clean out the animals and milk the goats and feed the baby seals.'

'Exactly. You worked all the time? From dawn to dusk.'

'Yes.'

'And didn't you get tired?'

'Of course we got tired.' Fabio scowled at him. 'What's wrong with being tired? Working like that was *good*. Everybody ought to do it instead of messing about at school trying to solve maths problems that don't have anything to do with real life and writing silly essays about people who are dead.'

When he found he couldn't drive the children into a corner, the ferret started on the aunts and it seemed as though there really couldn't be any hope. They *had* taken the children without their parents' knowledge; they didn't try to deny that. Neither Coral nor Etta were any good at telling lies.

And now it came to the end, to the summing-up, when the judge had to make the jury understand exactly what the case was about. Everyone in the court was silent, everyone knew the verdict would be guilty, but even those people who had wanted it at the beginning weren't so certain now.

Then Etta beckoned to the Christmas pudding man who was supposed to be defending them and whispered something, and he went over to the judge and whispered to him, and the judge nodded. No one knew what had been said but after a few minutes a clerk came in carrying two big dictionaries.

'Your honour,' said the pudding. 'I ask for leave to read out the two most up-to-date definitions of kidnapping. The first comes from the London Dictionary and it says: *Kidnap: To hold a person against their will.*' He turned to Minette. 'May I ask you to step into the box again.'

She did so.

'Would you say you had been held against your will?'

'*No,*' said Minette.

The question was repeated to Fabio.

'*No,*' shouted the boy.

The pudding picked up the second book. 'The definition of kidnapping given here is: *To hold a person for ransom. To demand money to secure the victim's release.*'

He looked at the benches where Minette's parents and Fabio's grandparents were sitting. Then he called them out one by one, and to each of them he said: 'Have you ever been asked for a single penny by either of these ladies?'

And crossly, peevishly, they admitted that they had not.

'In that case, your honour, it is my opinion that no kidnap took place.'

The jury were out for six hours and during the whole of this time Fabio and Minette absolutely refused to leave the building.

'We're staying till they bring in the verdict,' said Fabio—and nothing the police or the social workers or anyone else could say would move them.

So they sat on hard chairs in an office behind the courtroom and waited. They were so tired they could hardly stop themselves from slipping to the ground but they did it. It was like keeping watch when someone was ill or dying; it had to be done.

It was after midnight before the jury returned and everybody filed back into the courtroom.

'Have you reached a verdict?' asked the judge, leaning down from his box.

'We have, my lord,' replied the foreman in a solemn voice.

'And do you find the defendants guilty or not guilty?'

There had never been such silence. Not a breath was heard in the court; not a rustle . . .

The foreman raised his head.

'Not guilty.'

Oddly it was not Minette but Fabio who burst into tears.

CHAPTER TWENTY-FOUR

The Island had never looked more beautiful. The sea sparkled and danced, the sun shone through the green crests on the waves; and on the hill the blossoming gorse was a mass of gold.

The children had been allowed to come up for a week to say goodbye. Minette had to go back to her parents, but Fabio's mother was taking him back to South America. She had read about the trial and about Fabio's school and she no longer thought that her son needed to grow up as an English gentleman.

So it should have been a really sad farewell, but it wasn't because the aunts had called them into the dining room the day they came and shown them an important-looking document covered in red seals.

'It's our will,' they said.

The children started to read it but they couldn't make head nor tail of it and in the end Etta said: 'What it says is that we have left you the Island. To both of you jointly. When we die the Island will be yours.'

They had stood round them; all the aunts—Etta and Coral and Myrtle and Dorothy—and nodded in a pleased way.

'We know that you will regard it as a Sacred Trust,' they said.

The children could hardly believe it at first. It was too big to take in: the thought that the Island would one day be theirs, and they could live on it and care for it, and be together. It made the years in between seem unimportant. Minette was not so frightened now of her parents' moods—and they were trying to behave better. Time would go quickly—very soon now she and Fabio would return and their real lives would begin.

'Will you manage the work till we come back?' Fabio asked and they said, yes they would because Dorothy had decided to stay. She thought it was time to hang up her wok and she had decided to breed piranha fish in a tank so that if any more

Sprotts came to the Island she could see them off.

As for Herbert, he went on making himself useful as he had done ever since they escaped from the *Hurricane*. He polished the napkin rings and tidied Art's cutlery drawer and ordered some bedroom slippers for the Sybil from a catalogue.

But most of all he went on helping Myrtle. He showed her how to keep her hair tidy in a net, he stuck her loose sheet music together with Sellotape and every single morning and every single evening he saw that she put on Aunt Etta's bloomers and her rubber ring and had her swimming lesson in the sea.

All the same, Fabio and Minette, who had not seen him since before the trial, felt that Herbert had changed. He seemed to be working too hard, as though he was afraid of what might happen if he did not keep busy, and sometimes they caught him gazing out of the window with a strange look in his large brown eyes.

'He's homesick,' Myrtle whispered to the children. 'He misses the sea.'

The children were very upset. Herbert, after all, had saved their lives.

'Isn't there anything that can be done?'

asked Fabio.

Aunt Myrtle sighed. 'He *could* be turned back into a seal,' she said slowly. 'There is a way.'

'Not a knife?' said Minette, horrified.

'No. That might work but . . .' She shook her head. 'The mermaids say that if one weeps seven tears over a selkie when the moon is rising . . . Seven human tears . . .'

'But could you bear it?' asked Minette. 'I mean, he's your friend.'

Myrtle looked down at her Wellington boots. 'I could . . . bear it,' she said, biting her lip, 'if it is the right thing to do. One can always bear what is right.'

So they went to the other aunts and had a meeting and then they went to find Herbert who was cleaning the windows of the sitting room.

'Herbert, we want you to tell us the truth,' said Aunt Etta. 'Were you happier as a seal? Do you want to return?'

Herbert spun round, the polishing cloth in his hand. There was no need for him to answer. They only had to look into his eyes.

'He has reached the Rock of the Farnes,' Herbert said in a dreamy voice. 'But he swims slowly. I could catch him up.'

So then they realized that Herbert's thoughts all this time had been with the great kraken and that he longed to swim with him and be his escort in the work of cleaning the sea.

But when they told Herbert what the mermaids had said and that he could be turned into a seal again if someone wept seven human tears over him he shook his head.

'Myrtle stayed by my side when my mother died; she played music to me in all weathers. I couldn't leave her now.'

So then Myrtle stepped forward and now she was not a vague and dippy woman whose hair fell down. She was a heroine.

'If it is right for you to swim with the great kraken you must do so, Herbert,' she said and though there was a sob in her throat she held her head high.

They decided to do the turning in the crystal cave and of course everyone wanted to come. The Captain couldn't leave his bed but the stoorworm promised to tell him all about it and the mermaids insisted on being there, and the naak and even the boobries, though it wasn't at all certain that they knew what was going on.

They had to wait until the moon broke out of its covering of cloud—but when Herbert threw off his dressing gown and stood there only in Art's boxer shorts, everyone sighed because it was all so dignified and beautiful, like a ceremony in ancient Greece.

It was Myrtle of course who was to do the actual crying, and because the tears had to fall directly on his head, Herbert knelt before her . . . and then she began.

She remembered all the good times— the music on Seal Point, the silent evenings beside her friend watching the sunset . . .

One tear fell on Herbert's head . . . then two . . . then three . . . four . . . five . . . six . . .

Only one more.

But just when everyone was clutching everyone else ready for the great moment, the tears stopped.

It was most embarrassing. Myrtle sniffed. She blinked, she blushed. She had shed six tears; and she couldn't shed a seventh.

For the truth was (though she never told anyone) that at that moment she had suddenly realized that she need never again go into the cold sea in her chill-proof vest and her sister's navy bloomers. She still minded terribly losing Herbert—but the relief had blocked her tear ducts as thoroughly as if they had been plugged with cement.

It was a dreadful moment, but of course help was at hand. Minette only had to think of saying goodbye to the man who had saved her life and she was off.

She took Myrtle's place—and as the seventh tear fell on to Herbert's head there was a flash of blinding jagged light.

And when they looked again they knew they had done right. On the ledge of rock was a pair of crumpled boxer shorts—but streaking out of the cave into the open sea was a silver hunk of streamlined muscle which thrust through the waves like an arrow.

*   *   *

The next morning was the children's last on the Island and they got up early and walked along the strand as they had done on the first day when they woke up to find they had been kidnapped.

'You will come back, won't you?' Minette asked.

'You won't stay and become Prime

300

Minister of Brazil?'

She wanted to make him swear; to have a kind of ceremony—but then she saw his face as he looked out over the Island and saw that he loved it as she did, and she knew for certain that they would both be back. And the ache of parting became a different sort of ache—an ache of happiness—and then they turned and went back towards the house where the aunts were waiting.